THE COST OF CINDERELLA'S CONFESSION

JULIA JAMES

THE WIFE THE SPANIARD NEVER FORGOT

PIPPA ROSCOE

MILLS & BOON

First published in Great Britain 2022
by Mills & Boon, an imprint of HarperCollins*Publishers* Ltd,
1 London Bridge Street, London, SE1 9GF

www.harpercollins.co.uk

HarperCollins*Publishers*
1st Floor, Watermarque Building,
Ringsend Road, Dublin 4, Ireland

The Cost of Cinderella's Confession © 2022 Julia James

The Wife the Spaniard Never Forgot © 2022 Pippa Roscoe

ISBN: 978-0-263-30110-6

12/22

This book is produced from independently certified FSC™ paper
to ensure responsible forest management.
For more information visit: www.harpercollins.co.uk/green.

Printed and Bound in Spain using 100% Renewable Electricity
at CPI Black Print, Barcelona

THE COST OF CINDERELLA'S CONFESSION

JULIA JAMES

MILLS & BOON

For Nic—a huge thank you!

Julia James lives in England and adores the peaceful verdant countryside and the wild shores of Cornwall. She also loves the Mediterranean—so rich in myth and history, with its sunbaked landscapes and olive groves, ancient ruins and azure seas. 'The perfect setting for romance!' she says. 'Rivalled only by the lush tropical heat of the Caribbean—palms swaying by a silver sand beach lapped by turquoise water... What more could lovers want?'

Pippa Roscoe lives in Norfolk, near her family, and makes daily promises to herself that this is the day she'll leave the computer to take a long walk in the countryside. She can't remember a time when she wasn't dreaming about handsome heroes and innocent heroines. Totally her mother's fault, of course—she gave Pippa her first romance to read at the age of seven! She is inconceivably happy that she gets to share those daydreams with you. Follow her on Twitter @PippaRoscoe.

PROLOGUE

THE MEDIEVAL CHURCH was bathed in the warm sunshine filling the *piazza* in the ancient hilltop town in central Italy. Sunshine that did not warm Ariana. Instead, only cold filled her. Cold that almost had her shivering. Or something did.

Fear.

Fear of what she was about to do—what she had to nerve herself to do...steel herself to do.

Face set, hidden from view by the little veil that dipped from the deliberately stylish and very expensive hat, which went with the equally stylish and expensive tightly cinched suit curving over her shapely figure, she walked up to the arched entrance of the church, invitation at the ready.

The service had already started, and the choir were singing an anthem as she slipped unobtrusively into a seat at the back. She sat down, feeling sick with nerves, wishing with all her being that she could just bolt and run. But she *had* to do this.

She bowed her head, as if in prayer, but actually to avoid looking at the well-dressed congregation...or the figures by the altar rail. Another rush of fearfulness assailed her at the enormity of what she was about to do.

But there's no other way—none!

The anthem finished, there was a rustling among the congregation, and then the priest—a high-ranking cleric, as befitted so grand a society wedding—began to intone the words of the ceremony.

A dizziness filled Ariana's head, and her heart was hammering. She had to time this right—totally and absolutely right—to the very moment.

The dreaded moment.

The dreadful moment...

And then it came. The words that had never received a response at any wedding she'd been to. But today, right now, they would. They must...

There's no other way—however much I long with all my being not to do this!

She heard the priest say the words—her cue, her signal. Heard the dutiful pause that followed. Heard herself stand, step into the wide aisle. She started to walk forward, every step compelled from her by a strength of will to overcome her repugnance at what she was doing. What she was about to do.

She started to speak, forcing the words out through her constricted throat. The words she *had* to say, falling like a sacrilege across the sacrament of holy matrimony. Words to halt it in its tracks.

'*Yes!* I have an objection! And I will not hold my peace! This marriage cannot take place!'

She saw heads turn, heard the collective gasp of shock from the congregation as they stared at her, striding down the aisle on high heels that struck like nails on the flagstones, towards the two figures by the altar rail.

The bride, a slender column in white, her face invisible beneath a long lace veil, did not move. But the groom did. Ariana's fixed gaze saw him turn. Slowly, like a jaguar that had just heard something behind him move. Something that might be prey—or a fellow predator.

The cold inside her froze instantly to solid ice as his gaze came to rest on her. It was as if liquid nitrogen had just been poured down her throat. She felt her senses sway, and with every instinct in her body she wanted to halt and turn...and flee...

But she would not. *Could* not. She had to do this. Had to play it to the very end.

His eyes, like a basilisk, watched her approach. They were all that she could see.

Not the man who had given away the bride, now starting forward with an oath, nor the bride herself, still not turning, motionless like a statue. Let alone the best man, the half-dozen bridesmaids, flower girls and page boys all staring open-mouthed at her approach.

Not even the priest stepping forward now, his expression half concerned, because her interruption must, in light of his professional duty, be attended to, and half holding the collective outrage she could feel coming at her in waves from the congregation at her stupendous, scandalous social *faux pas* in doing what she was so appallingly doing.

The priest opened his mouth to speak, to demand the reason for her outburst, but she pre-empted him. She stopped dead, some way still from the altar rail and the front row of pews, and threw back her short veil.

And *then* she saw the basilisk eyes change.

Saw recognition.

For a second, a micron of time so short it almost ceased to exist, she saw something flare in the obsidian eyes. A black flame...

Then it was gone. Now in his eyes there was only a

blade so sharp she could feel it cutting the flesh from her bones.

He started forward, but she was already speaking. Her voice a clarion, heard by all present. Heard by the motionless bride, her back still turned to her. Heard by the groom, with tension in every line of his tall, lean body, every plane of his hard, stark face. In the sculpted mouth now whipped to a narrow line.

She pointed her hand as she spoke, praying that it was not trembling. An accusing hand. Directed at the groom. The man whose wedding she had to stop. Right now.

'He *cannot* marry her!' she cried out. 'I am pregnant with his child!'

CHAPTER ONE

Three months earlier...

ARIANA GLANCED AT her reflection in the mirror in the ladies' room of the uptown, upmarket Manhattan hotel, her peat-coloured eyes, a legacy of her father, deepened by eyeshadow and mascara, her generous mouth lustrous with lipstick.

Her grandfather would say she looked like a harlot, but she didn't care—he always thought badly of her. Nothing she could do pleased him. Even when she tried to dress demurely he still disparaged her. She was too tall, too full-figured, too curvaceous, too everything. And, worst of all, far, far too outspoken. Always drawing attention to herself in entirely the wrong way.

Unlike her cousin Mia.

It was Mia who was the granddaughter he approved of. Mia, so petite, so slender, with her long fair hair and angelic features. Mia, so gentle and sweet-natured. Quietly spoken, diffident—meek, docile and shy. Just as a woman should be.

That was their grandfather's opinion, and he did not balk at holding forth about it.

Ariana had heard it all her life, even as a child, and

certainly once she became a teenager. She should be inured to it, but it could still sting—even now.

Well, not tonight! Tonight she was four thousand miles away from her grandfather's grand *palazzo* in Umbria and she was going to enjoy herself. She'd just completed the refurbishment of her mother's new house in Florida, bought with her latest husband—number five, as Ariana had totted it up—and she'd flown to New York to catch up with her other American clients, including her hostess tonight: wealthy socialite Marnie van Huren, a friend of Ariana's mother, who was bubbly, sociable— and matchmaking.

'Come to my party, honey, and get yourself a nice man! You career girls are always too busy for romance!'

Ariana had smiled but said nothing. She focussed on her career for a reason—and it wasn't to compensate for a lack of romance in her life. It was to escape her grandfather's financial control.

It was a control that was not just financial, but emotional as well—a control he'd always sought to exert over his family. He'd done it with her uncle, Mia's father, who to his dying day had never stepped out of line any more than his daughter—sweet, docile Mia—did now. That hideous day Ariana's uncle and aunt had been killed in a car crash, when Mia was seven and she was nine. The tragedy had scarred them all, making her grandfather's stifling tyranny even more suffocating. He'd become determined to make Ariana like gentle Mia, wanting to chain his granddaughters to his side, not wanting them to have a cent that had not been bestowed upon them by himself even once they'd grown up.

Ariana had vowed never to be dependent, never to let her grandfather curb and constrain her as he did her timid, gentle cousin Mia. Nor to react to that crushing control in the way her own mother had. She had eloped at nineteen with a good-looking penniless wastrel who had soon abandoned her, freshly married and pregnant, in exchange for being bought off by an irate father-in-law, never to be seen again. Least of all by his daughter Ariana.

A succession of marriages interspersed with affairs had followed for her mother, all disapproved of by Ariana's grandfather, but fortunately always to wealthy men.

Ariana had no intention of copying her mother's solution to her grandfather's tyranny. She would never be dependent on a man's largesse, whoever that man was. She would make her own money, using her own talents.

It hadn't proved easy, and her precarious efforts to succeed in the overcrowded world of interior design were yet another source of contemptuous disapproval by her grandfather—yet another reason to condemn her. But she'd been dogged in her persistence and her determination, and now, at twenty-seven, she felt she could call herself a success.

It wasn't, of course, a success that earned her grandfather's approval—nothing could do that—but it earned her enough money to live a comfortably affluent life. The downside was that it was a life dedicated to her career. Though she dated from time to time, it was never a priority for her. Romance, for now, came a very poor second.

But when she finally had time for romance she would make sure it was the real thing. Permanent. She would not be like her mother, flitting from man to man, husband to husband. No, for her it would be different. One man, one love, one life—together.

One day I'll meet him! The man I'll make my life with—who will mean everything to me. The one man in the world who'll set me alight like a flame, to burn for him all my life!

It would happen one day—and in the meantime there was work and, like tonight, socialising.

She glanced at her reflection again. The figure-hugging cocktail dress showed her generous curves in a way that would have had her grandfather choking. Defiantly, she gave a toss of her head, sending rich brunette waves rippling over her shoulders as, with a final glance, she sashayed out on her five-inch heels and went to party.

Luca Farnese stood at the side of the crowded function room, which was noisy with chatter and the clink of glasses and bejewelled bracelets, and surveyed the scene. He would not be staying long at this high-society Manhattan shindig, only long enough to have the conversation he wanted with his host, and then he'd escape.

Even though he knew, without vanity, that he was being eyed up, courtesy of his darkly good-looking Italian features, his six-foot height and lean, fit body, he had no desire for any dalliance tonight. Or ever. He had already found the woman of his dreams—and she was all he had ever sought in the woman he would make his life with.

A memory of her across the ocean, waiting for him to return and declare himself to her, played in his head, conjuring up her angelical beauty, her fair hair, luminous blue eyes, her tender mouth and her soft, melodious voice. She hadn't said a great deal, had only hidden her doe-like gaze beneath demure lashes, but from the moment he'd met her—only a handful of weeks ago—he'd been captivated by her. The gentle sweetness of her nature had shone through, and the air of quietness about her had been serene and tranquil. What he had always dreamt of—longed for.

And he knew why.

Bitterly so.

Memory slid back down the years, the decades, and his expression tightened in painful recollection. Raised voices, doors slamming. His father's voice, pleading and placatory, his mother's angry and denouncing, vitriolic in its complaint and criticism, unstoppable in the full flow of her histrionics. Then a final slamming of a door and silence. Oppressive, echoing silence.

Himself as a young boy, clutching the landing banisters with clammy hands, his expression strained and anxious. Then going back to his bedroom with a heavy, forlorn tread, his insides knotted up, his heart thumping as he climbed back into bed. But not to sleep. To stare tensely up at the ceiling, hands clenched either side of his stiff body, trying to block out the echoes of the shouting and cursing.

He'd wished his mother wasn't always quarrelling with his father, yelling at him, storming out, making scenes wherever she was, in front of everyone, even in front of complete strangers, not giving a damn that people were looking, not caring about her son's mortification, her husband's cringing embarrassment. However badly his mother behaved, his father seemed to be in thrall to her, letting her endlessly get away with her outbursts.

As a boy he'd been unable to understand why—but as he became a teenager, and then a man, he'd come to understand the power his mother had over his father. The power of her blatant sexuality that his hapless father had never been able to resist.

Rejection of his father's endless surrender to his wife's sensual allure had brought Luca to a steely resolve for himself. His own marriage would be nothing like his tormented parents'. Never would he be in sexual thrall to a woman as his father had been, and nor would his wife be like his demanding, self-absorbed mother, who'd cared nothing for her hapless husband and her neglected son.

No, the woman he would fall in love with—his ideal since his teenage years—would be the very opposite. Quiet and gentle, sweet-natured and loving, never raising her voice to anyone. And all he'd want would be her happiness, as he bestowed upon her his devotion and his wealth.

Wealth he had made for himself, in the cut-throat world of high finance. Wealth of which he was now in continued pursuit—and he needled his glance through the guests, looking for fellow financier Charles van Huren, whom he had arranged to meet here.

Charles's business schedule was as non-stop as his own, and as Luca was flying back to Italy the next morning it meant that tonight, albeit at Charles's wife's birthday party, was the only opportunity they would have to discuss the joint business investment they were contemplating.

He levered himself away from the wall, intent on finding his host in the crowd. He gave a cursory glance into the room opening off to his left, from which throbbing dance music was emanating. As he did so, someone caught his eye.

A woman…dancing on her own.

Ariana could feel the slow, heavy beat of the music, the old, familiar number echoing in her pulse as she moved to it, murmuring the well-worn lyrics of the track with a nostalgic half-smile playing on her lips.

Without conscious volition she moved on to the floor, started to dance, not caring that she had no one to dance with, wanting only to feel the slug of the music, to give herself to it, her feet moving indolently, arms twining, serpentine, winding in and out of the intoxicating melody.

Feeling the luxuriant tresses of her hair loosened from their customary businesslike confines and moving across her shoulders like a silky cloud, she dipped her head, hair swaying, heartrate synching with the heavy music. Losing all sense of time, she was becoming one with the music, primitive, primeval, caught in its low, seductive beat.

Then the music ended, and lights flared in a blaze. She looked up, throwing her head back, catching her breath as her eyes focussed.

Straight into the watching gaze of a man standing at the edge of the dance floor, looking straight at her.

Luca stood immobile, his gaze fixed. Why the hell had he stopped as he had?

It was a pointless question to ask himself. He knew exactly why.

The woman was tall, her height accentuated by heels that threw her lush body, tightly sheathed in a dark red dress, into lusher curves yet, lengthening her slender legs. Her long, loose hair cascaded down her back, framing a face as breathtaking as her body, with huge dark eyes and a curving, wanton mouth...

The woman who had just stopped dancing would have drawn the eye of a saint.

And he was no saint...

He felt his body quicken with incipient arousal. He crushed it down. He wasn't in the market for an encounter of any kind. Not any longer. And certainly not with a woman like the one he was staring at.

Before, when he'd wanted…needed…a woman he'd picked carefully. Very carefully. Someone to dine with, talk with—politics, business, finance—and take to bed. High-flying women, nearly always working in the same field as himself, with whom it was therefore easy to converse. Sleek, svelte women who wore an evening dress as if it were a business suit, with short, smooth, styled hair and discreet, immaculate make-up. Beautiful women, obviously, but women who controlled their lives as rigorously as he did his own.

The woman he'd just been watching had not been controlling her life at all. She'd let the music control it. She had melded her body with it. Arms moving sinuously, body swaying, head bowed, lost to the world…

A world she had suddenly returned to as the music had stopped and her body had stilled.

For a second her eyes, dark and huge and smoky, lifted to his, looked right at him. Then, abruptly, she was turning away, raising her hands as she did so to lift the heavy tresses of lush dark hair as if to cool her neck. It was a very natural gesture, and a sensual one…

Luca's gaze narrowed slightly. The woman's movement had lifted her breasts, which now strained against the tight material of her dress, emphasising her generous cleavage. Again, against his will, he felt his body react…

Anger stabbed. This was way out of order.

Forcing his muscles to obey him, he moved sharply away. Across the main function room he saw Charles van Huren, finally finished with his duties as host, and made eye contact. Receiving an acknowledging nod in return, he headed forward, and moments later both men had disappeared into a deserted room and settled down to their business discussion, in brisk, time-efficient tones.

All thoughts of the lushly curved brunette with her smoky eyes, sensuous dancing and mane of wild hair, were forcibly banished.

Ariana let her hair fall again, heavy on her shoulders, and as if she were following through with the gesture twisted her head towards the entrance to the dance floor. She exhaled, relief filling her. He was gone.

That moment, brief as a casual glance, had been anything but casual. Her gaze had collided with his like a physical clash, and she knew with a sudden pulse in her veins that had nothing to do with the throbbing music that it had been fastened on her. Watching her dance.

Watching *her*.

With an intensity that had felt like a spear right through her.

Instinctively she'd swivelled away from him. She was used to men looking her over. But never a man like that…

A hollow formed in her stomach as she made her way to the edge of the dance floor, seeking, suddenly, the support of a wall to lean against. His face, so briefly glimpsed, burned in her vision.

Aquiline, high cheekbones, ludicrously good looking. And eyes like obsidian…cutting right into her.

She drew a sharp intake of breath, banishing the image, glad he'd disappeared. She wasn't here for a pick-up.

Done with dancing, she headed back into the main function room, ready to mingle and relax. Some forty minutes later she was doing just that, chatting to a middle-aged couple, acquaintances of her mother, when they were joined by a friend of theirs who was, as she disclosed to Ariana on being introduced to her, very bored with the current décor in her uptown apartment. Ariana gave her her card, and then, tactfully pressing no further, slipped away, helping herself to a glass of champagne just as Marnie sailed up to her.

'Ariana, I need you to help me out! One of my guests is trying to escape!'

Ariana felt her arm taken, and was inexorably borne away by her exuberant hostess. They were heading, Ariana saw, to Marnie's husband, who was talking to a man with his back to them. She got only a moment's warning, and then she and Marnie were upon them.

The man turned.

For the second time that evening it came. That searing gaze that had lasered her while she was dancing.

Ariana felt her breath catch, her stomach muscles clench, and immediately, out of some atavistic instinct, schooled her features into unbetraying immobility. Dimly, she heard Marnie throw some arch remark at her husband about not talking business at her birthday party, and then she was turning to Ariana.

'Tell your compatriot he can't possibly leave yet!' she gushed.

'Compatriot?' Ariana heard her own voice echo.

She was conscious that she was glad to look at Marnie, and not at the man beside Charles van Huren.

'Italian—like you,' Marnie confirmed.

Wondering vaguely if it were possible that the man who had been talking to Charles van Huren might have imperfect English, Ariana felt obliged to respond to her hostess's imprecation.

'Signora van Huren implores you to enjoy the evening of her birthday party with her most sincere wishes,' she ventured cautiously, in Italian.

It was a strain to look directly at the man, whoever he was, but she did it all the same. And as she said her piece something flickered at the back of those darker-than-dark eyes. She didn't know what—only that she found it disturbing.

But then she found everything about him disturbing. Up close like this, the impact he had made on her when she'd realised he'd been watching her dance was increased tenfold. He towered over her, even in her high heels, with his lean, taut body, and his hard-planed features once again made her breath catch.

The chiselled mouth gave a sardonic twist. 'Thank you for the translation, but I got it the first time around,' he said, in perfect, only slightly accented American-English. His voice was deep, and very dry.

Marnie gave a trill of laughter, and her husband shook his head resignedly. 'Honey, Luca only dropped by at my request. We had some business to discuss. He needs to get away now.'

His wife threw up her hands in protest. 'No, no, no! I won't have it! He's here now and I won't let him leave!'

She seized up a glass of champagne from a nearby waiter and thrust it at her unwilling guest. He took it, Ariana could see, with obvious reluctance. As he did so, she made to slip away. It was apparent her fluent command of Italian was entirely unnecessary.

But a diamond braceleted hand fastened around her wrist. 'Uh-uh!' countermanded her hostess. 'Not before I've properly introduced you!'

Ariana squirmed inwardly, but to no avail. It had suddenly dawned on her, with excruciating embarrassment, what Marnie van Huren was doing. Setting her up.

Well, she would not be rude, but she schooled her features to an expression of complete impassivity as Marnie happily burbled on, exchanging their names with each of them.

'Ms Killane...' The deep, dark voice sounded her name briefly. Inexpressively.

She gave an even briefer nod of acknowledgement, not troubling herself to echo his name in return.

Her hostess beamed all the same. 'Well, now the introductions are over I must circulate! Charles!'

She released Ariana's wrist and bore her husband off, leaving Ariana standing there like a lemon, the glass of champagne in her hand.

She gave a tightly controlled smile. 'So nice to have met you, Mr Farnese. Do please excuse me,' she murmured in deliberate English, her tone as inexpressive as his, and turned away.

She would not be complicit in her hostess's embarrassing matchmaking. Nor would she, even more excruciatingly, give the damn man any idea that she was complicit. Not waiting for a response, she threaded her way across the room, chatting animatedly with anyone she knew, even if only slightly.

She was done with the party, she realised. If Marnie van Huren was set on pairing her off, she didn't want to spend the evening avoiding her hostess's efforts. She set down her champagne, dived into the restroom, then went to the cloakroom to get her fake fur jacket and make her getaway.

She stepped out into the upper floor lobby, beyond the function rooms, and headed for the elevator.

Then stopped dead.

Luca Farnese, tall, dark, devastatingly good-looking and with those obsidian eyes that could cut like black lasers, had beaten her to it.

There was nothing else for it. She either had to bottle

it, and scurry back to the party, or else hold her nerve and make her escape as she'd planned.

She opted for the latter. Head high, she stalked to the elevator.

Luca Farnese watched her approach. His face was unreadable, completely masked. Did the man think she was chasing after him? She didn't care. Because she wasn't. He could think what he liked—it didn't bother her.

Bestowing upon him only the curtest of nods of acknowledgement, she stepped gratefully into the car as the elevator doors slid open. He followed her in.

'Lobby?' he enquired.

The dark, deep voice still had that sardonic tone to it, and Ariana knew exactly why.

'Please,' she said briefly.

He jabbed with a long finger and the doors sliced shut. The car descended. It seemed to leave Ariana's stomach somewhere on the function room floor as it did so. Or something did.

She did not look at her fellow passenger, staring fixedly ahead. As the doors sliced open again he stood aside, letting her emerge first. She stalked across the marble lobby towards the hotel's revolving doors. Out on the pavement the air was chilly, and she clutched her jacket around her. A doorman beckoned a taxi for her, opening the passenger door as Ariana stepped forward.

A voice sounded behind her. Deep and speaking Italian.

'Have dinner with me,' said Luca Farnese.

CHAPTER TWO

THE RESTAURANT WAS QUIET, and Luca liked it that way, it was why he patronised it when he was in New York. As the waiter bestowed menus upon them he found his thoughts flickering like a faulty circuit.

Why the hell had he gone and done this? It didn't make logical sense. He should have headed back to his hotel, dined in his suite and had an early night before his flight to Milan the next day. Then at the weekend he'd be heading south, into the heart of Italy, to Umbria. To change his life for ever.

With a woman as unlike the one he'd brought here as it was possible to be.

The faulty circuit shorted out. His gaze lifted from the menu to the lush brunette Charles's wife had so blatantly introduced him to. He'd been as dismissive about the introduction as civility permitted, and yet, when she had been similarly dismissive of him, he had been illogically put out. Was that why he'd made his impulsive dinner invitation to her?

His dark eyes rested on her now, as still he questioned himself. Her focus was entirely on the menu, and it allowed his gaze to linger. That fabulous hair, a wanton cloud around her shoulders, long and luxuriant, those huge, long-lashed smoky eyes, the full, wide mouth, lush with deep red lipstick to match the burgundy of her dress pulled tight across her generous breasts.

Sensuous, sensual… He'd known it from the moment he'd watched her dance. Unable to *not* watch her… And yet—he frowned inwardly—she was totally different from the kind of women he had affairs with—the sleek, corporate executive types, with sharp hair and sharp minds and slim, gym-fit bodies.

This woman, seated opposite him now, couldn't be more different. And not just from the style of women he was used to. In his head flickered a projected image of the woman waiting for him in Italy—half a world away. Angelically fair, celestial blue eyes…

The image flickered again and cut out. Gone. As if she no longer existed. At least for now.

Only the woman sitting opposite him remained, dominating his vision, his senses, his consciousness, blocking out everything else. Every*one* else.

Why? Why am I doing this when it is not what I planned at all? And why this woman?

The questions speared his head, seeking an answer from his keenly honed, coolly rational brain. Finding none.

He snapped his mind away from what he was doing and why he was doing it, forcibly returning his attention to his choice for dinner.

'Have you decided?' He closed his menu, setting it down on the linen tablecloth and looking across at her.

Ariana Killane. Her name hung in the space between them. Italian and Irish. A potent combination. He'd asked her about it in the taxi here. It had seemed like a neutral subject to begin their evening together.

'Killane? And yet you speak perfect Italian?' he'd thrown at her questioningly.

'Irish father. Italian mother,' had come the reply.

She hadn't looked at him, hadn't quite met his eyes across the narrow space in the cab.

Yet he knew she was as burningly aware of him as he was of her—it radiated from her. Just as it had when she'd so briefly met his fixated gaze when she'd stopped dancing, and when she'd immediately walked off after Charles's wife's blatant introduction, and when she'd stalked out of the elevator across the lobby. He felt it now, in the way she still didn't meet his eyes as she answered his question in a faux casual manner.

'I'll be predictable, I think…'

Luca heard her response to his question and was glad to take his thoughts away from where it was inconvenient for them to go.

'The *tournedos rossini.*'

He gave a nod. 'Good choice. It's mine too.'

For a moment her choice of such a rich dish surprised him. Then, his eyes going to her generous figure, he realised it did not. This was no stick-thin *fashionista.* This was a woman nature had bountifully endowed with a sensual appeal and a body to match.

He beckoned the waiter, watched the sommelier coming over too. After both had been despatched, he let his eyes rest on the woman he'd invited, without any logic or sense, to have dinner with him.

And whatever came after.

Ariana reached for her wine glass. She felt she needed it. What in God's name did she think she was doing? She'd let this man—a complete stranger but for his name—commandeer her taxi and bring her here to this oh-so-discreetly quiet French restaurant.

Beside the taxi she'd turned, astonished at his invitation, given that he'd clearly not even wanted to be introduced to her and that she'd stalked away from him. So what had changed his mind? Or hers?

I wasn't looking for this...

Yet it had happened.

'Why?' The question had fallen from her lips unbidden.

His expression had flickered. 'Don't be tedious.'

He had sounded almost impatient, as though she were irritating him by presuming to question why he had asked her to have dinner with him when the answer was obvious.

That single glance when I stopped dancing. Cutting right into me. Deep inside...

That was all it had taken.

As she'd sat in the taxi, unconsciously pulling as far away from him as the confined space had permitted, it had been impossible to deny. Out of nowhere, a single glance from a stranger had— Had *what*, precisely?

She'd been burningly aware of his presence a bare few feet away, conscious of the faint but evocative scent of his aftershave, of the sheer masculinity of the man, of the length of his outstretched legs, of his hand casually resting on his powerful thigh. She'd looked doggedly ahead, aware of her tight grip on her clutch bag but somehow unable to relax it, aware of the pulse thudding in her throat, the tightness of her lungs, trying to keep her breathing natural as she'd gazed sightlessly ahead of her at the stop-start New York traffic and the city canyons crushing around them.

Heading off for dinner with a man who was a complete stranger.

Luca Farnese.

The name rang no bells, but clearly he was one of

those people who moved in the same circles as the van Hurens—a banker or an investor or some such. She lifted her wine glass to her lips, still burningly aware of the man sitting opposite her. of the impact he was having on her, as she took in his chiselled profile, the blade of his nose, the high cheekbones, the sable hair, the line of his jaw. He was the whole damn package, from his lean, taut body to that subtly spiced aftershave and his intense, overpowering masculinity.

As to why—why him?—she still didn't know.

There were plenty of good-looking males in the world. But not a single one had ever had the effect on her that this one had—so that she'd upped and gone off with him when anything like that had been furthest from her intentions.

Well, why shouldn't I have dinner with him? I'm single and unattached. So what if I've only just met him?

Defiantly, her eyes flickered to him now, as she took a second jittery sip of wine. He was lifting his own glass.

'To an enjoyable evening,' he murmured, and his gaze, veiled and half-lidded, lingered on her fractionally before dipping as he took a leisurely appreciative mouthful of the doubtlessly expensive vintage wine.

She watched him savour it, then set down the glass, reaching for one of the poppy seed bread rolls in the silvered basket, tearing it open with his long, strong fingers, then spreading it with a curl of the yellow butter floating in an ice-water dish.

'So,' he began, glancing across at her, still with that half-lidded veil over his eyes, 'what took you to the van Hurens' this evening?'

The question was uttered in nothing more exceptional than a civilly polite voice, and Ariana was grateful. She needed to let the electric charge circling inside her dissipate. Conversation would do it.

'Mrs van Huren is a client of mine,' she answered.

They were speaking in English, and she was glad of that too. This was New York, and Italy was four thousand miles away.

And maybe I want to keep it four thousand miles away...

'Client?' Again, there was no more than civility in his question.

'I'm an interior designer. I recently did her house in the Hamptons.' Ariana answered with the same politeness that she might have used with any acquaintance. Or a complete stranger. 'She was kind enough to invite me to her birthday party tonight. I've just flown up from Florida, after doing some work for my mother there.'

'Interior design?' Luca Farnese said musingly, demolishing the last of the bread roll. 'Not my field. Tell me about it.'

There was a different note to his voice now. It was no less civil, but with a note of expectation in it that put it in the category of a business-based enquiry.

As if he were making an investment assessment, Ariana found herself thinking. Not that she required any investment funds. Nor would she ever seek them. She had not escaped her grandfather's hold only to put herself into the hands of control by investors.

Control by anyone, for any reason.

Her gaze flickered over him. Over the starkly good-looking face, where the hardness of his features was not softened in the slightest by being so ludicrously handsome, rather exacerbated...

If I ever did want investment funds—finance of any kind—you would be the very last man I would turn to.

There was an air of ruthlessness about him that she could sense. After all, hadn't he shown her that with his abrupt invitation to her tonight? Helping himself to something he wanted with little regard to the niceties of social discourse?

Every instinct told her that a man like that, surfacing from where she had no idea, would be a bad person to be beholden to. To be in his power…

She pulled her thoughts away. He'd asked a simple question—the kind that a man like him would ask about any business sector he was unfamiliar with—and she should answer him accordingly.

Their first course arrived—an assiette of *saumon fumé*—and she started to eat as she talked.

'What would you like to know?' she countered.

'Whatever you consider relevant,' he returned, attacking his smoked salmon. 'Do you work for yourself, or for a company?'

'The former,' she answered crisply. 'I would never work for anyone else!'

An assessing glance came her way. 'That sounds very definite. Can you afford that luxury?'

Ariana's mouth thinned. 'I make sure of it,' she said. 'I won't be dependent on anyone—or beholden to them.'

Even as she spoke she wondered at herself. Why on earth was she saying all that to a man she didn't know from Adam? Yet she was, all the same. And more.

'I'd rather starve in a gutter,' she said slowly. Unconsciously, she let her grip on her knife and fork tighten, and her jaw clenched.

Luca Farnese's dark, unreadable gaze rested on her, and he paused in his own eating. He said nothing for a moment, and then, 'You don't look like you're facing that possibility,' he observed, clearly taking in her expensive designer dress and overall chic appearance. His voice was very dry.

'I'm not,' she replied, her manner crisp again. 'I'm doing very comfortably, thank you.'

'Courtesy of the likes of Mrs van Huren…?'

'Yes, precisely.'

'Do you work only in North America?' Again, there was only cool enquiry in his voice.

'No, in Italy, mostly. I'm based in Tuscany. But I have clients here too. Some have properties in Italy as well—hence the link.'

'Where do you make the most money?'

'It's not a question of where, so much as from whom.' It was Ariana's turn to make her voice dry. 'Once I gain a client's trust and confidence, then she will often engage me for other properties, or to redo one I did some years ago.'

'So…' he glanced at her again as he resumed eating '…repeat business rather than growth of your client base?'

'Both.' Her voice was still crisp. 'There's a finite number of properties, even for very wealthy clients, no matter how often they're redone, so taking on new clients regularly is essential. I have to be careful, though, not to over-extend. Each client gets my exclusive attention, and I can't and won't dilute that.'

He frowned. 'You don't take on staff?'

'No—quite deliberately so. It would compromise my personal brand and give me headaches over management, employment law, et cetera. Even taking on freelance designers would be complicated, so I avoid it completely. I prefer it that way.'

'So what is your gross turnover?'

She blinked. 'And that would be your business because…?' she countered.

A thin smile indented his mouth briefly. 'Habit,' he said succinctly.

'Forgive me,' she said sweetly, 'if I don't satisfy your curiosity on that. Since I'm not a limited company, my accounts are my own business.'

A careless shrug of one shoulder was her answer. 'Like I said—habit.' A half-smile twisted at his mouth, not humorous so much as sardonic. 'I admit I find it curious to encounter someone who does not wish to expand their business or seek investment for such expansion.'

Ariana shrugged back. 'I'm comfortable where I am,' she said. 'I make a reasonable profit and, as you observed, I am not facing penury,' she added sweetly.

A waiter whisked away their empty plates and another deposited their entrées, while the sommelier reappeared to refresh their glasses. When they were finally left alone, Luca Farnese resumed his interrogation.

Why don't I mind him doing so?

The question fleeted through Ariana's thoughts, but she had an answer already. Several of them. Because it was giving them something to pass the time—a neutral subject that didn't matter.

But there was more to it than that, she realised. Memory stabbed of her pathetic attempts to get her grandfather to acknowledge her achievement in building a successful business from scratch. His response had been scathing. She would crash and burn, go bankrupt. It was inevitable—just a matter of time—she should have stuck to choosing colours and fabrics...

The old and all too familiar burning resentment rose in her, and with it came a realisation that she was actually enjoying being interrogated by someone like Luca Farnese. He was taking her seriously, doing her the courtesy of treating her like a businesswoman—not a silly little female, way out of her depth and making a fool of herself…

'How does your profit align with charging for your professional time? Or as against the uplift on what you supply to clients in material? And how do you manage cost differentials between suppliers and what you pass on to clients?' Luca Farnese was asking now, as both of them made a start on the succulent rich steaks of their *tournedos rossini*.

'Carefully!' Ariana acknowledged. 'I have to provide added value as a middleman, or my clients could go straight to the suppliers and vice versa. My USP is very often simply sourcing—knowing how to get what a client wants, from somewhere she hasn't thought of.'

'Do you carry inventory?'

'Some…but I have to be careful about that too,' Ariana answered.

'Dead money?'

'Yes, indeed. But it gives me agility and speed if I have something in stock that I know a particular client likes—I buy in anticipation sometimes.'

'Risky?' he observed laconically.

She nodded. 'That's why knowing my clients is key. I can sometimes be proactive—pre-emptive, even. If I see something—say, at an antiques sale—I can let a client know even if she hasn't considered that she wants it. Knowing my clients' tastes intimately is a big part of my value, and it helps keep them loyal to me.'

He went on to his next question, and Ariana realised she was finding it a stimulating experience. His line of questioning was keen, and without doubt reflected a surgical precision when it came to grasping the anatomy of any business. Interior design would be small fry to someone like him, of course.

Deciding she'd had enough of being the one under interrogation, she turned the tables. 'So, what about you? What do you do to keep yourself from penury?'

She made her voice light, but pointed for all that, to make it clear that she was done with this one-way discourse.

He looked at her speculatively. As if assessing her.

Does he think I should know who he is?

She took him on. 'The world of high finance, which I assume is your field, since you are a business acquaintance of Charles van Huren, is as unknown to me as interior design is to you,' she said to him.

'I invest,' he said shortly. 'I also speculate.'

Ariana raised her eyebrows. 'Risky?' she observed, deliberately using the word he'd applied to her earlier.

A curt shake of his head came her way. 'Hedged,' he said.

'Ah…' she took another mouthful of the melt-in-the-mouth tender fillet '…one of those!'

His mouth thinned. She could see it.

She knew he was about to speak, but she pre-empted him. 'I know…' Her voice was very dry, the look in her eye drier still. *"Don't be tedious?"* She eyed him. 'You were going to say that again, weren't you?'

'In my experience…' and Luca Farnese's voice was even drier than hers '…those who deride hedge funds are those who can't afford to invest in them or make the profits they bring.'

'Well,' she acknowledged consideringly, 'I have no complaints to make. I earn my money from women who are rich enough to afford beautiful homes, and you and your kind are very often those who make the money to pay for those beautiful homes.'

She gave a half-smile as she spoke, meeting his gaze.

Feeling its power. Wondering at it. And wondering, with almost a sense of confusion, just what it was about him that made her so physically...sexually...aware of him.

She'd known better-looking men, flirtatious and openly admiring, with handsome faces and good bodies—had even dated some of them when she hadn't been busy on client projects. But not a single one of them had possessed the dark, powerful allure that this man did.

She was ultra-aware of him—everything about him. From the way his cropped hair feathered slightly at the nape of his neck to the faint sign of incipient regrowth at this hour of the evening along the strong line of his jaw, the way he wore his charcoal business suit and the thin wrap of gold around his wrist in the understated but formidably expensive watch, the equally understated studs of his cufflinks.

But it wasn't the external things about him, nor even the darkly saturnine looks—it was more. Dangerously more...

It was the knowledge that the only reason she was here, having this unplanned, unscheduled dinner with him, was that he was responding to her in exactly the same way as she was to him. She wouldn't be here otherwise...

It was both a heady sensation and a disturbing one.

This has come out of nowhere. Two hours ago I'd never set eyes on him. Yet here I am, dining with him.

Dining—and what else...?

She slid the question aside. Unwilling, right now, to face it, let alone answer it. Instead, she asked a different one aloud—one to keep the conversation going.

'So...' she sliced off another delicious sliver of tender beef, dunking it in the rich, truffle-based sauce '... what about you? Do you have a base? Or are you one of those globe-trotting financier types?' She made her voice sound politely interested.

'I operate out of Milan,' he supplied.

'Milan I could live in, at a pinch,' she said musingly. 'But New York never. Far too modern, too frenetic.'

'I agree. But don't you care for Milan?'

She shook her head. 'Not really,' she conceded. 'Tuscany suits me better. I've lived in Central Italy all my life—my mother's family is from there.'

She knew there was an automatic constraint in her voice. She did not want to think about either her mother or her grandfather, in his opulent *palazzo* in Tuscany's neighbour Umbria. It was a luxurious prison for those her grandfather wanted to keep at heel. But her mother had escaped—rackety though her lifestyle was—and she too had escaped.

Only her cousin was still trapped. Poor little Mia, her grandfather's captive. Pampered and petted and kept in a cage she dared not break out of.

I offered her a way out—said she could come and live with me, work with me—but she turned it down. Didn't dare. Didn't want to lose our grandfather's approval.

She could not blame her. Mia had seen first-hand their grandfather's rage and his contempt for the granddaughter who had dared to break away from his control. Mia wasn't strong, as she was. Her meekness, her timidity, her gentleness—all counted against her when it came to breaking free.

She shook her head clear of thoughts that were useless. She could not help—not until there was something Mia actually wanted from her.

Luca Farnese was speaking again, and her attention went back to him.

'Killane...' he murmured. 'No other links to Ireland?'

'No,' Ariana said shortly.

She knew nothing about her father, other than the fact that he'd been good-looking, feckless, and had readily accepted a pay-off from her grandfather to accede to a speedy divorce the moment she'd been born. Where he was now was of no interest to her. Just as she had never been of any interest to him. Nor to her mother either.

She gave a mental shrug. She was used to not being wanted—neither by her parents nor her grandfather.

But one day I will be wanted—one day there will be a special person for me.

Who it would be she had no idea, but he was out there somewhere…

Her gaze came back to Luca Farnese. Something was happening between them…something that was impossible to deny, but that had been there from that first electrifying moment. She felt a frisson go through her. What had seared through her when he'd watched her dance—what she was burningly aware of in her every moment in his company—was like nothing she had ever encountered before…experienced before.

Could this be…? Could this possibly be…?

The question was trying to form in her head, but she would not let it. Too soon, too difficult…and far too uncertain…

Yet she felt strange currents swirling inchoate within her, bringing to the surface thoughts, wonderings, questions…

Her eyes went to him again as she cleared her plate and pushed it away, replete after the rich, delicious food, reaching for her wine glass. Against her own expectations she had relaxed—partly under the stimulation of describing her line of business, partly because this was

her second glass of wine, and partly due to a new aware-
ness taking shape in her, because he wanted her to relax.

Her expression flickered now. *It's why he got me on
to interior design. Knowing I'd let my guard down on a
subject familiar to me, something I'm so involved with...*

A question hovered in her head. *And just why does he
want me to relax...?*

She didn't need to answer that. It was in the way his
eyes were meeting hers, the way he was reaching for his
own wine glass, taking an answering mouthful. Holding her eyes just a little bit longer than the conversation
between them warranted.

*Beneath the surface something quite different is hap-
pening...*

His unreadable dark gaze rested on her and she felt a
sudden hollow open up inside her. It was not unreadable
at all. She felt her stomach clench, her throat tighten. Her
pulse quickened and her eyes widened. It was impossible
to prevent the tell-tale revealing dilation of her pupils.

As if a switch had been thrown, the rest of the restaurant disappeared and all the people in it. They simply
vanished. Only this man was here—Luca Farnese, sitting
opposite her, his long body lounging back, setting down
his wine glass with a click on the table, leaning forward,
reaching a hand out...

In a slow, leisurely manner, he traced across her cheek
with one fingertip, from her cheekbone to the corner of
her mouth.

'Stay with me tonight,' he said.

His voice was low. Husky.

His dark eyes were neither hard nor soft.

Only desiring...

CHAPTER THREE

LUCA FELT HIS gaze narrowing, pupils flaring. An instinctive, unstoppable reaction. As instinctive as the lift of his hand as he'd reached forward and made contact with that soft-sheened skin across which he had drawn the tip of his finger, to touch lightly...so lightly...on the swell of her lower lip. Then drop away.

He reached for his wine glass. Took a slow, leisurely draft, never dropping his eyes from her. He watched her face, watched the expression in her deep smoky eyes change. Saw her full, lush lips part slightly, heard an almost inaudible inhalation of her breath. Giving him the only answer he needed.

He felt his body quicken. Yielding to what he'd been keeping supressed—leashed—as he'd reverted with calculated determination to business, the subject he found easiest to talk about, even applied to a sector he was unfamiliar with.

It had served its purpose. Got them to this point.

To the decision he'd just made.

He wanted her.

It didn't matter that he didn't want to want her...that nothing about this tonight should be happening.

It was too late for such thoughts. What was happening was happening, and it was overriding everything else. Overriding all caution, all reluctance, all wariness. All reason.

Ruthlessly he put them all aside. Just as he had from the first moment he'd set eyes on her, sensuously dancing in a world of her own, drawing his eyes to her, dominating his focus. His response to her overrode them all.

His eyes rested on her now, feeling the power of her allure. Her mane of dark burnished hair, the deep smoky eyes, the lush mouth. Her ripe, rich beauty. A slow, potent curl of desire went through him. His body quickened again, arousal cresting in him, more powerful, more visceral than he had ever known.

His eyes washed over her. The dress that moulded her body was in the way—he wanted it gone. Wanted to see her full breasts spill free of it, wanted to peel it from her like a ripe fruit, to feast on what was concealed within.

He moved, restless suddenly, summoning the waiter, scrawling his name on the tab. He was known here. The invoice would be sent to his office for settlement. Then he was getting to his feet. Forgoing the usually required social civilities of asking whether she might like dessert, coffee, liqueurs. He had no time for that now.

Desire was unleashed in him—insistent and imperative. It shouldn't be there, but it was, and he didn't care that this was not what he should be doing, that this woman had no place in his life. That he should never have looked at her, should never have taken her to dinner. Should not now be intent on taking her back to his hotel.

I should put her in a taxi, send her off—consign her to nothing more than passing memory.

But he didn't want to.

Not now.

Not yet.

There was only one thing he wanted, and his hunger for it was increasing every moment.

'Let's go.'

He drew her to her feet, draping her jacket around her shoulders.

Out on the pavement, he turned to her. 'My hotel is on this block,' he said.

She made no reply, and he did not require one. All he required now was for her to do what she was doing. Walking beside him along the near-deserted sidewalk, not speaking against the traffic noise, her hands holding her jacket together, holding her clutch bag, keeping pace with his long stride on her high heels.

The charge between them now was so strong that it was like St Elmo's Fire, flaring around them.

Inside the lobby of the boutique hotel—small, discreet, ultra-luxurious and exactly the way he liked it—he guided her to the elevator. Still she said nothing, and neither did he. There was no purpose now in further speech.

Yet in the confines of the elevator he could hear her breathing, sense the tension in her. A tension he shared. Arousal was scything through him, blotting out everything else. He wanted to reach for her, release the tension racking within him. He was holding himself apart from her by sheer strength of will. Refusing to let himself even look at her as he stood beside her as the elevator soared upwards. Taking them to the only place he wanted her to be.

His bed.

Faintness drummed through Ariana. Not from the wine she'd drunk at dinner, nor the champagne at Maisie van Huren's party, nor even the upward whoosh of the elevator.

From what she was doing. And why.

Because there was only one 'why' in what she was doing. Though it made no sense. She did not do things like this. She did not go back to the hotel room of a man she had only just met. But she was doing it now.

With Luca Farnese.

But why? Why him? Why this man?

The question thrummed in her head, as it had all evening. Her eyes went to him. Fastened on him. On the aquiline profile, the sculpted cheekbones and the hard-edged jawline that was already darkening, the long-lashed deep-set eyes and the sensual mouth, the lines etched around it.

Drawing her as no man ever had before…

Knowledge flooded into her. Knowledge of exactly what she was doing—and why.

Because I want to. Because out of nowhere he's walked into my life, and for reasons I can't understand he has a power, a sexual potency I've never experienced!

But did she want to experience it? Did she want that dark allure of his to draw her closer? Did she want to give herself to its embrace?

She felt a sensation like electricity flicker along her nerves, felt the pulse at her throat start to race. Something she did not know—had never known—had happened as she'd lifted her head after the hypnotic rhythm on the dance floor, her gaze clashing with his. She had acknowledged that something was flowing between them. Impossible to deny. Primitive and primeval.

It was here again, now, in this confined space. Pressing all around her. Her and him. They did not speak, and he was not looking at her, but she could sense, palpably, the restraint he was exerting. It was visible in the set of his jaw, the compression of his mouth, the tension across his shoulders.

He's leashed—leashing the power he wants to exert. That he wants to release.

She felt the voltage of the electricity that was building up around them, between them, as if she were in the middle of a charged space, heat beating up inside her, flushing through her veins.

It was madness—she knew that. Knew that even now she should stop what was happening. She should break the electric silence, turn to him and say, *Actually, I'd better go back to my own hotel, I think.* Halt the elevator and send it back to the lobby. Get into a taxi and leave without a backward glance. Alone.

Leaving Luca Farnese to be nothing more than a fleeting memory of a single night in New York, having dinner with him and then walking away. Going back to Italy... back to her normal, predictable life. Familiar. Safe.

Yes, she would do it. She would do just that. The moment the elevator stopped she would do it. She would turn to the man beside her, whose dark presence was as tangible as if his hand were fastened around her wrist, whose aftershave was still catching at her senses, whose obsidian eyes she could feel slicing through her. She would turn and say that she was sorry, that she had made a mistake...

She felt her heart thudding, her breathing quicken, every muscle taut. The elevator stopped with the slightest judder. The doors slid open. She began to turn, to tell Luca Farnese what she must tell him...

A hand slid around her hand. Cool, strong fingers closing over hers. Silencing the words that died on her lips.

His head was turning to finally look down at her. His eyes held hers. Those dark, unbearable, obsidian eyes...

cutting into the very heart of her. Telling her nothing. Telling her everything.

Her breath stopped—her heart stopped.

Desire, like black fire, shone in the depths of his blacker eyes... Burning towards her like a black flame— a flame that consumed all that was reason and sense. Burning away everything but what was now left to her—a knowledge that was deeper than reason or sense.

This is what I want.

This was what had been engendered from the very moment she had seen him looking at her and felt him reach into the very core of her.

'Come,' he said, and his voice was low, insistent.

His cool, strong fingers meshed with hers, leading her forward to the only place she wanted to be now...tonight... She knew that with a certainty that burned away everything else in the world, in existence.

In Luca Farnese's arms.

His bed.

Luca watched her enter the room as he stepped in behind her, shutting the door and flicking on the two bedside lamps to bathe the room in a soft, low light. She was standing there, in the middle of the room. Not moving. Her eyes were huge, and smoky, and fixed on him.

He felt desire—arousal—kick inside him, hot and urgent. He was behaving as he had never done. Picking up a woman at a party just to have sex with her.

He thrust the crude description aside. Who the hell cared how they had got here, or how swiftly? It would be one night—one night only. One night of breaking every rule in his book.

Especially now...when you are on the brink of making a quite different life for yourself.

He thrust aside the warning that was trying to gain entrance. He didn't have time for it, nor room for it. Instead, he let his eyes feast on the woman standing there, full breasts straining beneath the fabric of her dress, hair a fall of satin and silk around her shoulders like a veil, parting to display the sensual beauty of her face.

Displaying it for him.

Displaying herself.

He walked towards her…halted. Her eyes were huge, lifted to his, fire flaring in their smoky depths. Her lips had parted and he could hear her breathe. See the pulse throbbing at her slender throat…

He slid his hand around it, thumb resting on her pulse, feeling it throb beneath her skin, feeling her tremble at his touch. He let his hand relax, easing it down sensuously to graze his thumb along the delicate length of her collarbone. He reached his other hand forward, trailed his index finger slowly, deliberately, down her cheek, seeing her pupils dilate, feeling the fine, subliminal tremble of her body again.

His hand slid over her shoulder, moulding the flesh beneath as he turned her around. He smoothed the fall of her tumbling hair from her back and she dipped her head forward. She knew what he was doing…what he was about to do. He could feel her still trembling, quivering, motionless though she appeared.

With a single unbroken movement he drew down the zip of her dress. As he did so, slipping the fastening of her bra, arousal flared in him more strongly, more urgently yet. He slid his hands inside the dress, around her body, beneath her bra. Cupping her breasts as they spilled into his palms.

She gave a gasp, head thrown back, and he began to pluck at the nipples, engorging at his touch. Blood surged in his body and she gasped again, head rolling. He gave a low laugh, his body responding as fully to hers as hers did to his, and pulled her back against him. The curves of her hips fitted against him, desire cresting at the lush softness of her against the hardening of his own body.

For a moment…a totally self-indulgent moment…he kept her there…

Then he released her, stepping away.

'I'll use the bathroom,' he told her, turning away, striding in, shutting the door behind him.

He took his time, methodically stripping off his clothes, draping them over the shower rail, putting his shoes beneath the vanity. The process gave him the pause he needed. The control he needed. Yet he could feel a nerve working in his cheek, knew how tightly his jaw was tensed, how focussed his gaze was as he reached for a towel to snake it around his hips.

For one long second he saw his own reflection.

It was that of a stranger.

I don't do this. I don't pick up women at parties and bring them back to my hotel room. I don't do it.

And to do it now—at this juncture of his life…

So why? Why was he doing it?

The question burned, demanding and accusing.

He got his answer as he walked out of the bathroom.

She was lying in the bed, half exposed by the pulled-back bedding, and her lush, ripe body was waiting for him.

For his possession.

The sheet was cold beneath Ariana's naked back and she welcomed it. Her body was a blaze of heat. Filled with an insanity she could not subdue. Because surely she was insane, to be doing this? Coming to the hotel room of a man she had never set eyes on before this evening?

She felt defiance spear through her. She was giving herself to this moment and she would not question why. A stranger he might be, but what was burning between them she could not—would not—be denied. Or resisted...

He is like no one I have ever known before! Whatever it is about him, it draws me to him. I just want him so, so much... I want him to want me and desire me...because I am burning with desire for him...

Restlessly, she moved her naked body on the cold sheet, arousal blazing in her. She had never, ever, felt it so strongly before.

Only now—with this man—he's setting me alight...

Anticipation, hunger, the longing for him, for his touch, his possession, made her breathing shallow, her heart race. She felt her arousal mount. Where was he? What was keeping him? She wanted him—she wanted him *now...*

And then, with a leap in her heart, a catch in her throat, she saw he was there. Walking out of the bathroom, his torso hard and muscled, wearing nothing but a towel snaked around his hips, which could not disguise the fact that what was possessing him was just as powerful.

His eyes were fixed on her, dark, and purposeful. He stopped by the bed, looked down at her. Her breasts were bare—there seemed little point in modesty now...not after his shocking, intimate possession of them. Her nipples were crested coral peaks, straining upwards above the sheet pulled across her.

Until he lifted it away.

He looked down at her completely naked body. His gaze seared her. Then in a single movement he had flung aside his towel and slid his smooth, powerful body, naked and aroused, down beside her, to start his possession of her. His complete and total possession...

Light was pressing on Ariana's eyelids. Bright and insistent. She didn't want it, but could not turn it off. Something had woken her—some noise. She opened her eyes, blinking, saw sunlight diffused through the window of the room.

The hotel room she'd just spent the night in.

With Luca Farnese.

She stilled, heat flushing through her naked body. Consciousness burning in her of the night she had just spent with him.

Dear God, did I really do it? Did I really fall into bed with him the very evening I met him? Fall into bed with him and have sex so abandoned, so intense, so absolutely incredible that I can't believe it was possible...

But how could she deny it? Or want to deny it...

It had been amazing, fantastic! Taking her to a plane of sensuality she hadn't known existed, had never known could exist! Just as, she felt her breath catch with wonder, Luca Farnese was a man she had never known could exist...not outside her dreams and longings.

She turned, reaching instinctively for him. Wanting to be in his arms again, to hold him close—hold this most incredible man, who had suddenly appeared in her life, setting her on fire for him....

A man, she realised, with a sudden hollowing of her stomach, who was no longer beside her in the bed.

She jolted herself up on her elbows, staring around. There was no one there. The room was empty. The only clothing visible was her own—her discarded dress and underwear on the chair where she'd left them.

Emptiness filled the room. The en suite bathroom

door stood open…the room was empty. She jack-knifed up, feeling her muscles and limbs protest at the sudden movement.

Limbs that had strained with their every fibre against the hardness of his.

Her hands had clung to his back, his shoulders, his hips, indenting deeply. Her neck and throat had arched as her spine had arched, as orgasm after orgasm had exploded through her, and her voice had cried out with it.

Memory drenched through her like scalding water and she gave a cry, her hand flying to her mouth. Between her legs a dull ache was throbbing, low and persistent. Testimony she could not deny.

Just as the empty room was testimony.

She stared around, feeling her heart start to thud with apprehension. Disbelief. Dismay.

Slowly, very slowly, she stood up, heart thudding more heavily. She looked about her. Apart from her clothes, the only thing she saw was her clutch bag on the unit beside the TV. And the note propped against the screen.

With shaking hands she snatched it up, opened it. Read the brief, curt words incised on the paper.

I have to go. Room service is on the tab for breakfast. I wish you well.

He'd signed it with his initials. *LF*. That was all.

She let the note fall from her hand. Numbly, still disbelieving that he had gone, she walked into the en suite bathroom, unhooked the towelling robe there and thrust her arms into it, knotting it tightly around her body. She could feel the thudding of her heart become a hammering. Feel nausea rising in her.

Like an automaton she crossed the bedroom, bare feet

sinking into the carpet, pulling open the door with nerveless fingers as she registered, belatedly, what the noise that had woken her had been.

Luca Farnese leaving. Walking out on her.

As if what had happened was nothing—*nothing*...

She stepped into the corridor, saw him standing a few metres away by the elevator.

'Why?'

The single word fell from her lips.

He turned, his expression masked.

He did not bother to ask her what she meant.

'Last night was a mistake.'

His voice was curt and clipped.

'A mistake?' Ariana's voice was hollow.

An impatient look crossed his face.

'It should not have happened,' he said. His mouth thinned. 'If you had any...expectations...please accept my regrets for the misunderstanding.'

Ariana's face convulsed. But he was not done yet.

'I wish you well,' he said. 'However, I can have nothing more to do with you.'

Her eyes were distended, her voice a bare husk.

'Why...?'

The single word came again, as if it had been ground from her out of broken glass.

The impatient look was on his face again—and something more. Absolute rejection.

'I'm returning to Italy today.'

He took a razoring breath. Eyes levelled on her, cutting into hers.

'I'm getting married,' he said.

Luca sat immobile in the hotel limousine driving him to JFK International Airport. His fingers gripped into the leather of the seat's armrest. In his head a scene was replaying. That tableau in the elevator lobby outside his hotel suite.

For a second—a fraction of a second—she'd held herself completely motionless, wrapped in a bathrobe, hair tumbling over her shoulders, face stark, after he'd said what he'd had to say…given her his reason for walking out on her as he had. Then a cry had been wrenched from her—a hoarse, gasping sound—and every feature had contorted. She'd started forward, hands clenched, hurling words at him like bullets sprayed from a machine gun.

'You *bastard*! You total, absolute bastard! You piece of—'

That broken cry had come again, and then she'd been surging forward, hands raised, closing the short distance between them to where he stood, rigid and rejecting, by the elevator doors. She'd pummelled his chest and he had seized her wrists, holding her away with main force and a face as black as night. She had tried to wrench her hands free, twisting her body frantically, repeating her denunciation of him, yelling at him, her eyes ablaze with fury.

And fury had seized him too. Fury that had come from somewhere very deep inside. From a place he'd never before allowed to get control of him. But which had possessed him then.

He had not spoken, only thrust her away, releasing her wrists as the elevator doors had opened. The car had been occupied, with hotel guests coming down from a higher floor, and he'd seen them react to the woman hurling vitriol at him, with her tangled hair all over the place, wild-eyed, features contorted, barefoot and wearing a bathrobe all but coming apart at her cleavage. He'd seen their shock, their embarrassment.

She'd still been yelling at him, but his own black, ice-cold fury had deafened him to it. He'd stepped back, moving into the elevator car as the doors sliced shut, blocking her out. Silencing her.

His rage had been absolute.

It still was.

With her, and with someone who was even more culpable than the yelling banshee he'd thrust away from him.

With himself.

For the criminal stupidity of what he'd done.

Ariana sank down on the bed, its crumpled sheets cruelly, viciously mocking her. She was shaking…shaking all over…her legs like straw, her body weak, as if she were made of tissue paper.

She felt eviscerated—as if talons had ripped her open. Humiliation seared through her like a wash of burning acid. To have done what she had—let herself be used as Luca Farnese had used her, so shamelessly, so ruthlessly, for a night of sordid sexual gratification! An empty, meaningless encounter that he'd *known* was to be nothing more—*could* be nothing more!

He had known all along. From the very first moment when he'd stood looking at her as she danced…to the moment he'd walked out on her, leaving her, used and discarded, in his tumbled bed.

In her head, his cold, dismissive words stabbed like an icy knife.

'I'm getting married.'

Those words had consigned her, in that instant, to being little better than a prostitute. And condemned himself, beyond any excuse, to being what she had told him he was, hurled at him in her rage and humiliation…

She wrapped her arms around her body as if to hold herself together.

He deserved it! He deserved every word I threw at him!

And she—oh, she deserved the other word burning in her throat. Choking her.

Fool. Fool, fool, fool...

To have done what she had done...

Yet even as she knew that, she knew something else too—something that cried from her. Something she dared not admit to...

That she wanted, with all her being, for him to have been the man she'd thought he was when she'd been in his arms.

Not who he'd proved—so cruelly and so callously—to be...

CHAPTER FOUR

LUCA SAT AT his desk in his Milan office, his expression stark. He *must* put behind him the insanity of the act he'd committed in New York. That night of sex with a woman so unlike any other he had ever been with. Sex so intense, so…so *torrid*—the hackneyed term twisted his mouth—and so explosive that it could still, a week later, burn in his head like a flaming brand.

Only sanity had prevailed. He had walked out on her. And when he had—when he'd stood by that elevator— he'd endured what he never intended to endure again. Her face twisted with explosive rage as she hurled her accusations. Her vitriolic condemnation of him. And behind him the shocked embarrassment of the occupants of the hotel elevator as they witnessed the scene.

Memory came from much longer ago. His mother, not caring who saw her in her rages. His father enduring it all, long-suffering, brow-beaten, doing nothing to stop the hideous scenes, endlessly trying to placate her, plead with her, making no difference at all to the way she behaved… And himself as a young boy, cowering, hating it, wanting his mother to stop—stop raging, stop being so *angry*. Wanting her only to hold out her arms to him… But she never, ever did. Never had…

He felt emotion from long, long ago clench within him.

Emotion from much more recently.

Both toxic.

His jaw steeled, eyes hardening. He would consign Ariana Killane and the disastrous night he'd spent with her to oblivion. Only one woman mattered—the woman of his dreams. The woman he was going to marry. And this very weekend he would stake his claim to her.

There was only one woman, from now on, whom he would ever permit to exist for him.

And it was not—*not*—Ariana Killane.

Ariana stepped back, staring at her colour board. With a frown of concentration she removed one of the fabric swatches pinned to it, replacing it with another from the clutch she held in her left hand. Yes, that was better. She reached for her camera, reeling off shots to send to her client, together with her detailed proposal.

It would take her till late this evening to complete it, together with the costings and timeframes, but she welcomed the work. Since returning from New York she'd done everything in her power not to let herself remember what had happened there. Yet every time she lost focus on work memory leapt—every searing detail of that unforgettable night…

Until she crashed and burned on the memory of what had come after it.

That was all she should allow herself to remember! That hideous morning-after, when Luca Farnese had shown her just what the night had meant to him.

Nothing—less than nothing…

A mistake. That had been his curt dismissal of it.

Whereas for her…

She felt an ache possess her—an ache for something

she tried so hard not to admit. An ache for what had never happened...

And yet it haunted her still with longing.

Waking in his arms, seeing him smiling at me, him kissing me, warmth in his eyes... Ordering breakfast—breakfast in bed—making love again afterwards... Then getting up and dressed...wandering hand in hand through Central Park...finding somewhere to have lunch. We'd talk about ourselves and tell each other everything, laugh and kiss... And he would tell me how glad he was we'd found each other, how amazing our night together was, how special I was to him...

Instead—

'*I'm getting married.*'

That was what he had said to her. It had been the indifference of his dismissal, the coldness in his face, his voice—the callousness of what he'd done to her—that had made her call him out for what he was, and her words had been as accurate as they were crude, as she'd hurled them at him in her fury.

The recollection of her blind, humiliated rage was her only comfort now—all that she could cling to along with the shreds of her self-respect. Yet it could not assuage the accusation still lacerating her, the knowledge of her own stupidity and the folly of what she had done.

Her expression hardened, face tightening. Well, she had learnt a lesson, that was for sure! One of the many in her life she'd learnt about not being wanted, not being valued.

Like her father wanting only her grandfather's money, not the daughter he had conceived. Like her mother preferring whoever her latest husband was to her daughter, jaunting off and leaving her with the grandfather who had only ever found fault with her. Like the grandfather so scathing in his condemnation of everything about her, with his endless unfavourable comparisons with her cousin, so meek and docile.

Like being used as some kind of disposable throwaway sex toy by Luca Farnese, before he headed back to the woman he was going to marry.

Her mouth twisted. Did that unknown woman know what kind of man she was going to marry? She pitied her, whoever she was. No woman deserved Luca Farnese. Not for a husband. Or for anything else...

Not even for a one-night stand in New York. For that, least of all.

'Signor Farnese—it is good to see you again. How is our business venture progressing?'

The elderly man rising with some difficulty from his armchair in the book-lined library of the resplendent Renaissance *palazzo* in Umbria was warm in his greeting.

Luca's handshake was brief and firm, and he waited politely for the elderly man to resume his seat before taking his own. For the next few minutes he made the required report to his host. His demeanour was respectful, given that Tomaso Castellani, even in his eighties, was a financial force to be reckoned with. But he knew that his own investment in the long-established Castellani import/export empire, broadening it into China and the Far East, was of greater value to his host than to himself.

But then, his interest in Castellani SpA was not confined to business matters.

It hadn't been from the very first time he'd come to the *palazzo*, some six weeks ago, at Tomaso's invitation, to explore the possibility of a business association between them. Lunch had followed their preliminary discussion—and it had put the matter all but out of his head.

There had been one simple, life-changing reason for that.

The angelically fair young woman who had walked into the ornate dining room as they took their places, her quiet manner as diffident as her smile was shy and sweet, her hesitant, low-pitched voice as melodious as her eyes were celestial blue, dipping downwards demurely as Tomaso performed his introductions.

From the moment he'd set eyes on her he had been lost, Luca knew. Captivated. This…*this* was the woman who had been in his dreams since his teenage years.

And now, today, he was going to make that dream a reality.

He felt his muscles tighten suddenly, as if a shot of adrenaline had surged through him.

And he would leave behind him, completely and permanently, all trace of that disastrous mistake he'd made in New York—and the woman he'd made it with. Who was out of his life—removed from it as precipitously as she'd entered it.

It was in the past, that night, and it was going to stay there. Locked away. Never, *never* to crawl back out.

It was one night—one night only out of all the years of my life! One night and one mistake. And it is over, finished—done with. All it has achieved is to make me surer than ever about what I want…the kind of woman I want. The absolute opposite of that one.

He wanted the woman who right now, at this very moment, was within his reach. And as he spoke to Tomaso Castellani, knowing what he said would come as no surprise to him, the approving, welcoming response of the elderly man only confirmed it—for why would he *not* be welcomed as so eligible a *parti*?

Genially, his face wreathed in smiles, Luca's host got to his feet, reaching for the silver-handled walking stick beside his chair. 'Come, my friend. First we shall lunch and then…' his smile deepened '…you have both my permission and my blessing, to make your proposal! And I do not doubt for a moment what her answer will be, so dear to me as she is.'

Nor did Luca doubt the answer he would receive. She was the woman of his dreams and he would devote his life to her and to her happiness. For him, no other woman would exist. None *could* exist.

For a fraction of a second memory flickered… Another woman—searing his senses…

He crushed it to oblivion. That woman no longer existed. He would not allow her to.

Ariana's expression was troubled as she stared frowningly at her phone. Mia did not often get in touch with her. It was not that they had grown apart, but it was difficult for Mia to see much of her, if anything at all. Ariana was not welcome at their grandfather's *palazzo*, and the more successful she was in her business the more unwelcome she was. It was a thorn in his flesh that she was not financially dependent on him.

Had it made him even more possessive of Mia? she wondered bleakly. Even more controlling of her cousin? Had her own escape from their grandfather's domination only increased that which he held over Mia? Although Mia had always been willing to be as meek and dutiful as their grandfather insisted, was she still content to be so?

If you can bear it, please, please come and visit, Ariana! So much has happened, and I long to see you again. I feel very alone just now.

Ariana's troubled expression deepened, and she searched her diary for a possible date for a visit. It would be tricky, for her diary was solid with work. Deliberately so. It helped to keep at bay the tormenting, humiliating memories that assailed her.

No! Don't got there! Just don't! You think that night with Luca Farnese was special because it wasn't something you'd ever done before. To light up like that, to fall into bed with a man you'd only just met just because he looked at you the way he did...touched you the way he did...made love to you the way he did...

Her mouth twisted. She was fantasising again! Luca Farnese hadn't 'made love' to her! He'd had sex with her—hot, torrid, searing, mind-blowing sex! She'd been a body to him—nothing more than that. A woman to sate his passing lust upon. A convenient female happy to roll into the sack with him—a last fling for a man before he hitched himself for life to another woman.

Her expression darkened even more. For him to indulge himself in a sex-fuelled one-night stand knowing... *knowing*...that he was going to be married, having committed himself to another woman and still thinking it was OK to tumble a stranger into bed... That... Oh, that was beyond despicable...

She dragged her angry thoughts away, focussing back on Mia. Her cousin needed her. Sudden decision filled her. If she dropped everything now, she could be at the *palazzo* in an hour or so.

Resolved, she texted back to her cousin. A moment later Mia's reply came. She sounded eager. More than eager.

Desperate.

Ariana's frown deepened.

Luca eased the gears of his car, a top-of-the-range sleek, silver-grey saloon, and moved off along the long gravel drive away from Tomaso's *palazzo*. Satisfaction filled him. And much more than that.

Relief—was that what he was feeling? Relief that he had finally achieved what he had longed for all his life?

Ahead, the wrought-iron gates, electronically controlled, started to open. But it wasn't because he was leaving. A car was turning into the drive, an open-topped sports car of a type popular with female drivers, in an eye-catching royal blue. It threw up gravel as it made the turn, accelerating forward to pass his car by. The driver was, as he'd expected, a woman, wearing a bright red suit, her head covered by a matching scarf. She had on huge sunglasses, her hands on the wheel in red leather gloves. She drove fast and purposefully, ignoring his presence.

He slowed to let her by, then found his eyes going to his rear-view mirror as she disappeared towards the *palazzo*. He frowned. Had there been something familiar about her?

He dismissed the thought, turning on to the highway and thinking no more about it. Dwelling, instead, on the woman from whom he'd just taken his leave.

His brand-new, absolutely perfect fiancée.

His ideal woman.

'What have *you* come here for?'

Ariana's grandfather's voice was harsh, his demand far from welcoming her arrival. Ariana shrugged, ignoring his reproof—because what else could she do?—peeling off her red driving gloves and removing her dark glasses.

'Mia asked me,' she replied, keeping her tone equable.

She tried not to rile her grandfather, though she knew that her very presence—her very existence—did so. She was after all, she thought, with a mingled stab of bitterness and pain, living proof of his errant daughter's unforgivable folly in not doing what he'd wanted her to do—making a suitable and well-bred match of his choosing. She had run away with a feckless wastrel instead.

Her grandfather's expression changed. Became pleased instead of disapproving. 'Hah! So she has told you her news? Well, go and congratulate her!'

Ariana halted in mid-removal of her headscarf. 'Congratulate her?' she echoed in a hollow voice.

'Of course! She is to be married!'

Her grandfather's voice was rich with approval. With satisfaction.

'*Married?*' Ariana felt shock reverberate through her. 'I had no idea…' she said limply.

Was this why she texted me? It must be—but she gave no hint of it!

Mixed emotions jarred within her. If Mia was getting married, that would explain why she longed to see her, as she'd put in her email. Ariana frowned. But then why would she have added *I feel very alone just now*?

'Where is she?' she asked her grandfather.

'Out in the garden—the gazebo,' her grandfather replied. Adding, 'The ideal place for a girl to receive a proposal!' he added, still in that voice registering strong approval.

Ariana's eyes widened. 'She's just got engaged *now*?' she asked.

'Yes, yes!' Her grandfather nodded irritably. His expression tightened. 'And it is as well you did not come any earlier. I would not have had her fiancé set eyes on *you*! He left just in time.'

Refusing to feel stung by her grandfather's criticism of her—when had she ever pleased him?—Ariana made the connection his words had instigated. That car she'd passed on her way in—sleek, black, with tinted windows. Her cousin's fiancé…

So, who?

Well, she wouldn't ask her grandfather.

Telling him she'd go and find Mia, she headed through the series of wide French windows opening off the grand *saloni* to the *terrazzo* beyond. The gazebo was situated on the edge of the huge stone pond, overlooking the regimented gardens with their straight pathways, severely clipped topiary and classical statues—not a garden for running about in or playing. But then her grandfather had considered any outdoor activity to be unfeminine, other than sedate walks up and down the gravelled paths.

The gazebo, at least, had been regarded as an acceptable destination, provided she and Mia had taken a suitable book with them to read there. Sometimes, when he had been particularly pleased with Mia, she'd been allowed to take her dolls and have a pretend tea party. Only when Mia had begged—prettily and gratefully—had Ariana been allowed to share in such a treat.

Ariana's expression was poignant. Mia had always been a sweet, sensitive soul. And she still was, Ariana knew only too well.

Please, please, let this engagement be welcome to her! Please let her text have been so agitated simply because she's feeling emotionally overwhelmed!

'Ariana, you came!' Mia's greeting was a cry, and she leapt up from where she'd been sitting, gazing out over the parterre, and ran towards her.

Her hug was tight—and clinging. But when she released her Ariana saw, with a shock of dismay, that she'd been crying.

And they were not tears of joy, as a newly engaged woman's should be, but tears of misery.

Luca depressed the accelerator. Shot off along the autostrada heading back to Milan. He was keen to get things moving. He wanted no delays. The wedding would take place as soon as it could be organised.

Personally, he would have been content with a swift civil service, but that was not what his bride would want. Nor Tomaso. So it would be a lavish church wedding, the whole event to be handed over to professionals along with a sky-high budget.

As discussed with Tomaso before he'd left the *palazzo*, it would take place in the beautiful medieval church in the nearby historic town. A picture-book setting that would show off his bride's shy beauty to perfection.

He gave a flickering smile of pleasure and his expression softened. How amazing it was for him to have found her as he had! Her angelic looks were matched by the sweetness of her disposition! Her shy smile…the cerulean blue eyes that looked so tremulously at him…her low, diffident voice. No wonder he'd been instantly smitten. She was everything he'd ever dreamed of—the perfect wife for him!

And, of course, Tomaso Castellani had welcomed his suit. Luca had made it abundantly clear to him that his precious granddaughter would be safe in his oh-so-devoted hands. That she would be as precious to him as to Tomaso, as protected and sheltered as she had been all her life.

'I'll take absolute care of her!' he'd promised, and he would keep that promise. *'Because she deserves it! She is as lovely in her nature as she is in her beauty!'*

There would never be any dissent between them—never any cause for concern, never any disagreement.

She will be my peace…

He could not wait to make her his bride. His wife.

Frustration bit at Ariana as she seized Mia's hands, sitting beside her on the stone bench of the gazebo.

'Just *tell* him! Tell him you don't want to marry him after all!'

Her cousin's face buckled. 'I can't! I *can't*!'

'But why not?' Ariana demanded. 'He's not a monster, is he?'

'No! Of course not! But… But he's…he's so…so *keen*…on me. I can't refuse him! Not after I've already said yes to him!'

Frustration mounted in Ariana, and she had to bite back her instinct to say, *Well, you should never have said yes in the first place then!* Instead she tried another tactic.

'Tell him you were overwhelmed! That it was so sudden, so unexpected, you didn't sufficiently take on board what was happening. Say that he rushed you!'

Her lips pressed tightly. 'Rushed' was an understatement—Mia had known the man less than two months and had spent very little time with him, nearly always in her grandfather's company. OK, so the man had been instantly smitten—given her cousin's exquisite beauty, Ariana could understand that! But surely he would see that Mia needed time—courtship, even—and that marriage was far too important to be rushed?

Didn't her own mother's sorry experience bear witness to that? Running off with her wastrel father and then promptly bolting with a replacement. And then a replacement for the replacement…

She realised her cousin was shaking her head, felt her grip on her hands tightening.

'I *can't*! Oh, Ariana, I'm not outspoken like you are! I can't tell him anything like that! He wants the wedding to be as soon as possible—he doesn't want a long engagement!'

'And what about what *you* want?' Ariana countered, her face working. 'Mia, you don't have to do what others want all the time!' She took a heavy breath. 'Talk to our grandfather! Tell him you don't want to marry! That you feel hustled into it!'

Mia's eyes filled with horror. 'No! That would be even worse! I can't! He's thrilled for me! Overjoyed! I can't do it to him—I can't!'

Ariana squeezed her cousin's limp hands. 'Mia, this is your *life*! You *cannot* marry a man you don't want to marry just because you don't want to reject him, and least of all because you don't want to upset our grandfather! You *have* to stand up for yourself!'

Even as she said that she knew how hopeless it was. Mia had never stood up for herself in her life. Up till now she'd never wanted to—had been content enough, so it seemed, to be their grandfather's favoured grandchild, fussed over and pampered and made much of. All that favouritism had never spoilt Mia, though—she remained as sweet-natured as she always had been.

Too sweet-natured…

She got all the honey and I got all the vinegar, Ariana thought ruefully.

She let Mia's crushed hands go. The thing was, she was just as protective over Mia as their grandfather was. She hated to see her as tearful as she was now.

She got to her feet, looking down at her cousin, her lovely eyes red with crying. There must be a way to extricate her from her predicament. It shouldn't be impossible—after all, Mia was only engaged, and engagements could be broken.

'OK,' Ariana said, sounding brisk and sensible, 'let's think. There must be a way of releasing you without causing anyone any upset.' She looked at Mia a moment, frowning slightly. 'Just to be sure—you *really* don't want to marry this man? I mean, this isn't just nerves, is it?

Are you not even a tiny bit in love with him? I mean, if it's got to the point of him proposing…?'

Mia shook her head. 'I'm not in love with him at all!' she exclaimed.

Her gaze slipped past Ariana and she looked out over the gardens through the open shutters of the gazebo. There had been an odd note in Mia's voice. Adamant and evasive.

'Mia? Is there something you're not telling me?' she asked slowly.

She put a hand on her cousin's shoulder, turning her around to face her again. Mia's eyes were filling with tears again.

Realisation dawned in Ariana. 'Oh, Lord,' she said in a hollow voice. 'There's someone else, isn't there?'

The tears spilled down Mia's pale cheeks. 'Nonno will never let me marry him! Never! He's English—a musician. He plays the guitar and he's been busking here in the town, for tourists—that's how I met him. I stopped to listen on my way to the hairdresser and we got talking, and… Well, we've somehow managed to spend some time together, and… Oh, Ariana, I've fallen in love—I truly have. And so has he, with me. But Nonno doesn't know anything about it. And he'd never approve—never! Matt hasn't any money…'

Ariana felt her heart sink. No, a penniless English musician busking for a living would not be their grandfather's idea of a suitable husband for Mia—not by a million miles.

Mia's voice rang out in anguish. 'And Nonno is so pleased that I am going to marry Luca! He's handsome and eligible and fabulously rich.'

Ice reached Ariana's lungs, freezing her breath. Yet

through her frozen airway she managed, somehow, to speak.

'Luca...?'

There are many other Lucas—thousands of them! Hundreds of good-looking, incredibly rich ones too... There must be!

But even as she prayed so desperately she heard Mia's answer. The one she knew she would give.

'Yes,' Mia said, getting the words out through her tears. 'Luca Farnese...he's some kind of financier in Milan.'

'Luca Farnese?' Ariana echoed, in a voice like death, and felt every last cell in her body freeze.

CHAPTER FIVE

LUCA WAS IN his office in Milan. He was leaving for Geneva that afternoon, but first he had something quite different from his business affairs to attend to. He pulled the freshly delivered folder on his desk towards him. Its pink and gold delicacy was quite at odds with the dark-grained wood surface. He flicked it open, glancing through the contents so carefully prepared for him by the extremely expensive wedding planner.

Whilst he didn't care about trivia such as floral arrangements and table settings, they would naturally be of interest to his fiancée. A copy had been despatched to her already—he would phone her from Geneva tonight and discuss it with her. Not that Mia would dispute anything—she always went along with everything he wanted without demur. The sweetness of her nature ensured that.

On impulse he picked up his phone, spoke to his PA in the outer office. He would order flowers to be delivered to the *palazzo*. More flowers. And at lunchtime he'd cancel his business appointment and take a look at some of the jewellers in the Galleria Vittorio Emanuele, the famous Milan shopping arcade full of prestigious boutiques. His fiancée already had a massive diamond and sapphire engagement ring, but he would find some pretty trifle for her and have it despatched today.

In his mind he saw her lovely face light up as she opened it. Delight in her celestial blue eyes...

'He keeps sending me things! Flowers every day now—and jewellery! I can't bear it!'

Mia's voice down the telephone was a plaintive wail.

Ariana tensed. Tension was her daily state now—tension and horror. And increasing desperation.

Dear God, Mia *couldn't* marry Luca Farnese! She just couldn't! It was impossible—unthinkable!

I have to stop it somehow...anyhow!

But how? She couldn't get Mia to break it off herself, no matter how hard she tried to persuade her. Nor would Mia go to their grandfather. And she'd almost had hysterics when Ariana had said *she* would tell him.

'No, you can't—you can't! He'll be so angry!' Mia had cried.

The word had tolled like a bell in Ariana's brain. 'Angry' would not be the word if she went to their grandfather and told him the real reason Mia could never marry Luca Farnese...

She shuddered. It was one thing to be defiant against his domestic tyranny—another to see in his face the disgust and the condemnation that would be there if she did tell him. And this time he would have every right to despise her.

Though no one can despise me more than I despise myself for my criminal stupidity.

But if she told Mia, would it give Mia the courage to tell Luca she would not marry him? With a heavy heart, Ariana knew it would not. Nothing would give her gentle, doe-like cousin the courage to do anything she feared to do, anything that would cause upset, make others angry with her...

Claws pincered within Ariana as she finally got Mia off the line. If her cousin would not break her engagement, then only one other person could.

Luca Farnese must break it off.

And, though dread and revulsion filled her, she knew there was only one way to get him to do that.

I have to tell him who Mia is.

Though she would have given a million euros not to have to do so.

Luca snatched up his ringing phone in no good mood. He was back in Milan after a night in Geneva, and to his annoyed disappointment, when he'd phoned the *palazzo* from his hotel to discuss the wedding plans, he'd been informed that his fiancée had retired early. Well, he would try again tonight—and if he needed to he'd drive down the following day to see her in person.

There was the honeymoon to discuss too. He'd already suggested a choice between the Seychelles and the Maldives, and he wanted to settle it. Mia had said she was happy with either, but there was still the resort to be chosen. Somewhere very private—that was his only stipulation.

Very private.

In his mind's eye he could see her…her pale, slender beauty enhanced by the azure waters of the shallow sea, like Botticelli's *Venus*, or the *Venus de Milo*, serene and tranquil. He would lift her into his arms, carry her into their shaded cabana, lay her down upon the waiting bed—

His vision cut out.

The woman had been replaced.

No pale beauty but sultry, dark-eyed, her hair a wanton cloud, her full breasts peaked and straining, her rich mouth lush and parted... She was lying there in his bed, waiting for him. A temptation impossible to resist...

Like a guillotine, he sliced away the forbidden memory.

'What is it?' His snap to his PA, who was calling him, was not civil.

'I am so sorry, Signor Farnese, but this caller is really most insistent. She gives her name as Ariana Killane—' she began.

For a moment that seemed to last for ever blackness filled Luca, obliterating everything else in the universe. Then it cleared.

'Tell Signorina Killane that her services are *not* required,' he said. He drew a sharp breath, indenting his cheeks so that they hollowed starkly. 'She is an interior designer I came across when I was in New York,' he went on, giving his PA an explanation that she could use in future, 'and she has been pestering me since.' His mouth compressed. 'Get rid of her.'

He replaced the phone, stared across the wide office. Black anger filled him. That she had the temerity to try and contact him *now*, all these weeks later...

Did she not get the message clearly enough? The message that I don't want anything more to do with her.

He sat motionless at his desk. It seemed to him that there was a precipitous drop in front of him. Ready to swallow him up if he did not keep very, very still.

Then he took another breath, slow and deliberate this time, and the sensation eased. His eyes dropped to the pink and white wedding folder. Just seeing it there was reassuring. Soon, in a few brief weeks, his fiancée—his ideal woman—would be his bride. And nothing...*nothing*...was going to stop that.

His eyes darkened. *She* was not going to stop it. The

woman he had left behind in New York. The woman he should never have indulged in—who had called him every name under the sun, yelling at him, making a scene...

Memories fused within him. The woman in the bathrobe, yelling at him in front of an elevator. The woman from much longer ago, yelling at his father...

No! He would not allow such memories. Not any more. Never again. They would not, *could* not touch him. He would live his life exactly the way he wanted to, taking total control over everything. Making life do what *he* wanted.

Always.

'Is that Ariana?'

The voice on her mobile was unknown to her, as well as the number calling.

'Yes,' she answered, in the language she'd been addressed in—English. 'Who is this?'

'Matt. I'm Mia's...friend. Look, I'm sorry to phone you, but I don't know what else to do. Mia gave me your number and I... I can't get through to her! She's not answering calls or texts—I'm worried! Really worried!' He paused. 'I'm scared she'll do something stupid.' His voice sounded choked. 'Or already has—'

Chill struck Ariana, but she kept her voice calm. 'OK, Matt. Listen. I'm in Brussels at the moment—at an antiques fair. But I'll phone the *palazzo*, speak to the housekeeper, and ask her to go and check on Mia. Then I'll get right back to you.'

She rang off and did just that. It took for ever to be put through to the housekeeper, and her anxiety only increased while she waited, but when she was finally put through she knew why it had taken so long. And the reason chilled her to the bone.

'Signorina Ariana!' The woman was breathless with agitation. 'Such a scare we've had! But it is all right now. The doctor has been, and Signorina Mia is perfectly well! He has forbidden her to take any more sleeping pills—she must have hot milk and honey, nothing more, if she has insomnia. Your grandfather will insist, so you have nothing to worry about, I promise you. There will not be another such accident.'

Somehow Ariana said what she had to say and rang off. Then she called Matt back, sticking to the housekeeper's interpretation of what had happened. Mia had been confused, forgetting she'd already taken a sleeping pill and taking another one as well…

But what if the overdose hadn't been accidental?

It didn't bear thinking about.

She flew back to Italy early, and drove to the *palazzo*—only to find her cousin not there. Her grandfather had insisted she rest completely, she was told, away from all the wedding preparations, and she had gone to a spa.

'Then I will see my grandfather,' Ariana said grimly.

The maid looked nervous. 'The *signor* is very occupied…' she began.

Ariana ignored her, marching into the library.

The scene that followed was hideous, but she did not flinch from it. Could not.

'You *cannot* let her go through with this wedding—not after this!' she threw at her grandfather. 'Even if it was only an accident…' she would not put into words her greatest fear '…what state of mind must she be in to make such a dangerous mistake? This isn't just pre-wedding nerves. She doesn't want this wedding to happen! You *must* see that!'

She might as well have saved her breath.

Her grandfather surged to his feet, face red with instant rage, banging his stick on the floor in fury. He rang a peal over her head, accusing her of jealousy, of wanting to ruin her cousin's happiness, of causing trouble as she always did!

'And do not think to spread your poison to your cousin directly! I have given orders that you are not to see her. You are not welcome—so get out. Get out!'

Ariana got out, her grandfather's vituperation echoing in her ears as she drove away, heaviness pressing down upon her. The wedding was in a week. What could she possibly, possibly do now to stop it as Mia had begged her to?

It was in the long, sleepless reaches of the night that it came to her. The only way. Unthinkable—but it would achieve what had to be achieved. Ugly, painful, desperate, and it would take every ounce of her nerve and strength of will to carry it out, so repugnant was it to her.

But she would have to do it.

There was no other way.

Somehow she must let her cousin know she would not fail her in her hour of need. However desperate the means...

Luca stood by the altar rail, watching with a softening of his expression as his bride approached on her grandfather's arm. Soon—very soon now—she would be his. And he would devote himself to her...to her happiness.

She will be my life and I will give her everything she wants! Everything she could ever want!

He could see it already in his mind. Their placid life together, peaceful and serene, devoted to each other...

My sweet, gentle Mia...

He smiled warmly at her as Tomaso patted her hand, then placed it on Luca's own. He felt it tremble and was moved by that. Her face was hidden by a long veil, and he was glad of that. The gown was simple, but beautiful, with a demure sweetheart neckline, and the folds of the skirt fell into a graceful train held by pretty little flower girls with wreaths in their hair. He had no idea who they were, nor her maid of honour—relatives, he assumed, or the daughters of friends. He was not concerned with his exquisite bride's family—only with his bride herself.

She was like a fantasy come true…

And just as perfect.

His smile of reassurance deepened. He did not mind that she appeared a little nervous, a little tense—he approved of it, even. Someone as delicate as she *should* feel emotional at her wedding…

He could not see her eyes through the veil, but that did not matter so long as she could see him clearly. He pressed her slender hand, to reassure her once more, and felt it tremble again. Then the priest began the service with a clearing of his throat, and Luca turned his attention to him.

His thoughts were strange as the ceremony progressed. Memories flickered across his mind.

Last night he'd dreamt that he was a young boy again, kneeling by the banister, filled with fear at the angry yelling coming from downstairs as his mother raged at his father, vitriolic and denouncing. And then had come the slamming of a door. And the silence. Deadly, ominous silence. And fear had bitten at his throat like a wolf…

He'd awoken in a cold sweat, and it had taken a while to bring himself entirely out of the dream and realise how different his reality was now. How it always would be.

His eyes went to the quiet, beautiful woman at his

side. A line of Shakespeare drifted through his head. *'My gracious silence...'*

Then the priest paused in his sonorous recitation of the words of the marriage service and Luca frowned, wondering why. What had the man just said?

'If any of you know just cause or impediment...'

Ah, yes, that was it—the infamous *Speak now or for ever hold your peace* bit.

For a second, a moment of time so brief it did not really exist, a memory flashed, so vivid, so intense, it seared like a brand across his skull.

A naked body, lush and wanton, a cloud of hair around a face set with deep smoky eyes, a rich scarlet mouth lifted to his... And desire, hot and humid, searing and urgent, scorching through him.

No! He banished it, obliterated it. Destroyed it utterly. It did not exist. He would not permit it to exist. Would crush it out of existence. It was in the past. Over. Finished as soon as it had happened.

No impediment...

No, none—because he would not allow it. He would allow only what was happening now. He drew a breath. Certainty filled him. No, there was no just cause or impediment whatsoever against him taking the woman of his dreams to be his wife...

Except...

From the back of the church came footsteps—like nails striking the flagstones of the aisle. A voice—harsh and strident—was breaking the hallowed silence. Heads were turning...breaths were being held across the congregation.

A voice was calling out.

Announcing.

Denouncing...

He felt his head turn. Felt his gaze falling on the figure of the woman walking down the aisle. A red suit exposed every curve of her voluptuous body. A matching pill box hat with a black veil concealed her face.

A veil she threw back as she approached.

At his side he heard Tomaso give a snarl of rage, start forward.

But he himself did not move. Could not.

He could only level his eyes on her with a fury he had not known he could possess—a fury that should strike her into silence if there were any justice in the world... any decency.

But there was no justice...no decency. There was only her voice, ringing out like sacrilege. Freezing him to the very marrow of his bones.

'He *cannot* marry her!' she cried out. 'I am pregnant with his child!'

The whole world had frozen. *She* had frozen. Ariana's hand dropped to her side, suddenly as heavy as lead. In front of her she could see the appalling tableau—her grandfather clutching his silver-topped stick, then raising it as if he would lunge forward and strike her. Luca standing there, as frozen as she, his eyes like pits, basilisk in their power to destroy her. And Mia—whose slight, slender body suddenly buckled...

Instinctively, Ariana lurched forward to try to catch her, but her cousin's bridegroom was there before her, folding her against him to stop her fainting fall. She saw her grandfather's stick clatter to the flagstones and then he was beside Mia as well, the priest too, helping her to a pew. Everyone was gathering around her. All across the church voices were raised...people were aghast, appalled.

Ariana turned. Fled. Filled with sickness and horror

at what she had done. What she had had to do...been forced to do...

Because there was no other way...no other way...no other way...

The words screamed in her head, circling like angry seagulls, shrieking and flapping.

She burst out of the church, desperate to get away, to find her car. It was parked in the next street, for the *piazza* had been kept clear for the wedding cars.

The bright sunshine blinded her—or something did. But she gained the edge of the *piazza*, saw her car pulled up against the pavement, one of many parked there by the guests. Urgently she fumbled for her keys, pressing the button to unlock, yanking open the driver's door.

An oath sounded behind her, running feet. Her arm was seized, her body hauled around.

Luca, his face black with fury, his hand closing over her other arm, was shaking her as if she were a rag held in his iron grip.

'How *dare* you?' he snarled. 'I will *destroy* you for what you did!'

Fury filled him—a rage so black it was flooding his veins, blinding his vision. But it was not obliterating the face of the woman who had done what she had just done.

'You vicious, jealous, destructive *witch*!'

He shook her again, as if he could make her disintegrate before his eyes.

But she was throwing her head back.

'I tried to talk to you! I *tried*! You wouldn't let me! There was nothing else I could do—'

The words were falling from her, defensive, vehement. Her eyes were distending, her face contorted.

He heard her take a ragged breath, plunge on.

'You wouldn't let me talk to you—warn you—'

'*Warn* me?'

Fury flooded him again. His mouth twisted derisively. He saw her face blench and was glad of it. Savagely glad.

'Warn me that you were so twisted and vicious that you would think nothing of destroying the wedding day of a completely innocent woman! Hurl at me a monstrous *lie*!' His mouth twisted. 'You're no more pregnant than a nun! I damn well used protection—'

His hands dropped away. To touch her, even in anger, was to taint him.

His eyes scored hers. 'Well?' he demanded, and there was ice in his voice now, not fury. 'Are you pregnant? Tell me to my face.'

Slowly, he saw her shake her head, and he felt again that fury engorge in his throat. His mouth twisted and he stepped away. It was not safe for him to be this close to her...

'Get out,' he said softly. It was a softness that he saw made her blench again. 'Get out. And if you *ever* come near my bride again, I'll—'

She gave a cry, throwing herself into the driver's seat, slamming the door shut, but opening the window. 'You *can't* marry her now! You *can't*!'

He leant forward, menace in every line of his body. 'I will do,' he said, 'exactly what I wish. I will tell her you were lying through your teeth in your despicable claim!'

'No! You *won't*! Because Mia is my *cousin*—and if you *dare* to think of marrying her now I will tell her what happened in New York! She will *never* marry you then! *Never!*'

He heard her fire the ignition, the throaty roar of the powerful engine silencing everything except the shock slicing across his brain. She shot off into the narrow cobbled street and he watched her go.

There was blackness in his soul.

And deadly, deadly rage.

Ariana was in her apartment over her office and showroom in a fashionable street in Lucca. She was staring at the text Mia had sent. It was simple, and brief.

Thank you with all my heart.

She felt sick.

Shakily, she flicked off the screen, dropping the phone on her bedside table. She was in a dressing gown, her hair wet around her shoulders. She'd been in the shower for half an hour, as if she might sluice from her body the memory of what she'd done that day. What she'd *had* to do.

Scandal, outrage—lies.

That showstopping lie in front of all the world to halt the wedding ceremony, to give Mia the chance she needed to escape her fate, to let her cousin faint dramatically to make it stop. Just make it *stop*.

And the other desperate lie—the one she had hurled at Luca Farnese, inverting the truth, desperate that he should believe it. Believe that Mia, who had been unable to face telling him she didn't want to marry him, would denounce him for having slept with her cousin…

She gave a choking sob. Only one person would be doing any denouncing. Her grandfather. And it would not be Luca Farnese he denounced.

She would take the fall for what she had done. She and she alone. For ruining Mia's wedding…for halting it in its tracks…for making it impossible for it to take place.

Well, she had succeeded in that—outrageous and drastic as her method had been. Had had to be.

And now… She shut her eyes, weary beyond anything in the aftermath of what she had done. Now there was just her life to get on with.

Her ordeal was finally over, and that, at least, was something to be grateful for.

Her grandfather would never speak to her again—but then how great a loss would that be? She had been condemned in his eyes long ago, by the very fact of her birth. This was only the finish of it.

As for Mia—well, she was free. And if she could find some way to elope with her beloved Matt…if she could somehow find the courage to do so…

I'll help her financially—I can afford it.

Wearily, she climbed into bed. She could sleep for a week after all the horrors of the day. So long as she did not dream.

Did not dream of the fury in Luca's eyes. The hatred in them. The loathing.

She gave another sob, pulling the bedclothes over her damp, tangled hair. Seeking the blessed oblivion of sleep…

CHAPTER SIX

LUCA REPLACED THE phone on his desk, a look of grim satisfaction on his face at what his lawyer had told him. Never had his features appeared so aquiline—he looked like a bird of prey, circling silently above its intended victim grazing unaware below.

Ariana Killane would pay for what she had done in that hideous, ugly scene at the wedding. And not just done to himself. To a victim completely innocent of anything. Mia—the sweet, gentle bride he'd longed for all his life—had done *nothing* to deserve what had been done to her that nightmare day. She'd even fainted with the shock, the horror of it all, on her very wedding day...

Done to her by her own cousin.

The fact that Ariana Killane was the cousin of the woman he'd wanted to marry was still unbearable to him. It had been thrown at him with such vicious spite, utterly destroying any chance of winning back his bride. How he could possibly marry Mia now, having taken her cousin to bed first?

She would hold me in revulsion—and rightly so!

He felt his guts hollow with self-loathing at what he had done that disastrous night in New York. That night he should never have indulged in, which had reached its tentacles across an entire ocean to entangle him here.

Meshing him tight. Destroying the marriage he could now never make.

Impossible to try and redeem the situation.

Only to level retribution upon the woman who had done this to him.

Destroy her life as she had destroyed his.

Ariana was in the office that opened off the stylish showroom she rented to show off selected pieces of furniture and artfully draped fabrics, as well as lamps, rugs and assorted *objets d'art* which might tempt potential clients to come in and book her services. She was going through her post, doggedly letting herself focus only on the usual mix of invoices and supplier notes, fabric samples, cheques and business correspondence, blocking her mind to anything else.

It was the only way to keep going—not thinking, not remembering, not replaying on an endless loop that nightmare day of Mia's wedding two endless, punishing weeks ago. It was over. It was done. That was what she had to keep saying to herself.

As for Luca Farnese…

She felt a chill inside her—and something more. Something that was like a cry of pain. The hatred in his face, the rage—the loathing… The memory was like knives stabbing her. Agonising.

Why? Why should it hurt that he hates me so much for what I did at his wedding? The wedding he deserted me for in New York…the wedding that he had intended to go through with even before he laid eyes on me! A man so despicable—to take another woman to bed with a bride waiting for him in Italy! But didn't I know what he was that morning I woke up without him? Didn't I know from that very moment what he was capable of?

She stared blindly at the next envelope in her in tray. It was marked 'Private and Confidential' and addressed to her personally, not to her business. She reached for her paper knife, sliced open the envelope, took out the typed letter within. It was from a firm of lawyers she had never heard of.

And as her eyes scanned the page she realised, with a sickening clench of her guts, just what Luca Farnese was indeed capable of...

'Signorina Killane, he accuses you of defaming him in a public place. That is the basis for his claim. He says you made a scurrilous accusation, knowing it was untrue, exposing him to the vilification and obloquy of all who heard you, materially damaging his reputation. You acted, so he maintains, out of malice and spite, ruining his wedding—a wedding upon which a great deal of money had been spent—humiliating him and alienating his bride, with the intention of revenging yourself for his perceived scorning of you following a highly transient sexual liaison of no duration and no emotional or personal significance whatsoever.'

The middle-aged bespectacled man addressing her across his desk steepled his hands, glancing down at the letter Ariana had shakily given to him, full of legal jargon, which he had just read. He shook his head.

'He is attempting to seek remedy in law,' he told her soberly.

'What can I do?' The words fell fearfully from Ariana's lips.

Her lawyer pressed his lips together and took a breath. 'Going to court is expensive, and you would run the risk not only of having to pay the damages he is seeking, but his legal costs as well as your own. I can only recommend attempting to settle with him out of court—as is set out here.'

'But he is demanding a fortune!' Ariana closed her eyes. The very air seemed to be choking her, as if it were toxic to breathe. 'I can't afford that sum,' she said. 'It would financially cripple me. Wipe me out.'

'Perhaps your grandfather—?' began her lawyer.

Her eyes flashed open. 'He'd see me starve in the gutter before he lifted a finger to help me!'

She got to her feet, her body as heavy as lead. 'I'll go to see my accountants—see if they can advise anything.'

That was indeed her next port of call, but she came away as dead in the water as she had feared. A loan of that magnitude…? Against her business…? Her accountant had shaken his head dolefully, saying he would do what he could but was not hopeful.

Bitterly, she made her way back to her elegant shop, walked into her office, sat down at her desk. She stared into space. There was a stone inside her. A boulder.

It would all go. Everything she had spent her adult life building up. Everything she had striven for, day after day, taking such pride and satisfaction in the fact that she was, by her own efforts, her own skills, gaining her independence from her grandfather, escaping his hold over her.

She set her face. Took a heavy, painful breath. Well, there was one thing at least she could be glad of. Matt and Mia were together.

After fainting at the wedding, Mia had been whisked off by their grandfather in a state of complete collapse to a private clinic, to recover from her ordeal and the ruination of her intended marriage. Ariana, of course, had been allowed no communication with her at all.

But she had stayed in touch with Matt, and had made over to him a sizeable sum of money that would enable him to launch his music career in London and rent accommodation there for himself and Mia, supporting them both. The next she'd heard Mia had discharged herself from the clinic and headed for London with Matt, planning to marry him the moment she could.

So at least what I did for Mia was worthwhile...

It was the only comfort afforded to her. Now she sat her desk, facing the ruin of everything she'd worked so hard to build for herself. All that was left was to wait for the axe to fall. Wielded by Luca Farnese. His killing blow.

In her head she heard his voice, black with savage fury. *'I will destroy you.'*

He would do so, she knew, without mercy or compunction. For what she had done to him.

Luca sat at his desk, an expression of grim satisfaction once more on his face. Now to spring the trap. The trap he'd set by issuing the writ for defamation, to which Ariana had responded in exactly the way he'd anticipated. She wouldn't risk a court case—she'd settle, just as her lawyer had informed his own.

Now it was time to contact her accountant. The man who was trying to find her a loan of sufficient magnitude to enable her to settle out of court.

Well, he was a magnanimous man—there was a limit to how much justice he would exact on Ariana Killane and what form it would take. He'd been the hard man with her. Now it was time for the softer approach. The generous gesture.

He smiled, picking up his phone. It was not a pleasant smile. Not pleasant at all.

Ariana's eyes widened.

'Are you *sure*?' she queried.

Her accountant repeated what he'd just told her and

her grip on her phone tightened. Could it be true? Had he really found a loan for her?

Fort the first time since that dreadful day of Mia's abortive wedding, three weeks ago, Ariana felt hope returning. She listened avidly as her accountant ran through the conditions. They were tough, with the interest rate high, the term short, but if she could keep her turnover going, could sustain her profit margins, then, yes, she might—just might—be able to stay in business, get clear of debt eventually, and emerge intact. She'd been warned that the loan was repayable on demand, but why would the lender do that if she made her repayments on schedule? Besides, without this loan she would go under anyway.

But I'll fight to save myself! Save everything I've worked for! I'll work every hour God sends!

'So, you are happy for me to proceed and give agreement?' her accountant was checking now.

'Yes! Oh, definitely, definitely yes!' she exclaimed immediately.

Ten minutes later, with the loan agreement signed by her digitally, it was done. Hanging up, she felt as if a crushing weight had been lifted from her.

As if to prove the stars were smiling on her, her mobile pinged. It was Mia.

'Ariana—darling Ariana! I couldn't wait to tell you! Matt's hired a recording studio! It's all set up, and it's all thanks to you! And we've got a date for the wedding! Please, please come—it will mean everything to us after all you've done!' Her voice changed. 'Are you quite sure you can afford all the money you've given us?'

'Of course I can!' Ariana lied immediately.

Gladness filled her as Mia chattered happily. Whether or not Matt ever found fame and fortune, he and Mia would be happy, for he was the man her cousin loved. And Mia was the woman Matt loved.

Her expression faltered a moment when Mia finally rang off. Mia, so sweet-natured, so angelic... Was it any surprise that Luca, too, had fallen for her?

The way he never fell for me.

Into her head stabbed Luca's harsh, scathing accusation. *'Jealous—vindictive.'*

Her face contorted. Was he right? Was she jealous of Mia and wanting to punish the man who had made it brutally clear that all Ariana had been was a meaningless one-night stand? Someone merely to slake a passing, momentary lust and nothing more than that? She pushed the thoughts from her head.

Luca's callous rejection of her was *not* the reason she had sought to stop him marrying her cousin! It wasn't!

I did it for Mia! Only for her!

The sound of the showroom door opening as someone came in stopped her self-tormenting inquisition, silenced the memory of Luca's condemnation. Getting up from her desk, she walked through from her office, putting a professional smile on her face for whoever had come in, whether it was just to browse or to make enquiries about her interior design services. Services she was now under desperate pressure to sell to as many clients as possible, if she were to have any chance of survival at all...

But as she walked in, without any premonition at all, she stopped dead.

The smile died on her face.

It was Luca Farnese standing there.

Luca saw the smile wiped from Ariana's face, and his eyes glittered. Hers widened in shock. Horror.

'You!'

The word shot like a bullet from her and a hand shot out to grab the door frame, as if to stop herself reeling back. Her other hand flew up in a gesture so automatically defensive he could have laughed. But his humour was tightly leashed—and so much else beside.

Calmly, he helped himself to the chair set in front of the elegant antique desk where clients could sit and discuss their requirements, crossing one long leg casually over the other and looking across at the woman standing framed in the doorway. He leashed his emotions tighter.

She'd gone pale as whey—the way she had when he'd confronted her by her car in the *piazza* outside the church, trying to flee the scene of her crime. The knuckles of the hand gripping the door frame were as white as her face, the nails as scarlet as her lush lips, parting now in the expression of horror crossing her face.

'I thought you might like to know the source of the loan you've just accepted,' he opened, enjoying every moment of this meeting with a savage sense of pleasure at what he was about to inflict upon her.

Justice, meet and fitting, for what she had done, the lives she had ruined—his and her innocent victim's… her own cousin! She'd had neither pity nor regard for her, callously and deliberately humiliating her in the worst possible way at her own wedding.

She seemed to sway, and in her distended eyes he saw realisation. The realisation that it was he, all along, sufficiently disguised through intermediaries, who had offered her the oh-so-convenient and timely lifeline of the loan that she had clutched at so eagerly. Given her binding signature to.

Giving herself into his power.

He smiled. She was not slow to understand—he'd give her that. Nor to cut to the chase.

'Why?'

She whispered the single word, and he answered it succinctly.

'You cost me my bride,' he told her. 'And you ruined your cousin's future. A cousin who had done *nothing* to earn your spite and malice.'

His tone was impersonal. He might as well be making some comment about the weather. He smoothed the material of his trouser leg, looking up at her again.

'But, unlike you, I'm not vindictive. I threatened to sue you for defamation precisely to get you to this point— borrowing money from me via a shell finance company I happen to own. You will pay the financial damages due to me. But,' he added silkily, 'there are other ways to pay damages that are not financial.'

He looked about him. The showroom held an ultra-tasteful display of expensive wares likely to induce wealthy women to wander in...perhaps to purchase some of them, perhaps to consider engaging Ariana Killane to refresh their assorted residences, either in Italy or further afield.

Memory plucked at him, of her telling him about it over that fateful dinner in Manhattan, when he'd crushed all his misgivings, ignored his knifing consciousness that had told him succumbing to the temptation he was indulging in would be a bad, bad mistake...

He pushed the memory aside—it served no purpose. There was only one purpose in him now: to exact his retribution from the woman who had taken from him the future he'd thought was within his grasp.

He heard his own accusation replay in his head. *'You cost me my bride.'*

His mouth tightened into a whipped line. His bride, the woman of his dreams—gentle, ethereally beautiful Mia, with her sweet nature and her quiet, tranquil ways—was lost to him. All that was left to him was this woman who had brought about that loss.

A woman who thought nothing of others. Who could spew vitriolic abuse in front of a crowded elevator and not care who saw or heard her histrionics. Who could play out her egotistical diva dramatics in the middle of a church, the middle of a wedding ceremony, leaving shockwaves echoing and the congregation aghast at the appalling scene, her aged grandfather near apoplectic and her own cousin collapsing in horror at the lie she'd hurled at her.

Well, Ariana Killane would pay for what she'd done to her own cousin, and to himself. He would destroy the business she valued so much in a fitting retribution.

But there was something else he was going to destroy too. His eyes glittered with dark intent. It wasn't just Ariana's business he would break. He was going to break her power over him—the power that had made him commit his greatest folly and cost him the future he'd dreamt of all his life.

I will break it because I must.

Because if he didn't…

His eyes fastened on her, standing there, still frozen, still ashen, her face stricken with shock and hollowing dismay.

He could feel his body's reaction to her despite his iron self-control, despite her white face. Her rich, sensual beauty blazed in his vision.

She was wearing a business suit in a deep royal blue, cinched at the waist, lapels curving over her full breasts, the skirt easing over her rounded hips, tight around her shapely thighs…thighs his hands had stroked, caressed, parted with his questing touch. The long, waving hair through which his fingers had sifted so lusciously that disastrous night in Manhattan was caught back now, confined in a net snood that begged to be ripped from her in order to let loose its glorious tresses, a living waterfall over her naked back and engorged breasts… Just as that confining, clinging suit begged to be stripped from her, to reveal the irresistible curves of her willing, wanton body…

But resist he must.

His jaw set, taut with effort, he veiled his gaze with equal effort. Resist he *would*… He would break her power over him. And break her as he did so.

Time to complete his retribution.

His gaze flicked over her. Still veiled.

'Tell me,' he said, resting his eyes impassively on her pale face, 'how long do you think it will take you to repay the loan you have just taken out to cover my claim for damages? I set the interest rate high, so you must take that into account. Given your current turnover—and, yes, I have a full dossier on you now…it was a condition I demanded of your accountant before I agreed the loan— and given your lack of assets to realise other than your stock… I am aware that this property is leased—that you do not own the freehold and nor do you own any other property. I would calculate it will take you five years at the earliest to be completely free of the principal of the loan I have made you.'

He was watching her face but her expression did not change, nor her skin's pallor. She stood there, immobile, knuckles still white, her free hand still raised as if to ward him off. Yet he could see, with satisfaction, that it had begun to tremble. It was as imperceptible as her shallow breathing but she was under stress. Extreme stress. He was glad of it. She deserved no less.

He waited, but she made no answer. After a moment, letting his words sink into her, he decided to continue. He had issued the bad news. Now he would feed her the good news.

But it will not prove good for her...

He felt his mouth tighten, his muscles steel, and deliberately relaxed his body, easing it back in the chair, never for an instant taking his eyes from her.

'Five years...' he echoed, musingly. 'Five years of being in my debt. Five long, punishing years. If, of course, I don't choose to call in the debt before then—I'm sure you understand that was one of the conditions I set.'

He took a breath, a considered intake of air, his gaze on her like a basilisk.

'But, as I said, there are other ways, Ariana.' His voice was gentle. 'Other ways to be free of debt.'

She did not move—not an iota. But the trembling in her upraised frozen hand was now discernible. Still she did not speak. So he spelt it out for her.

'You see,' he said, and his tone was nothing more than conversational, his gaze on her expressionless, 'you have ensured that Mia is lost to me for ever. So, since I cannot have the wife of my choice, I have decided to make do...' he smiled, the merest parting of his lips over his teeth '...with a mistress.'

He paused, savouring the moment. Savouring the flaring in her eyes...what it meant. His own eyes flickered over her again, and then met hers, head-on.

He went for the kill. 'You auditioned very well, Ariana—New York proved that quite adequately.'

He saw her eyes shut, then open again. Saw her whole body recoil, like a snake rearing to strike.

'Go to hell,' she said. Her words were ground from her, her mouth barely moving.

He shook his head. 'No, I don't think so. I want something out of this…this debacle. Something other than mere money, of which I have plenty. The loan itself is paltry—well, to me, at least. And besides, why should you object? You fell into bed with me the first time easily enough—and you enjoyed it considerably, to my recollection. So why not again? And besides,' he added, enjoying this moment too, 'this time around there will be an added bonus for you.' He paused. Then, 'If you please me sufficiently,' he said consideringly, 'I may make the loan a gift instead.' He got to his feet. 'Think it over,' he said. 'Then have dinner with me tonight.'

He gave her the name of his hotel and took his leave.

Only as he turned at her showroom door to take one last look at her did he feel something clench inside him, as if steel claws had sprung a trap. Which was strange, really—since it was he who'd sprung his trap on her. But the steel claws inside him clenched tighter, as if closing over flesh.

His own flesh.

Ariana dressed with care. A dark blue evening gown, sleeveless, high under her breasts, with a scooped yoke set with steel coloured beading, narrow skirts falling to her ankles. She wore it with a loose-fitting evening jacket in a filmy material, an even darker shade of blue, that skimmed her arms in batwing sleeves. She wore her hair up, in a pompadour style to give her extra height, along with four-inch satin evening shoes. Every centimetre helped.

She studied her reflection in the cheval glass in her bedroom, remembering, with a wash of nausea, how she'd sat at that vanity unit in the restroom of the Manhattan hotel, wondering if she'd put on too much make-up, worn too tight a dress.

Would it have made a difference if she hadn't? What if she simply hadn't gone to Marnie van Huren's party at all? If she'd made a polite excuse and gone for an early night instead?

So many chances to avoid this moment now, as she stood staring at herself in the long glass, wondering how she had come to this point.

And one chance above all.

She saw herself again, leaving that hotel in Manhattan, saw Luca Farnese turning to her.

'Have dinner with me.'

She felt her throat thicken. All she'd had to do was shake her head demurringly, murmur, *Thank you, but no.* And this moment would never have come.

But she hadn't. And it had.

And now all she could do was this: pick up her evening bag and leave her bedroom, walk out of her apartment on to the pavement below, get into the waiting taxi. Give the driver the name of the hotel.

Luca Farnese's hotel. Where he was waiting for her. Waiting to make her his mistress.

She felt emotion writhe within her, twisting like a snake. She silenced it, crushed it. She must not allow it. Must allow no emotion at all.

There was one purpose to this evening and one only.

Survival.

CHAPTER SEVEN

LUCA WAS IN his hotel suite, pacing up and down. He was not usually restless, and he tried to contain it now. But he could not be still. His mind was too agitated. The absolute self-control he'd exerted over himself that afternoon had taxed him to the limit.

With an effort of sheer will he stopped pacing. Looked about him. The reception room of the suite served as both sitting and dining room, and the table was set for dining.

Intimate dining.

Memory slashed at him...dining in that Manhattan restaurant with her. The woman he'd walked away with from that party, having had no such intention at all. His words inviting her to dinner—to so much more than dinner—had been out of his mouth before he'd been able to stop them or even want to stop them. And from that moment on—from the moment of her consent to let him take her to dine—the rest of her consent had been a given. Not once had she said no to him.

She wanted everything—everything that happened! Gave herself to it—could not get enough of it.

All night long.

It was like a wall crumbling. A wall he'd erected, brick by punishing brick, ever since he'd stood in the early morning in that Manhattan hotel room, looking down at her sleeping form, her hair tousled across the pillow, her body exhausted from their congress…her voluptuous, sensual body.

He knew every silken centimetre of it—had felt it shuddering beneath his, arching like a bow, straining every fibre, spread-eagled for his possession again and again and again… He had gazed down on it, knowing that he must leave her, whatever it took, whatever it cost. He must walk out.

Walk out and claim the woman he had left behind in Italy. The woman who had been lost to him now. Taken from him.

Now all that was left to him was to inflict his retribution on the woman who had cost him his bride—cost him so much more.

But *never again* would she have the power to do so. Not after tonight. Tonight would finish it. It *must*.

He felt emotion, powerful and raw, scythe within him. Blackness filled the dark sockets of his eyes.

Ariana walked up to the reception desk at the ultra-elegant boutique hotel, converted from a wealthy merchant's house in the *centro storico*.

'Signor Farnese,' she murmured.

Her head was high, her spine straight. She would do this in style. Whatever the depths of her humiliation.

The lift swept her up, and as she stepped out she saw the door to the suite opposite was already open—the clerk must have phoned through to announce her arrival. She could almost hear her heart beating, as if a bird were trapped inside her. One whose wings could never break free of its prison.

She walked inside, taking in the antique furniture, the floral display on a marquetry pier table. The only modern touch was a pair of sofas either side of a coffee table, on which was a bottle of champagne and two flutes.

But her eyes went only to the man standing by the window, open to the warm air of early summer. The man who was going to destroy her. Who already had.

Unless…

She felt emotion bite in her throat, bitter as gall. Poisoning her.

But she would not let him know. That, alone, would be her only salvation now.

'Champagne?' Luca made his invitation laconic.

'Why not?' came the equally laconic reply.

Ariana Killane strolled forward, approaching the coffee table, and picked up one of the empty flutes, a nonchalant air about her.

The flicker of a sardonic smile played around Luca's mouth. So that was how she was going to present herself—as if none of this mattered to her. Well, he would let her play it that way—for the time being.

His eyes rested on her. She looked magnificent. Appreciation purred inside him. Succumbing to her seductive allure in New York had been madness—every sane particle of his brain had told him so, even while his body had been inflamed by her, wanting only to possess her, to slake itself in her, in his searing desire for her.

But now—now it was very different. He would prove he was master of himself. Permit her no power over him. Only he had the power. And he would use it to the full.

He kept his eyes fixed on her as he opened the champagne bottle, filling both glasses. 'What shall we drink to?' he murmured, his eyes never leaving hers. It was a taunt, and he knew it—and so did she.

She didn't answer, and he knew she wouldn't—her

veneer of civility was rice-paper-thin, and he could see her tension in the line of her mouth, betraying the indifference she was feigning.

'Then I think that to an enjoyable evening is appropriate, don't you?' Luca posed the question with a lift of one eyebrow.

Again, she didn't answer. Her mouth only tightened minutely. In her eyes, deep in their smoky depths, he saw daggers... Swiftly sheathed, the blades concealed.

They only amused him. She had no power to strike him. He would grant her none. Never again.

He took a draught of the softly fizzing champagne, savouring its bouquet, watching her as she did the same, but taking only a small sip, as if it might choke her to drink more.

He lowered his glass, gesturing around the suite with his hand. He would select an innocuous topic to converse on, knowing it was as meaningless as their superficial civility towards each other. But it would serve his purpose all the same. Pass the time until he made his move on her. Broke her power over him.

'So, from your professional point of view, what do you make of this hotel?' he invited. It was an open question, posed in a socially inviting voice, deliberately so.

Was she grateful for such a neutral topic of conversation? Her expression gave nothing away. The mask she was wearing over that flawless face was perfect—except for that tell-tale tension in the set of her mouth, and the dark daggers in the depths of her eyes.

'It's been excellently and expertly done,' she said. Her tone of voice matched her air of cultivated indifference towards the reason she was here.

'Not one of your interiors, though?'

He spoke as if her answer might possibly interest him,

but knew she saw through it when she merely said, 'I don't do commercial work.'

Luca took another leisurely mouthful of champagne. 'And how is your business looking?' His smile was thin, his voice barely concealing the taunt. 'You will appreciate that I now have a vested interest in your turnover and profits.'

Memory snapped in him, of how he'd asked her what her turnover was that evening over dinner in Manhattan, and how she'd drawn back from his enquiry. Now she had no option but to tell him.

She did so coolly, in a crisp, businesslike fashion, outlining progress on current projects, indicating other prospects not yet confirmed, detailing upcoming costs, incoming payments. She answered all his questions fluently, holding her own under his probing interrogation.

Out of nowhere he found himself contrasting her to the woman he had intended to marry. What had he ever talked to Mia about?

Our wedding, mostly, and assuring her that although we would live in Milan we would make extended visits to the grandfather she's devoted to.

But what else had they talked about? He could not recall. Only that she had seldom said much.

But her quietness was what I craved.

He steered his thoughts away. Mia was lost to him. Taken from him by her own cousin's spite.

His eyes rested on Ariana, who was answering some question he'd put to her about the current stock value of the inventory she was carrying, and he heard himself interrupt her. 'Have you always been jealous of your cousin?'

Her expression changed. Closed like a door shutting him out.

'Mia is not a subject I am prepared to discuss,' she said. Her voice was clipped.

A stab of anger smote Luca. 'You ruin her life and presume to say that? To *me*, of all people?'

But her face remained closed, mouth set. 'I won't talk about her,' she repeated. 'What happened in New York made your marriage to her impossible. You wouldn't let me near you to warn you—'

His hand shot up. *'Basta!'* He would not tolerate her accusation! Her attempt to justify what she had done. The hideous debacle she had caused without a thought for her cousin—for how her words had caused Mia to collapse into a faint, prostrate with shock and dismay...

He took a heavy breath. He'd been a fool to turn the conversation to what she'd done. What did it matter that she sought to justify herself? It was impossible for her to do so. Her behaviour towards Mia was beyond contempt...

He fought for composure again and slammed down the emotions leaping within him. The anger she made him feel. He reached for the champagne bottle, refilling his own flute and hers without asking her. Then, crossing to the house phone, he gave the order for dinner to be served.

It came quickly, and he was glad. The serving of it gave him time to calm himself, get back in control. The control it was essential for him to exert to make her destruction complete.

How she got through dinner Ariana didn't know. She ate mechanically, which was an abuse of the gourmet dishes placed in front of her, grateful that the serving staff had not been dismissed. It gave her some shelter—frail but at least present—from being alone with Luca Farnese.

The man who had summoned her here to spend the night with him.

While the waiting staff were there he kept up a flow of small talk, to which she replied as mechanically as she ate. What it was about she had little idea—Lucca, mostly, and its history…the annual opera festival held in honour of its most famous son, Giacomo Puccini. She hardly knew. Or cared. All her strength was going into staying seated, lifting her fork to her mouth, making whatever replies were appropriate.

Not looking at him.

Not remembering.

As the excruciating meal finally finished, and she pushed aside her half-eaten *tarte framboise*, she heard Luca speak to the staff, telling them to serve coffee in the sitting area of the suite. Then he got to his feet.

'Shall we?' he said to Ariana.

His voice was smooth. Too smooth.

She stood up too, and walked across to one of the pair of facing sofas, sitting down on it with as much poise as she could muster, feeling the folds of her dress drape softly on the velvet upholstery. She had drunk very little wine, yet along with the glass of champagne earlier it had been more than dangerous. She could feel her heart rate increase, the tension racking through her.

Soon, very soon now, she would face her fate.

She watched the serving staff set out a coffee tray in front of her and clear away the dinner dishes, saw Luca presenting them with an obviously generous tip before they wheeled away the trolleys.

Leaving her alone with Luca Farnese.

And all that must shortly come.

The dread thudding in her heart grew heavier yet.

He sat down on the sofa opposite her. Without volition

her eyes went to him. Went to his aquiline profile as he leant forward slightly to pour coffee, the expensive material of his dark grey suit straining across his powerful thighs. Thighs that had pressed her oh-so-yielding body into the mattress that unforgettable night in New York...

Her eyes went to his hands now, as his long, strong fingers curved around the silver coffee pot handle—hands that had stroked her body, fingers that had expertly caressed her body's innermost secret recesses, drawn from her a shuddering ecstasy that had made her cry out aloud in gasping breaths her neck and spine arched impossibly.

She remembered her own hands digging into the supple sinews of his broad muscled shoulders as he brought her to a peak of pleasure that she had never known... only to realise she had not even begun to feel all he could make her feel as her body bowed, lifting for him, and he plunged deep within her in total, absolute possession...

Memory scorched within her, sending blood rushing to her face. She looked away immediately, willing her high colour to subside, digging her nails into her palms.

'Cream with your coffee?'

Luca's deep voice penetrated her agitation, and with forcible effort she turned to him, making her face expressionless.

'Thank you,' she said.

He handed her a cup, pushing the jug towards her, and she thankfully busied herself pouring in cream, stirring as she did so, watching, as if it were a fascinating movie, how the rich cream swirled into the dark, aromatic coffee.

'Sugar?'

Luca's deep voice came again, but this time Ariana shook her head.

'Sweet enough already?'

His jibe was open, and it made her eyes flash to him.

'And I have reason to be *sweet* right now because…?' she retorted, just as jibing.

Something darkened in his slate-grey eyes and she saw a momentary tightening of his mouth.

'Perhaps because I've thrown you a financial lifeline to save your business?' He matched her retort.

She was silent, jaw set, knowing she could not answer back this time. She lifted her cup with a jerky movement, took an unwise mouthful of hot coffee. But she made no show of how hot it had been. Made no show of anything she felt.

He was speaking again, his voice silky. 'So a little more appreciation of my…generosity…would not go amiss, hmm?'

His eyes were resting on her as he sat back, crossing one long leg over the other, making himself comfortable as he held his coffee cup, stirring the cream in a leisurely fashion.

What was in that gaze except a toxic taunt…? Oh, dear God. That rush of colour threatened yet again. There was a hint of what she knew must come… Both reminiscence over that fateful, torrid night of sex in New York and anticipation of a repeat performance.

Was he expecting her to reply to what he'd just said? The words choked in her throat and she dropped her eyes to her coffee cup, busying herself with taking another sip, less scalding this time.

He let her drink uninterrupted, and as she did so she could feel the caffeine start to hit. Bringing everything into focus. She lifted her eyes to the man sitting opposite her. His own eyes were still resting on her. In the soft light she could not make out their expression. But she did not need to. She knew what would be in them.

She set down her empty coffee cup, got to her feet.

His eyes followed her as she crossed the narrow space between them. He put down his own cup, got to his feet as well. Less than a metre from her. She caught the scent of his aftershave—the same as he'd worn in New York.

For a second she felt faint... Then she forced herself to speak. To say what she must say. Or lose what was most precious to her...

'You said...' Ariana heard her own voice as if it came from a long, long way away '...you wanted my...appreciation.'

He looked at her, his gaze unreadable, but she saw the tightness of his mouth, the steeling of his jaw.

'Tell me,' she went on, and she could hear the husk in her voice, knew why it was there, 'if I show you my...appreciation...what will you do for me? Will you write off the loan you hold over my head? So that I need not to repay it?'

He was standing stock-still, but he lifted a hand, reaching forward. His forefinger brushed down her cheek. Slowly, consideringly. It felt like a burning brand, searing her skin.

Branding me. Owning me. Body and soul.

He gave her his answer, his voice an open taunt, 'Perhaps that depends on just how appreciative you are.'

His long lashes dipped over his eyes, then lifted, and in their pitiless depths she could see all that she feared.

'Perhaps,' he said, and now he drew his forefinger down her throat, 'you might give me a demonstration?'

She felt his finger like the blade of a knife. As if it were drawing blood. He wanted *her* to make the move. Wanted *her* to commit the act that he required—her abject surrender. Her complete humiliation.

But she had been humiliated by him before.

And she would never, *never* let him do so again.

Never. Whatever it costs me!

Her business could go down the drain…she could lose everything she possessed—but not what was most precious to her. The one thing she would never lose again.

My self-respect. That is all I care about now—all that is vital to me. Essential!

Defiance blazed in her. A sheet of fury, white-hot and lethal. In a sudden jerking movement she stepped away, head snapping back, hands flying up to ward him off. There was denial in every line of her body. Scorn in her flashing eyes. Words spat from her. And there was absolute refusal in them, lashing like a whip.

'In your dreams! In your *dreams*, Luca Farnese—because you'll get nothing else! *Nothing!* I'd starve in a gutter first!'

Vehemence seared her like a branding iron on flesh as she reared back from him, from what he wanted of her, what he thought he could reduce her to. Begging from him with her body.

His reaction was so fast she could not foresee it, let alone avoid it. Hands snaked out, seized her shoulders, fastening over them like iron. And what was in his face now she had never seen before.

'*Dreams? Of you*?' A harsh, mocking laugh broke from him, cut off with a contortion of his features. 'Do you know why I summoned you here tonight? Let you think you could prostitute yourself for me?'

The iron grip of his hands tightened, his fingers digging into her. His voice had been a snarl, and it came again now.

'So I could do exactly what I'm doing now! Throw you from me like rotten flesh!'

His hands lifted from her as though she were poison, contaminated, and the movement was so sudden she reeled back as if he had actually flung her from him.

His voice was low, feral, his eyes like dark pits of fire. 'Do you think I would *ever* sully myself on you again? A woman like *you*?'

She stumbled back, hands flailing helplessly, trying to get her balance. Her face contorted. Mouth twisting as she heard what he'd just hurled at her.

Her voice choked as she spat back at him. It was all she could do. 'Go to *hell*, Luca Farnese! Just go to *hell*!'

She lurched away, snatching up her evening bag, half stumbling to the door of the suite, long skirts twisting around her legs, impeding her. She had to get out of there...she was suffocating, drowning...

From the moment Luca Farnese had told her to her face that he would take her to his bed again she had vowed to reject him with all the scorn and fury she was capable of. And all along...

All along he'd been planning a completely different kind of humiliation. Even crueller.

A choking sound broke from her and she clutched at the door handle, trying to yank the door open, fumbling with the catch because she was shaking, desperate, beyond anything, only wanting to escape—flee, get away...

She couldn't bear to be here—couldn't bear to breathe the same air as him.

Couldn't bear it...

A hand closed over her shoulder again like an iron vice, hauling her around. 'You're going nowhere!'

He towered over her, eyes like dark fire, face twisted in rage. Rage at her defiance? Her escape? She didn't know. Didn't care. Knew only that she had to breathe fresh air—or drown.

'Let me go!' Her voice was piercing—desperate.

Her eyes flared upwards, into his. And out of nowhere fear filled her. Not fear of his physical hold on her, which was lessening even as the fear seized her. But a fear that came from a far more terrifying place...

From herself. Her own body...

Treacherous—betraying.

The grip on her shoulder changed. His mouth untwisted. Only the dark fire in his eyes remained.

Pouring into her.

Burning into her.

For one endless moment they stood, frozen in time.

Then she spoke again: 'Let me go.' It was a halting, faltering whisper. A plea.

Slowly, infinitely slowly, her gaze agonising, she watched him shake his head.

'I can't.' A rasp broke from him. 'I can't let go of you—' he said.

And yet his hand dropped from her shoulder and she felt her body sway with the release of his grip. She must turn away—walk away—she *must*...

But she did not move. The world had stopped—so had her breathing, her pulse, the very beat of her heart. All had stopped. And still she could not move. His eyes were burning into hers, with a dark, dark fire in their bottomless depths. She could not wrench hers away. Could do nothing...

She heard him say her name. A hollow husk. Saw his hand lift to her waist. Felt weakness drown her...

His hand moved around her waist slowly, infinitely slowly, and she knew with what was left of any consciousness within her that she must step back—that stepping back, leaving, was the only sane thing to do...

But there was no sanity any longer. No sense, no consciousness...no rage or scorn or anger or fury. Only the flame beating up in her, burning all her senses, possessing her...

He said her name again, low and hoarse and broken. He stepped towards her, drawing her to him, his hand splaying out over her spine.

She was pliant, yielding...

Yielding to what was possessing her. Consuming her. Even as her mouth, lips parting, lifted to his...

CHAPTER EIGHT

HER MOUTH WAS VELVET. Velvet and silk and honey and nectar. He could only gorge on it. Everything dissolved around him. All sense…all shame. All purpose but this.

Somewhere he heard the sound of words shredding in his head like torn rags. This was not what he'd intended…

She was supposed to have come here—supplicant, desperate—and I was to have let her come, let her believe that I would allow her to do what she thought I was offering her. And then, when the moment came and she offered herself to me, I would thrust her from me—cast her aside. Show her that she had nothing that I wanted! Show her she had no power over me. Show myself that she has no power over me…

The very thought was a searing mockery to him now. She was in his arms, her body pressed to his, her mouth opening to his. His mouth was devouring hers and hers his. Desire—urgent…desperate—was leaping in them both. Desire that was impossible to deny. To defeat…

Her breasts were cresting against him and he could feel his arousal spearing him, widening his stance, could feel her hips crushing into his, feel the blinding flame of desire flare up in her as it did in himself. Unquenchable…consuming everything. His will, his reason, his conscious mind.

All evening he had fought it—from the moment she'd walked in, so incandescently alluring, just as she had been that first fatal evening when her lush, wanton beauty had inflamed him. But he had steeled himself, exerted his iron strength to see this through to the end. To the moment when he would complete his destruction of her.

By rejecting her.

Rejecting who she was and what she had done to him. What she would never do to him again.

What she was doing now…

Blindly he lifted her into his arms, felt the ripe lushness of her body pressing against his as he carried her into his bedroom.

Into his bed.

His whole body was aflame for her. Consuming him in its fire.

Light was filtering through shuttered windows. Light that burnt.

Ariana opened her eyes.

Luca was standing there, looking down at her. He had on a bathrobe. His jaw was unshaven. Eyes like granite. For an endless moment he simply went on looking at her, nothing in his eyes, in his face. Nothing at all.

Then he turned and walked into the en suite bathroom. Then silence.

She turned her head aside. Inside her chest her heart started to thud. The drum beats of a funeral.

Slowly, agonisingly, she made herself get out of bed. Made herself find her clothes, struggle into the evening gown that was on the floor, force her feet into her sandals. Made herself walk out of the bedroom, find her handbag, head for the door.

She was about to walk out of another hotel room, another hotel. Another city. But away from the same man. Déjà vu all over again…

Except for one small detail.

As she opened the door a voice behind her sounded. Harsh. Low. And taut as a garotte.

'I used no protection—I had none with me.'

Ariana turned, horror filling her.

It was the worst two weeks of Ariana's life.

If she had thought the days following her precipitate flight from New York unbearable, that was nothing, nothing at all, compared to each and every day now, that crawled with agonising slowness towards the due date of her next period. Only then could she be sure that any pregnancy test would be accurate and not a false negative.

Because she could not risk that! Could not risk feeling the desperate relief that the disaster of that hellish night had not resulted in what she feared most. She could not risk thinking she was safe—and then find she was not.

And when her regular-as-clockwork period failed to arrive she knew, with the same horror that had possessed her when Luca had thrown his declaration at her, that all her desperate hope had been in vain. A knowledge confirmed, like a vice crushing all the air out of her lungs, as she stared two days later at the vivid blue line on the pregnancy test stick.

Only one shred of hope was left for her to cling to. The lie she had managed somehow, with a strength she had not known she still possessed, to throw back at Luca before she'd made her escape from him.

'Don't worry—I'm protected!'

She had thrown it at him in a defiant snarl and from an impulse that had overridden everything else. Because there was only one thing worse than her being pregnant by Luca—and that was him knowing it.

Cold ran down her spine now as she took in the implications of that blue line. Pregnant. She was pregnant. She had conceived Luca's baby. She wanted to laugh—a hysterical, demented laugh. Because what other response could she give to such a realisation? Instead, she found her arms going around her midriff, in a protective gesture as old as time.

But there was only one person she must protect her baby from.

Its father.

Luca was working. He was working every hour God sent and then some. He was flying around the world. Working on the plane. Working in the hotels he stayed at. Working when he was back in his apartment in Milan, long into the early hours. Working to forget.

To blank. To block.

To deny.

Deny his own insanity.

Deny what he had done...what he had succumbed to. What he had committed.

How could I have done it? How could I?

He stared darkly and unseeing at his computer screen, the words and the numbers blurring into an incomprehensible mass.

A mess as incomprehensible as the criminal folly of what he had done.

Taken Ariana to his bed again.

The one woman in all the world he did not want to want.

Ariana was planning. Planning with an urgency that was driving her like a demon. First to work to a punishing schedule, finishing off every project, banking all the money she could—her survival fund.

It would not be much, but it would be essential. It would get her to the UK where she would try to live and work. Staying first with Mia and Matt, she'd use her contacts to get a job. See out her pregnancy, either as a designer or, at worst, a saleswoman. Her own business was finished—it had been since Luca had shown himself to be her mystery money lender.

Her own words seared in her memory.

'I'd sooner starve in a gutter!'

She gave a thin smile. Well, it would not be a gutter, and she would not quite starve, but everything would go—from the last bolt of fabric to her racy little car. Luca could pick the bones of her business clean if he so wanted. But that was all he would get.

Nothing else.

Instinctively—protectively—Ariana's splayed hand dropped again to her midriff...

Luca's mobile was ringing.

'Si?' His voice was curt as he took the call. He knew who it was, or he would not have answered.

'There is news, Signor Farnese.'

The caller's tone was neutral. Carefully so.

'And?'

Luca's expression did not change as he listened.

But something inside him changed.

His whole world changed.

Ariana gave a last glance around her bedroom. A pang smote her. She was losing what she had taken her adult life to build—an independence that was hers and hers alone. Now she must make a new life—for herself and her baby.

She hefted up her single suitcase—all she was taking with her. She gave a sour smile. Luca could make what use he wanted of her designer outfits. She would have no use for them as her pregnancy increased, nor in the penny-pinching life she must lead from now on. He could pass them on to the next woman whose life he destroyed.

But he didn't destroy Mia's life by marrying her—and he won't destroy mine.

That was all that mattered.

Face set, she walked downstairs, letting herself out on to the street. She would post the keys to her accountant—he could hand them on to Luca Farnese.

Except that would not prove to be necessary.

Because Luca was waiting for her on the pavement.

He could see shock whiten her face, deepening the hollows under her eyes. She did not look well. Her un-made-up face was gaunt, her hair pulled back into a tight knot. And she was too thin. Surely she should be gaining weight, not losing it?

His eyes went instinctively to her waistline. She was wearing jeans and a cotton sweatshirt. He frowned. Had his information been wrong? For a piercing second emotion stabbed him—but he did not know what it was and he put it from him. She was still standing there, frozen with shock, completely motionless.

'Going somewhere?' he asked pleasantly.

He levered himself away from the bonnet of his car, drawn up half on the pavement.

'Yes.'

A single word. Stony. As stony as her face.

'But not, however,' he informed her, his voice still

pleasant, 'where you thought you would be going.' He paused. Then spoke again. 'I've had you under surveillance since you walked out on me. You see, Ariana...' and now he made his voice like silk '...you have a habit of lying, and so I questioned your claim that you had been protected from pregnancy as you asserted. Your visit to a pharmacy to buy a pregnancy test might just have been caution on your part, to check you weren't pregnant—but your attending an antenatal clinic could only confirm that you were.'

Was it possible for her ashen face to whiten more? It did. He stepped towards her, taking her suitcase, tossing it into the boot of his car, then opening the passenger door.

'We need to get going, Ariana. I want to be in Milan this evening, and it's a three-and-a-half-hour drive.'

For a moment she only looked at him. The shock was lifting from her face, and something else was taking its place.

Closure. Complete closure. As if there were no longer a person behind the mask of her face.

She stepped forward, got into the passenger seat, did up her seatbelt as he took his own place behind the wheel and started the engine. He could still feel emotion running within him like an underground river, deep beneath the rock. Eating away at it from the inside.

She did not speak as he nosed the car forward. He did not care. Her response was not necessary. Her wishes did not matter.

Nor do mine.

The buried emotion jack-knifed in him like a stiletto thrust into his lungs. He thrust it back, down into his guts, where it must stay, its sharp edges like a razor embedded in his flesh. He would get used to its presence eventually. He would have to.

'Why are you doing this?'

Her abrupt question made his hands tighten over the steering wheel. He did not bother to ask what she meant by 'this'.

'The future has changed for both of us. It is necessary for us to accept the consequences of that change.'

He could see her head twisting towards him. In her lap, her hands were folded over her handbag. Only the white of her knuckles showed the tension she was under.

'It isn't a future that need concern you,' she replied.

Luca felt his jaw tighten—a sign of the self-control he was exerting. The self-control he always had to exert around her.

Except when it fails—catastrophically. And thus brings me to this point, now, where my life has been hijacked.

He wanted to laugh…a savage humourless laugh. Instead, halting at red lights, he simply glanced at her, his eyes flickering.

'Does the irony of it not strike you, Ariana? That the lie you told the world at my wedding has now become the truth?'

Her head turned away, dipped. 'Irony isn't the only word for it.'

'No,' he agreed, his voice low and tight.

The lights changed and he had to look ahead again. They were gaining the outskirts of the city. The autostrada awaited them, and then the long drive to Milan. And the even longer journey into a future that he had never wanted. That he had spent his life not wanting.

His grip on the steering wheel increased…the razor in his guts twisted.

She was speaking again, but not looking at him this time, her voice still low. Intense.

'Let me go, Luca. I will sign whatever disclaimers you require. Make no demands on you—financial or otherwise. Make no mention of you on the birth certificate. I will sever all contact with you, have nothing more to do with you. Leave you entirely free of me. Free of—'

She got no further.

'That will not happen.' His voice was hard. 'Because what *will* happen is this. We shall marry.'

Ariana heard him say it, but she did not believe it. It was impossible to believe. Impossible because it was…*impossible*.

Her eyes flew to him. There was only his profile, aquiline, carved from granite. Unyielding.

She shut her eyes, turning her head away from him, subsiding into silence. A profound weariness swept over her. These last weeks had been punishing—working nonstop, making what preparations she could, dismantling of her old life, ready for the construction of her new one. She felt….drained.

The smoothness of the car ride started to lull her to sleep, the sun streaming in warming her. Her thoughts wandered, become random, a blur. Her breathing slowed…

Her eyes were too heavy to open again. She wanted only to shut the world away.

Escape the only way she could.

Into sleep.

Luca slotted his car into his section of the underground car park at the block of luxury apartments in which he owned the entire top floor, parking it between his low-slung supercar and the top-of-the-range SUV he drove when heading for the Lakes or the Alps. Cutting the engine, he looked at Ariana asleep beside him. In repose, even in the dim light of the car park, she looked…

Beautiful.

The word was in his head before he could stop it. His eyes rested on her. Her head was tilted back, in three-quarter profile. The shadows under her eyes seemed less deep, the perfection of the sculpted features more accentuated. Her mouth more tender.

There was something familiar about her—and yet something *un*familiar. Something that was not her as he remembered her. Something…

Like Mia.

His gaze flickered. For the first time he could see the family resemblance. Their parents, after all, had been siblings…

He shook himself mentally. Cousins the two of them might be, Mia and Ariana, but in temperament, and in character, they could not be more different. And yet it was a disturbing thing, to see the faint resemblance between them, even though one was so dark and one so fair, one so gentle and one so—

Memory flared in him. Ariana, hurling her vitriolic denunciation at him in that elevator lobby in New York, her face contorted—as contorted as it had been at the hotel in Lucca—telling him to go to hell. The memories fused. Fused with more. His mother's rages…

He thrust open his car door to banish the memories—all of them—and the sound awakened Ariana. She opened her eyes, startled.

'We're here,' he told her, getting out of the car, going around to the boot to remove her suitcase.

She got out too, following him wordlessly to the elevator. It swept them up to his penthouse apartment. Inside, he led the way from the entrance hall down a short corridor, opening up a door.

'Your bedroom,' he said.

He went in, deposited her suitcase, and Ariana followed him in, gazing about her, saying nothing still.

'Freshen up,' he said, 'then join me in the lounge.'

She didn't answer, and he left her. Emotions were roiling inside him again, and he needed to be away from her right now.

He strode into his own bedroom—the master suite. It occupied the other flank, away from the entrance hall. It seemed prudent to put as much space between them as the apartment afforded.

More than prudent.

Essential.

CHAPTER NINE

ARIANA LIFTED THE lid of her suitcase, got out her toiletries bag, then disappeared into the en suite bathroom. It was as starkly modern as the bedroom. She washed her face and hands, staring for a while at her reflection. A blank-faced woman looked back at her with nothing in her eyes. Nothing at all.

Why did I come here? Why did I get into that car...let him drive me here?

Why had she not raged, or screamed, or run, or fought...?

But she knew the answer—had known it from the moment she had set eyes on him on the pavement. With a sense of exhaustion, inevitability—defeat.

There had been no point in not going with him. Now that he knew about the baby everything had changed.

She heard again his voice, saying what was unbelievable—unthinkable. Impossible even to contemplate.

'We shall marry.'

She pushed herself away from the vanity unit. Why had he even bothered to say it? Of *course* they would not marry...

Another wave of exhaustion ran through her—not physical as such, but far deeper. For now, all she could

do was what she was doing. Not thinking, not feeling…
not wanting to. It was all she had the energy for.

She emerged from the bathroom, feeling fresher in
face than in spirit, then left the bedroom, making her
way back down the corridor and into the front hall. A
huge reception room opened off it. Again, the décor was
starkly modern. Punishingly expensive. She could tell
that at a glance. Plate glass windows marched down the
far wall, and a wide terrace was beyond, illuminated with
bold lights. To the right, a dining room opened up, and
beyond it she could glimpse a kitchen.

Then Luca was walking in. He had changed out of
his business suit, swapping it for well-cut trousers and a
cashmere sweater, and Ariana frowned. She had never,
she realised, seen him in casual wear. In New York he'd
been in a tux, in Lucca in a business suit. And in church,
at his wedding, he'd been in a morning suit.

She hauled her mind away, not wanting to remember
that hideous scene. She couldn't bear it. A wave of depression swept over her. Had there truly been no other
way of saving Mia from a marriage she did not want to
make, but did not dare to refuse? A way that didn't end
in bringing herself here, like this? Pregnant by the man
whose wedding she had ruined, who loathed her very
guts for what she'd done…

'What would you like to drink?'

Luca's enquiry was polite as he crossed to a sideboard made of chrome and walnut, which Ariana had
disliked on sight.

'Mineral water—still,' she replied. 'I can't take *friz-
zante* any longer.'

He glanced at her.

She gave a slight shrug. 'I've had some morning sickness.'

His obsidian eyes assessed her. 'Is that why you've

lost so much weight?' His question sounded more of an accusation than an enquiry.

'I don't know,' she answered.

He opened a bottle of mineral water, poured it for her, and came across to where she stood in the middle of the room.

'It can't be good for you…losing weight. You should be putting it on.'

'I'm not even past my first trimester,' she said.

She took the glass from him, taking a sip. Her throat was dry, suddenly. To be here—here in Luca Farnese's ultra-modern, ultra-luxurious penthouse apartment in Milan—discussing her pregnancy, was unreal.

She felt emotion clutch at her and took another sip of water.

'I'm well aware of that,' was the only reply she got.

He'd returned to the sideboard, poured himself a shot of whisky from a bottle that she recognised as one of the most expensive single malts. He knocked it back, poured himself another, then threw himself down on a black leather sofa which Ariana had also immediately disliked. She disliked every aspect of the décor.

Yet it suits him.

The acknowledgement was in her head before she could stop it. The stark, unyielding décor was a perfect match for this stark, unyielding man.

He sat back, one arm thrown out across the back of the sofa, one long leg angled over his thigh. An apparently re-laxed attitude, but she had never seen a man less relaxed. Her eyes went to his face, and she felt her throat tighten at its impact on her. Protest against it as she would…

Why? Why this man? Why him? What is it? What does he have? Why does he do to me what he does and why do I respond to it? To him? Why do I just want to gaze and gaze at him? To drink in every feature, feel every impact of it? Why? Why am I so helpless?

The questions tumbled through her head but she could not answer them. Not a single one.

He was taking another mouthful of his whisky, then he looked at her straight on. 'Dinner will be here soon—there are kitchens in the apartment block that provide room service.'

She gave a slight nod, taking a seat on the sofa opposite him, clutching her glass of water.

He was silent for a moment. Then… 'We need to talk.'

She looked at him, saying nothing. What was there to say? Except… 'I'm not marrying you.'

The words fell from her lips and she was glad she had said them. Glad that she had made it clear. Where he had got the insane notion from she didn't know or care.

She saw his grip on his glass tighten. His jaw tightened.

His eyes lanced hers. 'Yes,' he told her, 'you will.'

She changed her expression changed, let it become one of genuine enquiry.

'Luca, why do you say that? Why do you even talk of marriage? It's so insane it doesn't bear thinking of!' She took a razoring breath. 'You cannot possibly want to marry me—'

'Of course I do not.' The words were stark. The voice harsh. 'You are the very last woman on earth I would want to marry.'

It was like a physical blow. As if he'd brought his hard, pitiless hand slashing down on her. But how could it be a blow? How could it? A blow—physical or verbal—would hurt, and how could she be hurt by what he'd said?

Not any longer. Not since that morning in Manhattan, when she'd run out of the hotel room to see him waiting by the elevator. Walking out on her after a night that had been so…so…

'But we have no choice, Ariana—neither you, nor I.'

He cut across the memories she must not have. Memories that were forbidden her, too cruel to remember.

His voice was still harsh and she could only go on looking at him, unable to turn away, to hide, to find any protection or shelter from him. Just as she had been unable to find any protection or shelter from the words he'd dropped like stones, crushing her, breaking her ribs, her lungs, as those elevator doors had opened for him.

'I'm returning to Italy to be married.'

With jerking hands she raised her glass to her lips, bone-dry again, and took another jolting sip, her eyes dropping down as if to protect herself from his rejecting gaze.

Rejecting her…not wanting her. Not wanting her for anything other than what he'd already had of her.

And not even wanting that now. Not even in his dreams.

In her head she heard his cruel, mocking words that night in Lucca, when he'd excoriated her with his rejection of her.

'Dreams? Of you? Do you think I would ever sully myself on you again?'

Her grip on her glass of water tightened to painfulness, numbing her fingertips with the pressure she was exerting. It was as if the pressure were around her throat, choking her. Choking her with the truth she had to face.

Luca Farnese—not wanting her…

Not wanting her that nightmare morning-after in Manhattan.

Not wanting her in that hideous scene in his hotel room in Lucca.

Not wanting her now, in this nightmare.

He was forcing himself to marry her—because for a second time she had committed an act of such criminal folly that she must pay for it all her life.

But my baby will not pay! I will not allow that!

Fierce emotion seared through her. Her eyes snapped up again.

'Yes—yes, we *do* have a choice! A choice I will exercise and to hell with you! I will have this baby on my own, and you will not have to force yourself to have anything to do with it—anything to do with me!'

She felt her jaw clench, her eyes burning with fire as she ploughed on, saying what had to be said—what had to be faced. By her—and by him. Her voice was ragged, but she would not let it break. By force of will she spoke vehemently, desperately...

'You've never wanted me for anything but sex! I've known that—and faced it!—ever since that morning in New York! You used me then like I was a whore—a sex toy—something to slake your passing lust with! Knowing all the time that you were going to be married to another woman—knowing it all the time you were having sex with me! And if you think...if you think that I would ever, *ever* let a man like that have *anything* to do with an innocent baby—*my* baby!—then—'

His voice cut across hers like a scalpel, eviscerating her.

'And do you think that I would ever want the mother of a child of mine to be a woman so jealous, so vindictive, that she would do what you did to your own cousin? A woman who had done you no harm—none! Who could never harm anyone! The gentlest, sweetest soul—'

A smothered cry broke from her and she turned away, gulping at her water, wishing it were whisky so that she could drown herself in its oblivion. She was shaking—shaking like a leaf—and she could not hold her glass steady. Water was splashing on to her chest, her lap…

Suddenly the glass was taken from her. Set down on the glass and chrome coffee table—another item of furniture she hated. But then hatred was all that was in her now…all that was knifing through her, hatred and fury and rage and destruction…

She felt the sofa dip beside her, felt her hands being taken. She was shaking still, but the hard, large hands folding around hers would not let them shake. Her eyes jolted upwards. Luca was seated beside her, his hands tight over hers. He was speaking—she could hear his words. But they could not be his, surely… For they were not harsh and hating…

They were weary.

'Ariana—stop. I will too. We must. Both of us.' A heavy breath was exhaled from him. 'Somehow we have to deal with this. We *have* to…'

He drew her to her feet, and she could not help but rise with him.

'Come and eat,' he said, and his voice was still weary. Dispassionate.

He let go her hands and they felt cold suddenly—which was strange, for surely they had been colder clutching the glass of water. She levered herself up, effort though it was, and followed him into the dining room. The table—more glass and chrome—was already set for two, and she sank down gratefully on the chair at its foot. Luca sat down at the head.

A moment later Ariana heard voices in the kitchen beyond, and the clink of crockery.

'There's an entrance to my kitchen from the service

elevator,' Luca informed her, as two young women came into the dining room, carrying small plates.

He murmured something to them and they both smiled at him. Ariana could tell they were impressed by him, responding to his lethal looks, his air of understated wealth and power. *Poor fools,* she thought, and then envied them for not knowing his true nature.

He gave a cool nod and they set down the plates. One of them fetched a bottle of opened wine from the kitchen, presenting it to him and receiving another cool nod in return, while the other wheeled in a trolley bearing two large plates with silvered covers, and two dessert plates containing *tarte au citron.*

'*Grazie,*' Luca said to them, and nodded in dismissal. They disappeared silently, closing the kitchen door behind them.

Ariana looked down at the plate in front of her. Some kind of vegetable terrine with dressed leaves. She wondered if she felt hungry, but she could not tell.

'You need to eat.'

Luca's voice came from the far end of the table and mechanically she picked up her fork and made a start. It was, in fact, delicious. Maybe she was hungry after all. Her eating had been erratic these last weeks as she'd worked every hour on finishing off client projects, snatching sandwiches here and there, nothing more than that.

Luca poured himself a glass of white wine, but did not offer her any. She stuck to water.

She went on eating, steadily demolishing the terrine and then reaching for a bread roll, consuming that too. It seemed strange to be dining with Luca Farnese again—although 'strange' was an understatement if ever there was one.

The third time I've done so.

But this time would be different from the previous two. This time… She felt her throat tighten. This time she would not be falling into bed with him…

She yanked her mind from the thought. Danger lapped at her like a dark, drowning tide. She pushed her empty plate away. Luca had finished too, and without speaking he got to his feet, picking up his own plate and collecting hers, replacing them with the larger plates, removing the silver covers.

It was chicken in a lightly creamy sauce, with new potatoes and French beans. It, too, was delicious, and Ariana realised she was eating with a will. But that was all. Otherwise an air of unreality was possessing her. Right now she should be landing in London, ready to remake her life. Instead—

Her thoughts cut out. It was impossible to think of anything right now.

Impossible to accept what was happening or where she was.

Impossible.

She heard Luca start to speak, cutting across her thoughts.

'So,' he said, 'where were you heading off to?'

She forked another mouthful of tender chicken. 'I was leaving Italy,' she said tonelessly.

'America, perhaps? Your mother? You mentioned that evening in New York that she lives in Florida now.'

Ariana glanced at him. 'My mother? No! She's the last person I'd go to!' There was more expression in her voice now. 'I know exactly what she'd tell me about my being pregnant. She'd tell me to get rid of it!' Something emptied out of her voice as she went on. 'The way she's always told me she wishes she'd done with me—'

She broke off, seizing up her water and taking a gulp.

Luca's eyes stayed on her. She looked across at him, meeting them square-on. If Luca Farnese wanted the whole sorry tale he could have it, and he'd be welcome to it.

'She got pregnant at nineteen by the man she'd run off with—my father. Who was a fortune-hunter. Plus a gambler and an alcoholic. She's always said he got her pregnant deliberately, in order to increase the size of the pay-off he was after from my grandfather.'

She paused, eyeballing Luca. His face was expressionless.

'It's not an edifying tale.' She gave a half-shrug of her thin shoulder. 'Well, he got his pay-off and I got his name—he had to marry my mother as part of the deal my grandfather insisted on. Then he got a speedy divorce the moment I arrived in the world. My mother went back to my grandfather, but bolted again the moment she could—yet another elopement. This time, luckily for her, with a man who could afford her. As for me... I was left at the *palazzo*.'

Her expression changed. Softened without her realising it.

'My uncle and his wife took me on. They lived there. My uncle was a gentle soul, and so was his wife—it's where Mia gets her sweet nature from, I suppose—and, unlike my mother, my uncle never defied his father.' She paused, and her eyes suddenly had a faraway look, as if she was back in a past long-vanished. 'I was happy with them... Even after Mia was born they were still kind and affectionate towards me. It might all have worked out OK, except—'

She broke off again.

'Except?' There was a new note in Luca's voice.

Ariana only gave that half-shrug again.

'My aunt and uncle were killed in a car crash when I was eight and Mia five. After that—' She swallowed and then went on, resignation in her voice. 'I reacted badly—I became "wilful and difficult", as my grandfather calls it. I was packed off to my mother, who was on her third husband by then, and living in Paris. She had absolutely no wish for me to be there, no interest in me. I was a nuisance to her and her latest husband, so I was returned to the *palazzo*—where my behaviour got even worse. I was sent away to school. A convent, where I was a boarder. I came home for Christmas, that was all, when I was allowed to see Mia—allowed to see that she had become my grandfather's most adored granddaughter. So pretty, so gentle, so pleasing in her manners...like a little doll.'

'And you resented her for that.' There was a harshness in Luca's voice.

Ariana did not answer. Resentment was the last thing she'd felt. She'd felt only a heart-wrenching, pitiful envy of Mia, so loved by her grandfather. Whereas she herself...

Unwanted—rejected. By my father, my mother, my grandfather. None of them ever wanted me. Cared anything about me.

She stopped remembering. There was no point to it. No point in explaining to Luca or even trying to. She knew what he thought of her. He would not change that...whatever pitiful tale she might trot out to him.

So she just gave another shrug. Went on eating...

'So...' Luca's voice came again '...if you weren't going to your mother, where were you going?'

'Ireland,' Ariana lied.

She didn't want him knowing about her plan to live in London. Didn't want him to know anything about Mia—that she had married another man, preferring Matt to him.

If he knew the truth about why I stopped the wedding—because his bride was desperate for a way to avoid marrying him—would he seek to punish her as he has punished me?

It was a chilling thought—and she knew she must do all she could to protect her gentle, fearful cousin. Luca Farnese could crush her and Matt like eggshells...

'To the Irish side of your family?' he probed.

'No,' she said shortly. 'I know nothing about them.'

He frowned. 'Your father...?'

'I have no idea about him—he could be dead for all I know. Like I say, he was an alcoholic. I don't know of any relatives, and even if I did I wouldn't want to know them.'

'So why go to Ireland?'

She shrugged again. 'It's somewhere to go.'

She saw him reach for his wine, a frown still on his face. 'Why leave Italy? Your work is based here.'

'Was,' she corrected. She set down her knife and fork. Looked straight at him. 'I won't be repaying your loan. So the bank will foreclose on me.'

'Obviously that won't apply now!' His voice was sharp. Then he set down his wine glass. Looked straight at her. 'Things have changed between us, Ariana. That much is obvious. I won't object to your continuing to work in moderation—for a while, at least. Afterwards, when the baby is born... Well, we shall see. Working mothers are not, after all, uncommon.'

She picked up her cutlery again, resumed eating.

'I'm not marrying you, Luca, and whether I am a working mother or not will be none of your concern. I won't be living in Italy, and I won't be asking for, let alone accepting, any child maintenance. You won't be involved in any way.'

She did not let emotion enter her voice. There was no

reason for it to do so. She was simply stating what was going to happen.

His voice cut across her grim, bleak thoughts.

'Do you want me to contest custody?'

CHAPTER TEN

IT WAS CALMLY SAID. Dispassionately said.

Ariana's cutlery clattered to the plate.

'On what grounds?'

Now there was emotion in her voice.

'On the grounds that I do not want my child raised in a foreign country. Taken from me.'

His eyes were levelled on her and they were not dispassionate. They were the very opposite.

'I will fight you with everything I have to prevent that.' He paused. 'And I have a great deal to fight you with, and good reason to do so. Do you doubt it, Ariana?'

She felt every muscle in her body clench, emotion biting in her throat. Then it died away, defeated. In any custody battle Luca Farnese would win. He would use his money, his power, to hire the best lawyers, drag out the process, contest any awarding of custody to her... It would go on and on for years...

I can't face that—I just can't...

That sense of weary, bone-tired exhaustion that had made her climb into his car that afternoon now assailed her again. Defeat dragged at her...

He was speaking again, and his voice was different.

'Ariana, do you really want that? Do not try and fight me on this. You will not win.' He paused again. 'And there is no need to fight me. We can do this civilly. There does not need to be any drama.'

There was something in his voice—something that made her look at him again. His face had no expression in it, nor his eyes, but there had been a tightness in his voice.

She dropped her eyes, picked up her knife and fork, resumed eating. Then she spoke. 'We don't need to marry, Luca.'

'Ariana.' His voice cut across hers. 'Understand this from the start. I do not tolerate chaos.'

She looked at him. Whatever it was that had been in his voice a moment ago was there again.

'If we married,' she said slowly, not taking her eyes from him, 'what then?'

She did not want to know for her own sake, but simply what it was that he thought might be possible—though it would not be, for she would not be marrying him anyway...

'We legitimise our baby, establish its rights in the world, regularise its existence, secure its future.'

'And us? What happens to us?'

Again, how did he see their future? A future that was not going to happen...

He did not answer at first. Then... 'We divorce.' His eyes rested on her like weights. 'I will not chain you to me, Ariana. And...' there was the minutest pause '...and you will not chain me to you.'

He reached for his wine and drained the glass, then looked at her again. His face was expressionless, as if carved from granite.

'We are toxic for each other. Destructive.' He paused again. 'And that is why,' he told her, 'I do not want you in my life.'

His eyes rested on her. Unreadable. Implacable.

Rejecting everything about her.

Except the baby I carry—the only thing he wants of me.

There seemed to be a stone in her throat, and she looked away. But he was speaking again, and she made herself look at him, eyes blinking suddenly.

'If we accept that it will be easier,' he said. 'There will no longer be any need for…for hostility between us.'

That stone was still lodged in her throat and she could not move it, could not swallow it. She pushed her plate away, reached for her water—as if water could dissolve the stone.

Once more she saw Luca get to his feet, clear their plates away and place their dessert on the table. Mechanically she started to eat it. It was something to do.

Luca was speaking again. His voice was calm, dispassionate. Remote.

'It will not be so bad, Ariana, you know. You will get used to living here. The time will pass. As I say, you can resume your work, if you want—providing you do not exhaust yourself. My schedule is busy, as you will appreciate.' He looked at her. 'We can make this work because we must. We have no option but to do so. Both of us.'

She met his eyes. She knew there was defeat in hers. Yet it was not victory in his.

What was in them she did not know.

Nor care.

A profound weariness of spirit possessed her. For now, that was all she could face. All she could cope with.

For now…

Luca lay in his bed, motionless but not asleep. The night was passing, but sleep did not come.

He was not surprised. Only resigned.

Consciousness consumed him. Consciousness that on the other side of the entrance hall, in the guest suite, was the woman he would have given more than was rational to give not to want. Not to desire.

But desire was irrelevant now. And so were her objections to what he had told her must happen. What either of them wanted was irrelevant.

He stared up at the ceiling, trying to work out what it was he was feeling. Then realised it was nothing. And that was the best thing to feel. The only sane thing to feel. The only thing he would permit.

Memory came to him, unwanted and unbidden, but in his head for all that. Memory from so long ago. Of lying in bed, not more than ten years old, staring at the ceiling as silence had finally fallen outside his bedroom door, the shouting and the yelling over—for that night, at least. Lying there, unblinking, hands clenched at his sides, willing himself not to feel…not to feel anything at all.

It was time to feel that way again.

Ariana gazed up at the front of the Duomo, its extraordinary triangular shape intricately carved into a myriad of convoluted tracery and statuettes, a miracle of Gothic art. She turned away, making for the city's other most notable construction, the Galleria Vittorio Emanuele.

She sat herself down at a café, ordered a decaf. She missed the caffeine hit of real coffee which had so often got her through a busy working day. But her busy working days were over now.

She slumped back in her chair, sipping the unappetising coffee. Feeling quite blank. Aimless. She would fill the hours wandering around Milan. It got her out of the bleak, stark apartment that Luca called home and that suited him so well.

She'd seen him briefly when she'd surfaced, leaving for his office. He'd informed her in neutral, inexpressive tones that he was taking her to see an obstetrician the following day and had booked her in for antenatal care. She hadn't bothered to reply, and he'd left the apartment. Soon after, she'd headed out herself.

The rest of the day passed as aimlessly as she had supposed it would. She walked a lot, glad of her padded jacket as she went up and down the streets, stopping for a sandwich which she ended up feeding to the pigeons. Eventually a weariness not just of spirit but of body drove her back to Luca's apartment. She went to her bedroom, lay down on the bed, stared up at the ceiling.

Luca found her there, gazing blankly. She turned her head to look at him. He'd paused in the doorway. Her expression did not change. Her eyes were not registering his presence.

'Are you all right?'

His voice was edged. Could there possibly be concern in it? It seemed unlikely.

'Fine,' she said, and turned her head away again, staring up at the ceiling once more.

'Ariana—you can't just lie there.'

'Why not?' She did not bother to turn her head this time.

'What did you do today?'

'I walked around. It passed the time.'

She heard him cross the grey-carpeted floor, felt the mattress sink under his weight, felt her hand taken. She tried to draw it back, an instinctive gesture, but his grip tightened. Imprisoning her.

'Ariana…' his voice sounded weary now '…you have to accept what has to happen. We both do. I don't want to marry either—I don't want anything to do with you nor do you with me. We know that. Everything between us has been a mistake and should never have happened. But it did. And now...'

She heard him take a breath—a heavy one.

'Now we just have to manage the consequences. What we want is irrelevant—only the baby matters. And we have to deal with that. Somehow.'

He let go her hand and it fell back onto the bedclothes like a dead weight. She felt him stand up, heard him walk to the door again. Walk out.

She did not turn her head or move. Only as her eyes stared up sightlessly in the darkening room slow tears started. Silent and scalding, and quite, quite pointless.

Luca opened the passenger door of his car.

'Ariana...' he prompted.

Silently, she complied, getting into the low-slung car. Just as she silently complied with everything—from going to the obstetrician to coming to the table for meals. Or, as now, getting into his car.

Ariana never contested anything he told her to do.

A rapier of emotion slit him as he slid into the driver's seat. It was like the ghost of the life he'd once thought would be his. Making a marriage where there would be no drama, no discord, no angry contestation or denunciation. A marriage of only co-operation, complaisance. Agreement. A quiet, tranquil marriage. With a wife who would never subject him to the histrionics he'd grown up with, as his father had endlessly tried to placate his always angry mother.

Why had he done that? Why had his father never stood up to her?

But he knew why. Had known since he'd reached his teenage years and discovered for himself the power of female allure. His father had been in sexual thrall to his wife—a woman he could not live with or without.

Luca felt his jaw tighten, his body tense.

That's what I feared for myself—why my dreams were always of a woman like Mia.

Yet it was not Mia he was now going to marry.

He gunned the car's powerful engine, exiting the garage, making his way slowly through the Milan traffic. The weather had brightened and he was glad. He needed the elements on his side.

'Where are we going?' Ariana's question was indifferent, uninterested, and she did not look at him as she asked it.

'Somewhere that might suit you better than here,' was all the reply he made.

She made no answer to it, only went on sitting there, her hands in her lap, gazing out of the window straight ahead of her. She didn't speak again. Stayed silent.

He gained the autostrada, heading north towards their destination. Lake Como. He drove steadily, enjoying the feel of the powerful vehicle under his control. His face set. There was not much else in his life to enjoy. Had his life gone to plan he would have had Mia at his side right now. It was for Mia he'd bought the lakeside villa on Como he was now heading for—a weekend retreat from Milan for them both.

Now it was for a different woman.

The woman replacing Mia.

Displacing her.

His eyes went to the woman at his side, pregnant with his child. So utterly unlike Mia. Yet now she was as quiet as Mia, uncontesting, docilely complying with everything he said.

He felt that rapier of emotion pierce him again, engendering a chill. The words of an old warning shaped in his head.

Be careful what you wish for.

Ariana looked about her. For the first time in unnumbered days—days that had passed one after another, each as dead as the previous day, days when she had felt nothing, because nothing was all it was safe to feel and all she had the energy to feel, days of just lying on her bed for hours—it was as if something were drawing her. She felt something stir within her—a gleam of interest.

Part of her wanted to ignore it, to let it sink down into the oblivion into which she, too, wanted to sink. But without her wanting them to her eyes went to the house Luca had drawn up at, a short drive from the snaking lakeside road, secluded and private on a small promontory over the lake.

Out of long professional habit, she categorised it as her eyes rested on it. A lakeside villa, late nineteenth-century, a picturesque summer retreat from Milan. Her gaze narrowed critically. Its condition was not pristine. The exterior paint had faded and flaked and there were uneven roof tiles, a sagging porch. The gardens were bathed in autumnal sunshine. And beyond, she could see the dark indigo of the lake, silvering to obsidian.

Luca was getting out of the car and she did likewise, hardly noticing that she was doing so.

'What is this place?' she asked, looking around her.

It didn't seem like a place that he would have anything to do with. Its ornate, fin-de-siècle style could not have been more different from that stark, bleak, modernistic apartment of his in Milan.

'I bought it for Mia. A place to come at weekends…

away from the city. I thought she might like somewhere like this.'

Ariana looked at him. 'Mia doesn't like water,' she said. 'She can't swim and doesn't like the sea. And she doesn't like glacial lakes. They scare her.'

She didn't wait for his response—because what could he have said other than that he had not troubled himself to ask her cousin what she might or might not like? But as she wandered off, wanting to see the villa from the front, she felt a shaft of sadness pick at her. How sad that Luca had wanted to please the woman he'd intended to marry and yet had had no idea that she would hate it...

Not that Mia would ever have told him.

And that was sad too...

She rounded the side of the villa, seeing the gardens that ran down to the water's edge, terminating in a broken paved terrace and a crumbling stone balustrade. She went to stand there, gazing out over the lake. The still, dark water was, indeed, something to fear, plunging down to icy depths so far below. But she did not share her cousin's fear of it.

She turned to survey the front of the villa, automatically itemising the work that would need doing. Inside it was probably also in need of work. She wondered what it looked like...

Luca was walking towards her. 'Shall we go inside?'

She gave a slight nod and he led the way, opening up the house for her. Inside, a flight of stairs ascended from a marble-floored hall. Some of the steps were chipped, and the walls were papered in a dated style that continued into the reception rooms, where its impact was worsened by an ugly patterned carpet and curtains. The furniture, by contrast, was antique, of the same period as the house, and it suited the ornate rooms.

Ignoring Luca, who seemed to be leaving her to it, she made her way over the whole house. Other than the dated style there was not a great deal to do, providing the plumbing and electrics were sound. Already in her head she was seeing it as *she* would do it. As if it was a commission.

When she finally re-emerged Luca was on the paved semi-circular upper terrace, and the setting sun was gilding the dark waters of the lake at the end of the garden.

'What do you make of it?' he asked.

She looked at him, then back at the neglected, run-down villa. 'It could be beautiful,' she said.

Was that wistfulness in her voice? She didn't know. Her eyes went back to Luca. He nodded. Maybe something in his austere face lightened—she wasn't sure. Or perhaps it was just the reflection of the setting sun.

'So, will you make it so?'

She started. 'Me?'

'It's why I brought you here,' he said. 'Ariana, you need a project. You're not used to being idle. You hate Milan, and my apartment. I thought this place might suit you better. That you might be less…less unhappy here.'

She swallowed, her throat suddenly tight. To have Luca Farnese show any sign of consideration for her…

But he was speaking still. 'I've talked to the obstetrician I took you to. He said…' He stopped and she saw his face tense. 'He said that you were showing signs of sinking into what might become depression. That would not be good for the baby.'

A stiletto slid into her lungs, puncturing them instantly.

It's not for me—it's just for the baby. That's all.

She swallowed again, as if she needed air.

Luca was speaking again, his words confirming that his concern was only for their baby, not herself.

'When we're married, and when the baby arrives, it will be the start of summer. This would surely be a good place to be then…fresh, clean air, away from the city…'

She made no answer. It was too much for her to deal with right now. She would not be marrying him, and she would not be living here, but there was no purpose in stating that now. She had no energy for it, no will…

For now, all I can cope with is doing what he wants— not fighting him, or contesting him, or defying him.

'So, will you take it on? Do up the villa?'

Luca's voice penetrated her wearying ever-circling thoughts and she heard herself speak—heard the familiar professional note enter her voice. It gave her something to cling to in what had become the alien landscape of her life.

'I can do an initial assessment for you…draw up some costings, provide some options,' she replied slowly. She wondered why she was offering, and then let it go. It would pass the time if nothing else.

Pass the time till when? Till you leave here and go to England, or anywhere at all? Till Luca accepts you won't marry him? Till the baby arrives…?

She heard the questions in her head but veered away from them. She didn't know and didn't have the answers.

'Good. Do so,' he replied, his tone brisk and businesslike. He got to his feet. 'Shall we go? It's getting dark and chilly. I've booked us into a hotel a short drive away.'

Ariana tensed.

Luca looked at her. 'Separate rooms,' he said drily. His expression changed. 'It's good that you've agreed to take on this villa. I'm glad it's come in useful after all.'

Was there an edge in his voice? She didn't know and

didn't care. Nor did she reply. There wasn't anything to say. As she had told him, Mia would have hated the place, and feared the water so close by. But she would have never told him so.

Poor Mia—poor, meek, biddable Mia. Pleasing everyone but herself. Letting herself be placed like a doll, never exerting any will of her own.

And now she herself was not exerting any will of her own either. She had let Luca take her over.

Have I been turning into Mia? Opting out of any agency over my own life? Letting Luca put me in his car, his apartment, while I turn my face to the wall, dissociate myself from the world, give in to his will...

She turned, looking at the villa, its faded beauty. It was unloved—sad and forlorn.

It needs a new start, a new purpose.

'Ariana?'

Luca was standing by the car, holding open the passenger door, clearly waiting for her to get in. She gave one last look at the villa, silhouetted against the darkening sky. Then got into the car.

She realised, with a strange sense of acceptance, that her mind was already running down a mental list of what the villa's refurbishment would require. That a sense of purpose was filling her...

CHAPTER ELEVEN

LUCA SAT BACK in his dining chair. They were eating at the hotel overlooking the lake, dark now except for the lights on a further shore. For the first time since the call had come through from the investigator keeping Ariana under surveillance he felt the tension racking him begin, fractionally, to ease its iron grip.

Ariana was talking, and all he had to do was sit back and listen, answering questions as and when required. She was talking about the villa, and had sketched out on hotel notepaper a new downstairs and upstairs layout. It was the first time he had seen any animation in her face since he had intercepted her planned disappearance and driven her to Milan instead, to begin the future that faced both of them.

Whether we want that future or not...

There was no choice about it. Not for him. Or for her. He had accepted it—she must too. His eyes rested on her now, his mouth tightening without his realising it. And she must not sink into the depression winding its dark tentacles around her, dulling her will to do anything other than lie on her bed, staring at the ceiling, hour after hour, going through the motions, nothing more, taking no care of herself or anything else... Passive and inert.

Docile.

The word plucked at him again, and he pushed it aside. The obstetrician's advice had been to do what he was now doing. Change the scenery and give her something to do—a project to provide her with some purpose other than simply waiting for the baby to be born. The obstetrician knew nothing of the dark conception of the baby, only that it was unplanned, unforeseen.

Into his head, disturbingly, came the memory of Ariana saying that her own mother had wished her never to have been born and her father had disowned her. She'd lost her surrogate parents, had found the loss difficult to cope with, had been sent away.

An unhappy childhood.

Like mine was.

His thoughts sheered away. He did not want to feel any similarities between them. Any kinship.

His eyes rested on her again. The new animation in her face was renewing her familiar beauty too. She had regained some weight and her face was less gaunt, cheekbones less sharp, complexion less wan. She was still not showing her pregnancy yet, but it was early days. Her first scan was still weeks away.

His thoughts sheered away again. A scan would make the baby real in a way that mere pregnancy tests and obstetric checks did not.

How can we do this? How can we bring a child into the world with parents between whom is such enmity, such discord—such anger?

But he knew the answer to that too. Had grown up with it.

Emotion stabbed in him. For that reason of all reasons he knew he must seek a better future for this child his own intemperate, disastrous weakness had created.

And that was what he was striving to do now. However

appallingly Ariana had behaved—wrecking her cousin's wedding as she had, just to spite him—he had to move on from it.

And she has to move on from my leaving her. As I did after our night together in New York—a night that could never have led to anything more.

But he must not think about that night or remember it. Let alone the night that had followed.

I was supposed to break her power over me—show myself that I was not in thrall to her allure, could resist the temptation she offers. That I could defy it—deny it.

Instead…

Yet again, he steered his mind away. It was too dangerous to remember. Too dangerous to do anything but pay attention to what she was telling him now, about the possibilities presented by the villa he had bought for the bride he no longer had.

Would Mia really not have liked it? Been afraid of being so close to the lake? Surely she would have told me if that were so—why should she not have?

He shook the question away, not wanting to think about it…about a future that was gone for ever now. Facing, instead, the future that did await him.

'If you want just a light touch,' this woman he was going to have to marry instead of her cousin was saying now, 'you can leave the layout as it is, but if you want something more radical then the bedrooms can be enlarged by knocking through, and the kitchen could become a kitchen diner.'

He shook his head. 'My preference is to leave well alone as much as possible.'

Ariana nodded. 'I'm glad…' She made a start on her food—grilled fish with polenta—while Luca cut into his lamb fillet. 'A house so untouched—well, apart from the refurb thirty years ago—is rare. The kitchen will need substantial updating, as will the bathrooms, but other than the external repairs the rest of the work is nearly all cosmetic.'

'How long do you estimate it will take?'

'Given the time of year, the exterior work needs to start as soon as you give the go-ahead.'

'Do so.' He nodded.

'I've a rough idea of costs, but obviously I will get written quotes for you to approve.'

He shook his head. 'Not necessary. The cost is immaterial.'

Ariana looked across at him. 'You'll get written quotes,' she said. 'Down to the last tin of paint.'

Her gaze moved away for a moment, and he could see her thin shoulders tense.

'I'd feel safer that way...with you signing off on all the work.'

He looked at her without comprehension.

'It will protect me from you,' she said.

'Protect?'

'I can't cope with any more anger from you,' she said. Her voice was low and strained.

He was silent. Her words echoing in his head. Then... 'I don't want to be angry with you,' he said slowly.

She made no answer, only went on with her dinner.

He shook the moment from him. Yet her words lingered.

But I have cause to be angry with her. So much cause.

For ruining his hopes of marriage to Mia.

For even more than that.

For desiring her when I do not want to desire her.

His eyes went to her. She was still making absolutely no attempt to accentuate her looks. She wore no make-up, her hair was tied back, her clothes were just a sweater and a pair of casual trousers. Yet still she turned heads. There was a sensuality to her, an allure she could not conceal. He'd seen it as they'd walked into the restaurant…male eyes going to her. It was effortless for her. She seemed totally unaware of it.

He heard again the word she'd used—the one that he'd echoed.

Protect.

His mouth thinned. He was the one needing protection. From his own self, his own intolerable weakness.

From the desire for her that destroyed the life I wanted to have… Leaving me with only this.

A woman he didn't want to want.

A child that should never have been conceived.

A future it was impossible to think of but which waited for him, all the same.

Luca returned to Milan the next day and Ariana was glad.

I will always be glad when he's gone. Glad when I'm free of him.

She swallowed. Of course she would be glad. How could she not be happy to be free of a man who caused her so much torment?

For a moment—a fleeting, flying moment—she felt pain stab.

It could have been so different.

She gave a violent shake of her head. How? How could it have been different? Only if Luca had been a different man…only if he'd never wanted to marry Mia.

If he'd wanted me, not her.

But it was sweet, gentle Mia that Luca had wanted.

Into her head came the words he'd said to her that first night in Milan.

'You're the very last woman on earth I'd want to marry.'

She felt the stab of pain come again—pain that had no logic to it. Not when it was *she* who was refusing to marry *him*.

She dragged her thoughts away. Pointless to think such things, feel such things. She turned her mind, with a sense of weary relief, to what Luca had provided for her distraction.

From her base at the Lake Como hotel she started making appointments for assorted tradespersons to turn up the villa. She hired a car—a sensible run-around—to meet them there, booking them in to make an immediate start. It was familiar work, and she stepped into it easily.

Back at the hotel she emailed Luca with an initial schedule of costs, and choices for kitchen and bathroom styles, receiving by return his go-ahead and preferences.

Thoughts flittered through her consciousness. Discussing costs, finance, business, was never difficult with him. It was common ground between them… Neutral ground.

Maybe that's what we need—something that is innocuous, harmless. Nothing to do with our bitter, toxic relationship.

Did Luca feel the same way? He seemed to, and she was glad of it when he arrived for the weekend and they went over to the villa to see what had been started.

His manner was low-key as he gave her his decisions on everything from colours to kitchen units. And unlike most of her clients he made his decisions instantly.

She heard herself say as much as he drove them both back to the hotel for dinner. 'So many of my clients can't make their minds up!' she remarked. 'The worst ever is my own mother—but then, why should that surprise me?

Given she can't make her mind up about her husbands, let alone her décor.'

She spoke lightly, but saw Luca glance at her as he drove.

'She seems to have made up her mind about not raising you herself. But then perhaps you were better off without her. Better no mother than one who doesn't care about you.'

There was real tension in him now. She could hear it, and did not know why. She drew an intake of breath. What had happened to neutrality? This was raw—going deep.

And not just for me—there was something in his voice then…

She heard his words echo…about mothers who didn't care. Her eyes flickered to him, saw his profile silhouetted.

What do I know about him other than the power he has over me to make me want him? And the fact that he does not want me in return?

She felt her throat tighten. Heard herself speak. 'Well, I got used to it. Got used to being not wanted—neither by my parents nor my grandfather. Which is why…' she forced the words from her '…not being wanted by you is just par for the course really.'

It seemed important somehow for her to say that.

Perhaps it will make it easier to deal with.

She kept her head turned towards him. Only the lights from oncoming cars illuminated his stark features. It was easier to say things in the dark. Things that were difficult to say yet which needed to be said. Things she was ready to say now. Ready to face. To accept—however painful.

'I have to accept, Luca, that you don't want me,' she heard herself say. 'That you hate it that we fell into bed—

twice—and that you hate me for stopping you marrying Mia. You hate, above all, that I am now pregnant. I am the very last woman, just as you told me, you'd want a baby with.' She looked away, meshing her fingers in her lap so tightly the blood flow was cut off. 'We can't help who we want or don't want in our lives.'

He did not answer and she did not expect him to. She turned her head away to look out over the dark, deadly waters of the glacial lake only a few metres from the road. Heaviness filled her, like a weight dragging her down into those deep, drowning waters, never to emerge again.

She felt tears prick in her eyes, but she could not brush them away or Luca would know that she was crying. Her throat constricted, tightening unbearably as she stifled the rising sob.

'Ariana…?'

She heard him say her name. His voice low. There might have been concern in it, but that was not likely. Well, not concern for her, at any rate. For the baby, yes, but never for her.

Never.

Luca Farnese would never be concerned about her. Would never stop resenting her presence in his life. Would never want her. Would never care about her.

She had known it since that hideous morning in New York, as he'd rejected her to go back to Italy and marry the woman he *did* want—her own cousin Mia. Who did not want him. Who'd turned to *her* to save her.

And save her I did—and thus earned the enmity of this man who never wanted to want me, even for passing sex. The man whose child I now carry.

She shut her eyes, feeling that heaviness press down upon her, suffocating her. The mess of her life…the mess

of his. Her thoughts burned with it. Her eyes burned
with it.

*It was a mess—nothing but a doomed, unholy, blighted
and accursed mess...*

Slow tears oozed again, scalding on her cheeks.

Then, 'Ariana—don't. Don't cry.'

Luca's voice was low, and what was in it was something she had never heard before.

In the darkness of the car's interior she felt him reach
out his hand, close it over hers, still twisting in her lap.
Stilling them.

'Don't cry,' he said again, and his palm was warm as
it covered her hands.

A single teardrop fell, splashing his fingers and hers.

He lifted his hand away, returned it to the steering
wheel. Drove on in silence.

Yet it seemed a different silence, somehow.

Luca stared down at the whisky in the glass in his hand
as he stood by the window of his hotel room looking out
over Lake Como, its surface dark except for where the
lights of the nearby houses fell on it in shimmering pools,
each separate from the other. Through the narrow wall
of his room was Ariana's. Separate from his.

His thoughts were strange. Difficult.

He had strived to break her power over him—the
power of his own unwanted desire for her—and he had
failed. Now she was beyond him anyway—her pregnancy
assured her of that.

In his head, the words she had spoken in the car circled.

'I have to accept that you don't want me.'

He wanted to laugh—savagely—at the irony of what
she had said. And that was not all she had said.

'We can't help who we want or don't want in our lives.'

He heard them afresh and lifted his glass, taking a mouthful of the fiery liquid within as if it might scour out what was inside him. Deliberately, he tried to conjure an image of Mia—but it would not come. It was as if she were already a ghost in his life—faded from reality.

He lifted his eyes, stared out over the dark and deadly waters of the lake. Faced the truth he could not deny. Whoever Ariana was, whatever she did, he would always desire her.

But what else was true beyond desire?

For a moment he recalled reaching out to press her hand, feeling a tear splash on his. Tears? From this woman who had so heartlessly destroyed her cousin's wedding? Why should he have felt what he had at that moment? A kind of pity...a weary sympathy for her as she had let tears fall?

He didn't know. Couldn't know.

He could know only that his future was mapped out for him just as he had mapped hers out for her. For the sake of this child that neither of them had sought to create they must somehow—somehow...

Be better parents than those we were given.

That was the truth of it. The only truth he could allow to matter.

With a sudden movement he downed the rest of his whisky, turning away from the window. Not wanting to think about any other truths... Truths too difficult to face. Too impossible to allow.

Ariana was talking. She was saying something about the villa's electrics and taking another pastry from the basket on the breakfast table. She needed to show Luca that whatever had happened on the drive back from the villa yesterday evening, whatever show of weakness or vulnerability or unhappiness—and, most of all, that strange, haunting moment when he'd taken her hand as her tears had started to fall—she was now back on the neutral subject of its refurbishment.

He heard her out, and asked several relevant questions, but when she had answered him he took control of the conversation.

'Ariana…'

She stilled. Tensing immediately. She could tell from his tone of voice, by the pause after her name, that she needed to be tense. She closed her face, veiling her eyes. Guarding herself from him. Protecting herself.

What was he going to say? What would he hurt her with now? Surely here, in the sunlit breakfast room of this expensive hotel on Lake Como, surrounded by other guests, he could not be too hostile?

His expression had changed.

'Don't,' he said. His voice was low suddenly. 'Don't, Ariana. There is no need.'

She looked at him, her fingers tightening on the knife she was about to cut her pastry with.

'No need to look like that,' he said. 'I only wanted to say—' He stopped. Then, 'In the car, you cried. I… I don't want you to cry.'

She swallowed, making words come, an acknowledgement come. 'Yes. I know. It's not good…' She swallowed again, more difficult this time. 'Not good for me to upset the baby.'

Something flashed in his eyes. 'It's not good for *you*,' he said. He took a breath. 'Ariana, I brought you here to the lake, to the villa, so you could do it up. In order to make things…to make things easier for you.'

He looked away, then back at her. Her expression

hadn't changed and her face was still closed, she knew, her eyes veiled. Because they had to be. Not because he was going to say something hostile to her, something harsh. But because there was something in his voice, in his eyes, that she could not bear…that hurt too much.

And yet he was not wounding her with his words… So why was her throat tightening, treacherous tears prickling again in the backs of her veiled eyes?

He was speaking again, in that same low, resolute voice, with that same watchful, intent gaze on her. 'And I want things to be easier for *us*. Because there *is* an us, Ariana! Whether we ever thought there would be or not, there is now. And I just want… I want…'

He fell silent, and she could not answer him or say anything. Then he was speaking again, in that same low tone, with that same holding of her eyes. Her vision was starting to blur, so fatally…

'Last night—in my room—I… I faced a truth. About us both.'

She felt her heart stop. Her breath stop. But she did not know why.

'We neither of us had parents who put us first as children…' his voice was sombre '…and that's why *we* must for this child we have created between us. It deserves no less.'

Ariana's heart started to beat again, her lungs to fill. Whatever it was that she had thought he might say, this was no reason for not breathing, for her heart to stop.

'Maybe for each of us,' he said slowly, his gaze turning inward now, 'our childhoods help to…to explain the adults we've become.' He paused, his gaze intent. 'You grew up without parents who cared about you, jealous of your cousin, wanting what she had. Not just your grandfather's affection…you were also driven to want—'

He broke off, but Ariana knew what he had been about to say.

To want the man she had. The man who wanted her, but not you.

She felt it burn in her throat, the bitterness of it all, but he was speaking again.

'As for me—' He broke off once more. Reached for his coffee, swallowed it. Set the cup down again. Looked back at her. He was different again.

'We have to go forward, Ariana, and deal with the reality of what has happened to us. We will never be close but we can be…civilised.'

He took a breath, his expression changing. Without realising his intent, she watched as he reached his hand forward, closing it over hers as it lay inert on the table-cloth, knife handle still in its grip. He patted it, as if reassuringly, then drew back, glanced at his watch.

He got to his feet. 'And now I must be on my way,' he said, in a brisk, upbeat tone. 'I have a meeting I can't miss. I leave the villa in your capable hands—keep me updated.' He raised a hand in farewell—a casual gesture. 'Until next weekend…'

He turned, striding from the breakfast room, and was gone without even looking back.

At the table, Ariana closed her eyes. They were shimmering with diamond dewdrops. Tears there was no point in shedding. No point at all.

Luca set down his phone. His expression was taut. The necessary arrangements were all made, the paperwork complete. Now all he needed was Ariana herself. He would be fetching her from Como that morning, and by the afternoon the deed would be done.

The deed that had to be done.

For a long moment he simply stared out of his office window, wondering what it was he felt. Realising he still felt nothing. The thing it was the safest to feel. Still the safest…

The words he had said to Ariana over a month ago circled in his head.

'We can be civilised.'

Because what else was possible between them?

And what was more civilised between two people who should never have had anything to do with each than doing what had to be done for a baby that should never have existed?

And what we feel or want does not matter. Cannot matter. Can never matter.

He got to his feet, strode through into the outer office and gave his PA his instructions for the rest of the day.

He was not thinking, not letting himself think, about what the rest of the day would bring.

CHAPTER TWELVE

ARIANA WAS SHOWING Luca the newly installed kitchen.

'A distinct improvement,' was his dry judgement, before she went on to show him the rest of the villa. Its refurbishment was almost complete, done in record time—weeks instead of months. She had worked assiduously, chivvying the workmen, taking up paints and paintbrush herself in some of the rooms, because it kept her busy, kept her going, kept her from thinking or feeling.

Outwardly she was brisk, businesslike. Dealing with things on a day-by-day basis. Nothing more than that. Keeping everything else at bay.

Keeping Luca at bay.

They seemed to have settled into some kind of truce, for want of a better word. They were civil to each other—civilised, indeed, just as he had said they should be—as if all the dark, dark waters just below the surface did not exist. Yet she was conscious all the time of their existence. How could she not be?

It was why she had to keep Luca at bay. She knew why she was doing it. To protect herself.

Not from his anger, as she had once said to him. But from something that was even more hurtful, even more wounding.

She heard his words to her that breakfast-time a month ago, carved into her.

'We can never be close.'

She led him upstairs, showing him the bedrooms, where the outdated wallpaper was gone, the patterned carpets replaced.

He would have brought Mia here. She'd have slept in the master bedroom, overlooking the lake she feared.

She put the thought from her.

'Which bedroom would you like for yourself?'

Luca's words penetrated, but she was confused. 'Me?' she said.

She would not be living here. She would be long gone. Living abroad was impossible now, Luca had made that clear, but she would settle somewhere on her own in Italy. Northern Italy…maybe Padua or Verona…so he could not accuse her of taking herself off too far. She hadn't thought about it much. Maybe she should start doing so.

He was glancing into another one of the bedrooms, filled with late-autumn sunshine, its walls a soft peachy tone, the carpet soft and deep. 'This would suit you,' he said, turning back to her.

She made no reply to that, saying instead that he should see the main bathroom, now comprehensively updated.

There were a couple of steps from the landing down to it, and in her hurry she caught her flat heel on one of them. Immediately a hand closed around her arm, steadying her.

'Are you all right?' There was concern in Luca's voice.

'I'm fine,' she said. She shook his arm off and headed

into the bathroom, showing off its new splendour. He looked around him, but there was a faint frown on his face.

'You've been working very hard,' he said.

'Hardly,' she said. 'The work has all been done by others!'

'That's not what I meant. You've accomplished a great deal in a short time.'

She gave a shrug. 'Well, I need to keep busy. Just like you said.'

He looked down at her. She was conscious, without her high heels, of how petite she was against him.

'But now you need to slow down,' he said. 'You're coming up to your second trimester, when your scan will be due.'

'I'm pregnant, not an invalid,' she said briskly.

He put his hand out to her again, taking her arm. 'Ariana—'

'I'm fine,' she said. 'Don't fuss!'

She shook his hand off. She couldn't bear him touching her. Couldn't bear his concern.

It's for the baby—just for the baby... Not me. Never me.

Those words he'd thrown at her were still audible in her head.

'You're the last woman on earth I would want to marry.'

She silenced them. What else could she do except what she was doing now.

'There's more to show you,' she said, keeping her voice brisk.

For a moment he didn't move, just looked down at her, his face unreadable. She stepped past him, avoiding body contact, and went downstairs to the drawing room, opening the glass doors to the terrace. It was chilly outside, even in the sunshine. Winter was coming.

I must be gone by then.

'I've had the terrace by the lake-edge repaved, as we discussed,' she went on in her brisk, professional voice, 'and the stone balustrade strengthened for safety reasons. There's been quite a lot of pruning done, but it will be best to wait and see next spring and summer what the garden has to offer as it is.'

Luca stepped out beside her, looking around him.

'It will be good, come the spring,' he said, nodding. He looked down at her. 'And in the summer, with the baby...' something changed in his face '...it will be ideal for you.'

She said nothing, moving to turn away instead. But her hand was caught. She tried to draw it back, but Luca would not let go.

'Ariana...'

His voice was different again. He spoke in the way he'd said her name upstairs, when he was fussing over her. He caught her other hand, holding them both together in his so that she had to turn towards him. She tugged to free them.

A frown formed on his brow. 'You pull away from me all the time,' he said. 'But I only want to reassure you—'

'I don't want you touching me!' The words broke from her. Sharp. Insistent. 'It was you who said it, Luca—that we should be civilised. But there's too much...too much anger...hatred...for there to be anything else.' She looked at him, unflinching now. 'You said it yourself—we can never be close.'

She saw his expression change. 'I should not have said that.'

'Why not? It's true.' She took a breath. Felt emotion

building in her. Finding its way to the surface. 'I know, Luca, that any concern you have is not for me. It is for the baby. I know it—and I understand it. I know that if I hadn't got pregnant I would never have set eyes on you again. I'd have let you take my business from me as punishment for what I did to you and gone off to starve in a gutter. And I would have been glad to do so if it got you out of my life! I curse the night I met you in New York! Curse that I ever let myself have anything to do with you! But now I have to. Because, as you said, we have to think not of ourselves and what we want—which for my part is to run like hell as far away from you as my legs will carry me!—but what this poor, poor baby is going to need…'

Her hand closed instinctively, protectively over her abdomen, which was starting to round now, to betray the presence of the living being within, who alone in all this mess was innocent of everything.

She would not cry, would not weep, even though she was cracking up inside, breaking into pieces. Numbly, she walked back inside, letting her torn and ragged emotions slowly subside, gaining mastery over herself again.

Indoors, she turned. He was standing in the open doorway to the terrace, looking at her, a troubled expression on his face.

She lifted her chin, squaring her shoulders. 'I've shown you everything,' she said, 'and now I'm hungry. Can we go and get lunch?'

Her voice was back to normal. The 'normal' she presented him with. The normal of being neutral and civil and civilised. The normal that had nothing to do with passion and hatred and destruction. Let alone anything else…

What cannot exist between us—what never will…

She walked out to his car, which was pulled up on the

driveway, leaving him to lock up. Then waited for him to join her, staring at nothing.

Luca secured the villa's front door with Ariana's words echoing in his head. Rearranging things inside it. Though how, he did not know. He knew only that...

That I didn't want to hear them.

His frown deepened. Hearing that sharp, repudiating rejection—*I don't want you touching me!*—had circled like a shark biting. It was *he* who did not want anything to do with *her*. He who had walked away from her that morning in New York. He who had told her, that ugly night in Lucca, that he would never sully himself on her again. He who had said they could never be close. That any 'us' was only because of the baby.

He heard her words: *'I curse the night I met you.'*

They bit into him, but why should they? He was the one with regrets over that night.

Because I was already committed to Mia.

His eyes went to Ariana as he walked slowly towards the car, his thoughts rearranging themselves in his head, a frown still on his face.

What if Mia had not been in my life then?

He stopped. Motionless. What if he'd been free in New York? Free to stay with Ariana after their night together—their searing, unforgettable night?

I didn't want to want her.

His expression darkened. No, he hadn't wanted to want Ariana—and he still didn't want to want her.

Not because of Mia—Mia, he knew, with a kind of haunting sadness, was gone from him for ever, faded back into his boyhood dreams of what the ideal woman should be like.

Did she ever really exist for me or did I just invent her

*for myself? Place upon her all that I thought I yearned
for in my ideal woman. Did I ever know her?*

She had spoken so little, given away so little of herself—he hadn't even known she would have hated the
villa by the lake…

Did I just conjure her from my dreams?

He tried to think now of what it would be like if it were
Mia standing by his car—but he could not see her. She
had gone…slipped away…a dream, a ghost…

Mia…sweet, gentle Mia…who had not deserved the
treatment her own cousin had so humiliatingly and so viciously subjected her to at her wedding. Cruel and heart-
less—jealous and vindictive.

His expression steeled.

That was why he didn't want to want the woman he
was going to have to marry now! The woman carrying
his child. That was what he must remember—that hideous scene in the church and only that! Not Ariana telling him she could not take any more anger from him,
with her tears falling on his hand, nor Ariana just now,
pulling away from him, not able to bear him to touch her
even when he meant her no harm…

He felt confusion well up in him…emotions dark and
difficult deep within. They were making no sense.

He made himself start walking towards the car again.
She was standing by the locked passenger door, staring into nothing. Her pregnancy barely showed under
her loose top. A pregnancy she would never have told
him about. If he hadn't discovered it she would have left
Italy for ever.

I would never have seen her again.

He stopped dead.

That had been his intention that morning in New York

as he'd left her there, lying in his bed. Never to see her again.

And if he hadn't—if he'd never set eyes on her again for the rest of his life...?

If that had been the reality, instead of this reality now...?

What would I feel?

He forced himself to close the distance between them. While inside his head all that he had been sure of was no longer there. Rearranged completely. But into what, he did not know.

Luca slowed to take a bend on the winding lakeside road, hemmed in between the plunging mountain slope to one side and the deep lake on the other, then accelerated again. His thoughts were inward, circling, as if he were an eagle high overhead, making no landing.

At his side, Ariana was studying her phone, looking at an invoice of some kind that she was scrolling through. Something to do with the villa refurbishment, he assumed.

His hands tightened on the wheel. He was not looking forward to the afternoon and what it would bring, but it had to be faced. It was all arranged.

She was closing her phone, slipping it back into her handbag. 'Where are we having lunch? Not too far, I hope. The electrician's turning up at three to put some more sockets in the utility room.'

Her tone of voice was as normal as it ever was when she was talking to him about the villa. But as he answered her he knew his voice was edged with tension. He would have preferred telling her over lunch, but she might as well know now. He had kept the preparations from her— it would be easier that way. It was something to be got through with as little fuss as possible—a mere legality for the sake of the baby they unwillingly shared, meaning nothing more than that. For either of them.

That was what he permitted himself to think about—not the questions circling in his head.

'You'll need to cancel him,' he told her. 'We won't be back by three.'

She turned to him, clearly about to say something, but he did not let her. He made himself say what needed to be said.

'We're going to Como, Ariana. We're getting married—it's all arranged. Just a civil ceremony, obviously, simply to get it done.'

He'd kept his voice neutral, inexpressive, as he made the announcement, but at his side he heard her gasp.

'Are you *mad*?'

He set his face, not looking at her, only at the twisting road ahead. 'It has to happen, Ariana. I made that clear from the outset.'

He didn't want an issue made out of it. He'd undertaken to complete the paperwork, assembled the documents, made the necessary appointment as methodically as if he were preparing a business dossier. Now they just had to show up for the occasion itself. As brief and as businesslike as he could make it. Then it would be done.

She swivelled in her seat. 'And *I* made it clear that no way was I going to *marry* you!'

He could hear the protest in her voice. He slammed down on it—hard. Slammed down on the biting emotion starting to rise up in him at her protest.

'We will marry for the sake of the baby, to regularise its existence. As I said, it's all arranged, I've seen to all the paperwork. You just need to show up, that's all.' He felt his teeth gritting. 'Ariana, this has to happen! You know it as well as I do.'

'Luca—no! No, it does *not* have to happen! And it won't.'

'It *must*. Don't make me keep repeating myself!' Against his will he could feel his own tension rising.

'There's no "must" about it! It's totally unnecessary!'

'Ariana—' There was warning in his voice.

In hers, there was grim objection. 'I'm not marrying you! Luca, listen to me—'

'There is nothing for you to say! So don't waste your breath saying it!' His voice was harsh, impatient. He wanted her to stop protesting, objecting—arguing. There was nothing to argue about—no alternative to what had to happen.

But she was insisting on speaking. Protesting, objecting—arguing. The way his mother always had...

'Luca, *listen*, damn you! I am not marrying you! I am not marrying you now or ever! *Ever!* Do you hear me? *Ever!*'

Her voice was rising. He could hear anger in it... felt anger rising in him as well. This was not what he needed—not now! He heard his own words again—*It has to happen*—he didn't want her arguing about it, making difficulties, making a scene.

Out of nowhere, memory flashed. Decades old. A car journey with his parents, himself in the back seat, his father fuming in the driving seat, his mother sulking beside him. Angry about something. Taking it out on his father, sniping at him with her vicious tongue. His father's face darkening as he refused to rise to it. The building tension like a cloud in a thunderstorm. His mother's fury breaking...her shouting at his father, angry and denouncing.

He'd put his hands over his ears, but it hadn't blocked her out.

He slammed the memory shut.

'Enough!' The harshness in his voice was rough, angry. 'This is going to happen, Ariana—it's not open for debate!'

He would not look at her, would not listen. Unconsciously, he accelerated—as if to get to the wedding he didn't want but had no choice about even faster.

'I said *listen* to me.' Fury was boiling in her voice, along with frustration and protest.

The yank on the sleeve of his suit jacket, took him by surprise and his head whipped around.

'I am not marrying you!'

Her words were vehement, her face contorted, her fingers digging into his sleeve. Angrily, he shook his arm, dislodging her grip, and accelerated again, his face set, jaw clenched. Not bothering to speak because he'd already given her his answer. The only answer that was possible. Deny it all she wanted.

'Do you hear me, Luca? *Listen* to me!'

The yank on his sleeve came again, and this time his movement to dislodge her was more violent. He let go of the steering wheel with one hand to shake her off. With only his left hand steering his grip on the wheel was skewed. The imbalance made the tyres screech, the powerful car swerve, and he swore.

'Ariana—*stop!*' His head whipped around again, and fury was blazing in him now, as he felt her grab at his sleeve once more.

His eyes flashed forward. A tunnel was coming up— one of many along this winding, narrow lakeside road set between sheer mountain and deep lake. She was still gripping his jacket sleeve, dragging at his arm, and he gave it another violent shake to get rid of it. She was distorting his steering. He felt the tyres screech again.

'You can't make me marry you! I won't! *I won't!*'

Her cry was vehement, but he ignored it. Ignored the dragging grip on his sleeve…pulled at the steering wheel sharply as he felt the powerful, speeding car move diagonally—dangerously—across the carriageway. Urgently, he twisted the wheel to compensate, to get back to his own side of the road.

But not in time. A lorry, headlights blazing, was emerging from the approaching tunnel.

He did not even have time to swear before the crash came.

Ariana's eyes were opening and closing, making sense of nothing. Lights, far too bright. Voices, far too loud. Her hands were flailing uselessly as the trolley she was strapped on was rushed forward. She tried to speak but could not. No one was paying attention to her. Only to each other.

She could hear words, medical terms, spoken urgently, orders given. She tried to move, but her head was immobilised in some kind of padded frame. Then the trolley was moving again, through doors swinging wide, and she could see the rounded arch of a CT scanner ahead of her. Alarm filled her and she tried to speak again.

She must not have a CT scan, it would be dangerous for her baby—she had to tell them.

And where was Luca? Where *was* he?

She tried to say his name, but that was hopeless too. The medics were sliding her into the scanner and she was told to stay still, quite still. It took only moments, and then she was being slid out again. A doctor was leaning over her. He was smiling.

'Your guardian angel was looking after you—and the car's air bags. There are no breakages, no internal injuries, only bruising and some lacerations. You'll be fine.'

He seemed about to rush off, but she made her hand snatch at him.

'My baby!' She forced the words from her throat, and this time they came out. 'Is my baby safe? I'm twelve weeks pregnant!'

The smile vanished from the doctor's face.

'Baby?' he said.

The doctor had given her painkillers to make her more comfortable, and they were keeping her in for observation as a precaution. But they would not say anything about Luca. Finally it was a nurse who told her, succumbing to her desperate pleading.

And when she did, the nightmare was complete.

'His legs took the full force of the impact. They were badly crushed. Surgery has stabilised him, but he will need much more.' The nurse paused, looking down at Ariana, her face strained. 'The surgeons will do everything they can, but...' she took a difficult breath '...it may be that they cannot save his legs.'

Horror drenched through Ariana—and a guilt so brutal she could not breathe.

She shut her eyes, as if that might stop the nightmare.

But nothing could do that.

Luca lay half propped up by his nurse against the pillows in his hospital bed. He'd been transferred to a hospital that specialised in orthopaedics. His rehabilitation had started, and soon the physiotherapist would be there to help him up...get him walking again on these strange, alien limbs.

But to what purpose?

He stared across the room. He had been here for weeks now, and it was as familiar to him as his own apartment. But he would be out of here as soon as he was able.

And then what?

He felt himself tense. As if he was guarding himself from the threat that was seeping into the room like a dark miasma.

He knew the name of it. Knew its power. Knew what gave it its power.

And it was not just the crutches leaning against the wall by his bed...

In his head, the words incised there by the letter left for him tolled with heavy blows.

He closed his eyes as if he could shut them out. Shut out both the words and who had written them. But nothing could. Nor ever would.

A soft knock on the door made him open his eyes again, unwillingly. A young nurse put her head cautiously around the door, not quite looking at him, and Luca knew why. Whatever appeal he had once held for her sex was impossible to detect any longer. His eyes were sunken, cheeks gaunt, face haggard.

As for the rest of him...

His mouth twisted.

'I know your physio is due, Signor Farnese,' the nurse began, sounding diffident, 'but you have a visitor who is very insistent on seeing you. She has come some distance, she says, and very much hopes you will agree to see her, however briefly.'

He froze. An emotion he would give no name to stabbed in his guts. Every muscle that still worked tensed like drawn wire. Slowly, he gave a curt, brief nod.

He steeled himself, his face a deliberate mask, as he fixed his gaze on the open doorway.

But the woman who walked through it hesitantly, uncertainly, was not the woman he'd thought it must be.

Shock went through him.

It was Mia.

CHAPTER THIRTEEN

ARIANA WAS SITTING on the narrow deck of the beach-front cottage, gazing out over the sugar-white sand that edged the flat sea beyond. She had been as touched as she'd been surprised when her mother had offered her this haven in Florida. But she was glad her mother was not actually at the grand villa behind the cottage, but was off skiing in Colorado.

She did not want to hear her mother say again, as she had on the phone, *'I know it's hard, but one day you'll be glad—'*

Ariana silenced her mother's voice in her head.

Glad?

Another voice came. The doctor at the hospital in Italy. Explaining, carefully—sensitively—what had happened.

Ariana had wept. Sobbed with a sense of heartbreak that had racked her body. The doctor had been kind, the nurses had been kind, everyone had been kind...

Yet still the sobs had come.

And a sense of bitter, bitter irony lacerated with a guilt so profound it had shaken her hand as she'd forced herself to write the letter she'd had to write. Guilt that would be with her to her dying day.

I caused it—I caused the crash. I and I alone.

Like red-hot skewers twisting into her, the self-blame came over and over again.

She shifted restlessly on her lounger.

I have to leave. I can't stay here for ever.

But where would she go and what would she do? Her business had been closed down—her accountant was winding it up. And as for going to London...there was no point now. Unconsciously, her hand splayed over her midriff. There was an ache inside her that could never be assuaged, shot through with guilt, regret and remorse...

She gazed blankly at the wintry sun reddening into a ball over the sea. Out on the beach a dog barked. Then another noise became audible. A motor of some kind... an electric hum.

She looked around. A wooden boardwalk ran down to the beach from the cottage and a motorised wheelchair was making its way along it.

Steering it was Luca.

He could see her. And he knew she had seen him. She had twisted her head around to stare at him, shock moving across her face. More than shock. Worse than shock.

Grimly, he powered on. The wooden boards were not ideal for the wheels of his chair, and the jolting, even though it was mild, sent pain shooting through him. He ignored the pain—it had become his habit to ignore pain.

He slewed onto the deck where she was sitting, still frozen, immobile, her knuckles white.

The woman he had thought never to see again.

But now he must.

Ariana felt the blood draining from her face. For a moment faintness whirled, then cleared. She jolted to her feet.

'What...what are you doing here?'

Her voice was a croak. The banal question she had uttered seemed so inadequate she could not believe she had asked it.

Did anything move in his eyes? There was no expression in his face, but that was not what she was looking at. What she was seeing was the greyness of it, the deep lines scored around his mouth—lines of pain. She felt emotion convulse inside her, seeing him looking the way he did. And another emotion too, that responded to it and made her pulse suddenly surge, countering the draining of blood from her own face.

But she must not feel that—she mustn't.

The mask over his grey lined face did not move.

'I've come to talk to you,' he said.

She stared at him, still not believing that it was Luca here, now, on a winter beach in Florida. She saw his hands tighten, one resting on the arm of the wheelchair, the other on the control panel. His arms, his torso, moulded by the sweater he was wearing, looked as strong, as muscled as ever. Involuntarily, her eyes dropped to his lower body. Long trousers covered his legs…

Her stomach clenched with horror—the same horror that had convulsed her when the nurse at the hospital had made that nightmare revelation to her.

He was speaking again. 'I've only just been released from hospital…' he took a sharp, harsh breath '…you left me a letter. I—'

She cut across him, voice twisted. Anguished. 'I had to tell you myself—not just leave it to the doctors!'

Something flashed across his gaunt face. 'I know,' he said. 'I understand.'

There was emotion in his voice now…emotion she did not want to hear. For it was the same emotion that was in her—one that could not be assuaged.

'But what I do *not* understand—' He broke off. Took another harsh, heavy breath, pinioning her with his gaze. As dark as obsidian…as searing as it had ever been…

Another emotion knifed through her—an old one…so old. And that, too, could never be assuaged…

He spoke again. His voice flat. 'Before I left the hospital I had a visitor,' he said. His eyes were behind that mask now. He paused, then said, 'Your cousin.'

'Mia?' Disbelief was naked in Ariana's voice. More than disbelief.

He gave a brief nod. 'She came to tell me some things.' His mouth compressed, and the expression in his eyes changed. 'Things you never thought to tell me.'

She swallowed. Unable to speak.

Luca's hand slammed down on the arm of his wheelchair. *'Why?* Why did you not tell me? Tell me that it was Mia who begged you to stop the wedding!' His voice was scathing. 'Because *she* didn't have the guts to do so herself!'

'That's not fair!' Ariana's defence of her cousin was automatic, immediate. 'Mia was distraught—'

'Distraught? She gave no sign of it! Do you understand me? Not one sign!'

Ariana shut her eyes, then opened them again. 'Mia's always hidden her feelings.' She swallowed. 'It's her way of coping with…with difficult situations…'

Luca stared at her. 'Coping with *what*, precisely? Being her grandfather's darling? What the hell was ever "difficult" about that?'

Ariana's face worked. 'You don't understand. Our grandfather smothered her…suffocated her. She was his favoured grandchild, but only if she was exactly the kind of grandchild he wanted her to be. She could never say no to what he wanted. Including…' her voice dropped low '…accepting your proposal of marriage. Because she knew,' she said sadly, 'it would make our grandfather happy. Then…then she felt trapped by it.'

'So she got you to do her dirty work for her and get her out of it. And you took the fall for it.' His voice was condemning.

Ariana swallowed. A sense of unreality was sweeping over her…to see Luca again…

She tried to focus, to keep only to listening to what he was saying. 'I had to find a way to stop the wedding without our grandfather realising Mia had never wanted to marry you. So that he would blame me instead.'

Luca's eyes were on her. It seemed unbearable to her that they should be.

'But it was not only your grandfather who blamed you, was it?' His voice was just as harsh, just as heavy. 'Not just he who accused you of acting out of vindictive jealousy.'

She looked away, giving a shrug. In her chest her heart was thudding. Her throat was tightening.

'Why did you not tell me the truth? That Mia never wanted to marry me!'

She could hear his incomprehension—and more. But what 'more' she did not know. Her eyes went back to him. She could see a nerve working in his cheek, haggard though it was.

'I… I didn't want your anger targeting her,' she said. She swallowed again. 'I knew I could take your anger, Luca. I've taken my grandfather's, so I could take yours. I'm strong—not like Mia. I wanted to protect her.'

'So you let me destroy you,' he said slowly. 'Blame *you*. Accuse *you*.'

She gave another shrug. It seemed so long ago now, in

another life. What did it matter any longer? How could it when...?

'Oh, God, Luca—I'm so desperately, desperately sorry!' The words broke from her, and then her voice dropped, became intense and sombre. 'The guilt will be with me to my dying day. I caused that crash—it was my fault! And when the nurse told me—'

She turned away, unable to bear seeing him. Her breathing was ragged as she wrapped her arms around herself.

There was a sound behind her, but the blood drumming in her ears deafened her to it. And then, as she stood there, shaking with the horror of what she had done to him, hating herself more than it was possible to measure, she heard him say her name.

She turned back towards him. He was no longer in his wheelchair, but standing upright. Her thoughts flew in confused disarray—then they made sense.

Cold went through her—an icy flood through her body.

Prostheses. That was how he was standing there. Prostheses covered by his trousers so you could never tell their presence.

Had she said the word aloud? She didn't know. Only knew the horror of his damaged body that *she* had caused.

His expression was changing again. She saw him take a breath.

'Is that what you thought?' he asked.

There was something strange in his voice now.

Her mouth was dry. 'The nurse said...said the surgeons might not be able...able to save your legs...'

He was silent for a moment, standing there. So tall, so upright.

Memory seared through her—his long, lean body covering hers, their thighs meshed in that unholy passion that had fused their bodies but nothing else…

He was speaking, and memory vanished.

'Well, as you see,' he was saying, and his opaque gaze was holding her horror-struck one, 'the surgeons were, after all, very good at their job…'

A choke cracked in her throat, but he was still speaking.

'OK, I'm still very weak, and I still need physio, so I use the chair for the time being, and there's enough metal in my legs to set off every airport security alarm I walk through. But *walk* is what I can do—and on legs that are mine. Still miraculously mine.'

Her hands flew to her mouth and that choking in her throat was now a sob, rising up unstoppably. Another followed it, and another, and then she could not stop them, choking and sobbing, pressing her hands against her mouth.

'Thank God—oh, thank God!'

Gratitude and thankfulness poured through her. He had been spared the ordeal she had so feared. Tears were pouring down her face now. Tears for so much. Tears not for relief, or gratitude or thankfulness. Tears of grief—tearing, unassuageable grief. For what had not been spared…

She felt arms come around her. Arms to hold her, to staunch her loss. *Their* loss. The arms of a man who had never held her as he held her now. To comfort her in her distress—in her grief at the loss of what she had once never wanted and now could only weep for. Such bitter, bitter tears…

She heard in her head the doctor's voice—kindly, sympathetic…pitying. And saw herself, not wanting to hear.

'It was not the crash. A silent miscarriage—that is

what it's called. The body registers pregnancy, pregnancy hormones remain, the body prepares for birth, but no embryo is developing—the body has reabsorbed it. You would have been told so at your first scan.'

She had wept then, as she wept now, for the tiny life that had had so short, so fragile an existence. For the loss she had had to tell Luca about in that stark, pitiful letter she had left for him.

Lucas's voice when he spoke was sombre. Strained. Filled with grief. Grief as deep as hers. 'Such a little life, and yet—'

He broke off, but she had heard the sorrow straining his voice.

She lifted her tear-stained face and when she spoke her voice was still choked. 'It seems so cruel! For our baby to have slipped away and we did not know…' She took a razored breath, making herself say what must be said. 'So cruel that I caused the crash that maimed and disabled you when we were driving to a wedding for which there was no reason.'

Her voice dulled and she pulled away. For he had no reason to hold her—none—and she had no claim on him, nor ever had.

'There was no reason, had we but known it, for you to have had anything to do with me.' Slowly, she shook her head. 'You're free of me, Luca—as I said at the end of my letter. That does not lessen my guilt about your injuries, though,' she said heavily. 'And all I can do is wish you a good recovery—'

She broke off, then made herself look at him. What did it matter now, with their baby gone, its fleeting existence snuffed out, whether he still thought her to blame for what she had done to stop his wedding to Mia? Guilty or innocent, it no longer mattered.

She spoke carefully, with difficulty. 'I'm... I'm sorry your hopes of Mia were dashed—I know she's the one you wanted. Have always wanted.'

He was standing motionless, stiff-legged, and the strain in his gaunt face was visible. She felt emotion knife in her, but made herself go on.

'I've known since that morning in New York, Luca, that I was nothing but passing sex for you. A mistake, just as you said it was. Regretted the moment you awoke.'

Ariana saw his expression change, the acknowledging nod of his head, and though there was no reason for it that she would allow, it was like a knife twisting in an unhealable wound.

'Yes,' he said. 'Regret has been my dominant emotion, I agree. Regret for a great deal. But most of all...' his dark, obsidian eyes rested on hers '...for my own blind stupidity.'

And mine! she wanted to cry—but what would be the purpose? Everything between her and Luca had been a mistake. Causing nothing but misery and the loss of an innocent life that should never have existed, and so very nearly maiming a man to whom she had been, and always would be, nothing.

She heard his words in her head, still twisting that knife in her side. *'We can never be close—you are the last woman I would ever want to marry.'*

He was speaking again, his voice cutting across her bleak and painful thoughts.

'Blind stupidity,' she heard him repeat. 'The blind and unforgivable stupidity of my denial of what has been there from the very first.'

His eyes were on her, opaque, unreadable, yet there was something in them that held hers to them as unbreakably as steel.

'My desire for you.' He drew a breath, harsh and heavy. 'A desire, Ariana, that I forced myself to deny from the moment I realised its overwhelming power.'

Her face contorted. 'And I know you hated yourself for it! You didn't want to want me! You said that to me! God, Luca, I know that—I know I meant nothing to you!'

'Because I would allow nothing else!' His voice slashed across hers and he took a breath, a shuddering one, that heaved in his chest as he exhaled again. 'Ariana, *why* do you think I walked out on you that morning in New York? If I'd stayed with you I would have been lost—'

He shifted position, a flicker of pain showing in his face as he did so. Abruptly, he spoke again. His voice was different now. Edged and guarded.

'Do you never wonder what made me want to marry Mia? Quiet and gentle and sweet and passionless.'

His expression changed again. There was a distant look in his eyes now, and they were shifting again, a bleakness in them.

'Because that was what I valued. Craved. To make a quiet, placid marriage! Totally unlike my own parents' marriage—' He broke off, his gaze turning inward. Then, 'Their marriage was hell. Thanks to my mother. She revelled in making scenes, raging at my hapless father, not caring what people thought, how they stared at her, shocked. She would make furious accusations, denunciations, storming at my father with her endless demands and complaints, and always, *always* my father tried to placate and appease her. He never, ever stood up to her—because he was besotted by her, abjectly in her thrall. And I *vowed* that I would never be like him! Never entrust myself to a woman who had any power over me.'

His voice hardened and his gaze opened to hers, returning to the present.

'Least of all sexual power.'

He drew a breath, harsh and heavy, his mouth compressing.

'And then I encountered you. And I found that my desire for you—which I could not resist that night in New York, though I knew...*knew*... I should—had the power to make me betray the quiet, gentle woman I had found in Italy, whom I had thought the ideal wife for me.'

His voice was condemning.

His face darkened.

'Everything you threw at me that morning...every accusation as I walked out on you...was true. And it burned like a brand on my skin that it should be so! I used that burn to tell myself how your rage and fury was the very proof of how impossible you were for me! How right I was to walk away...to go back to Mia thinking I would find the peace with her that I thought was what I craved.'

The expression in his eyes changed.

'It was the worst decision of my life.'

Ariana stood there, hearing him speak, unable to move a muscle. A pulse started to throb in her constricted throat. She saw Luca turn away, walk haltingly to his wheelchair, sink down in it. Pain flashed across his face as his legs bent, then relief as the pressure on them was lifted.

'Forgive me,' he said. 'I cannot stand for long yet.'

He lifted his face to look at her, and in his eyes was an openness she had never seen before. And his next words were an admission she had never heard before.

'Mia was a mirage, conjured out of my own fears. She was never real.' He looked away, out over the distant sea He paused, then spoke again with difficulty. 'I... I never knew her. Not the person she was. And...' he took a breath, also with difficulty '...and I nearly ruined her life as well.' He frowned, looking back at Ariana. 'I... I am glad she has found her own happy ending—her husband Matt was with her when she came to see me in the hospital. But as for me—' He broke off. Then, 'I should have stayed with you,' he said. 'I should have stayed, after our night together, and faced up to what had happened.'

His voice was harsh, and Ariana felt herself swallow, as painfully as if a stone were lodged there. 'We had sex, Luca, that was all.'

'No.' It was a blunt, one-word contradiction. 'That was not all.' He closed his eyes for a moment, then they flashed open again. 'You know it was not all, Ariana! You know that had I not walked out I would never have gone back to Italy to marry Mia. She would have become meaningless.'

And now his voice was different again, and his eyes fastened on hers with so dark a power she could not break it, so dark a power she could no longer breathe.

'Because since that night only one woman—only one!—has had any meaning for me at all.'

He drew in a breath, a rasp. His hands tightened on the arms of the wheelchair.

'You, Ariana. The woman I did not want to want. The woman I could no more *not* want, *not* desire, than I could not breathe, could not see or hear or taste! The woman who fills the world for me.'

'You said I was the last woman you would want...' Her voice was a whisper.

'I lied. I lied to save my own sorry skin. I lied to make the lie a truth. A truth that had died the first time I set eyes on you.' He shut his eyes for a moment, then opened them. 'Oh, God, Ariana, I have been the world's fool! You gave yourself to me in passion and in flame and I threw you away! I lied to myself, and to you, over and over again. Told myself I was glad—dear God—*glad* that you had proved my fears of you right, that you had acted out of jealous rage at your innocent cousin!' His voice changed. 'I told myself that the only reason I took you to Milan was because of the baby. That that was the only reason we were together.'

'But there is no baby, Luca. Not any more.' Her voice was sad.

She looked out to sea. The sun was setting now in a golden orb. Memory came of how she had stood watching the sun over Lake Como when Luca had first taken her to the villa. It seemed a lifetime ago.

'No. But there is us, Ariana.'

Her gaze came back to him. He was looking at her with something in his face she had never seen before, something that stopped the breath in her lungs.

His voice as he spoke again was low and strained. 'I've screwed up with you from the very first to the very last,' he said. 'I have neither hope nor expectation.' His mouth twisted in a simulacrum of bitter humour. 'I haven't even a sound body to offer you.' Something changed in his eyes. 'And yet all the same whatever I have, I offer you, Ariana. If any of it should by any chance be of any use or worth or value to you, then it is yours.'

She looked at him as if she had never seen him before. Because the man she saw now had never existed before. The man within the man. The man who had, in a single moment, said the most precious words to her. Precious beyond all measure—because she had never hoped for them. Never dared to hope for them.

Emotion welled within her, rising like a tide long stopped, long held at bay. Now no longer.

'There is us.'

She felt her throat constrict…her heart crushed within her. The world stopped. She walked up to him, reached out her hand. But not to take his.

'There is only one part of you that is of any use or worth or value to me,' she said. 'And it is this.'

Slowly, carefully, she placed her hand on his chest, where the beat of his heart could be felt. And she felt it now, strong and quickening. Felt his hand lift from the arm of the wheelchair, flash out and close around hers. Her legs buckled and she went down on her knees on the deck, her other hand lifting to his face, cupping his haggard cheek, then dropping away.

Words came, halting and painful, confessing and self-castigating. 'You kept rejecting me, Luca. Always rejecting me! From that first hideous morning in New York, after the most incredible night of my life. You had swept me off my feet and into your bed, to fall asleep in your arms and dream that in the morning would begin the greatest romance of my life, with a man who was like no other in the world, the one man for me! And then—' Her voice cracked. 'To wake and realise you were gone…just gone. You walked out on me, discarded me. And then— oh, God—worse still was what you threw at me. That you had slept with me *knowing* you were going back to Italy to marry…'

The words were choking her, but she had to say them—*had* to. Because they were gutting her, eviscerating her…

'And after I stopped your wedding that hatred in you for me, that deadly rage… You did all that you could to have your revenge on me, to destroy me. And you did. And then that nightmare night in Lucca, when I wanted to hit back at you in the only way I could, to reject *you* as you had rejected me…but I couldn't… I just couldn't—'

His voice cut across hers. Harsh—but not at her. Never harsh at her any more. 'Nor could I reject you—though I loathed myself for my weakness!'

She gave a cry that was half a sob, felt tears starting to burn in the backs of her eyes. 'And you loathed me, too! And you went on and on rejecting me—even when you were forcing yourself to marry me you were telling me that I was the last woman on earth you would ever want! Always rejecting me—*always*!'

She bowed her head.

'And I didn't know why it hurt so much! I'd been rejected so often in my life—by my mother, my father, my grandfather. I was used to it! Your rejection should not have hurt me as it did—so why did it? *Why?*'

She screwed her eyes shut so tight the tears on her lashes scalded her cheeks.

'I've faced it now—faced what I never wanted to face! That you could only hurt me, Luca, because…' she swallowed, and it was agony to do so '…because I loved you.' Her voice dropped. 'Though I cursed myself for it.'

'And you cursed the day you met me.' Luca's voice was heavy. He took a ragged breath, his hand tightening on hers. 'When you said that to me it was like a knife going into me—though I did not know why. Not then. But now—'

He broke off. Took her other hand, curled defensively in her lap, folded them within his, protectively…cherishingly. She heard the catch in his voice as he spoke again.

'Be mine. Be mine, Ariana of my heart. As I am yours, loving you as I now know I do—fool that I have been. Be mine as I am yours. Be *mine*.' His voice was choked now, and her tears flowed faster yet. 'And when we conceive in love and joy, in passion and desire, the child *will* come—for the sake of the baby we lost…'

She clutched his hands more tightly, her face uplifted to his. 'It seemed such a dreadful sign,' she said, weeping still for so much…for the child that had not been. 'It seemed like a sign of what had created it in the first place—a sign that it should never have existed, never *could* exist between us…so toxic, so poisoned…'

He silenced her—silenced her with a kiss so gentle it was like a breath of air, no more. A kiss such as had never been between them till now.

'We shall make right all that was wrong,' he said. 'It will be a second chance for us. And I promise, Ariana of my heart, with all my being, that I will never, ever bring hurt to you again—only all the love in my heart, for ever.'

She smiled at him mistily, tears brimming yet again. Her heart was overflowing with all that he had said. With all the wrongs that had been made right. It sang inside her, a paean to him.

'I ask only one promise of you,' she said. 'That you will never leave me.'

'Never,' he agreed.

He turned his head, looking about him. His gaze swept around from the beach, where the sea was pooling with the setting sun, turning to bronze, and the white sand was darkening to gold, back to the little wooden cottage. Dusk was gathering towards coming night.

'Could we start my never leaving you right now?' he asked, and there was something different in his voice which made her catch her breath, quickened the pulse at her throat.

She felt the wash of his eyes over her, a heat beating up in her as he brushed his mouth against hers and lifted her hand in his.

She straightened, getting to her feet, keeping hold of his hand as he got to his feet too, their eyes never leaving each other, her hand tightening in his.

'Oh, Luca, man of my heart—yes...*yes*!'

His arms came instantly around her, folding her to him, and it was bliss, oh, such bliss, to be in his arms again. Bliss to lift her face to his and be kissed by him. Softly, tenderly, sweetly... And then with more than tenderness. So much more...

She led him indoors. Into the rest of her life. And his.

'I don't want to hurt you...' Ariana's voice was anxious.

'You can never hurt me. Not now that I know I am yours, and that you have forgiven me for what I did to you.'

Luca's voice in the dusk, in the dimness of the bedroom, as he lay beside her on the bed, was husky.

'But it could be that you make the moves,' he went on, smoothing the waterfall of her hair from her brow as she lifted her mouth from his, and she could hear the wry and rueful note in his low voice.

'Every one,' she promised him, her voice warm, and so, so loving.

And so she did make the moves, with gentle hands and fingertips that explored in glory the wonder of his body, that smoothed with a little cry of grief for the scars scored into his stricken legs. But he would not let her weep again for him. He would only let her move her body over his, carefully, slowly, to ensure that all she brought to him was pleasure and not pain.

Slowly, sensually, as the night darkened around them, she made love to him, took his body into hers. Bestowed herself upon him. Wound her arms around him, felt his arms around her, holding her close, so close...

The moment when they came together, with a soft, breaking cry from her, a low, helpless groan from him, their bodies were meshed and fused and melded together, so that parting was impossible. For they were made one flesh. One body. One being. One heart beating...

She wept again, knowing how long and terrible a journey it had been to this moment, knowing all that it had cost them both. Including the little life they had created, so pitifully lost to them...

Surely another little life would come? She hoped so with all her being, even as Luca, careless of his scars, his still wasted muscles, his bones knitted together with steel and the patient skill of surgeons, swept his body over hers so that it sheltered her, stroking her hair, cradling her to him, murmuring to her of all that was and always would be.

One love between them.

For all time.

EPILOGUE

CAREFULLY, ARIANA LOWERED herself into the padded chair on the semi-circular terrace outside the villa's drawing room. Beyond the gardens sunlight glittered on the lake's dark surface.

It was good to be out of the maternity hospital.

Good to be home again.

Home.

Though Luca still had his ferociously modernistic apartment in Milan, it was the lakeside villa that was home—and it was glorious. Spring was ripening into summer, and the gardens were lush with flowers and greenery. She felt emotion pluck at her. Had she really once thought she would never live here? That it was nothing to do with her?

Her eyes went to Luca, stepping through the open French windows, a precious bundle in his arms. The two people she loved most in all the world. Her heart turned over, and she felt love and happiness and thankfulness drenching through her.

'Here he is,' said Luca, carefully lowering their adored baby into her waiting arms. 'Wide awake again.'

His voice was tender, doting, and Ariana loved him all the more for it. Loved their son all the more, too, overcome by a wave of tenderness. She smiled, gazing as dotingly as Luca at the tiny infant wrapped in his cotton blanket, his starfish hands waving slowly, his little mouth mewing.

'And hungry again!' She laughed, slipping the buttons on her maternity blouse, feeling her milk come in.

He latched on hungrily, and for a while neither she nor Luca did anything but gaze in wonder and mutual adoration. And thankfulness. Such thankfulness.

Without volition, Ariana felt tears prick the back of her eyes. Luca saw them, and hunkered down beside her, taking her free hand as she cradled their nursing child.

'I like to think,' he said, his voice low with deep-felt emotion, and knowing why she had become tearful, 'that he is the baby we lost—this time come again safely and healthily.'

She pressed her fingers into his, gazing across at him, eyes misting. 'How blessed we are, Luca,' she said.

She looked about her at the gracious house she'd restored, the gardens lush all around them, the dramatic lake edged with the mountains beyond—and the man beside her whom she loved so, so much.

And he loved her. As she had never thought he could—or would. And yet he did.

He leant forward, kissing her softly. 'Blessed indeed,' he said, straightening, then sitting himself down opposite her, crossing one long leg over the other.

His legs had healed almost completely, and that was another cause for her profound gratitude. It was a gratitude that Luca had shown in a massive donation to the hospital whose surgeons' skills had saved his limbs, and to the orthopaedic centre where he'd regained the use of them.

And that was not the only use his money had been put to.

Ariana smiled fondly at him. 'Your investment in Matt's career continues to pay off—he and Mia are charting with their latest release, she tells me.' She paused a moment. 'She says she wants us to visit when she and Matt are next in Italy.'

Luca looked at her. 'I will do so gladly.' It was his turn to pause. 'Ariana, she was a dream, a mirage—unreal in herself to me. I wronged her almost as much as I wronged you.'

His voice was sombre, and Ariana hated to hear it.

'It's in the past, Luca—and both she and I have found our happiness!' Her expression changed. 'I still find it astonishing that it's turned out to be Mia who is the secret to Matt's success! That she has such a beautiful voice. And,' she went on, 'how wonderful it is that our grandfather is now reconciled to her!'

It was true. A penniless musician and an eloping granddaughter had turned into a commercially and artistically successful musical duo—one for Tomaso to be proud of and one who made sure they spent a lot of time in Italy with him at his *palazzo*.

And although Ariana knew wryly now, rather than bitterly, that her grandfather would never be proud of *her*, in having a granddaughter who had married Luca Farnese—even if it was the wrong one!—he could not be as scathing of her as had once been.

'I think you'll find,' Luca was saying drily, 'that you too have gone up in his approval ratings by providing him with his first great-grandson…'

She gave a wry laugh. 'I doubt my poor mother will ever forgive me for turning her into a grandmother—however glamorous!'

'She'll love him when she sees him,' Luca promised her. 'As will your grandfather.'

On cue, their son unlatched, gazing up at them, then started to mewl again.

'Time for *dulce*,' Ariana said, and busied herself swapping him to her other side, conscious, with a little colour in her cheeks, of how Luca's eyelashes dipped down over his dark obsidian eyes as his gaze rested on her exposed breast. It would be a while yet before he could do more than look, but Ariana was already impatient...

She met his gaze as it returned to her face, remembering in vivid detail the passion that burned between them. For the moment it was only a memory—but soon...

'Don't look at me like that...' Luca's voice was husky. 'New fatherhood is miraculous, but it has its drawbacks...'

She laughed, tossing back her hair, cuddling her suckling infant closer to her breast. The necessary days would pass, her post-partum body would heal, and then... Oh, then...

Luca leant across to kiss her. Lightly and gently. With the promise of so much more to come.

The promise of eternal love and happiness for all their days together.

And all their nights...

Definitely all their nights.

* * * * *

THE WIFE
THE SPANIARD
NEVER FORGOT

PIPPA ROSCOE

MILLS & BOON

For Nic, thank you for the friendship, wine and trip down memory lane that planted the seed for this story. (There is no such thing as too many Aperol Spritz!)

And to the beautiful family holiday that helped it grow. Javi, I hope I've done Frigiliana justice!

xx

CHAPTER ONE

JAVIER CASAS LEFT the extravagance of In Venum—Madrid's newest and hottest nightclub—two marble steps at a time, rubbing at his tired eyes. *That's what happens when you push yourself too hard,* taunted the warning his closest friend had uttered only days ago. Javier huffed. Santi was filming his latest blockbuster hit during the day and finishing post-production on another in the evening—he was hardly one to talk.

'Casas!' a predatory female voice called, halting his steps. He couldn't claim not to have heard her in deserted Spanish streets at two o'clock in the morning, even though he was tempted.

He turned. She was two steps above him, but barely at eye level with his six-foot four-inch frame. Behind her, he caught the eye of the bouncer framing the door at the top of the steps and discreetly shook his head. Javier would deal with the woman himself. She'd managed to ignore all of his subtle and then not so subtle refusals so far that night, making the entire evening a practice in avoidance. He hadn't even wanted to come tonight, but he couldn't miss the grand opening for a bar that he owned forty-nine percent of—*silently.*

She reached out, red-nailed fingers gripping his shoulder. 'I thought that we could go somewhere.'

She licked her lips in a move she probably believed was sensual, but to Javier was deeply disturbing. The light from the club's entrance created a painfully bright aura around her, illuminating rather than disguising her ravenous desperation.

'You need to go home, Annalise.'

'There is a lot that I need, Javier, and I think you could help me with that.'

'Annalise—'

'I want your hands on me,' she whispered, leaning closer, and before he could stop her she had her finger on the zip of his trousers. He cursed, twisting free of her clutches.

'Basta ya!' But she didn't stop. He clasped her hands to keep them from grabbing other parts of his anatomy and stepped back as she tried to press herself against him. 'I'm *married*, Annalise,' he growled between gritted teeth.

She rolled her eyes. 'You are never seen with anyone on your arm, so we all know that's just a ruse. Unless you keep her locked up in your house and never let her out?'

He frowned, his brain trying to work out who 'we' was and whether she was joking or not.

'You could keep *me* locked up, if you like?'

He didn't have time for this. His driver was waiting and he had a meeting in five hours. He didn't bother responding. Instead he nodded to the man by the entrance, who appeared and gently prised her from him.

'Make sure she gets back to wherever she's staying safely,' he ordered over his shoulder, knowing it would be followed without question, and continued towards the car waiting for him.

'Don't look at me like that,' Javier groused when he

reached Esteban. His driver's expression hadn't changed a bit, but wry amusement came off him in waves.

'Didn't say a thing, sir,' his chauffeur replied.

Once settled in the back of the car, Javier checked his phone for the upcoming day's meetings, making sure that everything was on track to start bang on seven a.m. He scanned the two hundred emails his personal assistant had already filtered and checked the family message group he had with his half-sister and his mother—but neither distracted him from the sudden unwanted thoughts about the wife he hadn't seen for six years.

Angry with himself for not having more restraint, he pulled up the newspaper article that had been published last month. *More Than Just a Pretty Paintbrush—UK's hottest new interior designer making waves.* He scanned the puff piece that was more patronising than it was illuminating. He'd read it almost ten times now and each time his gaze snagged on the photograph of the woman who had left him on an evening that should have changed their lives for very different reasons.

The black and white picture showed her in a white shirt, holding a cup of coffee, looking towards the camera as if she had a delicious secret to share. Her eyes sparkled in a way he barely recognised and it infuriated him beyond belief that the way her hands cupped the mug concealed her ring finger.

Did she still wear it?

The car slowed and took an unfamiliar turn. Javier frowned, catching the flicker of his driver's eyes in the rear-view mirror.

'Badly signed roadworks. We're going to have to—'

The entire world shifted in an explosion of screaming metal and shattering glass. Swept up in a wave that crushed the confines of the car, Javier found himself upside down, choking on a vicious pain in his side. Time jerked back and forth between shocking speed and incomprehensible slowness. A piercing light cut between blue and white, making him wince as a figure he couldn't be sure was actually there knelt in glass. Blood dripped into his eye, but he couldn't move his hand to wipe it away.

Something bad had happened. Something awful even, but he couldn't understand what. He caught words like 'hospital' and the oddly irritating reassurance that everything would be okay. To the left he saw his phone, a shatter across the screen and, beneath the broken shards, an image of Emily about to tell him her secret, just before everything went black.

'Okay, that's it, ladies and gentlemen, time to leave.'

'But, boss—'

'It's one in the morning. Don't you have bars to drink in? Dates to go on? Homes to get to?' Emily teased. She loved her small team; they were eager and hungry, just like she was, but she knew how quickly hunger could morph into burnout and a healthy team was as important to her as their income.

'But we haven't finalised the tiles in the bathroom, the colours for the third and fourth bedrooms, and—'

'It can all wait until tomorrow.' She gathered up the coffee cups, cutting them off from the only thing that had kept them going this long, and one by one her two designers, one architect and her much loved assistant made their way out of the door.

Once alone, Emily sighed. They'd done good work on the Northcote project in the Cotswolds but the restaurant in San Antonio was niggling. It was still early days but she hadn't found *the thing* yet. And Emily would continue to be unsettled until she found *the thing* that brought the project together.

It had always been like that. Ever since she'd finished the evening course with the Design Institute. Returning from Spain, full of heartache, with nowhere to live and no idea what to do, had been awful. Until Francesca, her best friend, had invited Emily to stay in her home while she went travelling with her boyfriend. The only proviso was that Emily 'oversaw' the renovation of the kitchen/diner. Desperate for a distraction from the hope that her husband would come for her—that her sudden and shocking absence might finally make him notice her—Emily had first shadowed the interior designer and then become more of a project manager, coordinating the revolving door of tradespeople.

Through the months of the renovation, Emily had realised Javier wasn't coming for her. That the man she loved with a desperation that had almost ruined her had accepted her absence from his life as easily as a change in the weather. The devastation had very nearly ruined her, but as Fran's project came to a close the interior designer—Maggie—had encouraged her to take the Design Institute's course, insisting that Emily had an 'eye for it'.

So Emily had thrown herself into the world of interior design. She'd studied at night, working with Maggie during the day, learning from anyone she met. And when she had taken on her first job? It had been terrifying, with steep learning curves and intense hard work, but it had been a resounding success. And word of mouth had soon spread. People loved Emily's dedication and ability to reach beyond what her clients wanted to what they *needed*. And that thing that held an entire project together? Identifying it had become an integral part of Emily's process, but one that couldn't be forced.

Needing a little decompression time before she went

to bed, she opened the fridge and poured herself a glass of white Rioja. Leaning against the kitchen's countertop, she relished the silence of the large warehouse floor in Bermondsey that was all hers. The office, where scattered paper and laptops lay on a long industrial table, was partitioned off from her living area by wide factory-style windows and carefully placed planters bursting with greenery.

A sprawling white fluffy rug lay in front of an L-shaped sofa that was more comfortable than her bed. The magazine, open at the article she'd done last month, shimmered beneath the overhead light and Emily cringed. They said there was no such thing as bad publicity, but the puff piece had been written by a man who had sacrificed integrity for alliteration, and had focused on her appearance rather than her talent. But she couldn't deny that they had seen an increase in traffic on their website.

They were already beyond a healthy capacity, Emily knew, but she couldn't resist the lure of security that more work offered. *'Just hire more staff.'* The directive came with a typically Spanish shoulder-shrug. *'I'll give you the money.'*

The voice, sounding very much like her estranged husband, failed to grasp how important it was to Emily that she ran her business on *her* terms. But then he'd always done that—seen things the way *he* saw them, not bending for anything or anyone. So, no. She'd make it work with what she had until she knew absolutely that she could afford to expand.

She took a sip of wine and looked out of the window and down onto the deserted south London streets. Small boutique coffee shops punched above their weight next to international chains. Luxury apartments stared down defiant Victorian terraces and artist studios filled the docks next to Michelin starred restaurants. It was chaos in all its London beauty. But, for all the affection she felt for the area and the success she'd achieved with her career, Emily couldn't deny that something was missing. It had been creeping up on her in the last few years, as if, now that professionally she was beginning to feel secure, a new need, a new yearning was on the horizon. A more personal one.

Placing the glass of wine on the windowsill, she looked at the simple gold band on her ring finger. They'd been in such a hurry to wed, as if, even then, they'd worried that time might change their minds. She'd known that Javier would have preferred something grander, the ring *and* the ceremony. But she'd been quietly happy, the plain gold band more meaningful than a precious jewel that wouldn't have suited her at all.

She splayed her fingers, indecision warring deep within her. As if this were a line in the sand, as if removing it would be an act she couldn't take back. Gritting her teeth, she took off the ring, placing it beside her glass on the window ledge. She inhaled through the feeling of unease and took a sip of wine to cover the taste of tension on her tongue. She shook out her hands and flexed her fingers, hoping to dispel the sudden and intense feeling of *absence*.

Her phone's ringtone made her jump—the sound unusual and alarming at this time of night. She caught the Spanish area code in the unfamiliar number flashing on the screen as she went to answer it and a sense of foreboding cut into her breathing, quick and sharp. Responding to the caller, she confirmed that yes, she was Mrs Casas, and then the glass of wine slipped from her numb fingers and shattered on the floor.

Pain.

It gripped his head like a vice and when he breathed it was as if the devil himself had thrust a red-hot poker between his ribs. A lifelong habit had him stifling the groan that threatened to escape his throat. Javier knew he wasn't alone, and he *really* wanted to be alone.

Earlier—he couldn't say exactly when—he thought he'd heard his mother, which had been, unsurprisingly, enough to send him back under. Now he tried to hold onto the voices; a man was speaking in hushed but frustrated tones. So his mother *was* there.

Javier breathed as deeply as he dared and nearly cried out loud from the pain in his chest. Somewhere in the room a monitor beeped noisily, halting the conversation until the sound returned to a steadier rhythm and the voices resumed.

Why couldn't he remember what had happened?

He was in a hospital, that much was clear.

'He should be locked up!' his mother cried, shrill and overly loud. For a moment, Javier wondered if Renata was talking about him.

'He has spoken to the police, assisted them in their investigation and is not currently under any suspicion,' the confident male voice explained.

'But how can that be?' Renata demanded. 'He was driving!'

Esteban. They'd had an accident? Was Esteban okay? The beeping monitor increased in speed again, frustrating Javier beyond belief. He wanted to ask but he couldn't seem to make his mouth do what he wanted it to.

'It is clear to everyone that it was not his fault and he will be discharged later today.'

'While my son stays here?' There was a pause, as if the room's occupants tried to fathom Renata's illogical response to the different injuries sustained by the two men. 'I want to talk to your boss.' His mother was practically screeching now.

'I am Chief of Surgery.'

'Who is your boss?'

'Mrs Casas, why don't we go to my office?'

'I will not leave my son!' The outrage in her voice was horribly familiar. That, more than any pain, brought a cold sweat to his brow. Renata was difficult, truly difficult, and the only way he'd found to successfully navigate her personality was to put distance between them. He would have put the moon between them had it not been for his sister Gabi. His jumbled brain threw up a memory from his childhood that would have nearly buckled him had he been standing.

Please, Mamá, it hurts.

He went back under.

The next time he woke the sounds were slightly different, there was a silence in the room that encouraged him to risk a peek through heavy-lidded eyes. The bright white disorientated him for a moment and he closed them before the agony pressing into his brain became too much. But the quiet gave him enough space to think. He had been out—In Venum. The launch. He'd been there and…

I want your hands on me…

An unpleasant shiver ran through him at the memory. He'd got to the car with Esteban and…the roadworks. Javier braced, remembering the moment of impact, the way the world had swung and swayed. Blood in his eye…

'Who is Emily?' an unfamiliar female voice asked.

The monitor trilled again as his heart jumped awkwardly at the question.

'He's been saying her name over and over.'

Had he?

'No one,' his mother replied, sharp as steel and just as cutting.

For a moment his brain went blank and he thought he might have blacked out again, but his senses were still full of the room.

'Mother!' his sister said, outraged. 'Emily is his wife,' his sister explained to the stranger.

Anger filled him, tension cording his neck and fists. His wife was a lot of things, but most definitely never *no one*. No, he hadn't been surprised that Renata had been unhappy with his choice of wife—an English girl, barely twenty, who couldn't speak a word of Spanish. But his wife was *family*.

'That girl was nothing more than a—'

He forced his eyes open and whatever his mother had been about to say was cut off by the sudden flurry of activity around his bed. Fingers prodded and poked and someone shook his shoulders, not gently enough for him to ignore but not rough enough to hurt, tying him to the room when all he wanted to do was go back to the black.

'Mr Casas? Can you hear me?'

The woman was insistent and he raised his hand to ward her off, but his arm didn't move more than an inch. His throat thickened with frustration and he wanted to howl. Goddammit! Why wasn't his body doing what it was supposed to?

'Mr Casas, do you know where you are?'

He tried to speak but nothing came out, so nodded, which hurt enough to make him stop.

'We're going to get you some water, okay? I want you to try and take a sip for me.'

A straw appeared in his vision and, after a few attempts, he managed to get enough down him to soothe his throat a little.

'Okay,' the man said—Javier recognised the voice

from before. 'Let's try that again. Do you know where you are?'

'Yes,' Javier managed.

'Do you know what brought you here?'

He narrowed his eyes, trying to make his mouth say the words in his mind. He was on the brink of forcing the answer from his lips when the man fired another question at him.

'Can you tell me the last thing you remember?'

Javier frowned, the weight of expectation in the air different to the previous questions. His gaze flickered around the room—his mother, sister, the doctor and the nurse—but snagged on the doorway.

'Emily.'

Standing in the doorway to his hospital room, Emily was stunned by what she saw. In a pale blue medical gown, attached to monitors, Javier lay propped up, a vicious bruise slashed across his cheek, a cut marring the planes of his proud forehead, but it was the paleness of his skin that really shocked her. Javier was *never* pale.

Through a crazy dash to the airport and a nerve-racking flight, Emily had told herself that Javier was fine. Because there wasn't a reality in which Javier was anything other than a truly powerful force of nature. She could only believe that there had been some kind of misunderstanding. But the two and a half hour flight had given her too much time to think.

She'd tried not to read too much into the fact that she was still his next of kin, hating the way it made her heart leap. Because it was too familiar. Too similar to the hope she'd nursed in the first months after she'd returned from Spain. And then, in the blink of an eye, the time she'd been back had eclipsed the entire time she'd known him, and he'd not come for her.

She'd arrived at the hospital and found her way to the private ward, nearly passing the room completely when the sight of him had pulled her up short. Her heart in her mouth, she'd listened for his answers to the doctor's questions, needing to know that he was okay. He *had* to be okay. Her thumb had reached to stroke the ring she'd retrieved just before leaving her apartment when she'd heard her name on his lips.

Her eyes snapped to his, frozen in place by the intensity of his gaze until—

'Amnesia!' his mother screamed and Emily, tired and wrung-out, rolled her eyes. She thought she saw a glimmer of a smirk from Javier but a blink and it was gone.

The doctor saw her standing in the doorway and nodded his acknowledgement.

'My baby has amnesia! Do something.'

'Mrs Casas.' The doctor's firm tone snapped Renata to attention and she allowed him to gesture her out of the hospital room into the corridor, where she turned an ugly shade of red the moment she caught sight of her son's wife.

'I don't know what *she* is doing here,' Renata rushed out in rapid Spanish.

'She is Javier's next of kin.' He turned to Emily, seemingly unaware that to call her 'Mrs Casas' in front of Renata would incite violence. 'You *are* Mr Casas's wife?' he asked in Spanish. Emily was about to answer but his mother interrupted.

'She doesn't speak Spanish.' The disdain in the older woman's tone was unmistakable.

Emily bit back a retort. No, she hadn't spoken Spanish at the beginning of her relationship with Javier but she had made the effort to learn it, even after she'd returned to England when she'd thought she might still need it.

Renata stared straight at the doctor as if trying to cut Emily out of her line of sight and Emily was surprised it still hurt. His mother had never been anything but barely tolerant of her presence at the best of times, and this was *not* the best of times.

Deciding not to challenge Renata's statement, she allowed the doctor to bring her up to speed in English. The accident had caused a fracture of three ribs, some very nasty cuts and bruises but miraculously no broken bones. Most of his injuries were considered 'superficial', leaving Emily a little concerned by their definition. Over the doctor's shoulder she saw Javier arguing with the nurse about the electrodes he was trying to remove from his chest.

Taking advantage of his distraction, her hungry gaze consumed the rest of him. His massive frame looked almost comically large in the bed, but there was nothing funny about the collage of bruises across skin that was a shocking shade of grey. From the very first moment she'd met Javier, he'd been an explosion of life and colour—a vivid virility mixed with a charm that bordered on lethal, one that she'd surrendered to utterly and irrevocably.

The moment she felt Javier's focus shift from the nurse to her, she looked back to the doctor. Javier's attention might have been as gentle as a caress but it was as hot as a flame and just as dangerous.

'You are concerned about his memory?' she asked, unaware that she had interrupted Renata.

Both she and the doctor ignored the older woman's huff of outrage. 'Yes. He has a concussion. Scans show a little bruising that will go down in time, but we will need to run more tests to know if there is cause for significant concern.'

She forced herself to meet Javier's eyes through the window to his room, but what she saw in his gaze stopped her thoughts. Calculation. Determination. There was absolutely *nothing* hindering Javier Casas's mental processing. But the doctor didn't seem to see what she saw.

'What does this mean? If it is…amnesia?' she asked.

'It will depend on how much he remembers, *what* he remembers. But, in rehabilitation terms, the main goal is to make him comfortable and keep things familiar without forcing a return of memories.'

Emily tried to get at what the doctor wasn't saying, but knew it was pointless until they knew more. 'Run your tests.'

The next few hours passed in a blur. Emily waited outside the room while the tests were conducted, which was fine by Javier's mother. His half-sister Gabi came out and sat next to her without speaking. Emily was surprised when the young woman she remembered as a beautiful teenager took her hand and held on tight. It was as if neither wanted to say anything until they knew what was going on.

What would she do? Whatever the outcome, Javier would need help. Maybe he'd hire someone to stay with him? She'd read that he'd moved into an apartment in Madrid, ashamed by how greedily she'd consumed information about him in the gossip columns over the years. He'd be fine, she reassured herself like a mantra, over and over and over. That was all she needed to know and then she could leave. If she was lucky, she might make it back to London having only missed a day.

But…she knew that was a lie. Six years might have passed since she had last seen her husband, but she felt it. Time was up. There would be no more hiding from her marriage to this Spanish billionaire. An icy finger was tripping its way down her spine when the doctor came out, looking a little puzzled but hopeful.

'Mr Casas is doing well. Cognitively he's retained all normal function. However, the last few years are almost a blank to him. At the moment, his brain is struggling to cope with the injury, so the goal is to create a peaceful and quiet environment. To reduce any further risk, it's going to be important that you are with him at all times. There may be periods where he gets frustrated with his rehabilitation, where he asks the same thing repeatedly. It will be wearing and difficult, so it's important that you have support and help too.'

'Me? Why would I need support?' Emily's tired mind was taking too long to catch up.

'Because you will be allowed to take him home in a few days and you'll be caring for him, no?'

Her head snapped to Javier, his gaze on her steady and waiting.

Emily tuned out the doctor's words as she realised what it meant. What was expected of her. What Javier had forced her into. It was a *knowing*. Deep in her gut, and low in her heart. There was no amnesia. The look in his eyes told her that he remembered everything. Worse, it was the anger simmering in that gaze. An anger that she had never seen before, but knew categorically had been put there by her departure six years before.

Her husband, it seemed, was playing games and it infuriated her. Was this his way of punishing her for leaving all those years ago? His final act of revenge? Oh, she had no doubt that he had cast himself the innocent in his mind. But Javier Casas—the man who was *never* wrong—had made a fatal mistake this time. She was no longer the unconfident young bride of before. She had changed and if he wanted to wilfully and carelessly mess with her life then it was only fair that she do the same.

Entering the room, she went to his bedside, taking his hand in hers. For a second, she thought she saw a flare in his irises, the surprise contact shocking them both. But this wasn't her caring husband, the man who had swept her off her feet at nineteen and offered her the world. No. It was the man who had shown her the world only on his terms. And now she was going to do the same. She leaned forward, sweeping his thick dark hair from his forehead in seeming affection, his skin warm beneath the cold of her fingers, and leaned to his ear.

'If you think for one second,' she whispered, 'that I believe a word of this, you are sorely mistaken. And you *will* regret it.'

CHAPTER TWO

EMILY LEFT THE HOSPITAL, saying that she needed time to prepare for Javier's return. She had meant with regard to their house in Frigiliana, but in reality she needed that time for herself. Because if things went the way she thought they would, then these would be her last days as Mrs Javier Casas.

Emily pushed against the iron gate that opened into a small courtyard at the front of the house. The slash of fuchsia bougainvillea was stunning against the brilliant white of the wall, but the build-up of leaves and bits of rubbish blown in by the wind hinted at a neglect Emily felt in her soul.

She had *loved* this house. With an enthusiasm and fervour that had been all-consuming, she had spent hours filling it with her early forays into decorating, unable to quite believe that this was theirs. It was a far cry from the small two-up, two-down in Morden she had moved to when her mother had married Steven. Her stepfather liked things practical, and practical usually involved beige in one form or another. But this, she thought as she shook out the front door key, this had been her *home*.

For less than a nanosecond she paused, key half turned, wondering what she would find on the other side of the door. Would there be a woman's shirt in the bedroom? Lipstick, toothbrush…? But that didn't ring true. No matter what had passed or not passed between them, Javier had a moral line that would not be crossed. No. He would have remained faithful, but from fidelity to his vows rather than her.

She pushed against the door and was hit by a wave of nostalgia so strong and so powerful it rocked her where she stood. Even the smell was the same. Thoughtlessly she put her keys on the small side table to the right of the door as if she'd last done it only yesterday and walked towards the dining room table they'd spent two argumentative hours and five thousand euros on. The price was still inconceivable to her but she couldn't deny how stunning it was. Carved from a single piece of oak, it was the colour of honey and warm to the touch, no matter what time of year. Even now she couldn't resist reaching out to run her hand along it. They had feasted in this room, laughed until they had cried, they'd even made love on this table, so caught up in their desire for each other that plates had smashed against the floor. She'd bet that if she looked down she would still see the stain from the red wine they'd spilt that night. Instead, she looked into her memories and saw herself sitting here night after night alone, as she'd waited for her husband to come home, one lonely dinner after another.

The stairs in the left corner led up to the master and spare bedrooms, but she chose to follow the hallway on the right that led through to a stunning living area with floor-to-ceiling windows and a view that literally stole her breath. Although the house was a stone's throw from the heart of Frigiliana, it was situated at the top of the road that led away from the cobbled streets and lively restaurants and down to the bottom of a large gorge. Clinging to the edge of town, their home looked out onto the deep green foliage of the other side of the gorge and, if lucky, you could spot the occasional mountain goat.

Emily had spent hours staring out at that view. She had never seen such vibrant greens, set against a blue that no man could recreate. To the right of the room was a small white and green tiled patio that overlooked the lower level and swimming pool. Her mind threw memory after memory at her. She heard her own shocked cry turn to laughter as Javier swept her up fully clothed and jumped into the water with her. Laughter that had turned quickly into moans of delight and pleasure as he had peeled off her clothing piece by piece until there was nothing left between them.

Standing there now, looking down at the pool, Emily wondered if that had been the last time she'd made love to her husband, feeling that there was something so incredibly sad about not knowing. Her heart aching, she turned back to the room. Nothing had changed, she thought, as she looked up at the large rough-hewn white walls. A blank canvas she'd thought she'd paint her future on. A future that had never come to pass.

He hadn't changed a single thing, but the entire house was clean of dust—as if someone came at least once a week to air it. And it made her unaccountably angry. Angry that her departure had cost him nothing like the years of agony it had caused her. Angry that he had not changed a single thing, while everything in her life had been thrown wildly off-course.

And he'd done it again. His 'memory loss' had upended her entire life, disrupting her work schedule, and for what? So that he could have fun at her expense? So that she would return to his bedside and nurse him back to health as if nothing had happened? As punishment?

Well, a lot had happened and while some things had

changed—she had built a successful career and found a self-confidence she had desperately needed—some things hadn't. And one of those things was access to their joint account. And suddenly Emily wanted to see just how much he *couldn't* remember.

Javier fisted his hand as the car took another corner on the winding road leading to Frigiliana, ignoring the concerned glances the driver flicked his way in the rearview mirror. It didn't matter that Javier knew every twist and turn on this road by heart—he probably could have driven blindfolded—but the moment he felt his stomach lurch he was back in the car that had been hit so hard and fast by a truck whose driver hadn't seen the poorly lit sign for the roadworks it had rolled the car mid-air and landed Javier and Esteban upside down.

The moment his sister had enticed his mother away from his hospital room, he'd reached for his phone and called his driver. Thankfully he was okay, aside from feeling guilty and fearful, no doubt thanks to Renata. It had taken almost ten minutes and more energy than Javier had expected to reassure Esteban that he was still employed.

The moment he'd ended the call, the *policía* arrived. The two uniformed men had been quick to assure him that he was under no suspicion and that they just wanted to know what he remembered from that night. Reluctantly admitting that he had been less than truthful with his family and doctor about his memory, he'd told the officers what he knew, refusing even for a second to put Esteban in a vulnerable position.

The officer had nodded without even a blink. 'Happens more than you think.'

They'd departed, leaving Javier wondering just how often billionaires faked amnesia.

Javier wasn't entirely sure why he'd gone along with it. Initially it hadn't been intentional. He'd seen Emily standing there and his mother had misunderstood. But the fact that Emily *was* there, that she *had* come… It had shocked him into silence. She looked exactly like she had in the picture in that magazine. Older, more assured, with just a little hint of cynicism that hadn't been there before. *Before* she'd left him without a thought or second look.

Then the damn monitor had kicked off, happily declaring to the entire room just how much her presence affected his blood pressure. He'd nearly ripped off the electrodes then and there. But even he'd seen that she'd been as affected as he had.

And then had come the fire. Oh, it had been incredible to see. He'd always known it was there—she couldn't have been capable of the incendiary passion that had kept them in bed for the entire first week of their marriage otherwise. But she'd never let it so close to the surface.

If you think for one second that I believe a word of this…

In the back of the car closing the distance between him and Emily, Javier smiled. It was the powerful woman he'd always known her to be, but hadn't seen before. From the first moment he'd laid eyes on Emily, he'd fallen hard. It was the strangest thing—just *knowing* that this was the woman he'd marry, the woman he'd spend his life with. A knowing that had proved wrong. So utterly and incomprehensibly wrong it had threatened to shake the foundations of his sense of self.

So why had she come? She could have easily had the hospital contact Renata or Gabi instead. Yet she hadn't. And, judging by the time of her arrival, she must have been on the first flight out. Thinking back to the hospital, his first reaction had been one of shocking relief—and then such an intense state of confusion. Because she had left him, walked away from him without a word or a second glance, the memory of her abandonment making him want to lash out. To punish her. He had been tempted to allow this amnesia thing play out, curious as to how far he could push the wife who had abandoned him, but his conscience had overruled it. He'd known that he'd have to come clean with her the moment she'd left the hospital. He wasn't so much of a bastard as to completely upend her life to suit his own needs.

But he wouldn't have been discharged from hospital on his own, and he refused to convalesce at Renata's house. He rubbed at the scar on his collarbone. He knew exactly what kind of care he'd have received there. His stomach turned—this time not from the bend in the road, but the argument he'd had with her.

'A son should be with his mother.'

Not *Let me look after you*, or *Let's get you better*. Once again, as it always did, the world turned around Renata. His sister had shot him sympathetic looks, the siblings bonded by an understanding of their mother that no one else would ever share. He hated the idea of Gabi being subjected to Renata's tantrums, but when he'd asked her to come and live with him years earlier Gabi had rejected his offer, insisting that Renata needed her. Javier drew a deep breath. His mother's manipulations were extensive, but if she followed her usual pattern she'd be silent for at least a good few days. And then she'd be in touch as if nothing had happened, asking him for money.

Which gave him the time he needed to finally deal with Emily once and for all.

'We all know that's just a ruse.' Annalise's accusation from before the accident ran through his mind.

Jaw clenched, hand fisted, Javier had ignored the past for too long and it couldn't be avoided any longer.

His phone rang just as the car navigated the roundabout and along the narrow cobbled road through the lower part of town. His assistant, aware of the true state of his memory, was convinced that one of Javier's bank accounts had been hacked.

'That is impossible,' he replied firmly, knowing just how much he paid to protect his considerable assets.

'Sir, no. I don't think it is, because in the last three days nearly nine thousand euros has been spent.'

'Three days?' he repeated, his mind snagging on that rather than the amount of missing money.

'I'm sorry, sir. It's not an account that I've seen activity on before and because you were in hospital I—'

'The account number?'

Darien reeled off a series of digits Javier knew by heart. It was an account he co-signed and it hadn't been touched for years, even in the months before Emily had left Spain. He was about to ask Darien what the purchases were when the car turned down the winding road that led to the house he'd once shared with Emily and he began to suspect he knew *exactly* what the money had been spent on.

Emily bit her lip. She *might* have gone a little too far with the last of the purchases. She looked around the space she had spent three days and an inconceivable amount of money transforming. She nearly grimaced at the bright pink slash of colour from the two massive canvases she'd installed in the main room. But they weren't as bad as the five-foot ceramic parrot. Even with memory loss, Emily was sure Javier wouldn't believe that he'd allowed the monstrosity into the house.

It had been a terrifying waste of money and when she succeeded in getting Javier to admit that he was lying she would pay him back every penny. She might even use some of the things in future projects. The pieces themselves weren't terrible—parrot aside—just not right for the house at all. She was wondering whether she might be able to use some for the San Antonio project when she heard the crunch of tyres on gravel outside the house and a shiver ran down her spine. She was being silly, she thought as she fanned the sudden rush of heat to her cheeks. But now that he was near, she also felt a thrill of excitement—she was flirting with danger, taunting Javier. And it was the most alive she'd felt in months.

The sound of a car door closing cut through her thoughts as she fussed with the heavily—and quite horribly—laced linen tablecloth she had regrettably covered the beautiful table with. It had been strange to use her skills in interior design to cultivate chaos rather than calm and she blamed the jarring sense of aesthetics for why she jumped when she heard the knock on the door.

She opened the door and all her planned responses burnt to ash in the bright afternoon sun. *That* was what caused her to squint up at the man who filled the doorway, she told herself. Not the impact of seeing him standing there. Nostalgia, not desire, flooded her veins, bringing a flush to her skin and an extra beat to her heart.

But for just a moment she forgot. Forgot how, after the honeymoon period had worn off, she had spent far too many hours here alone while Javier worked all the hours God sent. Forgot how isolated and lost she had felt here with no friends and no easy way to make them, fearful that she'd become exactly what she had never wanted to become—a woman who lost herself to her husband, who was totally dependent on him, just like her mother had become on her husband.

Dressed in a white shirt and tan trousers, Javier looked nothing like the easy-going, charming boy she'd fallen in love with. There were hints of him, the self-confidence that had always bordered on arrogance, the stubborn determination that had seen him win any argument he'd wanted to…but there was more of the man now. In the breadth of his shoulders, the slight creases around his eyes, bracketing his mouth, even the few—*very* few— silver threads in his hair and stubble that added authority and experience and diminished nothing of the raw power that swept at her like an unending tide.

His thick dark hair was swept back from his forehead and the natural jut of his jaw that made him look almost perpetually defiant was both familiar and heartbreaking and she had the maddening urge to kiss him. To reach for him and pull him across the threshold by his shirt, just as she had done so many times in the first few months of their marriage. A flash of glitter in his eyes, the ever so slight tightening of his jaw, fired warning signals in her brain and with a primal sense of self-preservation she stepped back to let him pass into the house.

'Welcome home,' she said, her gaze fastened to his, searching his face for any sign of surprise that might betray him.

What. Had. She. Done?

The words sounded in his head, even as he broadened the smile on his lips purposely to disguise the utter horror that struck him. Hard. In the three seconds he'd allowed himself to take in everything he could see—and he could see a *lot*—he had to work harder than he ever had before to school his features.

'Well?' she asked, one foot tucked behind the other, a slight lean to her head that dared him to call her on the changes she'd made to their home.

He frowned, as if a little confused. 'Have you done something different?' he asked, looking around as if he meant the house. He turned back to Emily in time to see her leap on his statement, her mouth open and ready to accuse, but he pushed on before she could. 'It's your hair. It's shorter?'

The flash in her cobalt-blue gaze burned like lightning across the Alboran Sea. Fuming. She was fuming and, petty that he was, he kind of enjoyed it. After all, *madre de Dios*, she'd made their home abhorrent. He fought the urge to wince.

'Longer, actually,' she replied with a little growl that nearly made him smile.

He gestured to his head. 'I'm sorry, this memory thing. It's got me turned around.' The lie rolled off his tongue as easily as his wife seemed to have destroyed their home. He stalked over to where she leaned against the wall and his gaze flicked from an ugly linen tablecloth on what was possibly his favourite item of furniture through to the flashes of fuchsia in the living area that, frankly, scared the living daylights out of him.

He turned his attention back to the real threat. Emily looked pretty in a white shirt and denim jeans rolled up from the ankles, but it was the bare feet that poked and prodded at his memories—the way she used to giggle when he captured them in his hands, pressing kisses against the arch of her foot. The memory fired a familiar anger in him. One that cried out loud at her betrayal—at her abandonment. And, bastard that he was, he wanted to push her, taunt her with the only connection he knew still burned bright between them.

He leaned down towards her, crowding her personal space in a way he couldn't bring himself to feel guilt over. She craned her neck, staring up at him, watchful and wary, eyes becoming larger and larger, her pupils flaring under his attention as he bent towards her, so slowly that she had time to move, but so confident that she wouldn't. He felt it, the thickening of his blood, the slow burn that had never gone, no matter how long or how far apart they'd been. The warm scent of her skin teased him, pushing and pulling at desires he'd thought he'd long forgotten. As he drew even closer, her lips opened on a little gasp that he felt against his own before, at the last moment, he turned to press a kiss to her cheek.

The roil of his stomach muscles sliced at his ribs and he couldn't prevent the sharp inhale of pain. Anger turned to worry in the blink of an eye and she placed her hand on his arm, stopping him when he would have turned away.

'Are you okay?' Emily asked, genuine concern in her tone.

'Yes,' he said, dismissing her question despite the tidal wave of ache that brushed over him again and again, and the exhaustion that threatened to suffocate him. He'd never felt anything like it and he hated it. Hated the weakness in his body.

If he'd hesitated for even just a second he would have seen the hurt shimmering in the blue depths of her gaze as he closed himself off from her, but he didn't as he pushed himself through his own discomfort.

Awkwardly he made his way through to the living area, squinting to lessen the impact of the bright pink of the paintings Emily had brought into the room. He was sure they'd cost an obscene amount—partly because his

wife had always had good taste, even when she was trying to make it bad, but also because he knew how much
she'd spent in the last three days.

He sat down gracelessly on the new and deeply uncomfortable banquette seating covering the far wall, undeniably impressed by what Emily had achieved in just
three days, but nevertheless ready to pay any financial
amount required for the return of his sofa. The firm canvas cushion offered no respite from the tension and ache
that was growing closer to pain by the second. When he
finally lifted his gaze, he found himself staring down a
five-foot white ceramic parrot.

His wife had been possessed by a demon.

The swift inhale thrust another needle into his lungs.
He'd been ready to admit that he'd lied, even willing to
apologise to her for having her come all this way and for
interrupting her life. But this?

This was an act of war.

She was making changes to their house to *taunt* him,
to force him to admit that he was lying. Well, she should
have known better. Because Javier Casas did not lose and
he was one hundred percent determined that soon, very
soon, she would be begging, no, *pleading*, for mercy.

CHAPTER THREE

EMILY MIXED A salad dressing while trying to shake the horrible feeling that she'd got it all terribly wrong. He'd not said a thing, not reacted to any of the changes she'd made at all. And she was *sure* that the parrot would have done it.

Could he really have amnesia?

The only thing she hadn't missed was the way he'd tried to hide the pain he was in. Its shadow had whispered across his cheeks and she remembered well how much he had always hidden any sign of weakness. At the beginning of their relationship his stoicism had attracted her, but by the end she had resented it. The doctor had emailed her a list of the medication and the doses he would need over the next two weeks before they returned for a review, with instructions to contact him if she needed anything. She stifled a laugh. She needed a dictionary, a calculator and her own headache tablets.

Emily nibbled at the nail of the thumb on her right hand, unseeing of the feast she had gathered for dinner. She had, in fact, made him the meal he'd most hated from their time together, but that had been thrown into the bin the moment he'd sent her fleeing from the dining area and that kiss. She raised her hand to her cheek. Her heart was pounding as if he were still standing not an inch from her, heat in his eyes that burned into her soul.

The sputter of the peppers in the pan snapped her attention back and she removed it from the heat, with only a little bee sting from the oil. That was what she got for not paying attention. But as she ran the peeler over the courgettes, adding them to the fresh green salad with pistachios that was a favourite of Javier's, she wondered. What if he *did* have amnesia?

Could she do it? Pretend that all the hurt hadn't happened? The hours, days and even weeks sometimes when he hadn't come home. She'd been alone in a country that wasn't hers, unknowing of the language or people who could become friends. The gifts that he'd left in his wake—expensive, absolutely, exquisite, quite probably—but nothing that she would ever have chosen for herself and most definitely poor compensation for the loss of him.

But when they were together… A flush rose to her cheeks that had nothing to do with the heat of the kitchen. There had been a time when they had been pure intense passion. But Emily had soon discovered that it wasn't enough to hold a marriage together. They had needed more. *She* had needed more.

She finished the salad and plated the Padrón peppers with a sprinkle of sea salt and took them out to the table on the green and white tiled patio. The sun was beginning to drop towards the dark craggy outline of the range across the gorge and in the far distance she could see a sliver of the sea, sparkling like a jewel. And, even though her emotions were all over the place, her soul recognised this as home.

In sickness and in health.

The words gently whispered into her mind and she

knew that she would give Javier the help he needed. She just wouldn't, couldn't, give more of herself than that. Not this time.

Javier watched his wife standing on the patio from what had once been his favourite room in the house and was now a child's drawing of scribbled colours that hurt his eyes and his head. Gritting his teeth, he braced himself as he levered himself up, enticed more by the prospect of painkillers than food.

He had half imagined that Emily would have made his most hated meal—some evil concoction called corned beef hash that he'd disliked on principle. Meat should never, *ever* come in a tin. Even just the thought of it turned his stomach. But the scent wafting in from the open doors was mouth-wateringly familiar and he couldn't help but be drawn to the table Emily had prepared.

But it was her he gravitated to. As she stood there, staring into the distance, Emily felt as far from his reach as when she'd been in London. His conscience stirred.

'Are you okay?' he was unable to stop himself from asking.

She turned, a rueful smile on lips that had seduced him, had loved him and then cursed him. 'I was about to ask you the same.'

He nodded, allowing them both to avoid the question.

'Morcilla, salad, Padrón peppers, roast aubergine, Manchego... *Dios*, Emily, this is a feast.'

Taking in the table, he was suddenly famished. He didn't know where to start. As if sensing the sheer force of his hunger, she shook her head, a small smile pulling at the corner of her mouth. 'Just go for it.'

And he did. He filled his plate with portions of everything, each part of the meal a delicious taste. The citrus of the lemon-dressed salad, the sweetness of the quince paste for the creaminess of the semi-hard cheese, the salt of the morcilla and the fleshy aubergine.

'I think you have made every single one of my favourites.'

'Yes,' his wife replied as if it were obvious.

He looked up at her, leaning back in her chair, glass of white wine in hand and something in her eyes he'd thought he'd never see again. It poked at him and he didn't like it. But she must have misread the confusion in his gaze.

'It's what you do when someone is not well.'

'What?' he asked, this time definitely confused.

She frowned at his response. 'You make the person's favourite foods.'

The taste of Manchego and *membrillo* dried on Javier's tongue and he reached for his water. He nodded and looked up to find her watching him. He smiled at her and speared a piece of aubergine, filling his mouth to prevent a retort.

No. That hadn't been what his mother had ever done for him when he'd been unwell. She'd either refused to accept any sign of illness, or had drowned him in lavish, overwhelming and completely disproportionate concern—aimed at garnering attention for herself rather than her son. The idea of something as simple as making his favourite foods was strange and somewhat painful to consider. It made him feel awkwardly envious and resentful, as if he were on the outside looking in on how *normal* people lived.

'What did your mother make you?' he asked around the dry sand in his throat.

His wife held his gaze. 'Corned beef hash.'

He nearly choked on the mouthful until he saw the humour star-lighting her eyes. He swallowed around his smile and, more out of habit than curiosity, asked, 'How is she?'

She knew what he'd done, changing the conversation to distract her. But she'd felt such a sense of *pain* following the careless comment she'd made about making him his favourite foods it shocked her. In the past, Javier had been so adept at hiding his feelings but this time she felt his confusion, his loss, as if it had been her own. Yet, despite this, Javier looked at her expectantly.

Her mother. Emily felt the familiar tension across her shoulders and looked away from the table, out over the gorge to the sprinkle of early stars dusting the dusk sky. She had gathered herself by the time she looked back to Javier.

'She's much the same. She and Steven are still in Morden and...' she shrugged, not quite sure what else to add '...they're good,' she concluded. Javier's hawklike gaze focused in on the pause like a sign of weakness. The last time she had seen them had been just over six months ago. Before Christmas, because her stepfather liked their annual 'cruise at Christmas'.

The memory scratched at a wound that was only slightly dulled by time and Emily felt foolish for nursing the hurt. She had been sixteen when she had incorrectly assumed she was to join them on their Christmas holiday. She'd never forgotten the look in her mother's eyes as she'd silently begged Emily not to make a fuss, not to say anything. So she hadn't. She'd stayed behind because she was old enough, and had spent the entire festive period alone. And the following year there hadn't been any question of her joining them.

Each year was a fresh hurt over an old ache and she would feel foolish and guilty, because she knew that her mother was happy. She loved Steven, of that there was no doubt. So how could Emily resent her mother finding happiness after all that she'd been through? It had been just her and her mother for the first eleven years of her life and, while her mother had made it magical and wondrous, even as a child Emily hadn't been blind to the hardship and the exhaustion and the financial worry that her mother had tried to hide. So Emily's conscience poked and prodded, reminding her that her mother deserved to be happy.

She felt fingers wrap around hers where it held the stem of the wine glass and jerked at the unexpected contact, sloshing the wine over the edge, and let out a startled laugh. 'Sorry,' she said, reaching for a tea towel to mop up the spill.

'Things are not better between you?' Javier asked, concern clear in his gaze.

'They're fine,' she said again, the bland words dull on her tongue.

'So they haven't let you redecorate? I thought you would have painted over every inch of beige in that house.'

The tease pulled a smile from her, which faded at the memory of how her mother and stepfather had behaved when she and Javier visited to let them know they were married.

'I'm sorry. I'm *still* sorry,' she clarified, 'at their behaviour during that visit.' She shook her head, even now wondering if that had somehow been the beginning of the end of their fantastical romance. 'Steven has the emotional intelligence of an amoeba and the social skills of a toad.'

'But it is such a delightful combination, *mi cielo*,' Javier said, the sarcasm playful and the endearment intimate. 'And, of course, you have met my mother. There is no competition,' he said, the sweep of his free hand clearing any further debate.

Mi cielo.

It whispered into the night, reminding her of a thousand sighs and kisses and touches, warming her body beneath the cool breeze. She pulled her hand from beneath his and *still* the feeling of heat brushed across the back of her neck.

'So, the doctor told me that the last thing you really remember was Gabi's sixteenth birthday?'

The turn in the conversation was sudden and jarring. There was a hint of wariness in the question that hadn't been there since she'd opened the door to him. He resented the intrusion of that unease. For just a moment, he had felt the connection he'd shared with Emily flare to life once again, deeper than just the sense of attraction that was a dull throb across his body. His wife *hurt* and he wanted to take that away. But she wouldn't let him.

The thought took him back to the last months they had shared under this roof. The way she had retreated further and further from him and, no matter how hard he'd worked, tried to provide for her, he'd known—felt—time running out. It had been as if she were slipping through his fingers like sand and nothing he'd done had been able to stop it. For just a second, his lungs seized with the same kind of helpless anguish he'd experienced in those last few months of their marriage. That sense of inadequacy that cut right through to his deepest vulnerability.

Alto.

She was looking at him expectantly, and he shook off the thought. She wanted to know what he remembered, and he would have to be *very* careful about how he answered.

'Yes. The doctor advised me not to ask questions, or force the memories of what has happened since then.'

In fact, Javier's doctor had been just as suspicious as Emily seemed to be, though unwilling to specifically call him on it. His advice had been full of hypotheticals. *'If you can't remember...' 'If you feel that...'* All coming on the heels of a warning.

'I have met your mother, so perhaps I understand a little. But your wife is a different matter, Mr Casas. She looks like she'd fight fire with fire.'

It had been a timely warning and one that he reminded himself to heed.

'Is it as if the party was only yesterday for you?'

'Not quite,' he hedged. 'More as if that's the last thing I can remember. It's clear that time has passed. We look older, and there are some things I know,' he said, making it as ambiguous as possible. 'Yet things don't fit together coherently.'

She watched him steadily.

'But I remember what you were wearing that night,' he said truthfully. The image was as clear to him now as if it *had* been yesterday. She had been stunning in a white jumpsuit with a neck that veed tantalisingly deep. Cuts in the sleeves allowed the material to drape either side of her forearms, looking timeless and elegant. 'How you looked, how the scent rising from your skin hit me here.' He thudded a fist to his chest. 'How it reminded me of the first time we met and how all I wanted to do that night was take you to bed.'

Her pupils flared at his praise, the flush to her cheeks familiar and filling him with an aching want that he knew wouldn't be appeased that night. Once again, her lips parted ever so slightly, and he stopped himself from reaching across the table to plump her bottom lip with the pad of his thumb.

He'd clung to Emily that night, his gaze, his focus expertly blocking out his mother's hysterical attempts to steal her daughter's limelight on her sixteenth birthday. Hysteria that had been blessedly in remission for the three years preceding. But with the breakdown of her third marriage Renata Casas had returned to form.

Heart still pounding from the force of his adamant memory of her that night, Emily felt herself swaying towards her husband. It would be so easy to pretend that the last six years hadn't happened. To indulge in a passion that was still utterly undeniable.

Touch. It wasn't only what she'd missed about him, but it was a significant part. His touch had brought her to life, had shown her what passion could be, that it had colour, texture, taste and scent. That passion was luxurious and powerful and empowering… He had taken her from that drab beige, unhappy world of hers and thrust her into Technicolor. He had magicked her into a real girl—living and breathing and passionate. And then he had abandoned her.

Desperate to hold onto any thread that would keep her sane, she forced her thoughts away from dangerous ground.

'Gabi was worried about you,' she said, unable to forget the way his sister had held so tightly onto her hand, sure that the strength was hers to give to Gabi rather than the other way round.

Javier's penetrating stare threatened to smother her, accusing her of avoiding the shocking sensuality caused by the scattering of his words. For a moment, she wondered whether he would push the issue. He had in the past. He had wielded their passion like a conductor wielded his baton, deft fingers setting a pace and rhythm that could nearly have ruined her, pulling a melody from her soul that she was unable to deny.

But instead he nodded, a darkness shadowing his gaze. 'I worry about her. I believe that she is still living with my mother?'

For a moment she was about to admit that she didn't know. But if he had lost his memory, then he would want to know *why* she didn't know because she would, wouldn't she? A lack of sleep, a fury of adrenaline, a sense of...*something* building on the horizon all added to what promised to be a spectacular headache. She ran her fingers across her forehead, trying to soothe the tension, a gesture Javier didn't miss.

'Yes,' she eventually answered, having gathered that his sister was still living with his mother from the few exchanges she'd overheard in the hospital.

A frown flickered across Javier's brow but he did not share his thoughts. Which was another thing Emily remembered from her time with him. How closed-off he had kept her from his family. At first she had thought that they were not particularly close, but over the months of their marriage Renata had called again and again and every time Javier would go. It was a strange thing—as if it were duty, a weary one. But Emily had been reeling from her own hurt from a mother who barely saw her any more. That, combined with a husband who had spent more time away from her than not, had left her feeling vulnerable and lonely. In fact, this was the longest she remembered Javier spending without looking at his phone.

'What about work? Your businesses...will they be okay?'

She could imagine the panic and fear of his employees and company boards caused by the prospect of his memory loss, temporary or even perhaps lasting. She had lost count of the articles she'd seen over the years about the number of businesses he now owned.

He discarded her question with a sweep of his hand. 'Yes, I've spoken to my assistant. It will be fine. Would you like more wine? I'll get some,' he announced, excusing himself from the table before he saw Emily's reaction.

As if she had been struck, Emily froze—his words turning her to stone.

'It will be fine.'

The Javier Casas of six years ago would never, ever have said such a thing. In fact, the Javier Casas of six years ago would have already spent four hours working, desperate to catch up with his business affairs. So there was absolutely no way that the Javier of six years ago would think for even a second that his business would be fine without him.

The bastard.

He *was* lying. And this time she knew it with such force she practically trembled with rage.

Javier was congratulating himself on how well it was going as he retrieved a bottle of white wine from the fridge. He was tempted to have a glass, but doubted that mixing alcohol with strong painkillers was a good idea. And although he had navigated the tricky waters of his memory loss with Emily well, he knew that he would need all his wits about him. As it was, he was already fighting a tiredness that was shocking in its intensity.

He took the wine back out to the table to find Emily looking out at the gorge rising above the Higuerón River.

And he stopped. Struck by a shocking and unwelcome wave of déjà vu, his lungs seized and the knife twisted.

How many times had he imagined her here, at the house in Frigiliana, standing just like that, in his mind's eye? Whether he'd been in Madrid, Barcelona, whether he'd been further afield in Svardia, or Tokyo, or Pakistan, somehow he'd always imagined her here.

Javier had achieved incomparable success in the business world—more than half of which was a closely guarded secret. From the first company he'd owned, given to him by his uncle, who knew Renata Casas would never share the textile empire she considered solely hers, Javier had been driven. Driven to pay his uncle back, to prove that he was worthy of the gift he'd been given. And, with one heart-stopping investment, he'd made enough money to do just that, and more. He had expanded from one business to two, then three and so on. But if his mother had the slightest inkling of how much he was worth...carnage. It would be carnage.

But back then Javier had been driven by the need to prove himself, working like the devil himself, spending every hour he could, just to have something that couldn't be taken away from him. Something that was his...to share with his wife. But she had left him on the very night that he'd planned to tell her of his success. His hand tightened around the bottle of wine.

Javier had meant his vows, determined not to make the same mistakes as his parents. He had wanted a family. A wife, children, the laughter that had so drawn him to Emily from the very first—he'd wanted that sound in his life every day. How had he forgotten that? Looking at the silhouette she made against the night sky, he put the bottle of wine down and made a decision. Enough was enough. It was time for Emily to come home. And if he had to play the amnesia game to make it happen, he would. He would remind them both of how great they'd been together. There had certainly never been a problem with their attraction—the spark of desire had always burned like phosphorus in pure oxygen—molten, bright and white-hot.

He would—

'I think I'm going to head to bed.' His wife's words cut short and twined with his thoughts and a smile pulled at his lips.

'That would be delightful, *mi amor.*'

A different sort of smile painted Emily's lips and something sharp blinked in her eyes before it was gone.

'I shall see you tomorrow then.'

'We can go together?' he said, leaning in, unable to deny himself the hint of honeysuckle in her perfume. She looked up at him, his gut clenched. How had he forgotten how petite she was? Suddenly his mind was awash with erotic images that stole his mind and his breath. Her hand rose to press against his chest, where she would surely feel the thunder of his heartbeat. He felt claimed by it, until she opened her mouth.

'Javi...' The sing-song tone of her voice was at odds with the sensual web he was caught in. 'You know that the doctor ordered separate beds.'

'I know no such thing!' His outrage was swift and clear.

'Well, *that* was what he told *me.* You'll be okay getting to bed on your own?' Emily asked, knowing that Javier would see it as a challenge.

His response, 'Of course,' was a relief. She really didn't think that she could help him to bed. Not now that she knew he was lying to her. Anger, a hot and wild thing, unravelled in her and drew pinpricks of heat across her skin that hurt.

Emily got to the spare room, readied herself for bed and changed into her nightgown, lying down on a bed in a room that she had once hoped to make a nursery with the man she loved. With a man she had loved. But that man had been taken away from her and the thief was sleeping in the next room. A tear escaped and a line was drawn.

And as Javier Casas planned a seduction for his wife, Emily Casas planned their divorce.

CHAPTER FOUR

JAVIER WOKE UP feeling a sense of serenity he hadn't known in years.

His wife's redecoration efforts hadn't stopped in the lower sections of the house, but here in this room it had been something wondrous. As if Emily couldn't bring herself to make it awful. What had once been simple white walls accentuating the stunning greenery of the gorge through floor-to-ceiling windows was now...magical. There was no other word to describe it, and Javier was not one to use that word lightly.

The room was still sparsely furnished, the simple lines of the large wooden bedframe and the curved arch doorway to the en suite bathroom deeply satisfying. But she had bridged the area where the wall met the window with a thousand plants. Ones with trails, or little balls, some heart-shaped and others like tongues, but the sense of this room—it felt *alive*. As if she'd drawn the outside in and there was no glass, no separation between them and the rich landscape beyond. It softened a space he hadn't realised needed changing.

He threw back the covers and felt fire. A sudden, painfully bright, piercing jabbed into his ribs, catching his lungs in a death grip and tightening already bruised muscles along his side.

Cabrón.

He waited for the tremors to subside, the waves of pain to retreat, and forced his breathing to slow. He hadn't felt this helpless since he was a child and even the thought of it had him gritting his teeth. He forced himself up and, although it was slow going, made it to the bathroom, where he stared down the painkillers he'd left on the counter.

Emily hadn't made any changes that he could see to the room, but that didn't mean he trusted her not to have booby-trapped something. The thought had him expel a laugh that hurt more than he liked. So he reluctantly reached for the pill bottle and dry swallowed a tablet.

The light behind the mirror glowed golden across the unusual paleness of his skin and for the first time since the accident he took in the damage to his body. The bruise across his cheekbone had settled into a yellow-tinged purple which looked far worse than the angry red it had been, even if it was a sign of healing. He winced as he gently prodded the dissolvable stitches used by the plastic surgeon his mother had demanded—but his healthcare had paid for—on the cut on his forehead.

Javier had never been a vain man and he was always amused by how that surprised so many people. Scar or no scar, his only concern was how infuriatingly itchy the area was. Healing, again. He'd been warned. But… Not enough. He'd not been warned enough. Or maybe he just hadn't wanted to listen.

In the next room, Emily was probably sleeping and the thought of it made a mockery of all the times he had delighted in waking her up with kisses that turned into gentle touches, and caresses that turned into sighs of pleasure and the taste of her on his tongue. In mere seconds, Javier was hard and angry.

She had taken that away from them. Years of time

they could have been happy. He turned on the tap and splashed ice-cold water across his face, wondering just how long it would take for the painkillers to kick in and just how quickly he could bring his wife to his mercy.

He thought of the flare in her eyes last night, as he'd reminded her of Gabi's sixteenth. He thought of the need building within him and the urge to take advantage of the passion that had been like nothing else he'd ever known from the very first moment he'd seen her.

But he wouldn't.

No. He would never.

But he also thought of the concern and confusion he'd seen in her eyes. She had started to doubt her belief that he was faking, he knew it. And through the course of the evening he'd persuaded her that his memory loss was real. He'd felt it, her softening, melting, the way she had done in the past whenever she'd argued about the money he'd wanted to lavish on her or the gifts he'd bought her to compensate for the hours he'd worked. A slow, inevitable yielding as he'd got his way. A victory of sorts—one that was only marginally less sweet than what it would feel like to have her back by his side and in his bed.

Emily stared at the steam unfurling from the second espresso she'd made since finally giving up on sleep and trying to stop the circular thoughts from spinning around her head. Javier was punishing her, she was sure of it. Punishing her for leaving him, even if she hadn't wanted to. Even if she hadn't intended to. Because really she'd thought he'd come for her when he realised she'd gone. Thought that he'd rush to her side with apologies and promises that their marriage would be like it had been at the very beginning. But he hadn't. Not once had he reached out to her.

It's not as if you reached out to him.

No, she thought, she hadn't—*couldn't*—bring herself to call him. Because it would have hurt too much to beg, to plead with him to see her, to love her. Emily's heart throbbed. *That* was why she'd needed him to come for her. Why she'd needed him to make the first move. So she would know that it hadn't been a mistake. That they hadn't just been caught up in the passion of it all. That there was something real binding them together. That it hadn't just been *her* in this marriage alone.

She heard the slap of his bare feet on the stone steps leading down from the first floor, gathering herself in a panic. Javier clearly thought she believed his act. But he had forgotten how well she knew him. Nothing would keep him from his precious businesses. Not his sickbed and certainly not fake amnesia! So, no. He had underestimated her and this time she would have him at her feet, begging for forgiveness.

The steps, slow and hesitant, an unusual amount of time between them, poked and prodded at her conscience, but the gleam in his eye last night as he had teased her with the almost desperate sensuality between them cast her will in iron.

A perfect smile was on her lips as Javier rounded the corner and an almost imperceptible pause stuttered his steps, before they doubled in speed as he came down the remaining steps.

'Good morning, *mi amore*,' he said, reaching her, only a slight wariness in his gaze as if he were trying to predict what she might do next.

The fire that had kept her up all night fizzed and sparked, driving her towards an impulsiveness that she was unaccustomed to. He had thought to subdue her with desire and it was maddening. But she wasn't the only one who had been enslaved by their passion.

If he was surprised by the way she stood up from her chair, pressed herself against his body, wound her hands around his neck and pulled him into a kiss that could have scorched all thought from both parties, then he didn't show it. As if it were the most natural thing in the world, his arm swept around her waist and pulled her against him as Emily's intention only to use his own tactics against him spun wildly out of control.

The moment his tongue laved her bottom lip she was helpless to refuse him. She barely had a moment to prepare for how he took ruthless possession of her mouth in a way that made her pulse pound in her heart and between her legs. The growl that purred from his throat lifted the hairs on the back of her neck as his hand gripped the hair above her nape, angling her firmly back to allow him deeper, to allow him more of her and—helpless and wanton—she let him.

Anger and desire melded as she wrestled for control, biting down not so gently on his lip. His eyes sprung open and *burned.* For a frantic second she teetered on the brink of a precipice, wishing she hadn't been so impulsive… But then he walked them back against the dining room wall, pressing her, crowding her, tormenting her as his hands ravished her body, palming breasts with nipples hardened to peaks, fisting the flesh of her backside in a way that would be worth every ache.

This, she thought. *This* was what she dreamed of at night when her lust-addled mind taunted her with erotic pictures from before he had begun to work all hours, before the doubt and worry had crept in. Before she questioned if she had given up everything for a man who was no longer there.

Her head fell back and she felt feasted upon. He drew her against the rock-hard length of his need and she gasped, biting her lip to prevent the plea on her tongue. Words that would beg and bribe lodged in her throat as her heart ached and wanted and angered all at once.

He sneaked deft fingers behind her knee and drew her leg up to hook over his hip, gently pressing his way deeper against the throbbing ache that was almost painful in its intensity. She was helpless to stop herself from pressing back, from shifting in a way that caressed and eased and tormented her own arousal whilst teasing and hardening Javier's.

His eyes flared open, pinning her with an incomprehensible gaze that whispered only one word to her: *more*. She felt her orgasm begin to build beneath his watchful gaze, urged on by the voyeuristic enjoyment he found in her pleasure. Muscles tightened on an emptiness deep within, but outside everything burned, wanted, needed. More. She wanted more. Because she knew how good he felt deep within her. Knew what it was to be possessed by this man. To be owned.

As if a bucket of ice-cold water had slapped over her, she tensed. A scream stopped in her throat. No. She could not be owned by him. Not again. She'd not survive it.

'What?' Javier whispered, alarmed by the sudden change in Emily. His hands went to cup her face but she wriggled from them.

'Sorry, I've...' and she sneaked beneath his arm, escaping the circle of his embrace.

His breath straining in aching lungs, he stared at her, trying to ignore the sliver of hurt that cut more deeply than any wound from the accident. 'Are you okay?'

'Of course,' she insisted, spinning back round to face

him, a smile on her lips as fake as the five-foot ceramic parrot in the sitting room. Lips that had teased him to the point of near orgasm only seconds earlier. *Cristo*, he'd not been this out of control since their first time together.

'I just forgot that I have to go out.'

'Out?'

Javier detested intensely that he was sounding like an idiot, reduced to monosyllabic questions. But it was taking him a worryingly long time to get his usually hair-triggered brain out of the lust-fuelled fantasy of taking his wife on the table once again.

'Yes, out,' she said, her eyes wide, blush riding high on her cheeks, hair in disarray from where he had gripped and—

She reached blindly for her keys.

'What are you going out for?' he asked, amazed that the words formed some semblance of order.

'Food.'

'But we have—'

She spun away from him and was out through the front door before he could finish.

'—food,' he said to an empty house.

He swallowed, an act he both felt and heard. The sound of the door closing behind her had snapped a thread on the rope tying his emotions down and he felt something crawling, clawing, trying to get out. Shoving it down with more force than usual, he stalked into the kitchen and made himself a coffee.

He needed something to cover the taste of lust on his tongue. He rearranged his trousers to relieve the pressure against the wildfire ache Emily had drawn from him as if she were a magician pulling his desire like silk scarves from her pocket. The moment she had pressed her lips against his he'd been lost, only returning to his sense of self when she had fled his embrace.

He took his coffee out to the patio, wondering at the effect she had on him, when his phone buzzed in his pocket.

How is OP AM coming along?

He typed back to Santiago.

OP AM??

Operation Amnesia. I'm prepared to offer for the movie rights.

Javier stared at his phone, trying to work out if his oldest friend was joking. Clearly he had taken too long because the next message came through before he could reply.

Is Emily back?

Santi had been there the night he'd first met Emily. They had, in fact, been at the bar so that Santi could finally work up the courage to ask out Mariana—which had taken perhaps a little too much whisky, but had been successful nonetheless. Santi had been insufferably in love then and had been more than a little smug in the intervening years with his exceedingly happy marriage— to the point of trying to meddle in his own.

They had almost come to blows when Javier wouldn't go after Emily. It was the first—and only—real argument they'd ever had. But even his closest friend couldn't understand the devastating betrayal of Emily's sudden, silent departure from his life. How it had made old wounds run with fresh blood. No. Javier could never have gone after her.

Santi hadn't understood that, but it didn't stop him from being closer to him than a brother, one of the best filmmakers in the world, *and* the reason that Javier had made his first million. The nail-biting seven months Javier had to wait to find out whether his investment in Santiago's first film would pay off had been the most stressful of his life. He had been so unsure of success that he'd worked nineteen-hour days to cover the financial gap in his business in case it didn't pay off—unwilling to tell his uncle what he had done, knowing Gael wouldn't understand, and knowing that he could never have admitted to Emily that he had taken such a risk.

But Javier had known it would work. And it had. Spectacularly. From there on out, Javier became one of Santiago's main investors—the revenue from the film industry a small fortune in its own right. And in Javier's hands money turned into property and investments and companies, ranging from import to technology, communications and media. *Infierno*, he doubted even he could say the names of all the companies he part owned or funded.

He had amassed a fortune that had brought him to the attention of the highest—and sometimes most secretive—echelons of society and he had determined to do as much good as he could with his wealth.

But somehow that didn't matter a damn when Santi had asked, *Is Emily back?* His fist tightened around the phone as he jabbed out his reply.

Not yet. But she will be.

Emily's calves were hurting after stalking the upward winding cobbled streets of Frigiliana, but it was a good hurt. A physical one. It somehow soothed the emotional hurt she'd felt before fleeing their home. She had overreacted, she realised now. Not to Javier, not to the situation. *That*, she felt justified in. But she was embarrassed by how quickly her plan had backfired. Clearly she couldn't be trusted anywhere near Javier's lips, or hands…or body for that matter.

Even now the thought of it made her pulse leap, her skin flush and filled her with that indescribable yearning that flared low in her body. She looked up in time to dodge a tourist couple taking photographs in front of the spectacular bougainvillea pouring down the white walls of the town like a fountain.

She'd had no particular destination in mind when she'd left, but now her feet traced paths she'd taken with Javier when they had first come to Frigiliana, hand in hand, or tucked under the wide protection of his shoulders. The way his hand would trace the hemline of her skirt, caressing her thigh secretively and sending her wild. The way he would stop and talk to almost every shop owner or business owner, a question and an interest in everyone and everything. And she hadn't minded. She'd just soaked it all up.

Six years ago she'd unfurled beneath the sun and Javier's heated touch. She'd felt herself becoming the woman she was always supposed to be. Colourful, bright, happy. It had been so different from the beige, bored silence of the home she had shared with her mother and Steven. And she'd found herself angry with her mother all over again. Not for herself but for what her mother had lost. Because she too had once lived in the bright colours of summer. When Emily was young, her mother had been bright and bold. She had laughed and loved and lavished her attention on her daughter. But Steven had stolen that light, dimmed it. After they married it was as if her mother laughed to fill a silence, not because there had been joy. And the betrayal that Emily had felt…it had devastated her and confused her, scratched at her heart, making her feel guilty, angry, hurt and selfish.

She was suddenly the spoiled only child who didn't want to share her mother. But it wasn't that. Not at all. It was just that the woman who married Steven wasn't the same woman who had been her mother. And it had felt like the slowest loss played out in front of her each night as, hour by hour, her mother changed into someone who revolved only around her husband, as if she were sacrificing slices of herself over and over again until there was nothing left of the mother that Emily had once known.

Emily went to brush away the sudden trail of ice on her cheek, only to realise that a tear had fallen. She shook off the memories of the past and looked around at the town that had changed only a little in the last six years. Some of the shops were different, but there was still the silver jewellery shop on the first fork in the path, the bakery that would sell out before nine in the morning, the tourist shops with racks of sunglasses and hats for the unprepared. But it was the patterned cobbles that she loved the most, the little courtyards tucked off the main walkways behind peeling iron gates, and the Hand of Fatima door knockers standing out against painted doors.

As she continued down the cobbled street she saw a shop she didn't remember. SpaceWhale's doorway was framed by large green palms and snake plants, enticing Emily into the welcoming shade and away from the intense heat of the mid-morning. Inside she found a cornucopia of delights. Stunning prints and photographs, hypnotic incense and candles, jewellery, books, stationery. Not knowing where to look first, she found herself drawn to the scents and couldn't resist picking up a small bottle of perfume that was rich and sensual and felt as if it belonged to the wife of Javier Casas more than herself in that moment. Without questioning it, she paid for the perfume and took the shop's card—instinctively knowing that she would come back, either for herself or for her clients.

On her way out, she noticed a board pinned with announcements and local adverts. A picture of the most hideous cat she'd ever seen had caught the attention of several passers-by and a lot of laughter. As she drew closer, she read the announcement.

Ready for rehoming.
Be warned, this cat is possessed.

Emily hid a laugh behind her hand, but couldn't resist reading on. It warned of an evil cat that hissed, snapped, bit and clawed. It had been placed with seven different homes now and not one had lasted more than two days. Notoriously violent with men, the notice concluded with the challenge of rehoming...*if you dare.*

Eyes narrowed, smile pulling at the corner of her lips, Emily began to plan.

Two hours later Emily was unloading bags, boxes, trays, cases and more bags from the taxi she'd had to get to drive her home. She'd had to pay the driver extra because of her precious cargo, so she was surprised that he got out to help her unload, until she realised it was so he could get rid of them as quickly as possible.

Deciding it was safe to leave the bags outside while she unlocked the door, that giddy thrill of doing something wicked fizzed in her bloodstream again. Meeting Javier's nefariousness with her own was becoming an addictive game. One she warned herself against enjoying too much because, for the first time in a very long time, she was *enjoying* herself. Pitting her intelligence against Javier's was exciting.

She opened the front door and hooked it back against the wall and—

Gasped.

Javier was on the floor with his hand pressed against his head. She rushed over to him, horror flooding her veins and a sob stuck in her throat.

'Javi! Are you okay? What happened?' She cursed as she reached him, her hands shaking and her whole body trembling.

His unfocused eyes found hers and his expression changed to one of concern. He reached out and caught her wrists to steady her, his eyes snagging on the tears of shock filling her vision. 'Emily, what's wrong?'

Infuriated, she reared back. 'Javi! You are on the floor, what is wrong with *you*?'

He winced and gently rolled his head from side to side until he stared at the door, confusion once again filling his gaze.

'Emily. What is *that*?'

CHAPTER FIVE

HE WAS GOING to take great satisfaction in destroying that ceramic parrot. After he found out what the hell it was that was hissing at him from inside a small cage.

Mierda, his head hurt. Coming through from the patio, he'd had his phone in one hand, coffee in the other when he'd startled at the sight of the big white bird. Not that he would admit it to any living soul, but he'd jumped, spilling the coffee, and then— humiliatingly—had slipped on it and fallen. With his hands full and his stomach muscles already bruised, his body had reacted more slowly than usual and he'd landed on the floor, winded and aching.

He looked up at Emily, her expression unsure and guilt painting slashes of red over her lush cheekbones. She flicked her gaze between him and the cage and bit her lip.

'It's…it's…your…erm… It's our…'

Her eyes grew wider each time she tried to explain, the words seeming to bottleneck in her throat, and curiosity and pain were the only things that stopped him from laughing out loud.

Oh, God, what fresh hell was this?

He peered at the crystalline eyes glaring daggers at him from the small crate and the clawed paw that looked alarmingly threatening.

'We have a cat?' he asked, knowing full well they didn't.

Emily nodded quickly, blonde hair quivering around her like a shimmering halo.

'She's been at the cattery. While you were...' Her hand slipped from where he still held it, and gestured in circles—and a memory surfaced of her doing exactly the same thing when she had lied about something silly years before. One thing was for sure. His wife should never play poker.

But, he realised as he gently rested his head back down against the floor, his wife apparently *didn't* believe his amnesia and had found a new way to torment him. The cat—without a shadow of a doubt—was one of the ugliest things he'd ever seen.

He wanted to ask where the cat's fur was, but instead he asked, 'Her name?', while his mind recalibrated this new information about his devious wife.

Emily paused for a second, flicking the cat a glance and only releasing the pin of teeth on her lip to answer, 'Diabla.'

And this time he *did* laugh. *She devil.* It seemed appropriate.

Emily had barely got over her shock when it morphed into anger again. But she refused to give him the satisfaction of knowing how worried she had been. The stubborn, mule-headed, infuriating man deserved every single thing coming to him.

When she'd first seen him lying on the floor, her heart had stopped. Actually stopped. Only to start again with a whoosh that sent electric sparks shooting around her body, tingling her fingertips, pricking her heart and trembling her hands.

It was the second time he'd done this to her and it was too much, she'd decided angrily as she'd let Diabla out of the cage. The animal had burst from her confines, pausing only to hiss at Javier before rushing off at an alarming speed. To Emily's surprise, Javier had only laughed even harder.

She'd gone to the freezer, grabbed a bag of peas, retrieved his painkillers and stood over him as—still on the floor—he'd swallowed down two tablets. After that she had gone to her room, shut the door and ignored his attempts to speak to her.

Opening her laptop, she spent an hour fielding emails and assigning workloads to her staff, silently promising them all a pay rise when this was done. She'd never been away from her work or staff this long since she'd started the company and it tore at her to be away from it now.

She remembered Javier's swift dismissal that his businesses would be 'fine'. Well, she was glad *his* interests were fine. They couldn't all have a million and one assistants to cover their vast empires, she thought angrily. And then regretted her thoughts. That was uncharitable and mean. He had always worked hard, despite the money he had been born into. Javier was nothing like the rich men she knew from London: entitled, lazy, loud and bordering on brutish. No, Javier's work ethic had been inspiring, until it had become almost obsessive, until it had taken him away from her for days on end.

At some point Javier left some lunch outside the room, which she'd retrieved and absentmindedly eaten as she'd scanned the plans for the San Antonio project. The mood boards were her starting point, gathering any imagery that was associated with the client and the location. Because she had to bring it *all* together. The client wanted what they wanted, but if it didn't fit the space, if it worked *against* the location, then whatever she created would stick out like a sore thumb. It might, on the surface, be fine, but beneath it would be simmering discontent. So she threw herself into colours and moods and textures and, before she knew it, four hours had passed and her back ached.

But it had been worth it because Emily had finally got that feeling—the thrill of finding *the thing*. And suddenly everything slotted together: the patterns she wanted to use, the light fittings and the wall panels, the textures for some of the furnishings, even the style of crockery, all coming from a paint colour called Mountain Dawn.

It had caught her eye because she'd seen exactly that same rich buttery yellow that morning, creeping over the hill line above the gorge. It was a yellow that fitted against a dusky blue and a rich blush, a deep cobalt and a startlingly clean white. And the range of colours were perfect for San Antonio and her client. And now she was happy and eager to press on…but not until she'd seen where the next two weeks would take her.

Changing into a bikini she'd left behind the last time she was here, she hoped that the pool's cool water might soothe the anxiety skittering beneath her skin. She wrapped a robe around her and slipped quietly down the stairs, wanting to make it to the pool without alerting Javier. She just wasn't ready to confront him at the moment. She was bruised by his lies, and scared by her concern for him, a man she was seriously considering divorcing.

Because, really, what kind of relationship was this? She had wants and needs that couldn't be put on hold for another six years—a home, family, children… People she wanted to love and be loved by. What had started as a yearning a few years ago was becoming stronger and harder to ignore. She owed it to herself to try for more. She deserved more than this strange limbo she had been in since she'd left.

She snuck into the kitchen to retrieve the cat food she'd bought for Diabla. Emily shook the dry biscuits so the cat would know that food was there, her heart jumping a little as she caught sight of the clear blue gaze peeking around the door frame. She poured a large helping into a bowl and placed it on the little balcony, wondering why the cattery had given her such a bad reputation. Deciding that Diabla was simply misunderstood, while vainly hoping that she might scratch just a little at Javier, Emily made her way outside, where the early evening sun still had enough heat to warm the skin.

She sat at the pool's edge and took in the natural quiet that was particular to Frigiliana. Birds twittered, leaves rustled, a goat bleated somewhere in the distance, and it was the most restful kind of quiet she'd heard in years. She inhaled the scent of lemons from the fruit trees below and wondered if she had been wrong to leave this place.

Strange that it had all been because of a dress. Full of sequins and sparkle and Javier's expectation, it had been both beautiful and terrible when she'd seen it on the bed next to an invitation to a film premiere three days later. Beautiful because it was truly gorgeous, and terrible because the gift had come the very same evening he had left her waiting on a private runway for three hours, having completely forgotten that he'd agreed to come to her friend's party.

That night she'd realised that she'd never be able to go to Santi's film premiere, never make it through the night without breaking down. Part of her had worried that all the months of loneliness and desperate need to be loved would come pouring out in humiliating desperation, but the larger part—the far greater fear—was that, even if she did, it wouldn't matter. Because, deep down, she worried that she had tied herself for the rest of her life to a man who would never love her back.

She brushed a tear from her cheek and kicked her legs in the water. Heart heavy and thoughts swirling, she took a deep breath, let herself fall.

Javier had worried the entire time his wife had locked herself in her room, hating the way that it made him feel on the outside looking in. *Cristo*, it was worse than when she'd been in London.

He knew he'd scared her. For a moment, he'd scared himself. He rolled the shoulder that had a new ache he could add to his collection. He'd not had an accident or hurt himself since…he rubbed at the scar on his collarbone…since he'd learned not to, he thought darkly.

At age seven, he'd walked around with a broken collarbone for nearly twenty-four hours until his teacher had noticed something wrong and sent him to hospital. He'd fallen the day before on his bicycle, but his mother had told him he was trying to ruin her day, trying to take the attention away from her. She'd demanded to know why she had been sent such ungrateful, mean children: Gabi who cried all the time and Javi who just took and took and took. She'd called him a succubus and though he hadn't known the word, he'd understood what his mother had meant.

Things might have been different if it had happened on one of her 'good' days. Renata would have rushed him to hospital, primarily so that she could bathe in the lavish praise of being the perfect mother she sometimes liked to be seen as. But it hadn't been a good day. Renata had just split with her second husband and she was always especially difficult when that happened. But he'd still asked her.

Please, Mamá, it hurts.

The memory of it brought a visceral nausea that threatened to overwhelm him, even now. He'd never told anyone what it had been like growing up with his mother. Santi had guessed enough but even he didn't know the truth of how terrifying it was not to know what mood she would be in. Obsessively loving could flip to vicious jealousy in the blink of an eye. Most of her erratic behaviour had been excused by her family as *dramatic*, but Javier had always suspected that his uncle knew.

In his father's absence, his mother's brother, Gael, had taken Javier under his wing and instructed him in the wider family business. Javier had worked in some capacity in every one of his uncle's businesses since he was fourteen years old, before being entrusted with a small delivery service company on his eighteenth birthday.

Gael's gift had been more than Javier had ever expected, because his mother wouldn't willingly relinquish control of the textile empire she had inherited from her father. He remembered the time he'd had the temerity to ask her if one day he might run it, like she did. Renata had looked him dead in the eye and, with more seriousness than he'd ever seen from her, replied, *'Never.'*

No. She would never relinquish control of that company. Anything Javier had achieved was because of his uncle. But the difficulty there was the anger. An anger he tried to bury against the man who had allowed his mother to get away with what she did. But it was because of that anger that he'd impetuously used money from the start-up property business to invest in Santi's first film.

The complex emotions seethed through his veins, making him feel close to an edge he didn't want to approach. Being with Emily was forcing him to feel things that he had managed well enough to leave alone for the last six years. And now he was beginning to wonder if it hadn't been stubborn pride keeping him from her, but that it had been easier. His conscience stirred painfully in his chest. Because he'd known that things hadn't been okay between them. Each time he'd come home it was as if another shard had been chipped away and all he'd felt was that he was failing. Letting everyone down—Emily, Gael…he was failing.

'You're just like your father. A coward. A failure.'

He pounded the wall with the side of his fist. No. He was nothing like his father. He wasn't a failure and he didn't walk away. He would fix this with Emily. She would return to his side and they would be happy, dammit.

Because he knew she cared. He'd seen it in her eyes when she'd found him moments after he'd fallen. He'd felt it on his tongue in the taste of her, in the way she'd gripped his shirt and pulled him against her in the kiss that morning. He'd counted it in the pulse rate he'd felt when he'd grasped her wrist. He *knew* it.

He took the steps two at a time down to the lower level and the swimming pool. He could feel it in him, the anger, the argument, the words that they'd never said, the disagreements they'd never had. Oh, they'd had passion in spades but in their last few months together she had taken slow backwards steps away from him and she'd fallen through his fingers like sand. But not this time.

Rounding the corner, he burst out onto the patio to find it…empty.

He frowned, looking around, and couldn't see Emily anywhere. He knew she was out here—he'd seen her from the window.

There was a flash of white at the bottom of the pool—the swimming costume he'd talked Emily into buying six years ago. He'd made her promise to wear it at least three times a week, swimming pool or no, just so he could peel it from her delectable skin.

He looked closer, seeing Emily at the bottom of the deep end of the pool—hair floating around her like golden silk, eyes closed and hauntingly still. He waited for her to surface, something disconcerting needling in his chest. His breath started to become short as he imagined how her lungs must be feeling and still she didn't surface. Alarm quickly replaced anger, a fist to his gut, and his mind skipped over the thought that this was what she'd felt for him after his accident. Maybe even that morning.

Alarm turned to panic and—

Basta ya!

He launched himself into the pool.

Something wrapped firmly around her arms and Emily screamed in shock, water rushing into her mouth the moment it opened. She was dragged up out of the water coughing and spluttering, looking up to find herself staring at a very wet, very close Javier.

Heart pounding and angry from the fright, she slapped at his arm.

He shook her, not to hurt and it didn't hurt, but she felt it—his frustration, his fear, mixing with hers—and she slapped him again.

'What was that for?' he demanded.

'You deserved it!' she bit back.

'Probably. But why?'

Because you're lying to me. Because I've left everything in London for you—again. Because you make me want you when I don't *want to*, her inner voice screamed silently.

He shook his head, perhaps realising she couldn't answer his question. Not with this game they were playing.

'What were you doing down there?'

'Breathing,' she snapped sarcastically.

She saw the flex of his jaw, one of the only tells Javier Casas had, and reflexively she swallowed.

All the emotions, the drama and the worry of the last few days, the memories of a husband who hadn't even cared enough about the one thing, *one thing*, that had been so important to her... The ache spread out across her chest and crawled up her throat, her heart hurt all over again, bruised and raw, it thudded under the tide of memories washing again and again over her soul.

'*Mi vida,*' Javier said, sweeping a damp twist of hair from her cheek. 'What's wrong? Please tell me,' he begged.

But here? Now? Javier had encircled her with his arms, that legendary focus and determination all on her, the concern she felt press against her in waves. This was the man she had first met; this was the man who wanted to know her secrets and share them, her desires and make them happen, her hurts and make them better. This was the man she had fallen in love with and she so desperately wanted to pretend. Pretend that he *did* have amnesia.

Pretend that he hadn't lied to her and upended her life for his own selfish reasons. Pretend that the last six years hadn't happened. Pretend that it would be the most natural thing in the world for her to make love to the husband she had given her heart and soul to one Spanish summer's eve. She didn't want to worry about what would happen tomorrow or the next day any more. She wanted the here and now. She wanted her husband.

His hand cupped her cheek, and he was looking at her as if trying to unravel some great mystery she wasn't anywhere near ready for him to see. The white linen shirt he wore had turned see-through, clinging to his skin, and his dark trousers abraded her legs beneath the water. They were both breathing hard with the force of staying afloat in the deep end and, in unspoken agreement, Javier swam them back towards the shallow end, keeping her within the circle of his embrace.

He powered them easily through the water, creating a delicious slip and slide between their bodies, until she felt the gentle curve of the edge of the pool at her back. Encased in his arms, she didn't feel trapped but protected, sheltered, hidden… And here, as dusk was falling, in a pool hidden from the sight of passers-by either on the road or on the gorge, she felt that anything could happen. It whispered like a delicious taunt in her mind and soul until she wanted not just anything, but *everything*.

Intensity zipped from his gaze to her body, she felt it like a carnal stroke over her breasts and beneath the waterline. Javier braced one hand against the stone and held her with the other, even though she could now stand. His fingers burned the flesh at her side through the water and shivers racked her body.

'Are you cold, *querida*?'

She bit her lip and shook her head, her eyes fastened on his, so that she caught the way his gaze flickered between her lips and her eyes. The way his nostrils flared on a swift inhale and his pupils burst wide, the molten depths promising heat and hardness—all concealment ripped away from his intense gaze showing her a world of want she was so tired of fighting. She wanted, she needed, so Emily closed her eyes and surrendered.

'Kiss me,' she pleaded, no longer caring that she was

begging. He had always done this to her. He had always made her feel like this, *want* this. With complete and utter submission.

Javier Casas, the man who the press had dubbed as 'having it all', had never wanted anything more in his entire life. His wife was in his arms, asking him to love her. But he couldn't. Because he was lying to her. That she knew it didn't make a bit of difference. His conscience wrestled with the sheer force of his need for her, the request on her lips an invitation to the sweetest of sins.

'*Please.*'

The word escaped lips he'd kissed a thousand times and it hadn't been anywhere near enough. Memories of the way she would laugh beneath his mouth, the giggle he could bring forth with the lightest of touches in the most specific of places, the sigh when he slipped his hand between her legs, the moan that built with her orgasm, the sound of his name on her tongue as she came, it built until the wall of his desire for her loomed so large it blocked out all reason.

If he'd been worried that she'd be startled by the passion with which he claimed her lips, he was so very wrong. Emily was *inflamed* by it. Her mouth opened to his before he even closed the distance between them. Where he would have held her still, she came alive beneath his touch, raising onto tiptoes, twining her arms around his neck, pressing into his chest, making the blood roar her name in his veins. The taste of her was like manna from heaven and he hadn't realised just how lost he had been until Emily found him in that moment. His heart beat so profoundly that for the wildest second he thought to press a hand against his chest to hold it in place.

Encouraged by the small needy groans she made at the back of her throat—the ones he'd used to learn every single one of her favourite places to be touched and teased—he pulled her against the hard ridge of his arousal, satisfied by the little whimper that tangled in their kiss.

With his nose, he nudged her head back so that he could take tiny nips along her neck and shoulder, then chased the ripple of goosebumps with his tongue across her skin. He hooked the strap of the bikini top with his forefinger, sliding it down her shoulder, smiling to himself. If she'd known how much it had cost, she never would have worn the obscenely expensive item of swimwear. But he'd kept the cost from her because he'd known how good it would be to peel it from her skin.

'The moment I saw this,' he said, his finger releasing the strap and following the curve of the top, '*this* was what I imagined doing, over and over and over again.' He pulled down the cup covering her breast and took it into his mouth, relishing the way she leaned back, pressing her chest forward, wanting, needing more. Cupping her breast, his thumb teasing the taut nipple, he pressed open mouth kisses and went to the other, unable to resist the pull of wanting to have it in his mouth.

Her legs wrapped around his hips and brought his arousal deliciously against her core.

'When you wore this,' he said, between teasing her to distraction with his tongue, 'to Santi and Mariana's engagement party, I nearly had a heart attack,' he went on, smiling at the memory. 'You are never to wear this in public, *mi amore*. I told you that when I gave it to you.'

'Santi and Mariana's engagement party?' Emily asked, pulling back from his embrace and staring at him with startlingly dull eyes.

'Yes? You remember.'

She shook her head and slipped from his arms, bracing her hands against the pool edge and levering herself backwards out of the pool. 'I do,' she said as she reached for her robe. 'But you shouldn't.'

He watched her walk away—brain completely blank—until arousal dissipated and he realised what had happened. He cursed, striking out, sending a wave of water that covered half the patio. Santi and Mariana's engagement party had been only weeks before she'd left him and long after Gabi's sixteenth birthday.

The game was up. There was no more pretending.

He glared at the reflection of himself in the window, frustration and fury rippling out across the water in the pool. It was a good thing, he told himself. Because now? Now *nothing* would stop him from getting her back by his side.

CHAPTER SIX

EMILY PRAYED HE wouldn't come after her. That he'd just let her be—let her recover from the pool. Water dripped down her back from the ropes it had made of her hair. She was trembling with cold now, making a mockery of the intense desire that had shivered across her body before.

'*Kiss me.*'

She had begged. Shame coursed through her. The man who had left her alone, who had shown a selfishness that had cut so very deep, and she had *begged*. She would have pleaded for more if his words hadn't crashed through the fragile shell-world they'd created from his lies. She would have taken everything he had offered and given more of herself than she would ever have wanted. Her fingers rose to her lips, swollen from kisses that would have only had one logical conclusion: sex. He had kissed her with utter and complete possession, he always had. She shook her head at her own weakness. The fact that she couldn't trust herself around him was humiliating.

'Emily!'

His angry shout echoed around the stone-walled house and she wanted to run. Not because she was afraid of him, but because she didn't know what would happen now that the lies were broken in pieces on the floor. For six years, they had avoided this. Avoided why she had left…why their marriage was broken.

Oh, God.

She wasn't ready for this, not dressed in a bikini she was holding together, soaking wet, and still trembling with desire for him. She ran up the stairs just as she heard him come in from the pool, and slammed the spare bedroom door behind her. Grabbing the cover from the bed, she wrapped it around herself, trying to stop her legs from shaking.

'Emily,' he growled through the door.

'Don't you dare get angry with me,' she yelled back.

'What?'

'You're the one who faked having amnesia!'

'And you're the one who filled our home with tat,' he accused from the other side of the door. 'There is *no* excuse for that ceramic parrot.'

She could almost see the angry slash of his hand as if the door had been invisible.

'Having a husband who lies about a medical condition *is* the excuse!'

'Open the door, Emily.'

'No.'

'I will *not* have this conversation with you through a door!' She could tell he was angry, his accent had thickened and, although she would never be afraid of him, she wasn't quite sure what he would do.

'I… I don't want to see you right now.'

'No? Like you didn't want to see me six years ago when you left me waiting on a red carpet?' he demanded.

'Yes. Pretty much,' she replied glibly.

'Stand back,' he growled.

'What? No, I—'

The moment she heard the wood splinter, she leapt back away from the door. She hadn't been that close to it, but the shock of it startled her. Wood snapped as another bang cracked it from the hinges.

'Javi! What are you doing?' she cried. The door fell into the room, half swinging on the last remaining hinge as Javier, barefooted, white shirt and trousers still plastered to his skin, shoulders heaving, looked ready to explode.

'I am making sure, *wife*, that I can see you when you tell me why you left me. So that when you finally explain why you walked away from me without warning or explanation you can't hide this time.'

'Me?' Emily demanded, fury rising like a phoenix in her soul. 'You're accusing *me* of hiding?' she asked, closing the distance between them, mindless of the destruction at the side of the room. 'Javier Casas, you left me long before I even thought about leaving you.'

Shock blew his pupils wide and, rather than another angry outburst, Javier went completely and unnaturally still. It created a vacuum that pulled at her, that sucked air and breath and emotions towards the vortex that was *him*. She nearly stumbled towards him but he took a step back, stopping her in her tracks.

'How can you say that?' he accused, hurt mixing with anger and a palpable sense of injustice.

'Because it's true!' she insisted.

He shook his head, raising his hand to stop her, and then let it drop before he turned away.

'Wait, now *you* don't want to talk?' she demanded, stepping over a piece of broken door frame. 'You literally kick the door down and you're walking away?'

'I do not wish to say something I will regret.'

'I think it's a little late for that, don't you?' she hurled at his retreating back.

Inside, Javier was shaking with impotent fury. That he'd kicked the door off its hinges was terrible enough. But he'd been so mad, so infuriated that she would run from him again. Leave him with all these *feelings* and nowhere or way to get rid of them.

He clenched his jaw, forcing stillness through his body. This kind of hysterical behaviour, it was too much like his mother. A shiver of self-disgust tripped down his spine and turned his stomach. He had more control than this, he needed to have more control than this.

He stalked into the master bedroom, forcing the buttons of his shirt through the water tightened holes, sorely tempted to rip apart the fabric. Instead he yoked his feelings in time to hear Emily's footsteps enter the room that he'd woken in that morning with such a sense of peace.

He peeled the soaking wet shirt from his shoulders and it hit the floor with a soggy slap.

'We *do* need to talk.' Her voice from behind him was low, a whisper almost, resonating with an emotion that was so close to the wrong kind of surrender it turned his stomach.

He clenched his jaw to stop the denial roar from his throat. Because he knew she was right. Unable to turn until he had better control of himself, he nodded once decisively. It was enough.

'I will meet you downstairs once I have changed.'

His hands went to the button of the trousers that clung claustrophobically to the skin on his legs. Too tight. Everything was too tight.

'Javier—'

'Once I have changed,' he growled, turning to pin her with a stare that allowed no argument.

But he wished he hadn't turned. Because the insecurity in her vivid blue gaze, the way she held herself, a foot tucked behind an ankle, as if making herself as small as possible... A knife cut into his lungs. He had never wanted to see that in his wife: uncertainty, doubt. *He* had done that. He had made her feel those things. And more, his conscience taunted him.

You left me long before I even thought about leaving you.

He wanted to grip his head and make the words stop, but he wouldn't. Because he needed to hear them. He needed to know what had happened if he was going to save his marriage. If he was going to be better than his father. No. Unlike the man who had given him life, who had walked away in shame after failing his family, Javier was going to *fight*—and, no matter how Emily felt about it, she *was* his family.

Emily shifted in the doorway, yanking his attention back to her.

'Put on some dry clothes, or you'll catch a cold,' he commanded before turning to the en suite bathroom and closing the door behind him. But no amount of separation would remove the imprint of her seared into his mind. She had wrapped a throw around her shoulders, but it did nothing to disguise the way that water had clung to her thighs in droplets he wanted to lick from her skin. His fingers had touched and delved, but not nearly enough. *Cristo*, his need for her was like a madness in his blood. Even now, when they were emotionally as far from each other as they could conceivably be, he wanted her. He wanted to taste her on his tongue, to feel her writhe beneath him, to watch her find her pleasure. He could describe every single change that happened to Emily when she orgasmed.

The way that her head would fall back, her mouth would open on gasps that climbed higher and higher as she did, the way that she had learned to find ecstasy in her own sighs and cries and moans, the way that the closer she came, her breath would get caught in her lungs and she would reach for him, she would find him, her muscles quivering around him, gripping him and she would take him with her as she flew through her own orgasm.

He flicked the snap of his trousers angrily, releasing an erection he'd brought on himself from the confines of his trousers. *Por Dios*, he was supposed to be trying to fix his marriage, not lust over his wife like a naughty schoolboy. He shoved the trousers from his legs and rinsed off in the shower before grabbing a towel and hoping to hell that Emily had left his room by the time he emerged.

After he changed into clean and, more importantly, *dry* clothing he would turn his focus to the matter at hand. The goal? Convince his wife to return. Nothing else mattered.

Emily stood at the sink, gently dipping the herbal tea bag in and out of the hot water in her mug, strangely comforted by the way that Diabla wound herself back and forth through her legs. And she needed that comfort because the longer and longer that Javier took to come down from the bedroom, the worse her nerves became. It was as if six years' worth of ignoring everything had built up such a mass of tension and jumbled hurts and pains that she couldn't quite see right and she was genuinely worried at what might come out of her mouth.

All she knew was that, one way or another, things

had to change. It was just that she couldn't see her way through to anything other than…

'We will not divorce.'

Javier's pronouncement startled her as much as the cat and, with a screech and a hiss, Diabla disappeared in a flash.

Hot water sloshed over the side of the mug and down the back of her hand and a stifled cry caught in her throat. Javier cursed and came to her, taking the mug from her hand and turning on the cold water tap. Ever so gently he placed her hand beneath the stream, holding it when she would have flinched away, with all the care she knew him capable of. It was one of the reasons she had fallen so hard and so fast for the Spaniard. He had an innate sense of nurture he didn't know he possessed.

He placed her palm against his own, warming her hand from beneath so that the frigid water didn't bite as much. She was surprised when he huffed out a little laugh. 'Gabi did this once. She was trying to make me coffee and she burned her hand.'

She was distracted by the way his fingers encased her hand as if it were something truly precious. 'What did your mother do when she found out?'

His silence drew her gaze, but he was still focused on her hand—or so it seemed. Until the slightest of shakes of his head told her that his mother had done absolutely nothing. Her heart turned and she realised that she was not surprised, only more curious about Renata Casas than she had been before.

What she knew of his mother was arrogance, selfishness and disdain. But she had always presumed that came from a place of maternal snobbery—that Emily hadn't been good enough for her son. But now she was beginning to wonder if it was something else.

She was about to ask, when he turned off the tap and wrapped her hand in a clean tea towel.

'I'll get the arnica.'

She reached for him as he turned. 'Javier—'

'I mean it, *mi amore*,' he warned, his dark eyes glowing with intent. 'We will not divorce.'

And what rocked Emily more was the way her heart soared at his declaration. He returned before she could gather herself and pulled out a chair for her to take. After he sat, he reached for her hand and gently rubbed the soothing cream into her skin.

The circles his thumb made across her hand calmed her against her will. She wanted to stay angry at him. Needed to, but the care he was giving her was undermining her intent with the same intensity as the next words that came out of his mouth.

'I meant my vows.'

'So did I.' She'd expected her words to sound defensive and was surprised when they fell between them with a sadness that was painful to her own ears.

The flex of muscle at Javier's jaw told her he'd felt it too. 'What did you mean? About me leaving?' he clarified before she could ask.

He really didn't know. Emily didn't know whether that made it better or worse.

'You were never here, Javi,' she said, pulling her hand from the warm embrace of his fingers.

He frowned. 'I was working for us—to secure our future.'

'Our future *was* secure,' she insisted gently. 'We were together.' It was all she had needed. All she had *wanted*. 'We didn't need anything else.'

She almost read the thought in his eyes. *I did.* That was what he'd intended to say. And while they couldn't, wouldn't, say these things to each other, they didn't have a future.

'We needed money, *mi vida.*'

'We already had so much. More than I could even have imagined,' she reminded him.

'We needed security, Emily. My mother will never relinquish control over Casas Textiles. My uncle had given me a small start-up business but...' he looked away as if finding it difficult to discuss these things '...but I needed to make my own way. And then when Santi was looking for investors in his film... No one would fund him. He was going to have to drop it and I couldn't let that happen. So I took a risk. I invested heavily—*too* heavily. My uncle, if he'd known, would have taken back his business, thinking me reckless. But he'd have been wrong. I *prepared* for a significant financial loss. So I worked three times as hard, all the hours I could to counter any possible loss, all in order to have something of our own.'

'Javier...' She hadn't known anything of this. Only now was she beginning to realise just how much he had kept her truly on the outside of their marriage.

'It was okay ultimately, of course,' he said, but she knew that he must have been talking about money in the millions, not thousands. The pressure and the stress must have been...*had been* considerable.

'Why didn't you say?'

'Because it was *my* responsibility,' he said, bumping the flat edge of his fist against his chest. 'It had been my choice, my decision to invest in such a risky proposition, and for me to fix.'

'But as your wife, I wanted to share that burden.'

'No. As your husband, I wanted to protect you from such things.'

She tried to stop herself from growling. 'And *that* is

why I felt alone in this marriage. Because you didn't include me. You didn't share things with me—and you
were so focused on money and the future that you forgot
me and the present.'

'No! Everything was for you, Emily, don't you see
that? I didn't forget you ever.'

'No? What about Francesca's party? What about leaving me on a private plane on the runway for three hours?'

Javier looked at her, his face a mask of confusion. 'I
don't... I—'

Emily huffed out a bitter laugh. 'You didn't remember
then. I don't know why I'd think you'd remember now.'

'What are you talking about?'

'I'm talking about the night you bought me the se-
quin dress.'

Javier clenched his teeth, pressing down against a familiar wave of anger. He remembered that night *very*
well. It was the night Santi had told him how much the
revenue forecast was for the film. It had been beyond
their wildest imaginations. The premiere was three days
away and he'd bought Emily a dress of shimmering mid-
night. He wanted her at his side on the red carpet, so
that he could show her it had all been worth it. So that
he could show her his success. He'd got home later than
he'd planned because he'd arranged for the department
store to stay open so he could pick it up for her.

'But what does Francesca have to do with that?'

His wife looked at him with such hurt that an icy sweat
frosted his neck.

'The night you bought me that dress was the night you
had agreed to come with me to Francesca's party. The
night we were supposed to fly back to England. The night
I waited. And waited.' Javier's fists clenched as Emily's
words became thick and her eyes shone unnaturally with

unshed tears. 'I waited for three hours. And when you came home that night, barely minutes after I did, you gave me that dress and invited me to an event *you* wanted me to come to. Something that was important to *you*.'

She shook her head at him, sending a waterfall of golden hair shimmering in the late afternoon light, downplaying a hurt that he felt as his own, her pride both powerful and heartbreaking.

He desperately tried to remember it, her asking him to Francesca's party, but he couldn't. He knew that he had been drowning in work at that time, but had he made her wait like that?

'Why was the party so important?' he asked, hating that he couldn't remember the straw that had destroyed his marriage.

'Because I wanted my friends to meet you so that they would stop whispering about us and looking at me with pity as if I'd made a massive mistake.'

Cristo. 'It was *not* a mistake, Emily.'

'No? We were so young, Javi. I was nineteen, you twenty-one. We hadn't known each other more than three months when we married.'

But I'd known you only two minutes when I knew.

The concrete solid answer stayed in his mind though, that child in him still too hurt and fearful that she would leave again, not ready to say it out loud. He rubbed unconsciously at the pressure in his chest, unaware of how the action drew Emily's gaze.

'So instead of coming to the premiere of Santi's film…' He couldn't finish the sentence. He couldn't put it into words without the howling pain of her abandonment leaching from his voice. But Emily was telling him that he'd done the same to her?

'I left. I left, hoping that you would finally notice me.

I didn't care about the money, Javier. I didn't need future security, I cared about us,' she said, as if she'd sensed his attempts to justify his actions.

His senses went on full alert. 'Why are you talking in the past tense, Emily?'

'Because nothing has changed. You are still making decisions based on what you want. Not us. Not me. I can't live my life as if it is all about you,' she said, the jagged hitch in her breath so telling of how difficult this conversation was for her.

Ache. That was all he felt in that moment. Radiating out from his chest, everything hurt and from somewhere deep within a panic like nothing he'd ever experienced before was telling him to grab her now before she left him again. Because if she left now, he knew, *knew,* she would never come back. His pulse raged at his temples, blood pounding his heart in a frantic drumbeat.

How had he got things so wrong? How was he here?

He would fix this. He had to. He wouldn't, *couldn't,* fail this time.

'I should go,' Emily said, pushing the chair back from the table.

'Two weeks.' The words burst out into the open. 'Give me two weeks.'

'Javier…' His name on her lips was a perverted plea, the sound so wrong, but he wouldn't bow to it.

'You owe me that much,' he said, his voice hardened.

'And then what? After two weeks, what? You'll let me go then?'

'If that is what you want.' He forced the words from his lips, knowing that it was no risk. Javier Casas never made a deal he didn't know he could win. He might have underestimated Emily, but he knew his wife, he knew what she liked, what she wanted. All he had to do was give her those things and she'd be back by his side. He would have fixed it. He wouldn't have failed. The panic began to recede as he clawed back control.

'You'll give me a divorce?'

No. 'If that is what you want,' he replied again, his hands forming fists beneath the table. *It wouldn't come to that.* He would make sure of it.

'Then I have a condition.'

He caught his response before it revealed his surprise. 'Go on,' he invited.

'We will not have sex for these two weeks.'

He choked, actually choked, on air. 'No. Emily. Be serious,' he begged.

'I am serious,' she insisted, the blush riding high on her apple-round cheeks.

'*Mi corazón*, that is crazy. What is between us is—'

'Distracting, and always has been. If we have any hope of getting to the root of our marriage problems, you can't just sex me into forgiving you.'

'Sex you into… Emily—'

'No!' She put up her hand, firm and decisive. 'You do this, Javi. You come in all handsome and determined and…' she shook her hand up at him '…and *that* and you distract me from being mad at you.'

'Emily, if it's that easy to make you *not* mad at me, maybe you weren't that mad at me in the first place?'

'That is not a reasonable argument, Javier!'

He shrugged, really not quite sure that it wasn't. And although Emily had just made it that much harder to get his wife back, she had apparently forgotten that he was most definitely a worthy opponent.

'Define sex.'

'Excuse me?' Emily squeaked, her eyes wide with shock.

He shrugged again, enjoying unsettling his wife a little too much.

'Define sex,' he repeated slowly.

'Well, you know…'

There was absolutely no way in hell he was helping her out of this one. If she wanted to make such a ridiculous stipulation to their agreement, then she was going to have to define her terms. And if it left him any leeway at all, any, he planned to make full use of it.

'Intercourse,' she finally said, the word erupting from her mouth as if she'd held her breath around it.

'Agreed,' he replied swiftly before she realised how much room to manoeuvre she'd allowed him, 'but I have a condition of my own.' Her eyes narrowed, expecting him to be up to something. Good. She would need her wits about her. 'You will share my bed.'

'But we're not having sex.'

'No,' he agreed, wondering why she thought that the two were mutually exclusive. Yes, he'd always made love to his wife every chance he got, but… He clenched his jaw against the shockingly soft turn of his heart when he remembered what it had been like to wake up with her head on his arm, the curve of her body fitting so perfectly against his, the scent of her hair on the pillow. And now he was wondering whether he should take it back.

'You want to share a bed with me even though I will not sleep with you?'

He nodded, not quite trusting himself to speak or what else he might end up saying.

'Okay,' she agreed hesitantly, gingerly stretching out her hand for him to shake.

He nearly laughed, feeling almost guilty for something that would be so easy for him to achieve. He took her small palm into his hand, ignoring the warning sizzle and heat and spark.

'It is a deal, *mi reina*.'

Javier got up from the table, startling her.

'Where are you going?' Emily asked, somewhat dazed by the events of the past hour.

'I'm going to move your things.'

She opened her mouth to argue but nothing came out. She had—undeniably—agreed to share his bed, just as he had agreed—undeniably—not to sleep with her. And only now was she realising the torment she had just consigned herself to. She dropped her forehead to the table the moment he left the room.

What on earth had she done?

She was about to call him back, call it all off, call Francesca to arrange for someone to come get her, when she heard a distinctly feline cry and a uniquely male tirade of curses. Racing upstairs, Diabla speeding the opposite way in a streak, Emily rounded the corner to the master suite and gasped.

And then she laughed. She laughed so hard she started to cry, beautiful big joyful tears rolling down her cheeks.

'Oh, my…' she managed through her hysterics, bending double at the waist to try to relieve the pressure on her stomach muscles.

Javier turned, holding up what had once been one of his most expensive shirts, but was now barely strips of material. Fluff and feathers danced in the air from the absolute destruction that was the master suite. The look on his face was a picture! Miserably, Javier picked through the mess on the floor to retrieve a pair of his favourite trousers, setting Emily off on another round of impossible to stop giggles.

He turned back to her and stared as if she'd lost her mind. 'You can laugh, *cariño*, but have you seen what she did to your curtains?'

And then she stopped laughing.

CHAPTER SEVEN

EMILY SHIFTED HER LEGS, the satiny glide of the fresh sheets she'd put on the bed late last night decadent and delicious. Warmth and comfort surrounded her and she buried herself deeper into the plush bedding. The scent of sandalwood, mint and something peppery coiled a tempting tension in her sex, low and incessant. She inhaled dreamily and then screamed when Javier shifted beside her.

'I am right here, you know. If you wanted—'

She turned and slapped him on the arm. 'You scared me!' she accused.

'I was not hiding, *mi vida*.' Javier laughed, throwing back the sheets and getting out of bed.

The sight of his nakedness made her gasp, and slam her eyelids closed as quickly as possible.

'Emily,' he chided. 'It is nothing you have not seen before.'

'Yes, but that was different.' She felt the bed dip beneath his weight, as if he were kneeling beside her.

'Mrs Casas.'

He was waiting for her to look at him—because that was her husband. He commanded, demanded, complete attention. Gingerly, she prised one eyelid open to find him but millimetres away from her. The hypnotic depths of his brown eyes, fathomless and rich enough to drown in, seduced her sleep-addled brain and she allowed him to nuzzle her head to the side, to lean into the crook of her neck and inhale deeply from her skin—an unabashed declaration of intent mocking her sleepy sips at his scent from her pillow.

'You made the rules,' he whispered, his breath fanning out against her shoulder. 'The moment you agree to return to my side, we can get rid of this silly embargo and enjoy whole *days* of making love. Believe me, *cariño*, I want nothing more.'

And with that proclamation he was gone, leaving her in a melting puddle of desire and aching frustration in the bed they now shared.

Emily was not a fool and she wasn't used to lying to herself. Of course she wanted to sleep with her husband. The man was sculpted marble come to life in hot flesh. In six years, he had only become that much bigger and stronger. Javier had always been proud of his physique, relishing the power and strength he honed through disciplined workouts and hours at the gym—it was an energy he'd needed to expel she'd realised quite early on. Not that she'd once complained because he was simply mouth-watering. The breadth of his shoulders, biceps she didn't have a hope of circling even with both hands, the ripple of abdominal muscles that concertinaed when he laughed, or when he… She stifled that thought with a yank so severe she slammed her eyes shut. Even then, she could see the whorls of dark hair across his chest, remembered the way she had stroked and teased both herself and him as she tripped downward to the powerful jut of his erection.

Emily rubbed her thighs together, unable to prevent the pulse of need flaring at her core. Behind lidded eyes, she saw him in her mind, staring at her in *that* way, his lips a perpetual pout as if daring her to find fault in anything about him—and the infuriating fact that she couldn't. That challenge, it was a drug, a lure, a trap.

Because her husband was not above using sex to get what he wanted. And Javier Casas was simply a man who did not lose. But this was one game Emily couldn't afford to take lightly. She had meant what she said the day before. Nothing had changed. Javier was still a man who, purposely or not, put his needs and desires first. Not for nefarious purposes, not for greed or ill will but almost out of sheer stubbornness. It was strange that she hadn't really seen that before. Did it help that it was a thoughtless kind of selfishness or did it make it worse? Maybe if she understood a little more why… The thought made her feel embarrassed that she didn't know her husband as well as she'd thought she had. Was it possible to fall in love with someone before you knew them? They'd been in such a rush to marry, so full of passion and urgency and youthful confidence.

'I meant my vows.'

As had she, her inner voice insisted, feeling the truth of it sinking in. And being here, in their home in Frigiliana, she remembered. She remembered all the reasons she *did* love him. The power and care, the way he'd made her laugh, the way he had drawn an inhibited girl from London into a world of passion and colour and brightness and even the early stirrings of her own power. They *had* shared that. And she would never lie. Could not lie about this. She *did* love him.

But it hadn't been enough. Because she simply couldn't be like her mother. Couldn't and wouldn't lose herself to a man so much that she forgot her own child as much as she forgot herself. And that was why Emily pulled herself together and was gone by the time Javier emerged from the bathroom.

Emily was at the table when Javier came to a halt in the kitchen doorway. Diabla was peering at him from where she wove herself between Emily's calves. He glared at the beast that had done untold damage to his wardrobe and—the gall of the animal—she glared back before darting away the moment he crossed the threshold.

He bit back the low growl in his throat, realising that he might have to put more effort into winning over Diabla than his wife. With that in mind, he placed the bottle of sunscreen on the table next to Emily's breakfast plate as he pulled out his phone to order something online that might help him with the cat.

'What is this?' Emily asked, picking up the bottle.

'It's sunscreen.'

'Clearly.'

'You need to put some on. We'll be leaving in—'

A single raised eyebrow stopped him in his tracks and he stifled a much deeper growl this time. *Include her.* She wanted to be part of this with him. He had listened last night. He had heard what she'd said and it had cut him deep to know that he had made his wife feel so alone. He knew that feeling and never would wish it on anyone. But the rawness of that realisation, the realness of it was too much too soon. So he forced levity into his tone to hide the acid beginning to erode the rust on doors better left closed.

'Darling, I would love it if you would put on some sunscreen,' he said, pitching his tone at an alarming tooth-rotting level. 'I have somewhere that I'd like to take you and we would be leaving in about ten minutes—if that is something you would like?'

'I believe there was even a question in there, husband. I *am* impressed,' Emily responded, a light tease in her eyes, but also…a spark. A flash of joy that he had forgotten—one that lit something deep within him. Satisfaction. Peace. A joy of his own.

'Where are we going?' she asked.

'Somewhere I should have taken you a long time ago,' he admitted in a rare burst of truth.

Javier loved driving. Even the shock of the accident hadn't worn that away. The first ten minutes, settling into the car and the drive had taken a lot more of his concentration than usual. But when Emily had slipped her fingers around the death grip he had on the gear stick he had allowed himself to relax into the winding curves that would take them out and away from Frigiliana towards their destination.

With the top down on the matte grey convertible, the morning sun streamed down on them. Emily lost the battle to tame the strands of her hair and sank into the passenger seat, unable to hide her excited smile.

Shifting gears up and down to navigate the twists and turns, there was a happy silence between them, neither choosing to shout above the roar of the wind and the engine. And he wondered how long it had been since he had simply let things go. Thoughts of work, the endless turnover of meetings and emails, managing his mother from as far away as possible. The thought turned in his mind. This was the longest time Renata had been quiet. Usually by now she would have been after him for money to help prop up the business she seemed determined to drive headlong into the ground.

He felt Emily's fingers brush against his again, and forced himself to let go of the tension that had built shockingly fast. In the last few years his mother had been affecting him more and more. Whether it was because she was asking for more or whether over the years the weight of her had accumulated to become heavier and heavier, he didn't know. He pasted a smile on his face as he turned to Emily, just as she saw the turnoff sign for their destination.

She leaned up in the seat and turned to stare at him. 'Really?' she asked and suddenly he felt awful. Awful that she was so pleased by such a small thing.

'Really,' he insisted, promising silently to never make her wait for anything she desired ever again.

As they turned the corner, a pounding joy thumped in her chest. Emily had wanted to visit the Alhambra since she'd first come to Spain, yet somehow in the whirlwind of her romance with Javier it had never happened. But as they pulled into an empty car park Emily's heart dropped. She tried to tell herself not to be disappointed but, from the absolute quietness, it didn't look as if it would happen today. Notorious for mile-long queues and renowned for only high, very high, or extreme periods of activity, the empty car park was clearly a sign of closure.

'What is wrong?' Javier asked, seemingly unaware of the situation.

'Is it a bank holiday today?'

'No.' He frowned, confused. 'Why?'

Emily shrugged. 'It's a shame to have come all this way and for it to be closed.'

'It's not closed,' he replied easily as he got out of the car, came round and opened her door for her.

'Javier, there's no one here.'

He looked at her as if she were being obtuse. '*You* are here.'

Javier led them away from the large stone arch that formed the main entrance before she could read the signs placed across the door and towards a small man in a uniform. A regal bow greeted them and the staff member beckoned them through a side door.

Javier begged just a minute from her and disappeared with the older man, while Emily turned in a circle in the dusty courtyard that was surrounded by such incredible beauty. The Alhambra had been a military fortress and a royal palace, displaying both Islamic architecture and that of the Spanish Renaissance. The different styles juxtaposed should have created chaos, but instead it was a work of art.

She bathed in the warm earthy glow of the walls that had inspired the name of the sprawling building, The Red One. Perched up high on the hill, the exterior of the walled palaces appeared no less regal for its martial purpose. But it was the interior of the Nasrid Palaces that drew her—the intricate tiling, mosaics, carved wood and, her favourite, the mirador—arcaded porticos that brought the stunning view outside *in*. Here, the city of Granada, or the world-renowned gardens, appeared as if they were a piece of artwork displayed in the room.

She felt her creative well being filled with each breath and each new sight—creeping into her soul and feeding her heart. To be here—alone...it was as incredible as it was inconceivable. That Javier had done this—that he'd *remembered*...

'Well?' he asked, the crunch of his shoes on the gravel behind her alerting her to his presence long before his words. Beside him a young woman held a tray with flutes of champagne, glasses of what looked like fresh lemonade and small plates of tapas, exquisite enough to make her salivate.

She shared a delighted look with Javier and took a glass of lemonade and a few tapas, trying to swallow around the smile that pulled at her lips as Javier fussed over his choice. Finally satiated, he took a lemonade and, turning away from the staff member, he gestured towards the ancient buildings. 'Where shall we start?'

He had taken his sunglasses off, twirling them loosely in his hand, his head cocked to one side and a look of pure indulgence in his eyes. His white shirt, open at the collar, folded back at the sleeves, only served to highlight the bronze of his skin—already losing the unhealthy grey pallor from the accident. The bruise on his cheek was barely showing and the fall of his dark hair covered the stitches he'd received from the cut on his head. A different kind of excitement warmed her now. Heat in his gaze, an eyebrow raised as if sensing the direction of her thoughts.

'You know, we are completely alone, *cariño*...'

Frowning, she looked behind her to see that the woman had disappeared and she tried and failed—again—to stop the smile from pulling at her lips. 'You're incorrigible.'

'You started it,' he happily threw back, holding out the crook of his arm like a Victorian gentleman.

This. She'd missed it. The teasing, the lightness, the way the fun back and forth made her feel younger, happier, free. The years after she'd left Javier had been dark and heavy and hard. And being the boss of the small team meant that she'd had to make difficult decisions and pull rank occasionally. It hadn't exactly made space for...fun.

She took his arm and looked up at her husband. 'We can go anywhere?'

'Anywhere.'

'And it's just us?'

'Just us.'

She knew exactly where to start. She led Javier towards the Nasrid Palaces that had first caught her attention in school and held it, but even that years-long infatuation couldn't prevent the question that had been waiting impatiently on the tip of her tongue.

'Javi,' she whispered, 'just how rich *are* you?'

He looked at her for a moment, then threw his head back and laughed. Big, loud, joyous laughter that confused but delighted her.

'Very, is the short answer,' he managed with a rueful smile when he had just about recovered.

Emily, no wiser, simply waited and Javier nodded once and looked up over to the Sierra Nevada mountain range in the distance.

'No one expected Santi's film to be such a roaring success. Not even us.'

'If it was such a shot in the dark, why did you do it?'

'Because Santi is my brother,' he said simply. 'Not by blood, no, but we've known each other since we were six years old when we went first went head to head in the playground.'

'Who won?' she asked, entranced by the image of the two powerful, handsome men she knew as children.

'*Cariño*, you have to ask?' Javier scolded.

'Santi then,' she concluded in a tease.

He smiled begrudgingly before the smile dimmed a little. 'It was a huge gamble though. *Huge*,' he repeated as if he was still shocked by it even now. 'But it wasn't just because Santi had asked,' he admitted. 'I needed something that wasn't from Gael, or Renata. Something that couldn't be taken away on a whim. I needed to *succeed*.'

And for the first time in six years Emily felt the stirring of understanding deep within her. No, back then she wouldn't have understood. But now that she had her own business, poured blood, sweat and tears into it, she knew the sense of self it provided, the confidence, but she was surprised to hear that he'd needed to feel it too.

'And when Santi's film made over one hundred million at the box office...'

Javier opened his hand to the sky and shrugged. 'It was an incredible windfall. I invested again with Santi but also in other things. Over the years, I have lost some money but made an incredible amount more. Now I work with a group of people to try and put as much of that money back into the world as possible, but yes. I still have a lot of money.'

Emily knew Javier well enough to know that it was less about money and more about reaching that private, secret internal goal he'd set for himself. He had always been driven, in every single thing he did. Driven to a point of ruthlessness that bordered on selfishness. The thought turned something in her chest as they made their way towards the heart of the Alhambra.

'It is amazing what you have achieved, Javier. Really,' she said, her palm resting on the bare skin of his forearm sending sparks right to his chest. 'The success you have become is incredible.' His wife's simple words struck him with the full force of a punch that stopped his heart. His mind flatlined at the realisation that no one had ever said that to him. They had celebrated it, desired it, envied it more often than not. But recognising his achievements... Emily looked at him with silver sparks in her blue eyes that were all the more powerful for not being sensual. And then...

'Your mother must be happy,' she said ruefully.

Javier looked away. 'She doesn't know.'

Emily frowned, her steps stalling a little. 'What do you mean?'

'It is better that she doesn't know.'

Renata was a black hole that he could pour money into for the rest of his life and she'd never be satisfied. Whether it was for the business she'd inherited from her father, or for herself, money made Renata's cruelty vicious, the memory of it passing a cold shadow across the warmth of the morning.

But he knew that Emily deserved more of an explanation than that. So there, despite the gentle burn of the morning sun against his skin, he chose to walk into ice.

'She is…' he struggled for words that were honest, despite the familial guilt that nipped at the truth '…dangerously selfish. Oh, she can be gregarious and dramatic to the point of comedy—' he gentled his words with a small smile '—but beneath that is something…much more complex.'

He could see that his oblique descriptions were not enough to clear the confusion in Emily's eyes and suddenly he wanted her to understand, as much as he feared that understanding. He led her to a bench and gestured for her to sit.

'You asked me what food my mother made for me when I was sick as a child. We weren't allowed to be sick,' he said, swallowing the memories. 'It would either interfere with her plans or take the focus from her. We were told we were simply not ill and with such conviction…' He shook his head, marvelling even today how he had tried so hard to believe her. 'On the surface I imagine we looked like a happy family. But her thirst for attention was, *is*, unquenchable. It is worse when she is unmarried.' He clenched his jaw and his neck corded with tension, stifling the emotions that rose to the surface.

'And if we do not give her the attention she craves, she becomes harsh and vicious and unbearably cruel. But if we do, then she is *lavish*. She can pour love and attention on you. Before Gabi was born Renata would pull me out of school and we would go on luxurious holidays to Greek islands and the Caribbean. She would dress me in suits and teach me to dance. How to be a proper man. To bring her gifts and compliment her in just the right way.'

'What about your father?'

'He left before my second birthday, after nearly running Casas Textiles into the ground. Over the years, every time I made a mistake, or got something wrong, she told me I was just like him. A failure. For my entire childhood, I walked on the edge of making a mistake.' He was surprised when Emily uncurled the hand that had unconsciously formed a fist and slipped her fingers through his. She swept his hair back and cupped the side of his face. He captured her hand before it could do any more damage to his already weak defences.

'I would cut ties with her if I could…'

'But?'

Javier shook his head. 'Gabi. I cannot leave her to Renata's whims.' His jaw seemed clenched so tight, Emily was almost surprised when he spoke again. 'I asked her to come and live with me once. Gabi,' he clarified. The tension in Javier's body told her how hard it was for him to admit this. It was clear that his sister had chosen to stay with Renata—as clear as the emotional toll her decision had taken on Javier. The rejection of it must have been a devastating blow. He shook his head. 'For now the only way I can protect Gabi is by giving Renata the money she asks for, keeping her happy.'

Emily's heart ached for him. She couldn't imagine

feeling constantly held hostage by a parent, never knowing what to expect from the one constant that should be inviolate.

'But I fear that, in doing so, I've allowed her to become a monster.'

Emily shook her head at him. 'Javi,' she chided gently. 'You are her son, not her father or husband. You are not her equal and you are not her keeper,' she said gently. 'Her behaviour is not on you.'

He shook off her words and her reassurance. Emily didn't understand, couldn't. Yes, Renata had been abhorrent, but she was still his mother. She—unlike his father—had at least stayed. A flash of anger was unleashed and spread outwards with shocking intensity and swirled around the Emily who had also left, but he yanked it back with a ferocity that had him snapping his head up.

As if sensing that her words had not been heard, she turned back to look at the entrance to the Nasrid Palaces. 'Perhaps there is still time to do something for Gabi.'

Javier nodded, his jaw aching from keeping too much in.

'And maybe there is also a chance to change the way things are with Renata. Not her, I don't think that will happen,' Emily admitted, 'but perhaps you can change the way that you deal with her. Changing what you give her might mean you change what you get from her.'

His mind caught on her words but he wasn't ready to follow that statement through, so instead he followed her gaze to the sun-touched pinky-red richness of the buildings.

'So, are we talking *billions*? Because if so…'

A bark of laughter erupted unbidden but welcome into

the morning sunshine, lifting the anvil-heavy weight from his chest, making it something more bearable.

Emily tugged him from the bench and began explaining the history of a site he knew well but was happy to hear. Gently, easily, she described how the different influences had come to create what could easily be one of the Wonders of the Modern World.

He followed her as she entered Casa Real Vieja—the Old Royal Palace as opposed to the newer palaces erected during the Christian Spanish period of development. Each of the three palaces—Mexuar, the Comares Palace and the Palace of the Lions—was exquisite, and detailed with such intricacy he was mesmerised. But it was his wife that drew his gaze.

She had drifted away from his hold, eyes wide with awe and emotion as she moved slowly through each and every room. The sense of peace and serenity he felt as they moved on a stream of Emily's desire and curiosity, her surprised gasps of joy at something small but beautiful, the way she tugged at him to see what she saw, the way she shared her enthusiasm and excitement with him… He had missed all this because he had been too stubborn.

No. She had denied them this. She had taken this all away from him when she'd left.

He wrestled with the voice that sounded far too much like his mother, and far too much like the child who had been deserted by his father, lashing out in the face of such devastating abandonment. So he stifled it, thrusting it down, ignoring the hurt that the memories of his childhood had evoked, desperate not to be that lost, lonely boy again. His head began to hurt as his mind and soul veered between what had happened in the past and what he wanted from the future.

At that moment, Emily drifted towards an open archway that looked out at the incredible vista beyond. The interior of the chamber, shrouded in darkness with only natural light pouring through intricately detailed carving, made it appear as if the sun itself reached for her. The outline of her figure, the calf-length skirt nipped in at the waist a V-neck blouse was tucked into, and the way she had tucked her foot behind the ankle of her other leg hit him with such a strange blow—one of *jamais vu*.

He had seen her stand like that a thousand times, but this was the first that felt unfamiliar and out of reach. A cold sweat broke out across the back of his neck and a panicked pulse fluttered in his veins. The strange sense morphed into a certainty. As if he knew that this was his last chance to get it right or lose her for ever.

CHAPTER EIGHT

NEARLY A WEEK had gone by since they had visited the Alhambra, and Emily was both exhausted and inspired. Javier had taken her across Spain to visit some of the most incredible places, museums, galleries; anywhere she had ever mentioned a desire to visit, they had gone.

During the day they would feast upon Gaudí and Rothko, Jorge Oteiza and Eduardo Chillida, visiting the Guggenheim Bilbao and exhibitions at the Centre Pompidou Málaga, while in the evenings they would discover a world of culinary delights from Michelin starred restaurants to side-street vendors, delectable tapas to seven-course wine-tasting menus.

It was glorious, truly, and Emily could already feel the inspiration scratching at her, waiting to come out. So she had snatched the few hours Javier would allow himself to recuperate—his energy still startlingly low from the accident—to throw herself into her work as much as possible. Her team were doing wonderfully, and the energy and inspiration she felt at being here, seeing what she was seeing, allowed her to focus her creativity to the point where she was producing some of the best work she had done in the last few years.

The team missed her, but they were happy and busy. *She* was happy and busy…but it couldn't stop her mind circling back to what Javier had said when he'd opened up to her about his mother. He had shown her a childhood of hurt and neglect, with sporadic freedom in school or when his mother was occupied with a distraction. But, combining his descriptions with her own experience of Renata Casas and Emily had realised that the level of narcissism she portrayed was not a characteristic, but a very real trait. The kind of damage a person with such a brutally selfish world view could do to those around them, let alone a child...

As shocking as it had been, it had provided a real insight into him, allowing her to form an understanding of him that she'd never had before. She could see how he must have had to cling so incredibly tight onto his needs, his desires, to not lose them in the face of his mother's forceful personality. How hard he must have had to work to ensure that his wants were not obliterated by her demands. Perhaps so hard that he still clung to his needs with a strength that was too much sometimes. That understanding of him made her feel close to him...just as he seemed to be pulling away again. Since that day he'd kept her too busy to think, let alone ask any further questions. Questions that, she forced herself to admit, she was afraid to ask.

'What about your father?'

'He left...'

The two words had struck hard, leaving a shadow word ringing in her ear. *Abandoned.* Like, she was sure, Javier had felt when Gabi chose to stay with his mother. And exactly like he must have felt when she had left him six years ago. Guilt twisted her stomach into knots. But she had done so not knowing the whole story at the time. So no, Emily wouldn't blame herself for the decisions she'd made then.

But she *could* take responsibility for the decisions she made about the man she encountered now. He was as alluring, if not more so, than he had ever been. And, despite the caution she felt, she was swept up by her husband all over again. It was the little things that got to her. Three days ago, she had come down into the living room to find him reading a book. When she'd asked what it was, he'd tilted the cover for her to see—*Bald but Beautiful: Everything you need to know about Sphynx Cats*—tersely informing her that he was 'getting to know' his enemy. That his supposed enemy had started to follow him round the house was not something she felt like pointing out. Of course, it had nothing to do with the little trail of treats he would leave for Diabla even as he gently ignored her. Though it was less ignoring and more like gentling her in to his presence. Even if they visited the other side of Spain, Javier would make sure they returned that evening, no matter the time, because *he preferred their bed*. But she knew it was because he didn't like leaving Diabla alone for that long.

Yet, despite all his outward charm and attention, there was a sense of tension in Javier that Emily couldn't quite put her finger on. It was as raw and powerful and deeper than any tension she'd felt between them before. It was an undercurrent that both drew her and scared her, not physically but emotionally, and Emily was beginning to realise that with Javier that was perhaps the more dangerous of the two.

She knew she had been right to put that barrier between them—if she slept with Javier, if she made love with her husband, she feared she would be irrevocably lost. And he'd kept his word and not tried to sleep with her. But that didn't prevent the magnetic draw she felt to him, it didn't stop her from reacting when his hand lay upon her hip in the morning, gently tugging her back into the aroused warm body that thrummed with the same need, the same desires that whispered beneath her skin. It didn't help her heart and the way it jerked and pulsed and stopped and tripped when he emerged from the shower with a towel around his waist, or when he looked at her as if she were the only person in the entire world and he was just fine with that. Just a hint of that sandalwood scent, crushed mint and peppercorn, and her body softened, her defences melted just that little bit more.

And on a night like this, when he had covered the patio in tea lights, set champagne in an ice bucket, lit incense so that its heady scented smoke uncurled exotic thoughts and gentle music played from inbuilt speakers he was even harder to resist.

'You are trying to seduce me,' she accused as he came out onto the patio, Diabla weaving through his legs, both with such feline grace that neither tripped. If he was aware of just how much he'd won over the little she-devil, he showed no sign of it. Emily hid her smile in the turn of her head towards the champagne.

'But of course. What kind of husband would I be not to do so?' he asked, the charm present, but not quite able to mask that tense bass note in his voice.

'Is everything okay?' Emily asked, trying to ignore that feeling of once again being shut out by her husband.

'Of course, *mi reina*.'

He was lying again. He knew it. He was pretty sure she knew it too. But this feeling…he hadn't been able to shake it since the Alhambra. And it was *horrible*. A strange, angry frustration that he couldn't release. It was branded in his soul—and God knew Javier wasn't one for the dramatic, but that was the only way he could describe it.

She joined him at the patio's balcony and he hated that she could read him so easily, but also not at all. She reached up her hand to cup his cheek, her eyes asking to be let in, but his heart was bruised enough to deny her entry.

He turned his face to her palm, laying a kiss in the centre and reaching up to her wrist to feel the flicker of her pulse against the pad of his thumb. *Cristo*, she came alive beneath his touch. It was a temptation too far. His inner voice called him a coward but his stubborn nature ignored it bluntly and willingly hurling him into a course of action that would delight them both. He had agreed to her terms and, gentleman that he was, he would not break them. But that didn't mean she hadn't left him a leeway that he was determined to make absolute and full use of.

He swept his tongue out across the pulse point and felt the ripple of goosebumps across the skin of her forearm. Her fingers curled reflexively and the whisper of pleasure that fell from her lips was only encouragement.

'Javier,' she warned half-heartedly, 'we have a deal.'

'We do,' he agreed, even as his own arousal hardened to the point of near pain.

'We shouldn't be doing this,' she said, even as her body angled towards his like a flower seeking the sun.

He pulled back just enough to look into his wife's eyes, to see, read and know her desires, those on the surface and those much deeper. And the complexity of the layers in those depths, not just need, want and arousal, but warmth, comfort and connection and the yearning for more was what sent him deeper into this madness.

'Intercourse.'

'What?' The word was a choked laugh from his wife as he bent his head to place more and more kisses along her bare arm, closing the distance between them.

'You defined sex as intercourse. It was—may I say—rather unimaginative of you, Emily,' he teased gently, reluctantly pulling back to look at her. 'But I am not such a monster that I will take control from you—unless you will it of course.'

Stormy eyes sparked white heat at his words, and what had started out as pure distraction became an irrefutable need.

'One word from you will stop me,' he said, pulling her against him, the heat of her body raising the essence of her, jasmine and orange, filling his senses and driving him wild with torment.

'Stop me, Emily,' he all but begged, knowing that this would break the last thread of his control. He pressed his forehead against hers. She knew he was distracting her. He could read the accusation in her eyes as if she had said it out loud. But desire and desperation kept her silent long enough for him to press an open mouth kiss just above her collarbone and suck so that she melted in his arms enough for him to sweep her off her feet.

He carried her over to the chair, knowing that if they went inside, the deal, his honour and her clothes would be in tatters on the floor within seconds. He arranged her in his lap, her thighs naturally falling either side of his, and he gloried in having her above him. Her hair hung down in curtains, shielding them from the rest of the world—a glorious place where touch was erotic and thoughts were of nothing other than sin.

He drew her down against his erection, the delectable friction delighting them both as moans of need tangled in their tongues as they kissed. He promised her silently that he would keep to her deal—too much hung in the balance to not. But that didn't mean that he would let her go this night without punishing her in the most delicious of ways.

She hadn't helped matters, of course. The deceptively simple dress she was wearing had been designed with his torture in mind. The thin straps holding up the simple satin dress allowed the V at her neck to display the palm-sized flat between Emily's breasts in an invitation he couldn't refuse. He placed his hand there, against her sternum, even as his other hand slipped between the thigh-high cut in the satiny material, reaching behind her to pull her even closer, harder, deeper in a way that could never be enough to satiate his hunger for her.

He gripped and pressed, so that Emily would never know how much his hands shook with the intensity of his need for her. For this. Sheltered in the curtains of her hair, it didn't matter that he was blind with lust, he didn't need his eyes to feel, to touch, to taste.

His lips found hers with unerring accuracy and *devoured* in a roar of passion. His tongue thrust deeply into her open-mouthed acceptance. Positioned above him should have placed him at a disadvantage but he continued to possess, consume, *own* her mouth in the most exploitative of ways. And she let him. She simply opened herself to him as he sought to hide himself in her.

And that thought alone had him stopping. He shouldn't be doing this. No matter how much he wanted to, this was exactly why she had made the deal in the first place. Because he did this, used sex to distract her. And it was a line he didn't want to cross. He shifted his hands to her upper arms, trying to hold her in place when she would so willingly have closed the distance between them.

'Emily,' he said gently, trying to stop it before they lost themselves completely.

Emily shook her head. She knew that he was trying to stop this, but she didn't want him to. They were skating so close to the edge of the deal they'd made, and she knew it was madness to do so, but she was unsettled by the tension that had worked its way from Javier into her. Emily was as angry at him as he seemed angry at her, both too fearful of speaking a truth that would or could change everything.

So, instead, she was choosing this. Choosing to burn away her frustration in the most incendiary of ways. Choosing him and knowing that while it was cowardly it was also exactly what she needed. She kissed her name from his lips, teasing open his mouth and taking full advantage when he succumbed. The groan building in the back of his throat vibrated through her body until it flared deep within her, beckoning her thighs to open just that bit more, to press against him just that bit more, to demand from him *just that bit more*.

His head fell back in a surrender she knew better than to trust. But the cords of his exposed neck were too irresistible to her. She kissed and gloried in the taste of him, salt, spice and sweet, nipping at the muscles and shuddering at the little sharp points of stubble that had grown during the day—delighting in the scratch of it against her soft skin.

His fingers flexed around her biceps, neither pulling nor pushing, but the restraint was enough, the boundary—like the confines of their deal—something she wanted to push against, to test the limit of, to know his, to understand her own.

She pushed forward, letting him keep the steel bands

of his hands at her arms, returning her lips to his, laving the lush fullness of his mouth with her tongue, tormenting him with little kisses and teasing their arousal into something fierce.

Her hand went to his shoulder, fisting his shirt and grazing the muscles and skin beneath with her nails. In response his hand fisted the flesh of her backside, and a gasp of pure pleasure poured from her mouth to his. His inhalation was swift and deep, as if he were desperate to consume even her very breath, as if it were the most of her that he'd allow himself.

The thought had her almost cry out in protest, in denial. 'I want this,' she whispered desperately against his lips. 'I asked you before and that time I ran away,' she confessed, breathless and eyes closed. 'I'm asking again, and I beg you, please. Please don't stop this. Not this time. Not now.'

She knew it was selfish. She knew what she was asking, but the need for him was a madness in her blood. Gingerly she prised open her eyes to find him looking at her solemnly. It was a moment of stillness, the eye of the storm—his gaze searching for answers she didn't know how to give—the power of his focus, she feared, would penetrate to her soul.

'This is what you want?' he asked, his hand rising to sweep back a lock of hair that had fallen forward between them.

She folded her top lip beneath her teeth and bit down, nodding. *So much.* She wanted it so damn much she dared not speak it.

'Me rindo,' he whispered. *I surrender.* And he was looking at her as if there was no one else in the world.

His words lifted the leash holding Emily back and she claimed his mouth with such possession they would each remember that exact moment for the rest of their lives. Hands fisted in satin and cotton, tongues teased and tasted, lips parted and pressed, sighs and growls merged as they gave and took more of each other than ever before.

Javier held her in his arms as he rose, his display of strength enthralling, and while she might seem at his mercy, she knew he was utterly at hers. He guided her down onto the cloth-covered table, gently laying her across the surface like a dying man's last meal. Emily lifted her knees, rested her feet flat onto the table and watched her husband devour her with his eyes.

'*Tu eres mi reina,*' he vowed, his determined words fanning the flames between them.

She translated the Spanish in her mind and heart. She was his queen.

His hands pressed against the satin of her dress at her calves, sweeping easily upwards as he reached her knees and parted her thighs. Her sex pulsed with desperate longing, and nothing could appease it but him. He made space for himself between her legs, bringing the hem of her dress further and further upwards, sweeping circles with his fingers through the material in a silken caress, the whisper-soft touch delicately arousing with devastating effect.

He tormented her with his gaze, showing her in his eyes exactly what he wanted to do to her, warning her, building her anticipation, his silence more effective than any words ever could have been, in there a question— a warning. A line about to be crossed and, heaven help her, she consented with a desperate nod.

Bending, he pressed a kiss to her knee, smoothing the satin aside so that lips touched flesh, tongue tasted skin, fingers gripped and held. Her eyes drifted closed and she lost herself to Javier and the sensations he was raining down on her. His kisses drew closer and closer to the juncture of her thighs, the sensual anticipation sharp and tangy in her throat and fluttering in her chest. The sound of her breath panting from her lips, the gentle growl of delight from Javier as he pressed her thighs wider, only for her knees to fall aside and her hips to lift ever so slightly... It should have been embarrassing, it should have made her feel exposed and self-conscious but, in reality, it made her feel glorious. *Sensual.* An ownership over her own desires she had never let herself feel before.

Incomprehensible words fell from Javier's lips, but she didn't need to translate them. She felt it too. There was something about this moment that surpassed any other they'd shared before. As if the truth, the deal... these past few days had stripped away layers to expose a raw honesty that they had been too young to face all those years ago.

And then he kissed her through the satin strip of her panties, his hot wet tongue finding hot wet heat and all thought burned in a pyre of passion.

For a man who was not particularly religious, Javier had never before called to God so many times in such a short space of time. But, honestly, this moment was being burned into his soul and he felt every second of it. His tongue laved her through her underwear as her thighs quivered against the table, his palm on her abdomen, not just holding her in place but savouring every twist and turn of her body, relishing the way that pleasure rippled through his wife with pride and delight.

But it wasn't enough. Sweeping the material aside, Javier pressed an open mouth kiss to the flesh beneath the blonde cross-hatch of curls. Emily nearly came off the table and he couldn't help but smile—she had always been passionate and expressive but there was something different tonight. Unable to help himself, he teased her clitoris with his tongue, pressing against it firm and hard, relishing the answering pressure Emily provided, before little licks had her writhing beneath him.

Her arousal was like a fist around his erection—an exquisite torment. One that would not see release this night. Instead, he focused the entirety of his considerable attention on bringing her to orgasm. His thumb pressed gently at her entrance was the only warning he gave before he thrust his fingers into her at the same time as he drew his tongue against her clitoris.

Emily came up off the table with a cry. His name on her lips made him ache, but the one thing he would not do that night was break their deal. He had never wanted anything or anyone as badly as he did his wife, but he knew what was at stake and he couldn't, wouldn't, risk it.

Instead, he filled her with as much passion as he could, finding that place deep within her that brought Emily more pleasure than she could contain. He teased her, pressing her towards the brink of orgasm again and again until her pleas and sobs were indelibly imprinted on his tongue. And just as she promised that she couldn't take any more, he thrust his fingers deep and hard at the same moment as he nipped at her clitoris and Emily came apart on his tongue, pulsing around his fingers and sinking into a bliss he had been honoured to give her.

Wrecked. He had wrecked them both. Shaking off his stolen languor, he gathered her into his arms and, ignoring the pull at his damaged ribs and surrounding muscles, he took her to their bed, careful of Diabla weaving around his feet. Emily attempted a sleepy protest but he removed the simple satin dress and pulled the cover over her, not even telling Diabla off when she jumped onto the bed and made a little nest in the space between Emily's knees and elbows. He didn't know how long he stayed there, just watching his wife like that, but he knew that it was too long.

Emily woke, her body still rippling with gentle pleasure despite being thoroughly satiated. She smiled at the warm bundle that was Diabla, curled up in the small curve of her body. But behind her was nothing but the coolness of the night.

She turned, glancing at the clock to find that it was three in the morning, and a sense of wrongness filled her. It tasted a little like the tension she had felt from Javier since the Alhambra. Emily knew that if she left it, if she pretended it wasn't there, Javier would never explain it, stubborn man that he was. But then, perhaps she was the coward who let him stay like that, she thought as a tendril of sadness unwound from her heart.

Gently—so that she didn't disturb Diabla—she peeled back the covers, found her robe and made her way back downstairs. The house, shrouded in darkness and lit only by moonbeams, took on a different feel. Here in the living room she could see how jarring the changes she had made to their home were. She'd expected to find Javier asleep on a chair but, when she didn't, unease crept across her skin in goosebumps. If it hadn't been for the moon glow on his white shirt, Emily would have missed him sitting out on the patio.

She watched him for longer than she should, trying to find her courage, because instinctively she knew that whatever was said next could be a far more damaging line than the sexual one she had placed between them.

'I meant my vows.'

She had too. But she had also meant what she'd said

about divorce. Because neither of them could continue to live like this. She opened the door to the patio and, on bare feet, made her way over to where Javier sat on the steps that went down to the lower pool level. He didn't move, not even a millimetre, but she knew he was aware of her there. It was the imperceptible change—as if he became even more still.

She opened her mouth to speak but his words cut her off.

'Why didn't you come back?'

CHAPTER NINE

EMILY WAS GLAD that he didn't look at her when he asked. Glad that she couldn't read the expression behind the toneless question. But still her breath shivered from her lungs as she exhaled the hurt and guilt from the question.

This. This was what she had been hiding from for the last six years. She could tell herself that Javier had left her feeling lonely, had thrown himself into his business, but really…that was only half the story. And the lesser half at that.

She took a seat beside him on the step, not touching, but close enough to feel the warmth from his body. Barely hours before, she had felt stripped to raw honesty and she knew that she couldn't, wouldn't, betray him now by lying. They both deserved the truth now.

'Mum met Steven when I was about eleven,' she began, knowing it wasn't where he'd expected her answer to take them. She felt his gaze turn to her, but it was easier to look out into the shadowed gorge beyond. 'Before that, it had just been the two of us but I'd been happy with that. Mum…didn't know who my father was—she'd been seventeen when I was conceived. Angry at parents who stifled and disapproved of her, and looking for love in some very wrong places,' Emily said with a shrug, less embarrassed and more sad for her mother, who had been rejected doubly when she'd told her parents she was pregnant. 'They kicked her out.'

She heard the disdainful 'tut' which—for Javier—was expressive enough and she smiled ruefully.

'But I never felt the loss of it. Mum made everything magical. There were always stories of fairies, and parties and magic and colour. So much colour,' Emily said, remembering a childhood covered in glitter, finger-paints, mud pies and fun. The laughter and love of the years they'd spent—just the two of them—had been so, so precious to her.

'Not that it wasn't hard for her,' Emily said, nodding. 'She worked as much as she could—taking me with her on cleaning jobs until I was old enough for daycare and school. Money was...' she searched for a word that a billionaire like him would understand '...not there,' she settled on. 'But Mum made that work too. Though I saw how stressed she was when she thought I wasn't looking. The way she would bite her nails down to the quick. The way that she would drink hot water sometimes instead of lunch or have porridge for dinner. Things were hard without support from her parents and a kid at seventeen? It hadn't exactly broadened her social life. So, when she met Steven...'

The first thing Emily remembered was her mother's relief. Relief that she could share her burden. And although her mother would be devastated if she knew Emily had felt herself as such, she had. So Emily had promised herself that she'd make an effort with Steven.

'He made Mum happy. She found security with him.'

A security that had been the last thing on Emily's mind the morning of her wedding to Javier. That free-falling, reckless, *dangerous* feeling had been anything but safe. And, deep down, she'd revelled in the difference between her and her mother's wedding. Turning before the memory and the thought could take hold, she went back to what had really been behind her leaving Javier six years ago.

'I really wanted her to be happy,' she said truthfully. 'And I really didn't want to be the spoilt only child, jealous of her mum's new partner.' A tear escaped and rolled slowly down her cheek. Feeling shame and hating that it still hurt, hating the fact that she *had been* jealous.

'Mum changed. Slowly at first. Bit by bit she lost some of the colour she had brought to my childhood. I watched her losing little pieces of who she was to a man who didn't care.' An ache in her chest made the last words almost a whisper.

'It's not that Steven demands it or expects that she puts him first, but in some ways it's worse that he simply lets it happen. He takes and takes and takes and Mum won't stop. She orbits him like a moon around a planet,' Emily explained, her breath hitching in her throat. 'And that's what I feared I was doing with you.'

Emily's words hit Javier like a gut punch and a part of him regretted even asking the question. Earlier that evening he'd been so full of anger and resentment that it had felt like a poison running through his veins. Now, he'd almost welcome that feeling because it would be better than *this*.

'Emily—'

She held up her hand to stop him. 'I… It wasn't your fault, Javier. And I'm not blaming you,' she said quickly enough for him to believe it. 'But I didn't speak Spanish, and I didn't know anyone here. I put my degree on hold to stay here and my world became about you. It became waiting for you to come home, to have weekends with you so that I could talk to you and, even then, I had nothing to share other than what I'd maybe bought for the house or what I'd cooked that day.'

Javier frowned, confused and still defensive enough to sound it. 'I asked if you wanted to apply to college here.'

'You did,' she agreed, 'but I wasn't sure how much I'd get to learn without speaking the language.'

'You could have taken classes.'

'Yes…but you liked me to travel with you when you did business. I was due to start classes locally when we went to Seville for a week.'

'Yes, but—'

'And then the term after, we went to Zaragoza.'

Javier kept his mouth shut before he suggested something else that she refuted. He hadn't realised that he had done that. In fact, he disliked intensely looking back and realising that he hadn't even been aware of it at the time.

'Time just started to slip away from us and more and more you were working and I was left behind. And I thought if I returned to England and you came after me, I'd *know*. I'd know that you saw me. I'd know that it wasn't just me that revolved around you.'

I'd know that you loved me.

He heard the words she never said and, deep within him, he felt something start to shake, to tremble under the hurt and the pain they had both borne in silence.

'Why didn't you come for me?' she asked in a small voice.

He clenched his jaw, his teeth almost cracking under the pressure. 'I couldn't,' he said, ashamed of himself now.

'Why?'

'Because,' he said, the truth gravel in his throat, 'I had failed you,' he admitted finally and the anchor tying him to guilt and anger and grief loosened a little. 'All those years of desperately trying to succeed and when it came to the most important thing in my life—*you*—I had failed. And I couldn't face the possibility of seeing that when you looked at me,' he said, closing his eyes against the wave of pain as the soul-deep truth came out. 'So I didn't. Because if I didn't see it, if I didn't come and find you, then it hadn't happened. I hadn't failed you and you hadn't left me.'

He felt her hand cup his jaw and gently turn him to face her. She waited for him to open his eyes and, when he did, he saw the same complexity of understanding, guilt, forgiveness and hurt that gripped his heart in a vice. In the silence Emily placed her head on his shoulder and they stayed that way until dawn crested the gorge, burning away the darkness and pouring gold across blue, neither moving until Diabla howled at them for denying her breakfast.

Three hours later, after feeding Diabla and falling into bed, exhausted and sleep-deprived, there was adrenaline-inducing pounding on the door. Javier cursed viciously as Emily sprang up from the bed, worried that whoever it was would smash down the door. Still groggy from the emotional revelations the night before, it took a moment for Emily to collect her thoughts.

She looked across at Javier, who had thrown off the sheet and stalked from the room in a pair of black cotton trousers, trying to ignore the heat she felt from watching the way the muscles across his back shifted as he rolled his shoulders as if readying for a fight.

Bang, bang, bang, bang, bang...

The sound shot out like bullets, startling her all over again.

Javier yelled at the door and a shout came back, quick and hot, Emily just about catching, *'Abrete, bastardo,'* before Javier fired back something that would make the devil blush.

Emily was standing at the top of the stairs by the time Javier pulled the door open to reveal Santiago, hanging from the door frame, a bottle of champagne spilling onto the courtyard floor.

'Cristo, Santi, what time is it?' Javier demanded.

'Time for drinking, *hermano,'* Santi replied, before pushing his way into the house. He came to an abrupt stop when he caught sight of her at the top of the stairs and spread his arms open in welcome. 'Emily! *Mi hermosa!* It is so good to see you! What did this reprobate do to get you back?' Santi demanded.

'He faked amnesia,' Emily replied, unable to contain the smile that pulled at her lips from Santi's shocked outrage. An outrage that was perhaps a little too dramatic, making her think he already knew.

'Cabrón!' he exclaimed, punching Javier not so lightly on the shoulder. 'What is wrong with you?' he demanded in an award-worthy performance.

'Me? It's…' Javier flicked a glance to the watch on his wrist '…ten-thirty in the morning, Santi. What the hell is wrong with you?'

'Nothing, Casas. Absolutely nothing! *I,*' he exclaimed with dramatic flair, 'have been nominated for an ETTA,' he concluded, mock polishing his nails.

Emily gasped out loud, rushing downstairs to congratulate him. The ETTAs were world-renowned industry awards and only the best of the best were nominated. 'Santi, that's fantastic news!' she cried, embracing him warmly and missing the warning glare that Javier shot over her head at his best friend. 'Where is Mariana?'

'She's coming—she just had to stop at the bakery. The woman cannot pass a *churro* at the moment without eating it. Even the smell, I swear, *amigo*, it drives her *loca*.'

As the two men embraced, Emily felt a flutter in her heart as she remembered how distant she had kept herself from the beautiful couple. Mariana was generous and funny, while Santi's charm was infectious, but Emily had always felt awkward that they'd had to resort to English while she struggled with the new language and, just as she was beginning to get to know them better, Santi's work took them to Australia for a year and she had not seen them since. But now she wished that she'd not held herself back from the easy affection Javier's friends had offered.

Santi grandly placed the already open bottle on the table, turned to Javier and pulled him into an embrace.

'*Mi amigo*, I couldn't have done this without you. If you hadn't…' Santi stuttered, overwhelmed with emotion.

Emily watched as Javier shook off the praise, as she connected Santi's words with what Javier had told her since she'd come back to Spain. Javier had clearly invested a lot of money in Santi's first film and more, a risky move for a twenty-one-year-old, especially one who feared failure. But she could see how important it had been for both men, their bond irrefutable.

She heard Mariana shouting at Santi before she appeared at the doorway and smiled as she translated the accusation of Santi's desertion, just so that he could go and get his drinking buddy. She was at the doorway when she exclaimed at Emily's presence in much the same way as her husband had—and Emily found herself in a warm embrace, pressed up against a *very* pregnant belly.

'Oh, my…' Emily said, her eyes wide and her hands on Mariana's shoulders.

'Twins.'

'No!' she exclaimed in shock. 'When are you due?' she asked, fairly concerned that it was within the next hour.

'Not soon enough. It's all his fault,' Mariana groused affectionately. 'We're never having sex again.'

'Seems to be going around,' she heard Javier growl quietly and Emily couldn't help but laugh, a beautiful, loud peal that lightened her heart so much everyone joined in.

'Congratulations,' she said. 'Can I?'

Mariana grabbed her hands and placed them proudly on her round belly. 'Emily, meet Sara Torres,' she said, moving one hand to the left side of her bump, 'and her brother Óscar *Javier* Torres,' who was on the right.

Goosebumps prickled her skin as she took in the meaning of their son's name and she looked up to catch Javier's gaze on her and Mariana's baby bump.

Emily wanted this. With him. She wanted to be pregnant with his child, to feel herself grow round with their child and the love that increased exponentially. She wanted to get things right with their child—all the things that their parents had got wrong. She wanted to soothe hurts and ease mistakes with their love and what they'd learned about themselves…but she wasn't sure if they *had* learned enough. She wanted so much to make this work, to make their marriage work, but all the will in the world wouldn't amount to anything if they couldn't put the past behind them. Javier's eyes flared in understanding—as if he had sensed her thoughts—the connection acute and heartfelt until Santi severed it, demanding to know where the glasses were.

Javier sat back beneath the umbrella's shade, happy to find respite from the fierce afternoon sun. The table was littered with plates and glasses, bottles and corks, and *churro* crumbs from Mariana's side of the table. She and Emily had their heads bent towards each other, chatting away happily in a mixture of Spanish and English that had taken Javier by surprise.

'That sounds amazing,' Mariana gushed.

'Oh, God, no. It was awful. But the client wanted it, so she got it.'

'A green quartz bath worth…how much, again?'

'One million euros.'

Emily was enthusiastic about her business—talking about it, she came to life, her movements and expressions much more fluid and confident. She took pride in her work, in her company and her ability, in a way that he hadn't seen before. And he was suddenly curious. Curious about what her offices looked like, what her apartment was like. And he felt strangely awkward that, aside from the short, uncomfortable visit to her mother and stepfather, they hadn't spent any time together in England. He had been in such a rush to make their home here, in Frigiliana—away from his mother's house in Madrid, or his uncle in Barcelona, that he hadn't realised how difficult and lonely it had been for her. And that when she had wanted to return to England, even just to see a friend, he hadn't been there.

He fisted the cloth napkin in his hand and became aware of Santi's heavy gaze.

'So she found out that you were faking?' he asked, pinning him with an unsurprised look.

'What? You don't think that I came clean?' Javier demanded.

'Absolutely not.'

'Fair,' he admitted grudgingly. 'It has not been my finest moment, but she gave as good as she got.'

Santi raised an eyebrow in question.

'Did you not see the parrot?' Javier demanded.

'I saw the *cat*,' Santi replied. 'And I hope to never again,' he said, shivering and crossing himself.

'Diabla is a Sphynx cat and they are very much mis-understood. They happen to be incredibly affectionate,' Javier defended, unaware even then just how much he'd come to appreciate her.

'If you say so,' appeased Santi somewhat wryly. Javier ignored the bait. 'I am glad to see Emily,' Santi pressed on. 'You are always a bit more balanced around her.'

Javier frowned.

'You are my brother,' Santi swore. 'But I have no idea why you didn't go after her when she left.'

'It doesn't matter. She's back now,' Javier replied.

'Is she? For good?'

Javier didn't know the answer to that question. And for the first time in his life he feared that stubbornness alone wouldn't be enough. Thankfully, Santi let the subject drop and proceeded to tell them about his latest project, making them all laugh about the on-set drama from Hollywood's latest A-list celebrity. Mariana caught his eye a few times, always seeing deeper than the surface, but compassion was there as much as love and Javier knew that she wouldn't probe either him or Emily that day. It was enough to have this moment, the pure celebration of what his one true friend had achieved, he decided as he raised another toast to the film that had made them both.

The sound of his phone ringing cut through the moment, Santi exclaiming at the interruption as if it were a travesty. Javier glanced at the number and had marshalled his features by the time Emily looked across the table.

'My apologies. I have to…' He gestured at the phone and walked with it into the house, missing the shadow that passed across Santi's face and what he mouthed to the question in his wife's gaze.

'Mother,' Javier said, trying to keep his tone level despite the way his pulse lurched.

'Where are you?' she demanded, her tone imperious and shrill. Contrary to what one might assume, Renata didn't drink. There had been no warning signs for him growing up, no empty bottles to find, no trace of drugs to detect. All Javier had was the ability to distinguish the tone of her voice. 'Why are you not here with me?'

The needling would only last so long before it turned bitter and vicious. 'I am recuperating from the accident in Frigiliana,' he replied, hating the way his emotions seesawed, the child in him still wanting desperately to pacify his mother, to give her whatever she needed because, unlike his father, Renata had at least stayed. But he'd been fighting that yoke for years now. Rebellion hadn't worked. Emily and his marriage had also been an attempt to escape that, he could see now. He hadn't fabricated his feelings for his wife, but he had pushed them too far too soon.

'Have you not done enough of that yet? I need you here in Madrid.'

'Ma—'

A curse cut right through his word. 'Don't call me that,' she spat.

Javier took a deep breath. 'I am not coming back any time soon, Renata.'

'Don't talk such nonsense. I have an investment opportunity for us to look at.'

Us being a euphemism for herself. Javier wasn't going to give in this time.

'What about Luis? Can't you speak to him?' Javier

hoped that her husband could bear even just a little of the brunt of whatever was causing this meltdown.

'Luis? Oh, he's gone. Done.'

Javier pinched the bridge of his nose, pressing as hard as he could against the rapidly forming headache.

'What happened?'

'He was stealing,' Renata hissed. 'Draining our accounts. That's why I need you to come back. You need to fix this.'

'No.'

There was deadly silence on the other side of the phone line as he processed that he'd said that out loud, his mind distracted by the fact that this was exactly what she'd accused his father of doing.

'Don't be childish, Javier. I'll expect you tomorrow.'

'No,' he said again, furiously trying to temper his anger as too many things were surfacing. All the times he'd given and given and given and he knew now that it would never be enough.

'How dare you? After everything I have given you. You ungrateful, despicable child. The selfishness! Without me, where would you be? Just like your failure of a father, you'd be on the streets. And you think you can throw all my love back in my face? Let me tell you...'

Santi sighed as he placed the last of the plates in the dishwasher, having helped clear the table after lunch. 'I think it's time for us to be making a move, *cariño*,' he said to his wife.

Emily frowned. 'Oh. You don't have to,' she said, trying to keep the disappointment out of her voice. It had been so lovely sharing the afternoon with them, something she'd missed during her last time here.

Smiling sadly, Santi explained, 'Whenever Renata

calls and it takes more than two minutes it's never a good sign, Emily. She either wants money or to berate him, or both. Usually both. It is unlikely that Javier will come back out. But when you go to him, be kind?' The question struck her heart and Emily was quick to assure him that she would.

She bid them goodbye, with smiles and sincere promises to call Mariana soon, but the afternoon had lost its glow and Emily's chest ached for the man she had threatened to divorce not eight days ago. Suddenly the past didn't matter so much—or at least it *mattered* more in that she had seen a glimpse into the child that Javier hid within him, the one who had been so affected by his mother's behaviour and his father's abandonment, and she knew the way that knife cut deep.

She went into the house to find Javier staring out at the gorge from the windows in the living area, lost in thoughts only he could know. Perhaps in some way they had both been running from something when they'd married—hoping to find a bit of what they had been denied as children. It didn't make their feelings any less valid, but perhaps it could make her more forgiving of how young they had been when they'd made those choices. Perhaps leaving had meant only that they could use that time to become what they needed to be before returning to each other a little older, perhaps a little wiser, and a lot more secure. The thought soothed something in her, eased her path forward, and her decision was suddenly easy and clear.

But before she could speak of her feelings, before she guided them towards a future she wanted so deeply it scared her, she had to give Javier what he needed in this moment. She took his hand in hers, guiding him round to face her, and met him in the half turn. She placed her palm against his cheek and pressed her other hand against his chest, locking her eyes with his.

'Talk to me?'

She could see it—the desire in him to shut down, to close her out, just like he had done all those years before. But she could also see that he fought it, was struggling with the need to open up to her. That he was trying meant a lot to her, but that he won the battle gave her hope.

'I am done with her.'

CHAPTER TEN

FOR A MOMENT Javier wondered if he had conjured Emily from his deepest fantasies. He'd heard Santi and Mariana leave, knew that they would understand. Santi had known him long enough and well enough to know what he was like after one of Renata's episodes.

But he'd usually managed to hide it from Emily. For most of their marriage, Renata had been occupied with husband number three, so it hadn't been as much of a problem until she had left him, citing infidelity, nearly a month before Emily had walked away from Frigiliana without a second glance.

The warmth of Emily's touch anchored him here with her when all he wanted to do was howl and rage and burn.

'I am done with her,' Javier repeated with such vehemence he felt it in his soul. 'She is not a mother. She is not capable of such love. There is a selfishness in her that destroys. And no more. I will give her no more money and no more time.'

No more of me.

There was a fire burning in his words that rent the bonds he felt towards Renata. And while he felt the split down into his soul, Emily's open acceptance, the simplicity of her touch, the innocence of it undid at least some of the damage Renata had caused that day.

'I am sorry.' Her simple words doused the flames his mother had incited.

'It is not your fault,' he dismissed, wanting to hold on to his anger even as Emily's presence soothed, even as her words unravelled his fury.

'I am not taking responsibility. I am offering sympathy and understanding.'

He scrabbled to hold onto the bitterness and the anger, because if he didn't reach for that he would reach for Emily. And even in the grip of madness he knew that the deal he'd made with her was sacrosanct. She was the only good thing he had left and if he lost her...

'You should go,' he told her, trying to turn away from her embrace.

'No.'

'Emily, please. Go. Now,' he commanded, the hold he had on his restraint feather-light and failing.

'I'm not going anywhere,' she said, holding onto him through the storm of feelings that were thick and tangible in the air between them. She rose on her tiptoes and pressed hot, sweet lips to his. 'I don't need any more time, Javi,' she said against his mouth, in between kisses that destroyed him.

Sweetness turned salty and he realised that her tears had slipped between his palm and her cheek. She was crying. For him. And it nearly broke him.

'The deal—' he tried.

'The deal is done. I want to come home,' she begged as she teased his lips open with her tongue. 'Please. Let me come home.'

Shocked, he trembled with the force of his restraint—what she was offering, what he wanted to take, it was almost too much. Her final plea was his undoing and it tore every last shred of his self-control. As if freed from invisible bonds that he'd strained against for far too long, Javier launched forward, sweeping her up into his arms.

Emily's cry of satisfaction was lost in the passionate onslaught that engulfed them both. She wrapped her legs around his waist as he held her high against him, his arms beneath her thighs and his hands fisting her backside. She tore at his shirt, pulling and snapping buttons that went flying across the floor, whilst also trying to take off her own top at the same time. A few short steps had her back pressed against the wall of the living room— a momentary pause in the chaos created by the way he took her mouth. She offered no resistance, her mouth opening to his, wide and welcoming, her tongue beckoning him deeper, harder as it mirrored how he wanted to fill her elsewhere.

The moan of pleasure seeped from her throat into his mouth, catching his arousal in a velvet fist and squeezing. She leaned forward from the wall, the heat between her open legs pressing against the hard length of him. It was madness in his blood, how much he wanted her. Heat crept up from the base of his spine, reaching the back of his neck as his mind flooded with images of what he wanted to do to his wife. *With* his wife. But this raw primal urgency was something new to him and nothing like he'd ever experienced before.

He pulled back to look at Emily—her eyes wide, glazed with an eagerness that only served to goad him.

'Emily—' he begged with his last shred of decency.

'I want you as you are,' she whispered, her words staccato, in between sharp breaths. 'I want you like *this*,' she said, pulling at his shirt.

He didn't know himself like this, but in her eyes he could see that she was asking him to trust her. Trust that *she* knew him enough. It was all it took to break the final thread holding him back. Need coursed through his body in the space of a single heartbeat—wild and untameable by anyone but her. The feral thing that his desire had become demanded and keened his need.

He shifted his hold, letting her slide slowly, carefully, down the length of his body, enjoying the friction of her hips, her breasts, her hands clinging to him until her toes reached the floor.

He turned her in his arms, stepping them even closer to the wall, reaching for her hands and placing them on the wall either side of her, nearly losing control when she backed up against his erection, her head falling back against his shoulder, restless and needy. His curses littered the air as he ran his hands around her ribs and up over breasts that filled his palms to perfection.

Emily pressed against the wall to stop herself from trembling with the need that was a living thing unwinding in her. She was half terrified that it wouldn't be, couldn't be, satiated. It was too much to be contained. She had never wanted like this—this powerfully, this *much*. It consumed her.

Javier's hands cupped her breasts, his thumbs playing with painfully taut nipples, the ache and throb agitating in the most delicious of ways. Her entire body flashed over with heat, prickling and stinging, and Emily thought she might actually lose her mind to this, to *him*, and couldn't bring herself to care.

One hand left her breasts and, embarrassingly, she cried out at the loss. Feverish, she flexed her fingers against the stone wall, grasping nothing but more and more need. Then he pulled her against him and with his free hand he fisted her skirt at her thigh. Inch by inch he raised the material, as if teasing them both, until his fingers reached her skin beneath the bunched cotton. He palmed the back of her thigh, reaching higher and higher, her breath hitching in her chest—as desperate for what he was seeking as he seemed. He found the band of her panties and pulled, a hard jerk that tore the silk from her body in a way that made her hot and wet in a single breath.

The sob flew from her throat as he ran his thumb across her clitoris and down and back, her hips bucking and shaking, aware of the hard length of him pressed against her. Begging words, pleas, some intelligible, some not, fell from her lips but he was ruthless in his pursuit of her orgasm as if he wanted to punish her—*them*—with pleasure alone.

She felt him use her wetness to ease the path his fingers created, to gentle the delicious friction she craved. Her sex ached with the need to be filled by him as her climax climbed higher and higher. Carefully he pinched the bundle of nerves that throbbed and she cried out, her arms collapsing slightly, as he reached around her to brace them both against the wall.

Emily lost herself as a sea of sensation crashed over her in fiery heat and ice-cold shivers. Longing and need and desire ran through her veins, her body overtaken by pure instinctive feeling. She felt every single inch of her impending orgasm, building touch by touch, gasp by gasp, creeping towards her without mercy. Her whole body flushed with expectation and excitement and as her climax nipped at her toes and fingers she held her breath and…drowned in pleasure.

Waves and waves and waves of pleasure, urged on by Javier, who never stopped touching her, never stopped delighting in the orgasm that rolled through her body again and again. Utterly spent, her head fell forward against the wall, thankful for the way his body supported hers, preventing her from falling to the ground.

His hand returned to her thigh and backside, soothing her while causing goosebumps to scatter across her skin and her heart to jerk once more in her chest.

'Javier—'

'Shh… It's okay,' he soothed. 'I've got you.'

She felt him drop downwards and she tried to look around, but he gently slapped her backside and she understood the silent command. Shock and delight raged to life and pulled her back towards another orgasm.

'What—?' Her words were cut off by a cry of shock drenched pleasure.

Palms braced against the wall, Javier had nudged her legs apart and found her with his tongue. 'I can't… I'm not…' Her hapless protest died on her tongue and he laved her, filled her with the most intimate and carnal of kisses. The growl of his own satisfied pleasure vibrated against her core, and he whispered adoring words so at odds with the sinful act. Her breasts pressed into the cool stone, clashing with the heat coursing across her skin, her nipples aching from blessed icy relief.

He pulled her hips back slightly so that she fell even harder against his open mouth, and again she cried out. One hand reached upwards to claim her breast, finding her nipple, and he filled her again with his tongue.

She grabbed the hand that had claimed her breast. Pressing it against the lush roundness he tormented, she pleaded for him, to feel him inside her, to be able to orgasm around him, with him. She thought she'd said it out loud. She hoped she had, but once again that madness drew her and she wasn't sure, until she felt him withdraw and stand from the floor.

'Cariño—'

'Please, Javi.'

She reached behind her, impatient and desperate, grasping the button of trousers strained by the power of his need. A desire-drunk laugh escaped her husband and he batted her hands away, the sound of the zip being drawn down a musical promise.

She felt the heat of him against her back, the shiver of arousal passing from her to him and back again, as he gently pushed her legs wider, angling her where he needed her. Her heart pounded in her throat so hard with expectation she thought it might stop, until he bent his head and whispered indecently erotic descriptions of how she made him feel in her ear as he pushed so deliciously slowly into her from behind.

Her forehead fell against the smooth whitewashed wall as she trembled with the force of her bliss. He didn't stop whispering as he filled her, deeply, so deeply that she didn't know where she stopped and he began and somewhere in her soul she felt as if the indefinable thing that had been missing was suddenly found. She was surrounded by him, covered and possessed by him utterly, and she *revelled* in it, wanting, begging for more.

There was nothing familiar about this primal need coursing through her, verging on obsession. She had turned into a wanton creature—wanting his touch, wanting his words, his body to completely own hers. He began to thrust, slowly at first, bringing sweet sighs and simple pleasure slowly building towards an inconceivable point both out of her reach and worryingly close.

But then his clever fingers delved between her legs and sharp pinpoints of pleasure fired through her, raising goosebumps and uncontrollable shivers across her body. His thrusts became powerful, rapid, hurling her towards yet another orgasm that she wasn't ready for but wanted more than her next breath.

The sounds around them were an erotic cacophony of breathless pants, sweat-soaked skin slapping against sweat-soaked skin, a crescendo of growls and moans and prayers and curses that peaked on a roar as they came together in a soul-shattering moment that broke them into pieces mid-air and reformed them both into something new as they fell back to earth.

Javier was genuinely worried about opening his eyes—concerned that he really had hit his head in the car accident, that all of this was in fact some concussion-induced fantasy.

Bracing himself, he gingerly opened his eyes half an inch and had never been so happy to see that damn ceramic parrot in his entire life. And then Emily turned into his chest, sweeping her arm across it, and pulled herself into his side and he would have sworn on everything he had of value that his heart turned in his chest.

'Shh…' Emily whispered.

'I didn't say anything.'

'You're thinking too loudly,' she insisted.

He shook his head, unable to stop the smile from spreading across his lips. He peered down at her and she scrunched her eyes together. 'I'm sleeping. Stop it.'

But he couldn't. His hands roamed his wife's naked body as if imprinting every inch of her on them, in his mind and into his soul.

'Oh, God, you're insatiable! No more sex,' she cried in mock horror, turning away from him, causing him to laugh so deeply it hurt his ribs. She was warm against his body and he couldn't resist finding the angle where her neck met her shoulder and nuzzled kisses into it.

'I wasn't joking, Javi,' she groused, but moved her head to give him better access. 'And if I don't eat something soon, I might faint. I'm not joking about that either,' she said.

'Don't worry, *esposa*, you will have everything you could ever wish for.'

He got up from the sofa he'd managed to pull them towards with his last coherent thought before that delicious blanket of satiated need had blocked out all else, making sure the throw he'd placed over Emily was enough.

He ran a hand through his hair, refusing to look at the wall where he'd taken her so desperately and so madly in case he grew hard yet again. *Cristo.* Their lovemaking had always been extraordinary, but that had been something altogether different—new—and simply indescribable.

He grabbed his trousers and thrust them on, not bothering to fasten the clasp. He wasn't sure how long they'd stay on anyway, he thought a little smugly. As he pulled leftovers from the fridge—cold meats, tortilla, olives and Manchego—and put them onto a tray he realised he was trying to work out how much longer he could stay away from work.

They'd returned to Madrid for his checkup, where the Chief of Surgery had been more happy than shocked that his memory had miraculously returned. Javier had been given the okay to return to his local doctor for his final checkup, which was in two days. But beyond that?

He was surprised to find that the driving urge that had ridden him like a demon for so much of his life was strangely absent. He hadn't really noticed it until that moment. He'd not thought of work beyond a few emails that his assistant had forwarded requiring his input or authorisation. He'd received only one phone call from

Aleksander, regarding the next meeting of the exclusive and highly secretive charitable organisation he was part of. The King of Svardia had assured Javier that the event in Öström would run smoothly in his absence.

He smiled, wondering what Emily would make of the fact that he now rubbed shoulders with Kings and billionaires alike. So much had changed in six years, but they were still bound by the same thing that had brought them together in the first place. He was *sure* of it. Which was why he turned back to the idea that had needled its way into his post-orgasmic blackout.

He could definitely make it work. And fairly easily too, he figured, as he mentally sorted through what projects he had on the go and where they were at development-wise. In this instance he'd only need a couple more weeks off if he wanted to execute his plan. But the desire to think longer term was pulling at the edges of his mind.

Dusk had fallen, the moon rising into an attractive blue-grey sky, and stars were inking their way onto the canvas above the patio, but there was still half a bottle of champagne in the ice bucket tucked under the table, protecting it from the earlier heat.

He retrieved two clean glasses from the kitchen before returning to the patio, happy to find Emily leaning against the railings looking out at the gorge. The ends of her hair were a little damp from the shower she had taken. She was dressed in his shirt, which was far too big for her and covered all the things that would tempt him to take her right back to where they had been only an hour earlier. Even just the thought of it pulsed through him, hardening an arousal that was still shockingly swift and intense.

Raw. Primal.

There had always been a sense of that insatiability

between them, but never so...*carnal*. It had surprised him at first. He'd been fearful of intimidating Emily, shocking her, but instead she'd welcomed it, matched it, demanded it and more from him and he'd gloried in it. And more than a little of him was ready to indulge in her all over again.

As if sensing his thoughts, Emily cut him a narrow-eyed gaze and he shrugged and smiled. 'This is what you do to me, *cariño*.'

He paused only to pour them each a glass of champagne before joining her. He couldn't help but press a kiss to the juncture of her neck and shoulder, his chest mere inches away from her back in a chaste imitation of what had passed before, and offered her a glass.

'Now it is you who are thinking too loudly,' he chided. 'Care to share?'

Emily took the glass he offered, her gaze catching on the deep brown of his eyes, delighting in the invitation she found there.

'I was thinking about how much I want this to last.'

'Then let's make it last. Come away with me?'

'Away?' she repeated, buying time to cover the fact that he had misinterpreted her meaning. She hadn't changed her mind. She really did want to stay, to make a go of it. The thought of divorce turned her stomach and salted her tongue. But she couldn't help but wonder if they were just falling into the same pattern they had before. Rushing into things without taking the time to think them through. Talk things through.

But neither could she ignore how she'd felt seeing Mariana's pregnant belly, bursting with the children she and her husband were bringing into this world. The way she had glowed with the love binding her to Santi and to their future. Envious, Emily had realised that she wanted that so much, because then she might believe that Javier wouldn't one day grow bored of her like her mother had, wouldn't one day find something or someone else to love, leaving her lonely and wondering what she had done wrong all over again.

'Yes,' he said, guiding her over to the table, unaware of her thoughts. He sat without taking his eyes from her and pulled her into his lap. 'I want us to go away. Somewhere we won't be interrupted. Somewhere—' he nuzzled that spot on her neck he couldn't seem to get enough of '—I can do all the things I promised I'd do to you.'

A shiver ran through her body, the pulse at her sex throbbing wantonly all over again. Desire hazed her brain, fogging her mind. 'Where and for how long?' she asked half-heartedly, wondering about her projects and the workload that was racking up in her absence.

'I want to take you to Istanbul.'

Something in her heart turned. He remembered. After all this time, he actually remembered.

'We were supposed to go on our honeymoon,' she said, the words a little sad.

'Santi's movie came up and I had to work to cover the investment,' he said, cupping her cheek and gazing at her solemnly. 'And I regret that bitterly. So, let's do it properly this time. And *extravagantly*!' he said. Effervescent fizz and sparkle filled her bloodstream and a longing so deep and sure Emily was surprised by it. 'We will stay in the finest hotels, travel in the most luxurious style!' he promised dramatically.

'I don't need all that—I just need you,' she said, getting a little lost in the depths of that rich dark brown gaze staring back at her. 'But I'd really love to go to Istanbul,' she said truthfully, thinking—hoping—that she could juggle her workload to make it happen. There was a tendril curling in the back of her mind, unfurling with discomfort, with a wordless warning—but it was so quiet, it was easy to ignore. 'But what about Diabla?' she asked, realising that she was a new responsibility that couldn't be shirked.

Javier frowned and shrugged. 'She comes with us, of course.'

Emily couldn't help but throw her head back and laugh. 'You can't just bring her along,' she said, looking at him as if he'd lost his mind—over a cat that had hissed, spat, scratched and ruined at least six thousand euros' worth of clothing and property in the first two days of her stay here.

'Yes, I can,' he said determinedly. And, just like that, she supposed, yes. He really could.

CHAPTER ELEVEN

THE NEXT FEW days were a whirlwind of activity that struck her almost as frantically as the explosion of feelings and passion between her and Javi. They could hardly keep their hands off each other—and the way that it reminded her of how it had been in the beginning made her feel young and fun and deliriously happy.

Javier brought down his tablet and showed her the plans for their journey. They would take his plane directly to Istanbul. They would stay at a private members' club that he belonged to, once owned by a king, which sat regally on the banks of the Bosphorus. The pictures on the screen showed some of the most opulent, sumptuous luxury Emily had ever seen—a beautifully carved wooden bed, intricate tiling and mosaics that reminded her of the Alhambra, gold, marble and rich deep walnut. Her designer's mind went into overdrive and she had to stop herself from reaching for the tablet to pore over the images igniting creative fireworks in her brain. Javier only laughed, telling her that she'd be there in person soon enough.

They would spend three days there before travelling on to the Princes' Islands, where he had leased a sprawling Ottoman villa that looked more like a palace to Emily. It had staff and a private chef, and a private beach with water that looked like liquid turquoise. She'd never seen anything like it.

Her shock must have shown on her face because Javier asked her if she was okay.

'Javi, seriously. How much money do you have?'

He studied her, noticing the seriousness in her tone. 'More than I could ever spend in several lifetimes.'

'More than a billion?'

'Many more.'

'And while we're away, you're just content to let your billions...do their thing?'

He laughed. 'I have good staff. I trust them.'

'Mmm...' she replied, thinking of how her call to her own staff had gone that morning.

Javier left shortly after for his final doctor's appointment, while she remained on the patio, her hand soothing Diabla's discomfort at the sudden hive of activity. She smiled as the small feline butted her head against her palm until Emily picked her up and placed her happily in her lap, because in truth Emily needed the comfort as much as Diabla appeared to.

No, she thought to herself. The phone call with her office manager hadn't gone well. They were happy for her, of course, but she hadn't been prepared for the disappointment. The San Antonio client needed to move up their timescale, which would mean another site visit and condensed deadlines. They were willing to pay, but they wanted *her*. And they wanted her next week. And she couldn't do that. She was making a go of things with Javier, and she wanted their honeymoon. Wanted to explore all the richness that Istanbul had to offer. Her creativity, half-starved until she'd returned to Frigiliana, was ravenous now. At least that was what Emily kept telling herself. It was her creativity she wanted to feed, and to give her marriage to Javier the time and work it deserved.

So she was willing to sacrifice the San Antonio client, telling herself that she and her staff had already been stretched thin and that it was best to give their existing clients their focus rather than splitting it further. And while her office manager had tried to talk her round, Emily stayed firm. She was doing what she needed to do for herself and for her marriage. Even if it left her feeling a level of discomfort that was strangely familiar.

Diabla flicked her tail against Emily's legs in a syncopated beat that made her smile. The adoring look from the cat as Emily stroked and soothed her was soft comfort that she readily welcomed until Javier came bursting through the front door, declaring to the whole of Frigiliana that he was *free!*

'I have champagne.'

'More?' she asked, laughing.

'I would bathe you in it, if you hadn't taken out the bath six years ago.'

'It was the right move.'

'And yet I still miss it.'

'You have a pool!'

'I do not *wash* in my pool,' he said, mock outrage in his tone as he reached for her, dislodging Diabla, and pulled her into his arms for a kiss that went from welcome to wanton in seconds.

'As much as I would love to take this to its very logical and incredibly tempting conclusion, we must get ready.'

'Get ready for what?'

'Istanbul, of course. We leave tonight!'

Javier was moving fast. Too fast. But he couldn't escape the feeling that there was something coming. Something *bad*. Not usually a superstitious man, he couldn't shake the belief that if they didn't leave for Istanbul immediately, then whatever dark promise was on the horizon would catch up with them and change their lives irrevocably.

So he couldn't understand why—given that his wife had only come here with a suitcase with two weeks' worth of clothes—it was taking Emily so long to pack. He entered the bedroom to find her holding up a pair of trousers and frowning.

'What is it, *mi reina*?'

She shook her head and looked up at him. 'I don't have the kind of clothes that should be worn where we are going. I can't wear *these* to what was once a palace, Javi,' she said, pulling at her simple linen trousers.

'Darling, you can bring whatever you like. But I don't plan on you wearing much through the entire trip,' he said, ending on a growl that formed at the mere thought of her naked, on silk sheets, skin glazed bronze by the Turkish afternoon sun.

She batted him away. 'Seriously. I could really do with going shopping.'

'I will buy you whatever your heart desires...in *Istanbul*,' he stressed, throwing the pile of clothes from the side of her case into it.

'I can buy my own clothes, Javi,' she said with a little more bite than he'd expected. He could feel her scratch as if Diabla had taken a swipe.

'What is it, *mi amor*?' he asked, gently turning her towards him.

'I just...' she tried. 'I just feel like we're rushing this, Javi,' she admitted awkwardly. 'Do we really need to go tonight? Couldn't we take a little time so that I can,

I don't know, get the things I need? Like clothes, toiletries, cat food for Diabla?'

He smoothed back the blonde curtain that had fallen in front of her face as she tried to hide her eyes from him.

'Emily, I picked up the cat food on the way back from the doctor's. But—' he held up a hand to ward off her interruption '—if you want to take the time, we'll take the time,' he said easily. He might have been rushing, but the last thing he wanted to do was cause her hurt.

As if his being reasonable took the wind out of her irritation, she puffed out a breath of air that billowed a strand of her hair. 'I'm being silly,' she said.

'No,' he assured her. 'You're not. I just got caught up in the excitement of it, that's all. I'll cancel the car.'

'No, don't,' she said, stopping his hand from reaching for his phone. 'I want to go. I really do. Let's do it!' she said, and he watched the concern he'd seen in her eyes be replaced with excitement. 'After all, I want my honeymoon,' she teased, pulling him into a kiss with one hand and blindly throwing her clothes into the case with the other. The sound of their laughter dissolved into expressions of pleasure and they ended up keeping the car waiting for at least twenty minutes.

A short while later Javier followed Emily up the steps of his private plane, enjoying the way her satin top was pressed against her body by the wind whipping across the tarmac of the private airfield twenty minutes from Frigiliana. He took off his sunglasses and hooked them into the open neck of his shirt, unable to prevent himself from admiring the shape and tone of his wife's body.

'Stop staring,' she threw over her shoulder and Javier barked out a laugh. Lightness filled his chest and he couldn't contain his happiness as it slipped through his fingers and refilled in his hand as if he were taking fistfuls of sand.

'Never,' he promised her and his heart soared at the answering smile that pulled at Emily's lips. Lips that were still passion-plump from the afternoon's adventures. He invited her to sit as the staff stowed their small luggage, one taking very gentle care of Diabla's carry cage, and prepared for take-off. He retrieved his phone from his jacket pocket and it rang in his hand just as he was about to turn it off.

The only reason he didn't ignore the call was because of the name that flashed up on the screen. He frowned and answered.

'Gabi?'

'Oh, God, Javi.'

'Gabi? Are you okay?'

'No, I'm not. It's Mamá—she's...she's lost it.'

His stomach curled. Never before had his half-sister called him like this.

'What's going on?'

He could hear her taking giant gulps of breath before a sob emerged and then almost nothing but tears and incomprehensible words.

Emily stood, concern etched across her features. 'What's going on?'

'I don't know,' he said, shaking his head. 'It's Gabi. Renata's done something.' He turned his attention back to the phone. 'Gabi? Can you hear me? You need to breathe.'

Emily frowned at the sternness of his tone and gestured for the phone. As he half listened to his wife making gentle reassuring sounds to his sister, he fought the decision he knew he needed to make. He cursed. He should have known his mother wouldn't let their last call go so easily. But if he'd thought for a moment that Gabi would be caught up in the fallout he would have handled things differently.

He searched Emily's gaze, hoping his frustration and apology were enough, even as she nodded her understanding. He turned away, fighting the feeling that he had just messed up in the most fundamental of ways, and went to speak to the pilot about changing their destination to Madrid.

Emily was just as eager to get to Madrid as Javier. Gabi had been incomprehensible and inconsolable—nothing like the contained but gravely concerned young woman she had sat with outside a hospital room just over two weeks ago.

It's my fault. I shouldn't have tried... I shouldn't have done anything.

Gabi's words unfolded in Emily's mind and, no matter what questions she'd asked, she couldn't get Gabi to tell her what she'd tried, what she'd *done*. Javier's calls to his mother were going unanswered, which seemed to drive him into a frighteningly still kind of fury that Emily didn't think was healthy. At least the flight time was quick. While Emily secured promises that the air staff would look after Diabla, Javi arranged for a car to meet them when they landed and it wasn't long before Emily and Javier were walking down the private plane's steps towards a tall, uniformed man wearing sunglasses and with a jaw that to Emily looked as if it could cut granite.

'Esteban,' Javi greeted, surprise and something close to happiness flashed in his eyes before it dulled back to dark determination. 'You are well.' It was a statement rather than a question, and Javier's driver nodded.

'You?'

'I'll let you know when I've spoken to my mother.'

Nodding with an understanding that surprised Emily, the driver pulled open the door for them and once they were seated returned to the driver's seat.

Cocooned in the dark interior of the sleek vehicle, Emily reached for her husband's hand and tried to ignore the sting when he shifted out of her reach.

He didn't mean it. It's a hard time for him, so don't be selfish.

The phrase cut her deep, reminding her of how she'd felt as her mother had begun to change, to focus on Steven to the point where Emily had become near invisible. That familiar guilt and hurt began to rise in her chest as she felt shut-out again. Until he reached for her, taking the hand she'd left on the seat between them, his fingers cool but tight, and she knew how much that had cost him because it was priceless to her. That touch, it anchored her. She couldn't be invisible if he were holding her.

She cast a glance at him, the muscle at his jaw flexing rapidly, tension wound so tight through his body that it must have taken considerable effort not to crush her hand.

'Javier—'

'We're here,' he interrupted as the car turned into the open gates and a driveway that circled around a stone fountain before sweeping in front of a huge Tuscan-style estate. The designer in her quickly categorised the impressive building that must have contained at least twelve bedrooms. The front door was flanked by two tall cypress trees, the pink hue of the painted exterior plaster set off by the black-framed windows glowing as every single light in the house appeared to be switched on. She had never been here before. They few times that they had met with Renata, it had always been 'out', as if Renata hadn't wanted Emily in her home. Which, all considered, was probably correct.

Javier took the steps up to the front door in quick, angry strides and pounded on the door as Emily followed more slowly, which was why she could see Gabi when she opened the door.

She looked terrible. Her eyes were red and swollen from who knew how many hours of crying, but it was the hurt and fear in them that caught Emily the most. Her beautiful long brown hair hung in messy strands and, hunched in on herself, she looked small and so, so vulnerable.

'Where is she?' Javier growled.

Gabi put up her hand to try and stop him, but Javier pushed past her and stormed into the house, leaving Emily to gather Gabi into her arms just as she started to cry again.

'Oh, my love,' Emily said, pulling her into an embrace and sweeping the hair from her face. 'What on earth happened?' But Gabi only shook her head.

The moment that raised voices reached them in the grand hallway, Gabi ran off towards them, leaving Emily no choice but to follow. Hurrying to keep up, Emily found the living area where Renata, Javier and a man she didn't know stood facing each other.

Renata jerked her head up and with a look of such venom it nearly stopped Emily in her tracks said, 'Get her out of here. I never want to look at her ever again.'

For a moment Emily thought Renata was talking about her, but quickly realised from Gabi's reaction that her ire was directed at her daughter. Gabi turned and fled straight back into Emily's arms.

'That's rich,' the stranger in the room said, in heavily accented English. 'You send her after me like some Mata Hari and now you want to get rid of her?'

'Why would I want her?' Renata demanded. 'She's no better than a whore.'

Emily couldn't prevent the gasp of shock that escaped at Renata's bitter tirade—the way Gabi had flinched in her arms, it was as if she'd been struck. Whatever was going on here, Gabi didn't need to see or hear it. With a glance at Javier, who nodded his understanding, she drew Gabi back into the hallway, down the steps and into the car, refusing to let go of the young woman in her arms.

'It's not true,' Emily said, reassuring her with words of comfort. 'Your mother is wrong.'

'But she's not,' Gabi whispered through pale lips, and her tears became silent, which was so much worse.

Javier shook with a rage that felt endless.

'This is not how I heard you do business, Casas,' said the stranger. 'This? This is unacceptable. Appalling,' the man said, shaking his head in disgust.

'Who are you?' Javier demanded.

The man—as tall as himself—glanced at Renata and back to him again. 'You don't know?'

'I wouldn't have asked if I did,' Javier growled, just about done with this entire mess.

'Lady, you are crazy,' he said, turning his attention to Renata. 'My lawyers are going to go through everything with a fine toothcomb and when they're done…?' He let the threat hang in the air and Renata seemed to drain of all colour. 'She was trying to sell me shares in your company.'

'You mean Casas Textiles?'

'No. I mean *your* company. She's been using your name to secure business deals for months. As it stands? I already own fifty percent of Casas Textiles.'

The ringing in his ears was a warning of how close he

was to losing it. The man—apparently appeased by the shock that must have shown on his face—shook his head in disgust. He took a small white card from his pocket and handed it to Javier.

'I'll be in touch. Looks like you've got some talking to do.' And with that he left.

Without looking at the card, he shoved it into his pocket and turned on Renata.

She was trying to look defiant. In her mind, Javier reasoned, she probably hadn't done anything wrong. After all, she'd always behaved as if whatever was his was hers. He shook his head. She really was mad.

'Don't look at me like that. I am your mother.'

'Only when you want my money. What have you done?'

She shrugged her shoulder and touched a finger to the corner of her lip as if checking her lipstick.

'How could you speak to Gabi like that?' he demanded, unable to suppress the rage vibrating in his heart.

'It is true. She—'

'I don't care what you think she did, or even what she did do. You are *unnatural*,' he spat.

Renata's gaze turned ice-cold—a thing that would have terrified him when he was a child. Even now he fought his reaction to the bitter bite of it.

'How dare you—?'

'Me?' He let out a wild laugh. *'Me?'* He struggled to control his breathing and forced the words from his mouth. 'If this man chooses to press charges, I will not stand in his way. If there are more "investors" out there I will support them also. As for Gabi? No. You will never see her again. And if you try to contact me, or anyone associated with me I will call the police.'

Renata laughed, high-pitched and painful. 'Don't be so dramatic, Javi.'

'I mean it. For your own sake get some help, Renata.'

Javier turned his back on his mother and stalked through the estate that had never been a happy home, down the stairs—pausing only to grab Gabi's bag with her phone and wallet—and into the car where Emily sat, holding his still sobbing sister. He didn't need to tell Esteban to head back to the airport.

In the silence that filled the back of the car, Gabi's tears wrenched at his heart and no amount of sympathy offered by Emily's gaze could ease the hurt. He had let Renata's behaviour go unchecked, both with the business and his half-sister. Elbow against the car door and hand in a fist, Javier became almost completely motionless until they reached the airstrip. He opened the door before Esteban could reach it and helped Emily and Gabi from the car and into the private jet.

In clipped words he told the pilot to return to the airfield just outside of Frigiliana and entered the cabin, where Emily was covering Gabi with a blanket. She held a finger to her lips and motioned that Gabi had finally fallen asleep.

He looked at the small form of his half-sister, wondering how on earth he could have left her to fend for herself against Renata. He'd been so determined to shore up his business—to make himself such a success that failure wasn't a word that could be put even near him. And he had failed in the most fundamental of ways. His sister, his wife... No more. Mentally he drew a harsh line in the sand and in the quiet hour between take-off, landing and the return to their home in Frigiliana, Javier made plans.

By the time they had Gabi settled in the spare room, the headache that had started in the plane had lessened as, bit by bit, the decisions he made came together to form a cohesive whole. Quietly, he drew Emily outside to the patio, picking up two glasses and a bottle of the white Rioja she loved.

'I am so sorry, *mi reina*,' he whispered, keeping his voice low so as not to wake Gabi. He took her hand. 'I know how much Istanbul means to you, to *us*,' he hastened to clarify.

Emily smiled, easing the concern in his heart. 'It's okay. Gabi needed you, and your mother? Well… I think there's a lot of help that she needs, but not from you. At least, not right now,' she said gently. Javier nodded, so glad that their thinking was joined once again.

He leaned back in the chair, exhaling a long breath and taking in the scattered stars above. The plan, he reminded himself, bending forward again and, leaning his elbows on his thighs and turning her hand in his, he pressed on.

'I'm so glad you understand. Obviously, it's going to take a lot of work—and it will take a while—but moving to Madrid will make it easier, in the short-term and probably the long-term. The first thing I'll do is have my lawyers look through everything,' he pressed on as his mind turned over the order of things to ensure that nothing was left to chance. 'And you'll be able to help Gabi because she's really going to need support. God, I'm so glad you're here,' he said, love and plans clouding his eyes so that he failed to see the impact his words were having on Emily. 'I know that we've been apart and I've made mistakes, but I love you. *Cristos*, I love you. And having you by my side, here in Spain, is exactly what I need right now. I know it will not be easy, but it's the best way to—'

He paused only when Emily pulled her hand from

his, and he finally noticed that she was staring at him in confusion.

'What are you talking about?' she asked.

'Moving to Madrid, of course. Where did you think we would live?'

'I thought we might have a conversation about it first.' She half laughed, but the look in her eyes warned him that she was most definitely *not* laughing.

'But why would we need to talk about it?'

'Because I am your wife, not your cat.'

'Of course you are not my cat, Emily. What is wrong with you?'

'You haven't changed at all,' she accused, getting up from the table and brushing her hair back from her face, scrubbing at her eyes as if trying to wash something out of them. She looked back at him and shook her head. 'This was never going to work. How could I have thought that it would?'

CHAPTER TWELVE

JAVIER WAS LOOKING at her as if she had lost her mind. Perhaps she had, because she couldn't work out how she could have forgotten. Forgotten that *this* was what he was really like.

'What do you mean?' he asked, going impossibly still.

Oh, God, she had given up a lucrative commission for this. For a man who didn't even see how much the world revolved around him.

Her hands started to shake. 'I mean that this...' she gestured, between them '...you and me? Nothing's changed. It's all about you and what you want.'

'No, that's not—'

'What about my company? My business—my *life*—in London?'

For the first time that evening his gaze went blank. 'What about it?'

'Do you expect me to just bring it with me to Madrid? All my London-based staff—are they to come with us too? Or do I just get rid of it, and play nursemaid to your family?'

'That is not fair,' he said, standing up in anger and slashing a hand through the air.

'No,' she admitted, instantly regretting her words. 'Gabi does need help and support and I would never refuse her either. But you seem to think that I have nothing better to do with my time. I have a business that is just as valid as yours,' she said, his scoff enraging her further, '*even* if it does not make as much money as yours do. I can't believe that I turned down a commission for this.' She actually growled, grabbing her skirts instead of the hair she wanted to pull at her head. 'Javier! Don't you see?' she asked, allowing the hurt to enter her tone. 'Can't you see it? All the plans you've made, all the decisions, they're all about you and your family.'

'Emily, you are my wife. They are your family too.' His statement hit her like an accusation.

This was going so terribly wrong. Why did he sound so horribly *reasonable*? Something was building deep within her, emulsifying fear with guilt and hurt with anger. She'd done it again. She'd started to revolve around him. Because…because she *did* love him. She loved him so much that the worst thing about his plans was how much she wanted them. How much she wanted to move to wherever he was, how much she wanted to give everything up to make sure that Gabi was okay. How much she wanted to focus on a family with him. How tempted she was to let go of the company she'd built from the ground up. But fear made her harsh and put words in her mouth she would never have uttered rationally and she lashed out.

'So you would move to England then? You would run your empire from London? Bring Gabi and set up there instead?'

He tried to hold her gaze but he couldn't and when he looked away she knew it was lost. That she wasn't enough to make those sacrifices for.

Javier shook his head, disgust and bitterness in his eyes. 'You were just waiting for this, weren't you? Waiting for any excuse. You have *always* had one foot outside of this marriage, ready to leave when you wanted to. Even six years ago,' he accused. 'You could have talked to me at any point about what you were feeling, but you didn't then, and you're not doing it now—you're walking out on me *again*. There is no honesty here,' he all but spat.

'Honest? You want honest?' She laughed bitterly. 'Tell me, did you once think about my job or my life in London when you made your plans? Did you even think of talking to me about what I wanted from my future? No, you didn't because you're just like—' In shock she pressed her hand against her mouth—horrified by the words that she had only just held back.

'Say it,' he demanded, eyes turned almost black with anger.

'No, I didn't mean—' she struggled, back-pedalling furiously.

'You were going to tell me I was just like my mother.' He shook his head, absolutely nothing in his eyes now. 'Isn't that funny? Well, I guess no one could ever accuse you of being like your mother, because if you *did* love me you could never have said that.'

The hurt passing back and forth between them cut her so deeply that it would leave a scar for ever. 'Javi, this isn't—'

'You can go.' He dismissed her with a flick of his hand towards the door.

She went to him, tried to pull him round to face her, but he was as immovable as stone. 'I'm sorry, Javi, I honestly didn't mean that. You are nothing like her. You never have been.'

She tried to manoeuvre herself round to face him, but he kept shutting her out. 'Javi, you know that was not what I meant. Please. You accused me of not wanting to talk. I'm here, wanting to talk,' she pleaded. And just like that, in the space of less than five minutes they had repeated the entire cycle of their marriage. Passion, commitment, withdrawal, and silence.

She had no idea if he heard her or not, but after a long painful moment she knew she had lost him. The implication was too raw, too hurtful, and the argument with his mother far too recent. Tears filled her eyes, for herself, for Javier, for what they could have had...had he not been right. That she *was* scared. Scared of becoming like her mother—a woman who lost her entire sense of self to someone else.

She was by the front door when she heard his steps in the house behind her and she paused, thinking that maybe he'd call her back. Tell her that they were being silly. That they could start again. But instead he said, 'Esteban will take you to the airfield.' And he closed the door behind her.

Javier sat on the patio steps, head spinning and heart aching as the night passed overhead. Diabla wound her way between his legs, nudging the palm of his hand with her nose and meowing as if in mourning for what they had lost.

What had happened?

He ran through the events of yesterday again and again, trying to work out how he had lost so much in such a short space of time. He didn't know where to start because his mother's awful behaviour dived into Emily's accusations. They had hurled hurts at each other that should never have been said.

Emily had been wrong, he internally raged. He wasn't like his mother...but even he could see that in his determination to *not* be, he had become someone who would not bend, would not deviate from his plans. He'd had to be like that. Because growing up with Renata had meant orbiting around her—revolving around her moods and her whims or else.

But that word—orbit—reminded him of something Emily had said days before. The way she'd described her mother and her stepfather as if he were the sun to her moon. His gut began to curl. It was Emily's fear—he knew that. Losing her sense of self to someone else.

He'd not put the two together before, but now he had made the connection he realised that he *did* know what it felt like to lose himself to someone. He knew Emily's fear as a real thing that had happened to him and the thought that she feared that with him? That Emily feared losing herself to him?

Nausea swelled in his stomach. That he could have made her feel anything like that…

He hadn't known that she'd given up a commission to go to Turkey. But now he had to admit to himself that he *hadn't* thought about Emily's job—the job that made her bright and confident and a power to be reckoned with. He hadn't thought about her life in London when he'd blithely announced that they would move to Madrid. His only excuse was that he'd been so desperate to rectify his mother's mistakes—so determined not to fail, that he'd failed his wife. The one person in his life who he should put first, who he should sacrifice for, not force her to make sacrifices.

He gripped his hair in fisted hands and stayed that way until the sun peeked over the gorge.

'Javi?'

For just a second his heart tricked him into thinking that Emily had come back, but even before his pulse had leaped his brain recognised that it had been Gabi who had called his name.

'Are you okay?' he asked, turning to look at his sister.

'I was going to ask you the same question.'

Choosing not to answer, he checked his watch. 'It's early, what are you doing up?'

'I heard a scratching at the door,' his sister replied, her eyes still puffy and red from the night before. She was holding a blanket around her shoulders, looking the way that he felt, he admitted silently.

He lifted his arm and she came to sit beside him, nestling into his side, and then nearly jumped a mile high when Diabla brushed up against her calf.

'What is *that*?!' she screeched.

'*She* is Diabla,' Javier defended, reaching down to pick up the cat, who looked as if she was either going to run away or destroy the blanket that Gabi had pulled around her. As neither option was preferable, he soothed her with gentle strokes. 'She—'

'Has no hair!'

'—is a Sphynx cat,' he continued. 'They were bred that way and she has been poorly treated in the past and is very affectionate.'

Gabi continued to eye the cat with suspicion until Diabla turned in his arms and reached her paws to his shoulders and cuddled into him adoringly, causing Gabi to *ooh* and *ahh*.

'She was probably looking for Emily,' Javier realised, hoping that the cat wouldn't feel too betrayed by her departure. His heart clenched and Diabla meowed.

'Is she not here?' Gabi looked confused.

Javier grimaced and explained what had happened the night before. He realised that it was the first time that he'd spoken about such personal things with his sister and although it would do nothing to help the tear in his heart, it soothed the edges to say it out loud.

As they talked, Gabi made coffee and gathered a breakfast of sorts and he wondered if she realised how unconsciously nurturing she was being. How someone so soft, warm and loving could have come from their mother was a marvel.

'Will you go after her?' Gabi asked, stroking Diabla, who had now taken up residence on Gabi's lap, purring and dribbling her delight.

Javier looked out across the gorge, giving the answer he'd known the moment she'd left their home. 'No.'

'But why?'

'Because she needs to know her own feelings,' he explained. 'She needs to make the choice herself if she is ever going to come back. And I need her to make that choice,' he realised in that moment. 'I need to know that she's not going to leave me again.' *Like his father had.* 'So if she does come back, we'll both know. All this time,' he confessed, looking at his hands and then back to the gorge, 'I'd been telling myself that she was mine, that she'd come back, that our marriage would work because *I* wanted it to. Now I need Emily to want it.'

'Do you love her?' his sister asked, her eyes shimmering with emotion.

'So damn much it steals my breath and stops my heart.'

Two months later

Walking down the chewing gum dotted London pavement, Emily's teenage tears flashed through her mind. While her office manager brought her up to speed with the client requests from the Jenzes' residential redesign, which included a twenty-seater dining table for their extensive and beautifully boisterous family, Emily saw where she'd fallen on ice walking to school, she saw the bench she'd sat on hoping to calm herself after her mother had missed another school assembly because Steven had needed something, she saw herself waiting after a school trip because her mother had needed to take Steven a work file he'd left at home.

'Are you sure you want to do them back to back? We're doing the furniture presentation for the San Antonio project in the evening. We could schedule the installation for the Jenzes for the following day?'

'No, I want them done together as I want to scout out the Kleins the following day instead.'

'Are you sure, boss? I know we wanted to take on more work, but we don't have to do everything...' His words trailed off into silence as she held her words in. 'I'll put it in the schedule.'

'Good. See you tomorrow,' Emily said, ending the call on her mobile as she stared up at her stepfather's house.

She gritted her teeth, having put off this moment for as long as possible, and rang the doorbell. Something about that little *ding-dong, ding-dong* had always irritated her. As if it had never felt right for her and her mum. Or...not the mum that she'd known from a very long time ago now.

And with a start—as if she'd touched static electricity—Emily realised that her mother had been married to Steven for longer than when it had just been the two of them. And it cracked something inside her—cracked the hope that somehow she'd get her mother back. The woman who had laughed and painted with her fingers, who had cooked and made a mess that had delighted her as a child, the woman who sometimes had leaned into a childish silliness in the most joyful of ways...was not the same woman who answered the door in a camel-coloured cardigan and knee-length skirt on a Sunday.

'Darling,' her mother said, eyes crinkling, the blue bright, until she looked over her shoulder as her husband called out to know who it was. Her mother ignored him momentarily as she ushered Emily over the threshold. 'It's Emily, dear. You remember.'

Emily's brows nearly hit her hairline. Had he forgotten he had a stepdaughter?

Catching the look on her face, her mother whispered, 'That I *told* him about your visit.' Emily followed her mother through to the dining table, where two of the three plates already had food on them.

'I'm sorry, am I late?' Emily said, checking her watch and frowning to see it was only just twelve. She was sure her mother had said—

'No, we had to start early—Steven managed to get a tee time at the course with his friends.'

So they'd started without her. Emily bit her lip. She was an adult, a professional businesswoman, a wife even, but this? This cut her deeper than she knew it should.

'Pass me your plate and I'll serve,' her mother offered and even though the thought of food right now made her almost nauseous, she nodded. Her mother placed roast chicken, potatoes, carrots and peas on her plate as Emily watched Steven pour the last of the gravy onto his own.

'How is work, darling? Are you still doing that project in the city?'

It was an ambiguous enough question and could have referred to any number of now finished projects, but Emily didn't want to fight. She never had. 'Yes. It's going well. How are you both? Have you got plans to go away this summer?'

The banal question would have made Javier laugh.

Emily could almost hear him in her mind. *Cariño, you're going to have to do better than that.* But Javier's imaginary response was wrong. She didn't have to do better than that because the question occupied her mother long enough for Emily to watch, really watch Steven.

He'd always had this habit of looking straight ahead. Her mother had once explained that he didn't like eye contact and it was then that Emily had realised how much she did need it. For her it was confirmation that she'd been seen and heard. But now she noticed that he did it with her mother too and something curled in on itself in her heart.

Javier never did that. If they were talking, his focus was on her in ways she felt to the depths of her soul. If they were near each other, his eyes would find hers, his attention would be on her in a way she felt like a physical touch. He might have left her alone for days, weeks even at the worst point of his working life, but she had never felt as invisible as Steven or her mother made her feel.

Watching her mother talk for them both, not seeing how unengaged he was, Emily nearly dropped her fork. How could she have ever thought that what she had with Javier was anything like this?

She'd been so worried about losing herself to him, of becoming like her mother—a shadow of who she had once been—that she'd not seen that Javier was nothing like Steven. And more, Javier would never allow her to lose herself. Javier was so passionate, so dramatic, even in his stillness there was energy, movement. She could never have simply orbited him. Emily could only ever hold on for the ride, she realised. And that was it. It was a journey they had been on together. Yes, Javier might have been self-centred and stubborn, but he was not *selfish*.

There was a generosity to him, not just with his

wealth, but attention, friendship, passion...that he was capable of giving all of these things, despite the way that his mother had brought him up, was a miracle. Yes, he was rash and quick to act and made decisions without thinking sometimes, but none of those decisions had been about his wants, but what would be best for Gabi, Emily knew.

If she wanted easy, Emily could still walk away. She had her successful business, she was sure that she would one day meet someone who would be nice, great even. But they would never be Javier. Difficult, moody, stubborn...but brilliant, passionate, powerful. They would fight, probably at least once a day, but they would make love in the most spectacular way. There would be heat and spice and salt and sweetness and there would *never* be a dull one-sided impersonal conversation with their children ever.

Emily realised now that she had never lost herself to Javier. She'd never even been close to it. Instead, he'd been slowly guiding her to where she could know and see herself. And, just like when she was working on a project, she'd felt that *thing* click into place—the thing that held everything together. Love. Real, honest to God, all-consuming, utterly ludicrous and completely undeniable love. One that didn't erase her in the slightest, but instead made her *more*.

'What about you, dear? Any plans for a holiday?'

'Yes.' Emily nodded, putting down her knife and fork. 'I'm going to Spain.'

Diabla pawed at Javier's face, thankfully claws retracted, but she wasn't going to let him rest until she'd been given her breakfast. He growled. She meowed. He considered it a draw. She hopped out of the way as he threw the bedcovers back and stalked towards the bathroom, despite Diabla's attempts to herd him downstairs towards the kitchen.

'Wait, Diabla,' he ordered.

Standing in front of the mirror as the infernal cat drew a figure of eight between his legs, he noticed that finally the marks of the accident had gone. His skin had returned to a healthy colour, the doctors had given him a clean bill of health. There was only one reason for the hollows under his eyes, the loss of his appetite and the ache in his soul.

He ran a hand through his hair before stepping out of his briefs and beneath the powerful jets of the shower. Before she had left the day before, Gabi had made him promise that he would call Santi or Aleksander—his royal friend from Svardia. Not many knew about their association but in the last month and a half he and Gabi had talked *a lot*.

Focusing on his sister and the damage their mother had inflicted had been one distraction from the pain of Emily's departure. It had become achingly clear that, for all his stubbornness and determined focus on what was ahead of him businesswise, there had been a lot going on that he hadn't seen.

His insistence that Gabi should seek some kind of emotional support had been met with a deal—another that had worked to get beneath his skin. Gabi would only go if he did, so together they had met, once a week, with a young therapist to talk about their mother. Gabi visited her separately as well and she had worked incredibly hard to undo the damage that had snuck unknowingly into their lives.

He had not found it easy. *At all.* In fact, other than not going after his wife, it was probably the hardest thing that

Javier had ever done. Opening up, talking about feelings, was something he'd spent years purposefully stifling having learned from Renata that such a thing would only be met with derision or denial. But the counsellor was helping—no, he caught himself and rephrased the thought in his mind—the work *he* was doing with her was helping.

Turning off the shower and shaking the droplets from his head onto Diabla, who launched herself from the bathroom with an indignant cry, he recognised that arranging his businesses in such a way that he could take a six-month sabbatical had been the right thing to do.

Aleksander and their associates at the charitable organisation understood completely. Javier had begun to slowly and quietly downsize many of the other smaller and less important businesses, knowing that he did not need to, nor could he, keep up the punishing pace he'd set himself six years ago. His assistants and managers were seeing to that while he adjusted to life with a new perspective. So much had been tangled with how he had seen Renata and his childhood that he was having to learn and understand new patterns of behaviour as much as his old ones.

And every single day he had to remind himself that he was right not to go after Emily. That it was she who needed to know that if she returned it was because of her feelings, not his. And, he admitted to himself, he needed to know that too.

From downstairs he heard a smash and groaned, wondering what Diabla had managed to destroy now. Grabbing a towel and wrapping it around his waist, he was halfway to his wardrobe when he heard another crash.

It sent a spark of alarm through him as he cautiously made his way to the top of the stairs. There was definitely someone else in the house. Creeping down the stairs, the hairs on the back of his neck raised, he heard a thud coming from the sitting room.

Grabbing a long thin vase he'd never particularly liked, he raised it behind him, ready to defend himself and his house against whatever thief had mistakenly thought to steal from him. They could take the parrot, but everything else was *his*.

The first thing he noticed as he rounded the corner was that the two lurid fuchsia paintings had come down from the wall and that one was on the floor, the other missing. He frowned and glared at the parrot, until a noise behind him startled him into action.

As he turned, he swung his arm with the vase and—
Cristos!

Emily ducked just in time to avoid having the vase smashed over her head—a yelp of alarm pierced his ears and strangled his heart.

'What the hell do you think you're doing?' he roared. 'I could have killed you!'

She curled in on herself, crouched on the floor. 'I'm sorry. I'm sorry.'

Javier's heart pounded so hard he thought he might have a heart attack.

'Are you okay?' he demanded, fear coating his tongue with a thick salty bitterness.

She peered up at him and paled. 'Are you?'

'No, Emily. I am *not* okay.' He turned away, shaking his head, and put the vase on the floor, even though he wanted to smash it against the wall. That he could have hurt her in any way made him nauseous.

No, no, no, no, *no*. This was *not* how it was supposed to go! Emily stood on slightly shaky legs, guilty, awkward and upset. 'I'm so sorry, I just… I wanted to… I wanted to put it back,' she admitted morosely.

She'd wanted to undo all the damage she'd done before he'd come out of hospital. She'd managed to get one of the paintings in the small van she'd hired before Javier had appeared in the living room brandishing that vase she'd never liked much anyway.

Javier collapsed onto the awful banquette seating she'd put in nearly three months ago, wearing nothing but a towel, his hair still damp from the shower.

'Why are you here? I thought you'd still be at work,' she asked, getting her breath back.

'Why?' He frowned as if confused.

'Gabi said…' She trailed off as they both realised at the same time that Gabi had set them up.

Her heart beginning to settle from the fright, she went to sit beside him on the seat, her legs needing the support. Just at that moment Diabla launched herself onto her lap and started to pummel her, with claw sheathed paws. The purring and overexcited dribbling were more soothing to her heart than she could have imagined. Her hands swept around the small cat and she scooped Diabla into a hug, crooning adoring phrases and telling her how much she'd been missed.

She caught Javier looking at her with a raised brow and felt sheepish. Apologising, she put Diabla back down and turned to him.

'I'm sorry.'

'That's okay,' he said with a dismissive wave of his hand. 'I know you didn't mean to surprise me.'

He wouldn't meet her eyes. 'That's not what I meant. I'm *sorry*,' she stressed, trying to catch his gaze.

He clenched his jaw, as if trying to ignore her. How

much hurt she must have caused for him to do such a thing.

'I went to see my mother,' she said and waited for him to respond. Eventually he nodded and she took it as a sign to continue. 'It was…' she let out a small sad laugh '…exactly the same as it always is, but for one thing.'

She sensed that stillness that wasn't stillness take over his body. He was listening closely, his attention on her in a way that she suddenly felt as love. Tears pressed against the backs of her eyes. How had it taken her so long to realise this?

'I love you. I love you so much and not even that's enough. You are nothing like Steven and I will never be like my mother. Because of you. Because you wouldn't let me lose myself. You demand all of me whenever I can give it, but that requires me to be here. Not to lose myself like she did, and not to someone as unworthy as Steven. You are everything to me and I am *not* less for it, but *more*. I can't believe that I didn't see that before and I'm sorry that I didn't.'

The words didn't rush out of her, they slowly came, one after the other, so that Javier would know that she meant every single one of them. Because she wanted him to know, needed him to know how much she loved him.

'You are…insufferable,' she explained, the flare of surprise in his eyes making her smile. 'You are, Javier. I love you, but you are a pain in the arse,' she declared. 'You are stubborn. You act without thinking, you decide without asking, and you steamroll ahead before you look. But you are also absolutely and without a doubt the love of my life and I am not the same without you. You are passionate, driven, formidable and I wouldn't change a single thing about you because you are…the half of me that I didn't know I needed,' she confessed, tears escaping down both cheeks. 'And I love you so much it hurts when I'm not with you.'

Javier stared at her, his face unreadable. She swept away one of her tears, the small candle flame of hope that had kept her going since she'd arrived in Spain flickered in the silence. She bit her lip. There had always been the possibility that she'd come too late, that it might not be enough for her to tell him how she felt. Her heart ached and even then she nodded, accepting that she'd tried. Hoping that he might one day at least remember that he was loved for the man he was, not the man someone wanted him to be.

She stood on shaky legs and nodded to herself as tears clouded her eyes. She turned and stepped towards the door, when his hand snuck out to capture her wrist. She paused, not daring to turn, not daring to hope.

'You say that I am insufferable,' he accused, guiding her round to face him and pulling her to stand between his legs. Looking down at him, she should have held the power, but the reality was that she was utterly in his thrall. 'And you are right. I have been and—truthfully—will in all likelihood continue to be stubborn and selfish—'

'No—'

'Let me finish,' he commanded. 'I…became self-centred out of a need to protect myself, but I am learning that I no longer need that same protection. But I am *still* selfish, because I know that I want all of you. I will take whatever you think you can give me and demand more, because you are *it* for me. You are what makes me make sense, you are what I get up for in the morning and what I want to go to bed to each night. You could leave me a thousand times and I will always wait for you.'

'I will *never* leave you again,' she declared passionately.

'I'm still talking, Emily,' he said gently.

She looked down, biting her lip but utterly unrepentant.

'You were worried about losing yourself? You don't need to. Because you are here,' he said, thumbing his heart. 'Always. Whenever you need to find yourself, you are *here*. I know this because I am in your heart. Whether you will it or not, that is where I am and where I will stay for ever. I love you to distraction, Emily Casas. And if you'll agree to nudge me when I forget myself, when I become too autocratic, or selfish—or too much of a "pain in the arse", then I lay myself at your feet and beg you to stay.' Javier got to his knees, caught her hands in his and said, 'And I promise you will never have to ask or beg to be seen or loved ever again.'

Emily met him on the floor and—knee to knee—she placed kisses on his brow, his cheeks, his lips. 'And you will never have to look for me, because I will never leave your side. I love you, I love you, I love you,' she said, placing more kisses on his brow, his cheeks, his lips. Mouth to mouth, they professed their love until tears met smiles and heartbeats soared with a conviction and love that was simply transformative.

In the weeks that followed they put most of the house back to the way it had once been. The tablecloth left the gorgeous oak handmade table, the paintings in the living room were taken down and used for one of Emily's clients, the curtains so disastrously shredded by Diabla were cut down and made into cushion covers in what Emily declared was a stroke of genius and Javier declared was an abomination.

Emily made living in Spain and working in London a seamless affair, commuting twice a month and travelling to clients around the world when necessary. Her staff had come out to Spain for a week-long event that forged long-lasting friendships and working relationships, during which Javier waited on them all hand and foot, showing an interest in her staff and projects that practically made him a member of the team.

Javier had a slightly trickier transition to his lighter workload, but settled into it happily when he began to accompany Emily on her business trips. Gabi had come by for a short visit with so much news and so changed it had set Emily's head spinning. But it warmed her heart to see how close the bond had become between the two siblings and another building block in the family forming around her slipped into place.

It saddened her that her mother hadn't yet made it out to Frigiliana, but Emily was trying to focus on the relationship she had with her rather than the one she wanted and, bit by bit, it was hurting less. In Javier's arms and with the promise of his constant love for the rest of her life, Emily found a comfort, happiness and security she hadn't realised she was missing and never, ever needed to ask to be seen or loved again.

EPILOGUE

Four months later...

THE SCENT OF pine filled the spectacular penthouse apartment in Madrid so powerfully Javier had threatened to
open a window. Gabi had warned him against it on pain
of death, and he only relented when Emily pointed out
that Diabla wouldn't survive the fall if she became overly
inquisitive.

Although he had wanted to celebrate their first Christmas in Frigiliana, Emily and he had decided that Madrid
was much more suitable. It was big enough to house his
sister *and* the entire Torres clan, as well as being close to
the Puerta del Sol—the best place in the whole of Spain
to celebrate New Year's Eve.

Seeing Emily and Gabi occupied in the kitchen, he
decided that this was his chance to attend to his last festive secret and turned to leave, only to be smacked in the
face by a sprig of mistletoe. *Maldito*, did they not know
that the stuff was poisonous? Apparently his little sister
didn't much care, if the giggles he could hear from the
kitchen were anything to go by.

He looked around, seeing that what had once been a
sleek, chrome and black contemporary and technologi-
cally advanced haven at the top of one of Madrid's most

exclusive skyscrapers was now, thanks to his wife's creative talents, like the inside of Santa's grotto.

Navidad had truly come to their home—red velvet bows, green and gold tinsel and frost-coated glass baubles hung from every possible hook, nook or cranny. A tree that had cost an inconceivable amount of money to get up here brushed the top of the incredibly tall ceiling in the living room, leaving barely any room to put the little silver cat Emily had chosen to top the tree, rather than an angel.

Under the broad branches of the Norwegian Fir were mounds of presents. Some were for Santi, Mariana and their beautiful children Sara and Óscar, who were due to arrive in an hour's time. Some were for Gabi and her unborn baby, Javier having had to promise that he would respect her choice and not interfere in a matter he very much wanted to interfere in.

Many were addressed to his wife—from him, from his sister and even one from Diabla, who also had a few presents of her own under the tree. And no, he didn't care how much Santi teased him, Diabla *did* deserve her gifts.

He'd never really much cared for the festive period, the memories of his mother's past behaviour had always made it a difficult time. But three weeks ago he and Emily had talked a little more about her mother and Steven. Javier had asked if she wanted to invite them to Spain, but Emily had explained how her mother and stepfather would go on their 'cruise at Christmas', leaving her behind. He could see the pain it had caused her and how it had helped to impact their lives in ways no one could have imagined. But that day he'd promised her she would never spend Christmas alone ever again and that this— their first together—would be the very best. Which was why he was sneaking off to his office in order to plan a surprise present for her. One that he was sure would eclipse any other gift.

Her husband was up to something, Emily just knew it. Gabi gave her a smile that told her she suspected exactly the same.

'I think he's trying to out-present you,' she mock whispered.

'He can try,' Emily replied, confident that, no matter what her husband had managed to wrap, she definitely had the best one for him. She placed ham, chorizo, morcilla and Manchego on a large sharing plate. Lobster, prawns and crab would make up the main course, but even that couldn't take her attention away from the sweet nougat called *turrón* that she had come to crave with a need that was insatiable. She glanced longingly at it, Gabi catching her doing so and frowning for just a second. Before Javier's sister could put two and two together, Emily excused herself and went in search of her husband.

Moving as quietly as possible, she turned the handle on the office door and peered through the small gap, realising her error the moment that Diabla meowed, squeezed herself through the sliver of space and rushed towards her favourite human.

Javier turned in shock, quickly trying to cover the half-wrapped present on the table in front of him.

'What are you doing in here? I thought Gabi was helping you with the *entremeses*?'

'She is,' Emily replied, looking at the handsome man staring back at her. He always took her breath away. The rich deep longing she saw in his eyes reflected her own, it was addictive that look.

She pulled him round to face her in the chair and straddled him, much to his surprise and delight. '*Esposa*, we don't have time…' he complained, clearly torn between propriety and desire.

'Really, husband? All your shocking talents and you don't have time for this?' she asked, pressing herself against the hardness of his arousal.

Red slashes brushed across cheekbones that were the envy of many a person as he gripped a fistful of blonde hair at her nape and gently pulled her head back so that he could feast upon her lips. She groaned into his mouth, uncaring of the lipstick she had spent so much time on.

Turrón wasn't her only craving that had become insatiable in the last two months.

Slowing the kiss much too soon for her liking, Javier gently leaned back and levelled her with a searching look. Eyes narrowed, focus intent, it wouldn't take him much longer to work it out. '*Cariño*? What secret are you trying to keep this time?' he asked, his gaze confused, but— she was relieved to see—not hurt. Because he knew that there were no more lies between them now. Only joy and happiness and hope for a future she was excited to meet.

'Just one,' she teased gently, taking his hand and placing it low on her abdomen where the most precious of all Christmas presents would be making an appearance in about seven months' time.

Javier's eyes grew so wide and so round Emily couldn't help but laugh.

'No!' he said, as if too worried that he might be wrong.

'Yes,' she confirmed.

'Really?'

'Really,' she promised, and then squealed as he picked her up, stood from the chair and spun her round in his arms as Diabla danced between his feet.

'That's it. I'm never competing with you again. You

don't play fair,' he complained after kissing even more of her lipstick from her lips.

'No,' she replied, reaching up with her thumb to wipe off the hint of red on his bottom lip. 'I play to win.'

But she was surprised when he looked so happy with her reply. When she asked why, he replied, '*Mi amor*, when you win, we both win, and I wouldn't have it any other way.'

Santi and Mariana and the children arrived then, interrupting a kiss that would have led to so much more if left to their own devices, but Javier and Emily were happy to see them.

Later that evening Emily looked at the people sitting at the dinner table and realised that they were her family. Bonds formed by friendship, by choice, beyond blood, had made their family strong and powerful in a way that nothing else could. And there, in the candlelight, the magic of *Navidad* surrounding them, she looked at her husband and knew that this was the first of many Christmases to come that neither would ever forget.

* * * * *

COMING SOON!

We really hope you enjoyed reading this book.
If you're looking for more romance, be sure to
head to the shops when new books are
available on

Thursday 5th January

MILLS & BOON®

Coming next month

INNOCENT MAID FOR THE GREEK
Sharon Kendrick

His throat constricted. "Obviously, this changes everything," he said tightly. "I'm not having sex with a virgin," he snapped.

She was shaking her head, the glossy spill of copper curls tumbling down over her shoulders and he wondered if she had any idea how lovely she looked right then.

"I still don't understand," she whispered. "You want sex with me and I definitely want sex with you. A piece of paper says we're legally married – so what's the problem? Please explain it to me."

He chose his words carefully. "The fact that you haven't been intimate with anyone else is significant."

"How?"

He shrugged. "It suggests you still care for me and will read too much into it," he continued repressively. "And I really don't want that to happen."

Mia stared back, her heart slamming hard against her ribcage as she took in what he'd just said. "Of all the arrogant things you've ever said to me, Theo Aeton – and there have been plenty of those," she breathed. "That one really tops the lots."

Continue reading
INNOCENT MAID FOR THE GREEK
Sharon Kendrick

Available next month
www.millsandboon.co.uk

MILLS & BOON

THE HEART OF ROMANCE

A ROMANCE FOR EVERY READER

MODERN

Prepare to be swept off your feet by sophisticated, sexy and seductive heroes, in some of the world's most glamourous and romantic locations, where power and passion collide.

HISTORICAL

Escape with historical heroes from time gone by. Whether your passion is for wicked Regency Rakes, muscled Vikings or rugged Highlanders, awaken the romance of the past.

MEDICAL

Set your pulse racing with dedicated, delectable doctors in the high-pressure world of medicine, where emotions run high and passion, comfort and love are the best medicine.

True Love

Celebrate true love with tender stories of heartfelt romance, from the rush of falling in love to the joy a new baby can bring, and a focus on the emotional heart of a relationship.

Desire

Indulge in secrets and scandal, intense drama and plenty of sizzling hot action with powerful and passionate heroes who have it all: wealth, status, good looks...everything but the right woman.

HEROES

Experience all the excitement of a gripping thriller, with an intense romance at its heart. Resourceful, true-to-life women and strong, fearless men face danger and desire - a killer combination!

To see which titles are coming soon, please visit

millsandboon.co.uk/nextmonth